THE INNOCENTS CLUB

TAYLOR SMITH

THE INNOCENTS CLUB

MIRA®

ISBN 1-55166-544-1

THE INNOCENTS CLUB

Visit us at www.mirabooks.com

Printed in U.S.A.

This book could only be for Amy Moore-Benson,
with heartfelt gratitude for her insight,
her perseverance and her unflagging grace.
Here's to the wonder of new beginnings.

ACKNOWLEDGMENT

My deepest thanks to those who offered their
expertise and encouragement throughout this project.
If I played fast and loose with the facts, it's through no fault of theirs.
I am especially grateful to members of the Newport Beach Police Department,
who have been extraordinarily kind and helpful, particularly Dale Johnson,
Don Gage, Ken Cowell, Mike Jackson and Dave Sperling.
Thanks, too, to Dr. Ed Uthman, Ken Keller, Gary Bale and Luis Hernandez
for coming up with answers when I needed them.
For unflagging moral support, I thank Patricia McFall,
Philip Spitzer, the Fictionaires (Orange County's finest fiction writers)
and family members near and far (most especially
my wonderful Richard, Kate and Anna,
who make life a joy even on the darkest of days).

No one could be more thankful than I for the steadfast
commitment and hard work of the talented people
at MIRA, beginning with Editorial Director Dianne Moggy.
My warmest thanks to them all, most particularly
Randall Toye, Katherine Orr, Stacy Widdrington,
Greg Sarney, Heather Locken, Krystyna de Duleba
and her brilliant design team and, last but never least,
Alex Osuszek and his enthusiastic team, the folks
who bring stories and readers together.

To forget one's ancestors is to be a brook without a source,
a tree without a root.

—ancient Chinese proverb

Thursday,
July 4

Prologue

She was exhausted. Wounded, bleeding, swimming for her life. Lungs on fire. Thin arms and legs aching from cold and the effort of pumping against heavy surf. A silent cry arose inside her, fueled by equal measures of pain, fear and indignation: *I can't do this!*

As a young woman, Renata thought, she might have had a chance. She'd been fit then, and strong, albeit more than a little spoiled—the indulged only child of one of the world's wealthiest men. But she was sixty-one years old now, for heaven's sake. She hadn't the stamina she once had.

Her brain snapped an obvious response: *Swim or die, you fool!*

She glanced nervously over her shoulder as, behind her in the dark, deep voices sounded, exchanging terse, furious commands. Had they spotted her, a tiny form bobbing on the star-sparkled water? Were they following? They seemed so close.

No, she tried to reassure herself. Not that close. It was just an acoustic trick of the clear night air. They were far away, too far even to be seen very clearly, though the sweep of the searchlight told her they hadn't yet abandoned the hunt for her.

Only her?

A flash of shame passed through her as she thought of the young girl she'd abandoned on deck. What kind of woman leaves a child in mortal danger while she flees to save her own skin? Was it true what her husband had once said about her? Renata wondered. That there was something unnatural about a woman without empathy?

Her stroke slowed. Keeping low and still, she peered back at the boat, trying to distinguish between the silhouettes on the deck, but her vision wasn't what it had once been, either. If the girl was still on board, Renata couldn't make her out.

Perhaps, she rationalized, Lindsay, too, had managed to escape, leaping overboard in the confusion that had followed her own break for freedom. The girl appeared delicate, but they said she was a competitive swimmer. So, if she *had* gotten away, she had as much a chance as Renata herself of making it to safety. Maybe even better. After all, Renata thought resentfully, the girl had youth on her side.

Renata felt another quiver of guilt run down her spine. And if Lindsay hadn't escaped those thugs on the boat? There was little doubt what was in store for that lovely young thing.

Well, all the more reason to keep swimming. Renata turned back toward shore and paddled on with new resolve.

Her captors had miscalculated. All up and down the coast, from Dana Point to Long Beach, Chinese rockets, pinwheels and brilliant cascades were exploding in the blue-black sky, clamorous displays of Fourth of July patriotism. Dozens of other small craft bobbed on the water, observing the spectacle.

Those brutes may have counted on the noise and confusion to cover their escape, but they hadn't counted on one of their victims jumping overboard, had they? Renata thought smugly. And the pyrotechnics, far from making her more visible, seemed to have camouflaged her amidst watery shadow and sparkle as she made a clean escape.

Almost. But not quite.

At first, she hadn't even realized they'd fired on her, what with the noise of the fireworks. They had to have been shooting blindly, but one lucky shot had found its target. Renata winced at the caustic, burning sensation in her shoulder, but forced herself to ignore it. If she could just reach one of the small pleasure crafts lying in toward shore, she'd be home free. Then, she'd send back the authorities.

She slogged on, determined to get as far away as possible from the boat's searchlights before the fireworks finale, when her predators' eyes would readjust to the dark and have a better chance of picking her out. It would be a ridiculous way to die, flapping in the water like some wing-shot pelican. She wouldn't have it. It was as simple as that.

But her strokes were becoming more ineffectual. It wasn't just fatigue and the loss of blood. Her sodden dress was weighing her down. It would have to go, Renata decided. Her pumping legs kept her afloat while she wrestled out of it, wincing with pain. All she had on now were her sagging underthings, but her bra straps cut into her wounded shoulder. Her panties, too, drooped with the weight of the water they'd absorbed. In for a penny, in for a pound, she thought ruefully, slipping out of them, as well.

Then, she swam on, holding down rising anxiety by sheer force of her legendary indomitable will. It worked for a while, but between her injured shoulder and flagging strength, she made slow progress. Inevitably, panic began to creep up, and in spite of herself, Renata began to cry. She was so weary! She'd been paddling for what felt like hours toward the nearest boat, yet it never seemed to get any closer.

They must be moving off, leaving me all alone out here! Oh, God, I can't do this!

Her father's impatient voice rose from the deep recesses of her memory: *Stop whining and get on with it, girl! We make our own fate. Don't get mad, get even.*

He was right. Terrible to be so weak, Renata thought, angry with herself now. She'd become too sedentary, that was the problem. Her self-indulgences had once included scuba diving in the Mediterranean, all-night dancing and many, many men, but now they ran to more sedate pleasures—the latest gallery opening, a very good cognac, dinners at the White House. Certainly nothing that would prepare her to leap off a boat and swim, bruised and bloodied, toward a shoreline that was—what? Miles off, it must be.

She breasted a rising swell, breathing hard through gritted teeth, but her waning strokes no longer carried her forward

against the rolling sea. Renata paused to catch her ragged
breath and give her aching arms a rest.

Just for a moment. I'm so tired.

She lay back, arms spread, a tiny, naked crucifix on the
water's surface. Something warm seeped over her right breast,
a tepid rivulet trickling over her shoulder and down into her
armpit. Her fingers probed the wound's sticky edges. It should
hurt, she thought, but it didn't anymore. The narcotic effect
of sheer adrenaline, she supposed. She closed her eyes, trying
not to imagine how much blood she'd lost. How much was
still ebbing away into the great, insatiable ocean.

From somewhere deep inside her head came another voice,
low and drawling, offering stoic reassurance: *Just a flesh
wound, ma'am.*

John Wayne, she thought, smiling. He used to have a big
house just across the Newport inlet from their own summer
place. Her father had been a stocky, barrel-chested little man,
even in his elevator shoes, but his swaggering stride had always lengthened a little when he walked next to that famous,
side-loping amble. In the last few years of their lives, the two
men would often disappear together for a day of drinking and
deep-sea fishing. The Duke and Daddy—what a couple of old
bears.

Renata rocked on the waves, eyelids drooping, a profound
lassitude spreading through her body. A sleepy yawn built
inside her, but she stifled it, forcing her eyes open.

Stay awake!

Overhead, the sky arced like a great, speckled dome. It was
beautiful this far out, away from the city lights. Lazily, she
traced a constellation with her finger, her thoughts reaching
into the past for names she'd learned from Nikolos, the white-
haired Greek who'd crewed for so many years on her father's
yacht.

*Look, Renata, there is Sagittarius, the archer. And, there,
up high, next to Vega. Do you see him? It is Hercules, with
his foot on the head of Draco, the dragon.*

Good old Niko. So full of stories. Bunk, her father said.
Had he perhaps been just a little jealous, Renata wondered,
of her love for that kind old sailor with a thousand tales?

Listen! Do you hear it?

What, Niko?
The celestial symphony—music of the cosmos.
I don't hear anything.
You must listen harder, little one. It is the music made by the turning of the stars. The music that the angels dance to.

Renata smiled, closing her eyes so she could concentrate. The warmth at her shoulder was Niko's big, gentle hand, and she was a child again, lying on the smooth, rolling deck of her father's yacht. So peaceful. So—

A rude bump interrupted her reverie. A surfboard? Out here? Then, another bump. And this time, a sharp, stabbing sensation in her ribs. Renata opened her eyes and looked around, irritated.

Get away! You've got the whole ocean, for heaven's sake!

Another bump knocked her sideways. She righted herself in the water, but not before a thousand tiny razors sliced her left foot—a quick sensation, gone almost before her brain had time to register it.

Oh, for pity's sake! Move on! Now, before I call the police!

That did the trick. The ruffians scattered, and Renata was left in peace, rocking on the waves. Good riddance.

She was so very tired. She needed to rest. And then, when she had her strength back, there was something else she'd been meaning to do. What was it?

She lay back on the water, eyes fluttering as she searched the stars for the answer. They were so beautiful. Her trembling hand reached up. Almost close enough to touch. And then—

Oh, Niko! I think I hear it. I do! I hear the symphony!

Monday,
July 1

Chapter One

Renata Hunter Carr was not remotely dead when Mariah Bolt first laid eyes on her. Far from it. That condition was soon to change, of course, and Mariah would be the agent of that change. For those who believe in fate, the wheel was set inexorably in motion three days before Renata's ill-fated swim.

Three days and nearly three thousand miles away...

Jack Geist, deputy director of Operations, acted as if there were nothing unusual about summoning Mariah to his office on the seventh floor of CIA headquarters in Langley, Virginia.

His secretary turned the handle on the big wooden door leading to the inner sanctum, her other hand raised to Mariah, indicating she should wait. Through the crack between the door and the frame, Mariah saw the deputy at his desk, flipping through a stack of files. When the DDO didn't look up, the other woman cleared her throat softly.

"She's here, sir. Ms. Bolt? Who you asked me to call in?"

He raised his head slowly, looking distracted and irritated, and gave her a curt nod. She scuttled back out, nodding to Mariah, then pulling the door shut behind her as Mariah entered.

Geist's demeanor went through a transformation. He got to his feet and came around his massive desk, hand extended, lips stretching wide in a smile. "Mariah Bolt! I don't think we've ever had the pleasure. Jack Geist."

The smile stopped well short of his pallid green eyes, she noticed, taking his hand. He fixed her with a long, piercing look that could have been interpreted in any number of ways, none of which put her at ease.

His skin had the leathery texture of a pack-a-day man. When he finally released her hand and waved toward the leather sofa and chairs on one side of his wood-lined office, Mariah caught the scent of stale cigarettes only partially masked. She tried to picture the deputy huddled in the center courtyard with the rest of the agency's nicotine junkies, but the image refused to come. He didn't look the type to mingle with the masses, for one thing. Also, in her experience, covert Ops people played by their own rules, so she found herself looking around the office for the ashtrays she knew had to be there, despite the building-wide smoking ban—certain he'd have dismantled the office smoke detectors.

"Thanks for stopping by," Geist added, following her across the room.

"No problem." Not that this was anything but a command performance. Mariah passed up the deep leather sofa for one of the armchairs sitting at right angles to it around a low mahogany table. "My secretary said it was urgent."

In fact, Jane had pulled her out of an interdepartmental meeting to breathlessly pass on the DDO's summons. It wasn't every day analysts were called to the deep-cover side of the shop, not even specialists like Mariah, who supervised a weapons watchdog group.

Geist settled his own lank frame at the end of the sofa nearest her. His close-cropped hair was straw-colored, the kind that turns imperceptibly white with age. With his loosened tie and rumpled white cotton shirt, sleeves rolled to the elbow, he looked as though he might have spent the night on that couch, working on some unfolding international crisis. Did men like this have family lives? Mariah wondered.

Nestled in the corner between them was a low, intricately carved table topped with a hammered-brass platter. It looked like an acquisition from some Arab souk. Like the ruby Persian wool carpet beneath their feet, the water pipe on the credenza and the carved, mother-of-pearl-inlaid wooden boxes scattered around the room, the table was a souvenir, no doubt, of Geist's travels on behalf of the Company. On a lower shelf of the small table, she spotted another hammered-brass item—a bowl, empty at the moment, but its concave inner surface black with soot. The predicted ashtray. Bingo.

"The Last Days of the Romanov Dynasty," Geist said, getting straight to the point. "Ever hear of it?"

"Yes, of course," she said, nodding. "Largest and most valuable collection of Russian royal artifacts ever assembled since Czar Nicholas II and his family were assassinated by the Bolsheviks in 1917. Co-curated by the Hermitage Museum in Saint Petersburg and L.A.'s Arlen Hunter Museum. Starts a two-year North American tour this summer."

"Tomorrow, matter of fact. At the Arlen Hunter."

She resisted the temptation to say "So what?," already dreading where this conversation was heading. Did he know about her vacation plans? And then, another stomach-sinking thought: Did Geist have any inkling about her connection to the Hunter family? As spectacular as the Romanov exhibit was reputed to be, the Arlen Hunter Museum was the last place on earth she'd voluntarily choose to set foot.

"We found out this morning that none other than Valery Zakharov is going to do the ribbon-cutting honors," Geist said. "He arrives in exactly twenty-four hours."

"The foreign minister himself? I know the exhibit's an important revenue-generator for the Russian government, but that seems like overkill, doesn't it?"

"My thoughts, too, although Zakharov was due in L.A. later this week, anyway. The conference of Pacific Rim states opens out there on the fifth. There's going to be a big kick-off reception on board the *Queen Mary* the night of the fourth."

"Nice timing. They'll be able to see fireworks up and down the coast from there. The State Department should save a bundle on entertainment."

"No kidding. Anyway, we've spotted several known intelligence figures on the list of names the Russians have submitted for diplomatic visas.''

''That's not surprising, is it? Zakharov's ex-KGB, after all. Well, 'ex,''' she amended. ''Not precisely. It may be FSB now, but it's not like they've gone out of business. It's to be expected that Zakharov's entourage would include some spooks, I would think.''

''No doubt. That's why I want somebody there to keep an eye on things.''

''Isn't that the FBI's job?''

The deputy scowled. ''Funny, that's what our esteemed director said. Between you and me, Mariah, that man's so pussy-whipped by the oversight committees he doesn't take a piss without prenotifying Capitol Hill.''

Mariah said nothing. There was something tacky about a man bad-mouthing his boss to someone he'd never met before and who didn't even work for him. Given that the director had appointed Geist to his current exalted position, it was also more than a little disloyal. So what was that all about? A bid to make her feel part of his inner circle of confidants?

Geist had held the deputy's post only a few months. Like most covert operatives, he'd been little known inside the agency until his name had suddenly surfaced as the man who would take over the beleaguered Operations position. The press release announcing his appointment had said Geist was an eighteen-year veteran of the agency who'd served in a variety of positions, mostly in the Middle East. *Only* eighteen years, Mariah reflected—a relatively meteoric rise in a bureaucracy as large and byzantine as the CIA. It was safe to assume the man was both ambitious and ruthless.

''We have no mandate for operations on domestic soil,'' she said, pointing out the obvious. Was that why she was here? So he could keep his hands technically clean by using a non-Ops employee for whatever scheme he was brewing?

''Who said anything about an operation? I'm talking observation. Simply keeping an eye on Company interests. The FBI's worried about Russian moles and organized crime. Fair enough, but we've got bigger fish to fry. Zakharov's making a big push for the presidency. He's probably going to be the next man with his finger on the Russian arsenal. It's not much direct threat to us these days, but the Russians have plenty of potential for mischief. You, of all people, are well aware of that, Mariah. Why, just the level of their arms shipments to sleazy customers is enough to turn my hair gray.''

She was tempted to point out that the Russians would have to quadruple their activity to begin to approach the level of American arms sales abroad, nor were U.S. clients any less unsavory, on the whole. But she let it slide. Her job was to monitor the other team, not her own. In any case, she was curious to know where this conversation was heading. Curious, and more than a little uneasy.

"Zakharov is a thug, but if he's going to take over Russia, he's going to be *our* thug," Geist said. "We're already working to ensure he's in our pocket, but to be on the safe side, I'd like a little extra insurance. A reliable source in his inner circle would make me very happy."

A source in Zakharov's inner circle? That sounded suspiciously like co-opting a foreign agent—a covert operation if ever there was one. Mariah waited for the other shoe to drop. It didn't take long.

"That's why you're going to attend the Romanov opening," Geist said.

Bang. Just what she'd been afraid he was going to say. "Excuse me, sir—"

"Call me Jack."

"—this doesn't make any sense," she went on, ignoring the invitation to familiarity, which, she suspected, could only breed contempt. "If you're planning to mount a recruitment operation, you should send someone from your side of the shop with experience in this kind of thing."

"I understand you've done some work for us in the past."

Much to my everlasting regret. "Nothing of this order of magnitude," she said. "I wouldn't know where to begin identifying a susceptible target."

"Ah, well! That's the beauty of it, you see. The target has already identified himself. Someone you know. Yuri Belenko, Zakharov's executive assistant."

"Belenko? Really? I have met him," she conceded.

"Twice in the last year, if I'm correctly informed. First, at last fall's U.N. General Assembly session in New York. Then again in March, at the European security conference in Paris.''

She nodded. ''I was seconded to the State Department to work with their disarmament delegation, but—''

Geist leaned forward, elbows on his knees, fixing her once more with that intense, thousand-yard stare. ''Tell me about Belenko, Mariah.''

''I filed contact reports both times I met with him.'' It sounded defensive, she knew, but what did Geist think had gone on between her and the Russian?

''I know you did, but I want to hear it from you. What's he like?''

''He's...nice,'' she ventured, wincing internally. *Oh, that's brilliant, Mariah. What a wonderfully insightful analysis.* She tried again. ''Intelligent and personable. Well-educated, well-traveled. Forty-three. Divorced, apparently. Speaks excellent, idiomatic American English of the kind taught in KGB training courses—which we happen to know was his original stomping ground. We have to presume he still represents the FSB.''

''Personal quirks?''

''I'm not sure I know of any—unless you count the fact that he's an avid collector of proverbs and American slang. It's quite the running joke.''

''Proverbs, eh? What *else* does he collect?''

Mariah frowned. ''I don't follow your— Oh! Right. Well, yes, he is a bit of a ladies' man, I suppose.''

''You suppose?''

''As I said, he can be charming, and he tends to turn it on around women.''

''Especially you.''

''I beg your pardon?''

''I'm led to believe that our man Yuri's somewhat smitten with you, Mariah. Is that true?''

''What are you suggesting?''

''I'm not suggesting anything. I'm just waiting to hear what you have to report.''

''There's nothing to report,'' she said. ''Look, I don't know what you've heard from your watchers, but there's nothing between me and Belenko. The idea's ridiculous, not least because I lost my husband a year and a half ago, and my hands are full doing my job here and raising a teenage daughter. I'm hardly in a position or mood to carry on a wild social life with the likes of Yuri Belenko or anyone else.''

"You do get around, though.''

"How do you mean?''

Geist sat back and studied her for a moment. Then he got to his feet, walked back to his desk and reached for one of the files he'd been reading when she walked in. Withdrawing a piece of paper, he returned and stood over her, holding it up.

Mariah's heart sank. It was a photocopy of a *Washington Post* article that had appeared a few weeks earlier. The photograph accompanying the piece hadn't copied well, but she knew exactly who the two shadowy figures in it were.

"For someone who claims to be out of commission, you do lead a high-profile life,'' Geist said. He turned the article back toward himself. "The National Press Club awards. My, my! And there you are, recognizable enough, even though this is a lousy copy, gracing the arm of one of our top TV newscasters.''

"Paul Chaney's an old friend of my husband's. And mine,'' she conceded, realizing it was stupid to pretend otherwise, despite her own ambivalence on the subject. "He was getting an award that night. He needed a date and I went along as a favor.''

"This article's not about Chaney, though, is it? It's about you. And your father. There've been a couple of others since this one, too.''

"Unfortunately.'' She exhaled heavily. "Look, the whole thing was an accident. Some reporter found out I was Ben Bolt's daughter and latched onto a rumor that an unpublished novel of his had been found.''

She should never have gone to that dinner. Not for the first time, she cursed Paul for letting slip the information about her father and his papers. Not for the first time, either, she wondered whether his gaffe had been as accidental as he kept claiming.

"Your late father's considered to be one of the biggies of

American lit, I guess.'' Geist pursed his lips and shrugged. ''Not surprising news like that would create a stir.''

''I suppose, but I certainly never intended to get caught at the center of a controversy.''

''So? *Is* there a novel?''

She shrugged. ''There's a draft manuscript and some journals that showed up in an old storage locker. My father's agent is wading through the mess now, trying to see whether it adds up to much. I'm planning to see him next week to discuss what, if anything, we should do with it. In any case,'' she added, ''that's all beside the point. We were discussing Yuri Belenko, and I don't want to hold you up, sir. I'm sure you're very busy. Why would you think Belenko's susceptible to working for us?''

''Ah, well,'' Geist said, laying aside the *Post* article, ''that's what I was trying to get at before you went all coy on me, Mariah. I don't know if he's susceptible to *us,* but he certainly seems to be susceptible to *you.*''

''Why would you think that?''

''My people have been keeping an eye on him, and we've intercepted a couple of conversations where he's mentioned you in a most wistful manner. Also, did you know that when you were in Paris in March, he followed you back to your hotel one night? We think he was planning to pay a social call, only I gather your daughter was there with you...?''

''The conference was only a one-day affair, and she had spring break, so...'' Mariah felt a tremor run through her. ''Belenko was *following* me? He saw her?''

It was her old nightmare, come back to haunt her again— her child in danger because of her work. Deskbound as she was, it wasn't much of an issue these days. But when the March conference had come up, she and Lindsay had just gone through their second Christmas without David, followed by a rough winter. The appeal of springtime in Paris had overshadowed the risk of taking her daughter along on the short business trip.

Never again.

Geist leaned forward, elbows on his knees. ''My watchers said Belenko seemed real disappointed. Guess he decided he wasn't going to get to first base that night. We decided to start keeping an eye on him, though. Then, day before yesterday, we hit pay dirt.''

"Pay dirt?''

"He had dinner with his brother in Moscow. The guy's a literary critic for *Isvestia,* did you know that? Belenko told him he'd met Ben Bolt's daughter. I guess your father's novels are popular over there, too?''

Mariah nodded. "Your people bugged their conversation?''

"Yup. Belenko mentioned he was heading back to the States this week, said he was hoping to see you again. Maybe he was just trying to impress big brother, but from the way he spoke, it didn't seem like it was the finer points of modern fiction he was looking to pursue, if you know what I mean.''

Mariah sat back, momentarily stunned. Then she shook her head. "I don't think you're reading this correctly.''

"You never noticed Belenko had the hots for you? You're a very attractive woman, Mariah.''

She passed on the flattery. "That's not what this is about.''

"Why do you say that?''

"Because I've run into this kind of thing before. It's not me that's the draw, it's my father.''

"I thought he was dead.''

"He is. He died when he was twenty-eight.'' She sighed. "It's hard to explain. It's the phenomenon of being related to fame. There's a look certain people get when they twig to the fact that Ben Bolt was my father.''

"Certain people?''

"Certain grasping, upwardly mobile characters. Or, I don't know—maybe they're just fans. People like that want to get close to their heroes, even if only indirectly. Given the way Russians lionize poets and writers, Belenko could be very susceptible. As I say, I've seen it before. You can be ugly as a post and stupid as dirt, but if you're related to somebody famous, it never matters to those who are too easily impressed.'' Even though she herself found more to regret than celebrate in her connection to Ben Bolt, Mariah thought grimly.

"Be that as it may,'' Geist said, "it's a hook. I'm still thinking it would be a good thing if you ran into Belenko again. In fact, I think you should get to know him much better.''

''Are you saying you want me to seduce the man? Because if you are, I'm sorry, the answer is no. I interpret satellite data and write depressing reports on arms shipments that nobody reads. I wasn't recruited to be a swallow.''

His hand made solicitous ''there-there'' motions, patting the air. ''I didn't mean to offend you, Mariah. I'm not asking you to do anything you're not comfortable with. I just want you to reestablish contact with Belenko, see where his long-term interests lie. Feel him out. Note I said 'out,' not 'up,' '' Geist added, smirking at his own wit. ''If you get any hint he might be interested in joining forces professionally as well as personally, you let me know. We'll take it from there.''

''I'm not comfortable with this,'' she said, head shaking.

''You'll do fine. It's only for a day or so.''

''A day or so? I thought you just wanted me to cover the Romanov opening.''

''That's probably all. Foreign Minister Zakharov's going to be in L.A. for a few days, as I said, but we're not sure Belenko's staying the whole time. One way or the other, though, it's two days, tops. Promise. I know you've got a vacation coming.''

''What about the State Department? Secretary of State Kidd doesn't like Ops officers on his delegations.''

''I know, but that's the beauty of it. You're not Ops.''

Aha! Just as she'd suspected. The fact that she'd read him right gave her little satisfaction.

Geist went on. ''It's already been cleared with Kidd's office. Since you've worked with them before, he'll go along with it now. State has no idea about your approach to Belenko, mind you. We've said we want to use you as a quick conduit for intelligence briefings of the secretary in case the crisis heats up between Russia and Turkey.'' A small skirmish had been developing between NATO ally Turkey and the Russians over the latter's support to Kurdish rebels in Turkey.

It was hardly at the level of "crisis," Mariah thought, but Geist must have oversold its potential to get Kidd's approval.

"I suppose my own deputy has also agreed to this?" she asked, knowing full well that the well-meaning but ineffectual analysis chief was no match for a determined operator like Jack Geist.

"Naturally." Geist leaned back into the sofa and laced his fingers over his flat stomach. "All I'm asking you to do is help us take advantage of an opportunity, Mariah. If Belenko agrees to come on the payroll, my people in Moscow will manage him. I have full confidence in you to handle this."

Somehow, that was small comfort.

Mariah took her victories where she found them. The year and a half since David's death was just a blur, a blind succession of days filled with all the textbook stages of grieving, save acceptance. But denial she knew. And anger. And bargaining with fate: *Let this not have happened and I will live an exemplary life all the rest of my days.*

Fate wouldn't be bargained with, however, so the best she could do was allow herself a small sense of triumph at getting out of bed each morning—an act of sheer will, requiring a certain determined amnesia in order to ignore the losses strung like thorns along the beaded chain of her life.

This resolve to carry on was entirely for Lindsay's benefit. If she could have, Mariah would have sheltered her precious daughter from every harsh and buffeting wind, but she'd been powerless to keep David's life from slipping away on them. Lindsay had been robbed of a father's unconditional support at the worst possible moment, poised on the brink of adolescence, that moment in life when young people are already beginning to suspect that they've been duped and that the safe haven of childhood is an illusion fostered by a vast parental conspiracy. All Mariah wanted now was for her daughter to hold on to faith in the possibility of happiness, the constancy of love and the notion that people are mostly good—even if these beliefs held only the shakiest of places in her own personal credo.

At fifteen, however, Lindsay seemed equally determined most days to reject her mother's take on life, love and all other matters, great and small. This was one of those days when nothing Mariah did or said or wore or suggested was going to earn even the most grudging approval.

"Not the blue one, either?" Mariah asked, pulling yet another hanger from her closet. They were in her upstairs bedroom of the condominium town house Mariah had bought in McLean, Virginia, after it became clear David would never recover from the car crash that had ripped apart their family—a deliberate attack that had also injured her daughter, but missed its intended target: Mariah herself.

Lindsay picked up a magazine from the bedside table and began flipping through it, her beautiful, dark eyes avoiding both her mother and the dress. "Whatever," she said grudgingly.

Her hands were again decorated with ink doodling, Mariah noted, her nails painted blue-black. She'd been forbidden to go to school looking like that, but with school out for the summer now, Lindsay was testing limits again. Between the skin drawing, the hammered-looking fingertips and the third earring in one ear, her beautiful little girl seemed determined to transform herself into something out of Edgar Allan Poe. Why?

Mariah turned back to the mirror, gritting her teeth. They would not fight tonight.

From outside the flung-wide windows, the sweet, heavy scent of magnolia blossoms in the park-like condominium complex wafted across the warm evening air. But underneath that, the air crackled with the static charge of a storm brewing. July had arrived with all the restless, humid promise to which hormone-wracked youth are susceptible. Other people, too, perhaps, but not her, Mariah thought. That way lay only grief. She looked past her own reflection to her daughter's. It was going to be a long summer, and not all the storms would be outside.

Pulling her gaze away from Lindsay, she forced herself to concentrate on the task at hand. It was getting late, and she was damned if she'd stay up half the night agonizing over wardrobe choices for an assignment she'd been dragooned into. She should have said no, and not just because of the assignment. There was also the contact site: the Arlen Hunter Museum. Hunter himself had died several years back. Was his family still involved in the museum that bore his name?

The Hunter family. Mariah grimaced. It wasn't the *family* she was worried about. It was Renata. Would she be there? Well, what if she was? Why should it matter? Renata couldn't hurt her anymore. Had no power over her unless Mariah handed it to her, and why would she do that? Simple answer: she wouldn't.

She studied the dress in her hand once more. It was sleeveless and front-buttoning, with a high, Chinese-mandarin collar. The shimmering cobalt silk made a striking contrast to her softly cropped blond hair and cast her smoky eyes in an unusual light. It *seemed* suitable enough, but living with a teenager was enough to shake anyone's confidence in her own judgment.

"What's wrong with it?" she asked.

Lindsay's bare shoulder lifted in a dismissive shrug. She was wearing a black halter top over heavily frayed jeans. A full head taller than Mariah's five-three, with impossibly long legs, she was fair-skinned and fine-boned, with the doe-eyed delicacy of a Walter Scott heroine that belied an increasingly headstrong nature.

"A little fancy, isn't it?" Lindsay said without looking up. "I thought this was a work thing. Why don't you wear one of your suits?"

"It is work, but it's also a gala opening. I don't want to look like one of the museum guards, do I?"

Again, the shrug. "Wear what you want, then."

Lindsay tossed the magazine aside and flopped down onto

the big four-poster bed, thick curls washing like copper-colored waves down the smooth expanse of her back. As she landed, the corner of Mariah's eye picked up a tumbling dust bunny, expelled from under the bed by the exasperated whumphing of the mattress. She tried not to think how long it had been since the vacuum had made a house call under there. She wondered, too, how this maddeningly irritating girl could be the cornerstone of her happiness, her reason for living. Some days, motherhood felt like pure masochism.

Giving up all hope of approval, she lay the Chinese-silk dress on the bed, by the garment bag lying next to Lindsay. Her suitcase was on the floor, and it already held most of the things she'd need for their vacation to follow. Lindsay's own bag was packed, zipped and standing by the door of her bedroom down the hall.

"I still don't see why I can't come with you tomorrow," Lindsay grumbled. "I would have liked to see the Russian royal treasures, too, you know."

"I'll take you another time. The tour's coming through D.C. We'll see it at the Smithsonian."

"Yeah, right. Next year. You could have wangled me into the grand opening."

Mariah shuddered at the thought. It was bad enough she had to go herself. "The invitation list was tightly controlled," she said. "With the secretary of state and Russian foreign minister coming, the security contingent alone will take up half the hall. Anyway, this is no social occasion for me."

"I wouldn't get in the way. I didn't in Paris."

"That was different."

"Yeah, it was. Those were private meetings. This is a public opening. If I got dressed up, I'd blend right into the background. I look old enough. I don't even get carded at R-rated movies anymore."

Mariah frowned. "R-rated movies? I don't remember approving that."

"Mom," she said, rolling her eyes, "everything's R-rated

these days except Big Bird. I've told you about every movie my friends and I have gone to.''

Her friends included a six-foot, tank-size junior named Brent who'd started hanging around lately. Drive-in theaters and boys with shiny new driver's licenses were bad enough, Mariah thought. Now, add R-rated movies to the long list of subjects that she and Lindsay could argue about.

Not tonight, though.

''The point is,'' Lindsay said, ''I can almost pass for twenty-something if I get really done up.''

''That's all I'd need,'' Mariah said, rifling through her bureau, trying to find her travel makeup bag. She and David had bought the oak double dresser at a country estate auction not long after they were married. Now, for the first time in her life, she had more drawer space than she knew what to do with, and she could still never find anything. The bag finally appeared. ''I don't want to be worrying about some guy hitting on my baby girl while I'm supposed to be picking Russian brains.''

Lindsay's mouth rounded in a mock-pitying pout. ''Aw, poor Mom! Double-oh-seven never had to baby-sit while he was spying on Dr. No, did he?''

''Double-oh-seven, my foot. I'm just an old desk jockey who gets unchained from time to time for a closer look at the other side. Those visiting dignitaries, however, have roving eyes and hands. I'm not exactly going to blend into the background if I have to be beating them off you like some crazed fishwife, am I?''

Lindsay blushed, confirming the general wisdom that redheads look adorable in pink. ''Get outta here. You'll be beating them off yourself in that dress.''

Mariah was packing her toiletry kit, but she turned to her daughter with a look of mock astonishment. ''Oh, my gosh, is that a vote of confidence I'm hearing? You *do* think the dress is okay?''

Lindsay flipped over onto her back. ''It's fine. You going without me tomorrow isn't.''

"You're coming right behind me! Honestly, Lins, I don't know why you're making such a fuss. It's barely forty-eight hours."

"Because it's *boring* here. All right? And there's a party tomorrow night, and I'm not going to get to go to that, either! And if I don't—" She rolled off the bed and headed for the door. "It's not fair!"

The walls vibrated with the stomping of her feet down the hall and the slamming of her bedroom door, and then, the stereo came on loud. Very loud. Too loud for open windows and even the most well-baffled condominium walls.

Mariah massaged her forehead, trying to loosen the vise that was in the process of clamping down on her skull. When did the age of roller-coaster hormones end? It couldn't happen too soon.

She took a deep breath, willing herself to be calm. The neighbors were away. The music still had to be turned down, but she would not fight. Not tonight.

She zipped her makeup kit and tossed it on top of the open suitcase. Then, steeling herself, she went down the hall and knocked softly on Lindsay's door. No answer. The second rap was a little louder. Not aggressive. Just loud enough to be heard.

"What?" Lindsay snapped from the other side.

Mariah opened her mouth to ask if she could come in, but what if the answer came back no? Better to take acknowledgment as invitation. When she walked in, Lindsay was stretched on her stomach across the unmade bed, arms hanging down as she flipped through a pile of plastic CD cases on the floor beside her.

"We need to turn the music down," Mariah said. "The windows are open, and it's getting late."

"Fine," Lindsay said, but didn't move.

Mariah walked over to the desk and lowered the volume on the stereo. The chair, typically, was covered with clothes from the try-and-toss ritual Lindsay went through as she debated her image each day. Mariah made a move to start hanging them up, but if she did, she knew it would be interpreted as criticism—not that the mess didn't warrant it, but there was a time and a place, and this wasn't it. On the other hand, she wanted to sit down, and she couldn't bring herself to sit on top of all those clean clothes. She compromised and draped the whole pile over the back of the desk chair, then settled and looked around.

The decor was in a constant process of transformation. Nothing was ever removed, but layer upon layer was added as Lindsay's interests evolved. Between posters of rock bands and animals, new ones had been hung—book jackets and astronomical phenomena, two of the many passions of this difficult but incredibly bright daughter she was trying to raise. Images of the Milky Way and the Horsehead Nebula hung interspersed with others of writers as diverse as Jane Austen, George Orwell and Ken Kesey—and, Mariah noted, one whole wall of Ben Bolt, the grandfather Lindsay had never known.

Maybe it was just coincidence that she'd discovered her grandfather not long after losing her dad. Ben's novel *Cool Thunder* had been on her freshman English curriculum, after all. But Lindsay had taken her Ben Bolt study well beyond school requirements, reading everything by and about him that she could get her hands on.

Not surprising, Mariah supposed. At a certain point, everyone wants to know who they are and where they came from, and she herself hadn't provided much information over the years. Where Ben was concerned, she'd operated on the theory that if you can't say something good about someone…

"Why couldn't I stay at Chap's while you're working?" Lindsay asked sullenly.

Chap Korman was the literary agent who'd handled Ben's work from the start of his career. His house in Newport Beach, California, was only a couple of blocks from the cottage where Lindsay and Mariah were spending their three-week vacation. Since her own mother's death twenty years earlier, Mariah had become sole guardian of Ben's estate, and it was a credit to Korman that she felt as close to him as she felt estranged from the memory of his former client.

"There really wasn't time to arrange it with Chap and change your ticket—although, to be perfectly honest, Lins, I didn't even think of it. Carol was the first person I thought of." Carol Odell was the married daughter of Mariah's old CIA mentor and boss, Frank Tucker. The families had always been close. "She and Michael are really looking forward to having you there for a couple of days. So is Alex. Apparently, he's having sibling anxiety over the new baby. That little guy's crazy about you, and you haven't seen much of him lately."

"It's not my fault. I had exams and everything."

"I know. But when this assignment got thrown at me and I tried to think how to work it, Carol's just seemed like the best idea. I did try to call you," Mariah added, "but the phone here was tied up all afternoon."

"I was talking to Br—to my friends about the party at Stephanie's tomorrow. It's not fair I can't go."

"There'll be other parties. This couldn't be helped."

"It won't be the same! People won't be around later."

"People? Are we talking people like Brent?"

She nodded miserably. "He's going to Connecticut to see his dad. I won't see him again till school starts."

Mariah said a quiet prayer of thanks for that. She didn't think she was being overprotective. At eighteen, Brent was just too old and altogether too smooth. But she adopted what she hoped was an appropriately sympathetic expression and reminded herself not to let any dismissive platitudes pass her lips. The only safe recourse was to agree that this development was, indeed, as earth-shattering as it seemed from a fifteen-year-old perspective. "I know it's the pits," she said. September *was* a long way off, thank God.

Lindsay sighed, a real heartbreaker of a sigh. Mariah moved next to her on the bed and stroked that beautiful copper hair.

"Carol says Charlotte's just started smiling," she ventured.

Lindsay smiled a little at that. Mariah put an arm around her daughter's slim shoulders, bending to kiss her head. "I know how frustrated you are, Lins. Me, too. I'm so fed up with work these days, I could put a chair though the window. We really need this vacation."

It seemed they'd been planning it forever. A beach holiday, they'd decided, in a rare instance of total accord—three weeks of relaxing, swimming, tanning, shopping. Long walks on the sand. Maybe a few sailing lessons. California wouldn't have been Mariah's first choice. She'd have opted for the Hamptons or the Carolinas, but there had been advantages to going west, not the least of which was the chance to spend some time with Chap Korman, who wasn't getting any younger. That was certainly where Lindsay's vote had gone, in any case, so California-bound they were—with this one small wrinkle.

"Just be patient? I'll go do this job, and then we'll have three whole weeks to veg in the sun."

"Yeah, I suppose."

Mariah hugged her again, too grateful for the diverted crisis to listen to the doubts gnawing in the back of her mind. Doubts that should have told her there was something altogether too coincidental, too pat about this sudden call to duty on an old enemy's turf.

If she'd been less distracted, less weary, less defeated, she might have pulled her wits about her faster and found a way to turn Geist down flat. But she hadn't. And sure enough, it wasn't long before she felt an unseen hand clawing at the frayed threads of her life.

Tuesday,
July 2

Chapter
Two

Frank Tucker awoke in gloom and found himself crying. He froze, catching himself in mid-sob, and held his breath, ears straining. But the only sound he heard was a lonely summer rain pelting the roof like a sympathetic echo to his grief.

Though disoriented, his instincts were sufficiently honed to render him both wary and appalled at his lapse. He racked his brain to think where he was. His first thought was Moscow. Room 714, Intourist Hotel. Surveillance devices embedded in every wall.

Horrified to think the listeners might have heard him crying, he wondered if he'd been drugged to induce this sense of utter desolation. A dead weight of despair seemed to be bearing down on him, crushing his chest. He inhaled deeply, trying to cast it off, and as he did, the piney scent of wet juniper tickled his nostrils. This wasn't the typical Russian urban perfume of diesel, must and cooked cabbage, he realized. It was the smell of his own yard, drifting in through the open window.

Then he remembered flying back that morning. The unmarked aircraft had taken off from Moscow before dawn, Tucker the sole passenger. The only cargo had been one wooden crate. Picking up eight hours on the westbound jour-ney, overtaking the rising sun, the plane had landed at Andrews Air Force Base just in time for the morning capital commute.

The driver who met the plane on the tarmac had taken Tucker's suit bag and put it in the trunk of a dark sedan, watching while Tucker himself loaded the wooden crate. They exchanged hardly a word on the drive from suburban Maryland to McLean, Virginia, a chase car trailing close behind. Wending its way along the beltway, the convoy had turned off at the road leading through the Langley Wood, entering the CIA complex through a subterranean passage.

There, Tucker had carted the box to his sub-basement office. Prying it open with a crowbar, he'd flipped quickly though the moldering files inside before depositing the whole bunch in his heavy steel safe. After a quick call upstairs to confirm his return, he'd slammed the safe door and spun the dial, heading home to catch up on some of the sleep that had eluded him for the two days he'd been gone.

Now, with a warm summer rain splashing on the windowsill and the damp, earthy scent around him of a world washed clean, he was back in his own wide, empty bed in suburban Alexandria, fully dressed, only his shoes kicked off before he'd crashed on top of the covers.

How long ago?

The heavy curtains were drawn tight to shut out the light of day. Tucker glanced at the digital clock next to the bed: 11:33 a.m. He'd slept less than two hours before snapping awake to the sound of his own mournful cry.

The mattress dipped as he rolled onto his side, feet dropping with a thud to the carpeted floor. He exhaled a long, shuddering sigh, and the blade of his big hands scraped the tears from his cheeks—denying even this familiar room the pathetic sight of a middle-aged man reduced to tears. He had no recollection of the dream that had moved him to this state. All he knew was that it had left him with a profound sense of loss and longing.

He knew, too, that he was ludicrous—a brooding, barrel-chested hulk whose ferocious, black-eyed scowl had once struck terror in the hearts of fools and his more timid underlings. Now, here he was, reduced to whimpering in his bed like some self-pitying boy with a complaint about the unfairness of life.

He got to his feet and walked to the window, throwing back the drapes. The cloud-shrouded day cast a gentle light across the back lawn rolling down to the creek at the bottom of his property. The grass, dry and yellowing when he'd left forty-eight hours earlier, had already been transformed to lush green. On the borders of his lot, red hibiscus, white daylilies and blue hydrangeas were all in bloom—a patriotic display in time for the Fourth of July. The long fronds of the big willow by the creek swayed in the summer rainstorm, a slow, easy dance.

No automobile horns, no loud voices, no pounding jackhammers. After the noise and bustle of Moscow, the quiet was deafening.

Tucker passed a hand over his head, feeling stubble on a dome normally shaved bowling-ball smooth. He debated his next move. He was bone-tired, but even if jet lag was insisting it was evening, sleep wasn't an option. His dreams, obviously, weren't to be trusted. Anyway, he'd only meant to grab forty winks. If he went back to bed now, he'd be left to struggle with his bleak thoughts through the long, dark night to come.

He could get moving, he supposed. Shower, shave, see if he had any clean clothes. Drive back into work and tackle those old KGB files.

But what was the point? Nothing and no one depended on him. Now that he'd gotten his hands on them and spirited them out of Moscow, anyone could take over dissecting the files, for whatever they were worth. From here on in, it would be solitary grunt work, the kind meted out to old operatives who've lost the ability or the heart to wade through the secret jungles, waging covert war.

Tucker knew he'd been written off as a casualty of that war—wounded, though not quite slain. He'd toyed with the idea of early retirement, but at the last minute, he'd backed away from the abyss of empty years stretching before him. He was in disgustingly good health. If statistics were to be believed, he had a third of his life yet ahead of him. What he did with that time mattered to no one but himself.

His wife had been dead sixteen long years, although there

were days when he still half imagined Joanne would be there when he walked in the front door. He'd lost his only son, Stephen, a year and a half earlier. What family he had left needed little from him. His daughter Carol, and her husband, Michael, were a loving couple, hardworking, good parents to their two children. Sufficient unto themselves. All they required from him was that he put in an appearance at the occasional Sunday or holiday dinner.

Until recently, there'd been a woman in his life, helping to fill the empty hours and days, but that relationship had foundered and run aground like everything else. The extracurricular involvement with his secretary had started one night a few years back, when Patty had marched into his office after the rest of his section had gone home and demanded he take her to dinner after working her like a slave until all hours. Then she had invited him to her apartment. They'd kept on in a low-key way ever after, and when his son had died, she'd pretty much moved in, nursing Tucker through months of guilt and self-loathing.

Finally, though, understandably, she'd grown tired of the uneven arrangement, knowing there were prior claims on his heart and mind that she'd never dislodge. As the previous winter had settled in, Patty had announced one evening, with resignation but no rancor, that she was quitting the Company and moving to Florida. Tucker hadn't been invited to go along.

"It's not that I don't care about you," she'd said, her voice dusky as she busied herself with packing the suitcase on his bed. "Fact is, I love you. Always will, I guess, fool that I am."

Tucker was standing in the doorway, arms hanging stupidly at his sides, watching her and trying to get his mind around the prospect of her absence. "Then why are you leaving?"

She'd been part of his daily existence for nearly twenty years—at first, just sitting outside his office, running interference, holding back fools and whiners, keeping his expense accounts balanced and his files straight. Lately, he'd grown even more dependent on her.

She folded a sweater in a couple of brusque movements and laid it across the suitcase. Her hairdresser had taken to putting platinum streaks in Patty's tawny hair to camouflage the increasing gray, and they sparkled as she moved. Straightening slowly, she turned to face him. "I'm not leaving because I'm mad, Frank. Honest. I just can't live on a one-way street anymore."

He nodded. "I haven't been there for you. You stood by me these last months. You've done for me and done for me—"

"I was glad to."

"I don't know why."

She came over to him, smiling sadly, running a hand up his arm. "I do."

He cupped her cheek, thumb tracing the deep lines around her smiling mouth and hazel eyes. Her face was well lived in, but in the soft, forgiving glow of lamplight, he saw the pretty girl she must once have been, full of hopes and dreams that wouldn't have passed her by, if life were in any way fair. Her body, too, had lost the firmness of youth, but had acquired in its place the warmth and uninhibited generosity that comes to the best of women in middle age. "I haven't taken care of you," he said.

"It's not that. You take care of me just fine. You remember my birthday. You make me chicken soup when I get a cold. You sit beside me when I watch my stupid shows and never make fun when I blubber. You check the oil in my car, keep my brakes tuned and my tires aligned. There's not much you wouldn't do for me, Frank, I know that. Except the one thing I really want, and that's not your fault. You can't make yourself be in love with me."

He started to reply, but she put her fingers on his lips, saving them both the embarrassment of an empty protest.

"No, it's okay. That's just the way it is. I knew going in how things were with you. I guess I hoped it might change. Or, if not, that what we had would be enough." She shook her head. "But it's not. Not for either of us."

In his heart, Tucker knew she was right. She needed more than he was capable of giving her, and cutting her losses was probably the best thing for her to do. Knowing that didn't make it any easier, though.

She kissed him then, and he wrapped her in his arms, holding on just a little longer. The next thing he knew, they were pushing her suitcase off the bed. And it might very well have been the best lovemaking they'd ever had, but it didn't change the fact that afterward, Patty had finished her packing, loaded her Toyota and driven away.

Sighing heavily, now, Tucker stared at the big oak bed. His and Joanne's twins had been conceived there. She'd nursed them in the chintz-covered rocker next to it. Years later, Tucker had sat in that same chair, watching her life slip away. The Moroccan carpet beneath the chair was worn thin from the long hours of rocking.

His father had picked up the carpet in North Africa during World War II. A Marine gunnery sergeant, he'd somehow managed to cart the thing around for eight months before he was finally shipped home with a uniform full of campaign ribbons, a stump in place of his left arm and his stupid rug. He'd gone on to marry the hometown girl he'd left behind and raise six kids, of whom Frank was the eldest, all on a one-armed printer's wage—never, to the end of his days, uttering a word of complaint about his fate.

Tucker turned abruptly and headed for the bathroom, determined to shake off the sluggishness that enveloped him like a thick, syrupy mantle. *Clean yourself up, for God's sake. Give Carol a call, let her know you're home.*

But when he dialed his daughter's number a short while later, it was neither Carol nor Michael who picked up. It was Lindsay.

"Hi, Uncle Frank! You're home?"

"Just got in a little while ago." Taken aback at hearing Lindsay's voice, he fell into an awkward silence. She was the one who finally broke it. At fifteen, she had more polish than he did, Tucker thought ruefully.

"Carol's upstairs feeding the baby. I just read Alex a story and tucked him in for his afternoon nap. Actually, three stories. Four, if you count the one he made me read twice. I'd probably still be up there, except he fell asleep on the second reading."

Tucker smiled. His grandson was two, a whirling dervish.

"How was your trip?" Lindsay asked.

He hesitated. She had no idea where he'd been, of course.

Neither did Carol, nor anyone else for that matter. It had been a tiny group inside the agency that had studied the cryptic message that had prompted his sudden trip to Moscow. Not even the director had been briefed, so that if Tucker got himself arrested over there, or worse, the front office—and the White House, if it came to that—could claim he was a rogue operative who'd slipped the chain of command to settle some personal score. A burnout case, pushed over the edge by family problems that had nothing to do with official American policy toward its new Russian friends. Tucker had simply told Carol he'd be out of town for a while so she wouldn't worry if she didn't hear from him.

"Trip was fine," he said. "Dull. Is Carol going out? You baby-sitting this afternoon?"

"No, I'm staying here for a couple of days. Mom left early this morning for Los Angeles."

Tucker's pulse increased a notch. He'd recruited her mother himself. Mariah had worked with him for years in the old Soviet analysis unit, but their office partnership had ended when his career self-destructed. Since then, she'd moved on to bigger and better things, while he puttered on the sidelines, out of the field of action.

"I thought the two of you were going out there together," he said to Lindsay.

"I leave Thursday morning. There's an exhibit opening in L.A. tonight that she has to cover. The Russian foreign minister's going to be there."

"Oh, right, the Romanov treasures," Tucker said more casually than he felt. Why would Mariah be assigned to cover Zakharov's visit? That kind of thing wasn't in her bailiwick.

He had another sudden, uneasy thought. How coincidental was it that she'd been pulled into action just after he himself had received a mysterious summons to Moscow?

Tucker had started out in Operations, but had moved behind the lines when his wife first got sick. All these years, both he and Mariah had labored in the background, cranking out their intelligence assessments. But if there was one thing he'd come to realize on this Moscow trip, it was how much personal information the opposition had on him. And if on him, why not on her, too?

"Listen," he said to Lindsay, "tell Carol I called and I'm back, okay? I'll talk to her later."

"Okay. Will we see you soon?"

"You bet," Tucker said firmly.

He hung up the phone and went to find his car keys. Suddenly, it was no longer enough to let someone else examine what he'd thought were just musty records, selectively chosen and leaked to sway American thinking on the current power struggle in Moscow. He'd suspected, given his Russian contact's cryptic comments, that there was dirt on Foreign Minister Zakharov in there. Now he wondered if there was more to it than that.

He needed to know before anyone else saw those files.

Chapter
Three

As her plane touched down at Los Angeles International Airport, Mariah tried to tell herself that her only objective here was to do the job she'd been sent to do, and do it fast. Make contact with Yuri Belenko, see where his interests lay and file her contact report. If he seemed amenable to doing a little freelance work on the side, Ops would assign him a handler. Or not. Their call. As for her, she'd be free to pick up her rental car and the keys to the beach house, meet Lindsay's plane and get on with a much-needed vacation. End of story.

That's what she told herself. The truth was a little more complex, as truth tends to be.

They say time heals all wounds, but it's not entirely true. Some never really heal. On the surface, recovery may seem complete, but certain traumas leave a residual weakness that lurks in a troubled soul like a subterranean fault line, prone to unexpected eruption. There was such a susceptibility inside Mariah, unknown even to herself—a deep, dark place where resentment simmered and bubbled like hot, sulfurous magma. Until now, it had never percolated up to that place where liquid rage hardens into cold calculated action. But it's the nature of such fault lines to give way without warning, and the explosive results are nearly always devastating—even to innocent bystanders.

She checked into the Beverly Wilshire Hotel around noon, with an hour or so to kill before she had to head over to get the lay of the land at the Arlen Hunter Museum. The Romanov exhibit was set to open at six.

While she waited, Mariah decided to give Chap Korman a call. She tipped the bellboy who'd delivered her bag to her suite, then settled into a deeply upholstered wing chair, propping her feet on the bed's quilted floral spread, and dialed Korman's number from memory. In the twenty years since her mother's death, when Mariah had become the reluctant guardian of Ben Bolt's prolific output, she'd gotten to know the literary agent well.

"Mariah! I wasn't expecting you for another couple of days."

She smiled at the sound of his voice, although it sounded more wavery each time they spoke, Mariah thought sadly, anticipating the day when this last, best link to her past would be gone. Chap was alternately coy and grumpy about his age, but he'd been older than Ben by several years, so she calculated that he had to be at least in his mid-seventies by now. He'd long since left the bustle of New York to nurse his arthritic joints in the warmer climes of southern California, but he continued to represent a roster of longtime clients, even championing the occasional new one when he found a writer he believed in.

"I just got in. I'm staying at the Beverly Wilshire," she told him. "I was drafted for a short-term assignment, so I had to come early."

"Aha! A secret mission," he said delightedly. "Can't tell me what it is, right, or else you'd have to kill me?"

She rolled her eyes. "You read too many spy novels, Chap."

"Hey, this is exciting. You're the only spook I know."

"Big thrill. I could introduce you to twenty thousand other grunts who toil away in the same obscurity I do."

"So, is Lindsay with you on this covert job?"

"No, she's staying with friends. She flies in Thursday."

"Any chance you'll take me up on my offer? I'm just rattling around this big old place, you know. There's plenty of room."

Chap had retired to a lovely, bougainvillea-covered house in Newport Beach, of all places—an irony that never escaped her, since she tended to think of Newport as "the scene of the crime," having spent a fairly miserable youth there. Since she hadn't returned to the place in twenty years, she'd never actually seen Chap's house, except in photos. But his wife of fifty years had passed away the previous year, and Mariah knew he was lonely. She felt a twinge of guilt for not accepting the invitation.

"I really appreciate the offer. This cottage we've got is right around the corner. We'll practically be neighbors. That's the main reason I jumped on the place when the offer came up. I need some one-on-one with Lins, though. You know, kind of a mother-daughter-bonding-healing thing."

"I thought as much," he conceded, "otherwise I'd have gone all cantankerous on you. How's that little copper-haired honey of mine doing these days?"

"Oh, Lord! She's fifteen. Need I say more?"

"No, I guess not." Chap had raised sons, not daughters, but he had a good imagination. "What about Mom?"

"Day by day. Isn't that the conventional wisdom?" Mariah hesitated before confiding, "You know that assignment I mentioned? It's at the Arlen Hunter Museum—the opening of the Romanov exhibit. I'm supposed to help baby-sit the Russian delegation."

His heavy exhalation whistled down the line. "Oh, boy. I've been seeing ads for that show, and I thought of you. So? Is Renata going to be there?"

"I'm not sure. I imagine it's a strong possibility, though, don't you?"

"Probably. How do you feel about that?"

Good question. "Hard to say," she said truthfully. "I was under a lot of pressure to take this thing on. In the back of my mind, it occurred to me there was a good chance I'd run into Renata there, so I thought about digging in my heels and refusing. But you know what? Somehow I couldn't muster up the will. It's like morbid fascination with a car wreck or something. Part of me, I admit, is sick at the thought of seeing her after all these years. But another part of me is dying to get a look at the old witch.''

"Facing your demons, huh?''

"Maybe. Either that or pure masochism.''

Chap fell silent for a long moment. "Talk about timing,'' he said finally. "Did you get the package I sent you?''

"Package?''

"I overnighted it. I wanted you to see it as soon as possible. It should have gotten there today.''

"I'd probably left by the time it arrived. What was it about?''

"Your dad's manuscript. You know,'' the old man said thoughtfully, "it's a shame the press found out about those papers so soon.''

"I know. I'm really sorry about that. God knows, I didn't mean for it to get out. I was at a dinner with Paul Chaney. He was the only other person in the world besides you, me and Lindsay who knew they existed. He let it slip. We were in a roomful of reporters, so needless to say, the word spread like wildfire.''

"This Chaney—I've never met him, but he seems like a pretty savvy guy, at least on TV. And I thought the two of you were pretty close. Seems odd he'd do something so indiscreet, doesn't it?''

Mariah's free hand twisted the phone cord around her fingers until it began to cut off her circulation. "Funny you should say that. In my charitable moments, I try to convince myself it was an inadvertent blunder, but there are times when I think he did it on purpose. He had to know what a feeding frenzy the news would set off, and that I'd be forced to acknowledge the manuscript and journals existed.''

"Why would he do that?''

"Strangely enough, to try to be helpful. He thinks I should be making more effort to come to terms with Ben's memory. And I have, to some extent, Chap, mostly to satisfy Lindsay's curiosity. We went to visit Ben's grave in Paris, after all. I'd never done that before. But Paul thinks it would be therapeutic if I went further—got involved in promoting this new stuff, for example. I've tried to explain that there's a limit to how far I'm prepared to go with this father-daughter reconciliation, but he just doesn't get it.''

"I've been getting nipped by this media feeding frenzy myself,'' Chap said.

"I noticed you'd been quoted a few places. You seem to be holding them at bay pretty well.''

"I thought it best not say anything publicly until you and I had a chance to talk. But I got a letter from a prof out here at UCLA not long after the press reports started. His name's Louis Urquhart. He's working on a biography of your dad that's supposed to come out in time for Ben's sixtieth-birthday celebrations next year. By the way, I told you what the publisher's planning for the occasion, didn't I?''

"Repackaging and reissuing his whole collection?''

"Exactly. This Urquhart's not the only one interested in Ben's work these days. Might as well brace yourself, kiddo, because we're going to see a spate of books and articles about Ben over the next little while. He seems to be in vogue all over again with a new generation of readers.''

"I know,'' Mariah said. "Lindsay's English class studied *Cool Thunder* this year. So, what did this Urquhart have to say for himself?''

"It's a little complicated to go into over the phone, but he's making some pretty serious allegations. That's why I decided you'd better see his letter.''

"You're making me a little uneasy here, Chap.''

"Did you really not go through these papers of Ben's yourself, Mariah?''

"Not really. Skimmed a couple of chapters of the manuscript to see if it was something new or just an earlier draft of a book that had already been published. I told you, the only reason I even opened the box is that the rental locker where I've been storing my excess junk since I sold the house got flooded during the heavy rains this spring. I've been carting those papers around for years. When I realized they'd gotten damp, it was either chuck the whole lot or see if you thought anything should be done with them. I didn't have time to do it myself.''

Or the inclination, she could have added. She'd looked just closely enough to see that there was some sort of work in progress there, as well as more personal papers. She hadn't the competence to judge the fiction, she'd decided, and she certainly hadn't the stomach to read Ben's self-absorbed journal ramblings.

"I appreciate the trust it took for you to send these to me, Mariah," Chap said quietly.

She felt her eyes tearing up, and hated herself for it. "I know you'll do the right thing with them. Whatever you decide is fine with me."

"Thank you, sweetie. But I'm afraid it's not that simple. We may have a bit of a problem on our hands."

"How so?"

"Look, maybe the best thing would be for us to get together with Louis Urquhart while you're out here."

"Oh, Chap, no. Lindsay and I are supposed to be on vacation. I don't want to waste it hanging out with Ben's adoring public."

"I know how you feel, but this is not something we can ignore."

There was something in his voice, graver than Mariah had ever heard. "Okay, now I *am* worried. What could possibly be so all-fired important that—"

"Urquhart thinks the manuscript of the novel was stolen from someone else, Mariah. And he thinks Ben was murdered."

She answered with stunned silence.

"Now, I'm not saying I buy it," Korman added quickly. "I admit, there were a few surprises in those journals of Ben's, and the novel is unlike anything else he wrote. But it's a big leap from there to what Urquhart is alleging. Bottom line, though? Urquhart could have blindsided us by taking his allegations public, but he didn't. So I think it's only fair to hear the guy out, and then we'll decide together where to go from there. Okay?"

"But this is crazy, Chap! Murdered? We know how he died. At least, I always thought we did. Don't we? Wasn't my mother told that the French authorities did an autopsy when his body was found, and that he'd died of hepatitis?"

"She was, yes."

"So how did we get from hepatitis to murder?"

"I'm not sure. That's obviously one question we need to put to Urquhart—what evidence has he got to support his allegations?"

Mariah studied the nubbly, butter-colored wallpaper over the bed. "I don't know. This sure smells like a muckraking publicity stunt to me. Like this Urquhart's looking for a best-seller."

"If it were anybody else, I'd agree. But Louis Urquhart's one of the most respected literary academics in this country. His biography of Jack Kerouac won a Pulitzer Prize. I don't think he'd be building this murder theory if he didn't have some facts to back it up. Plus, he came to me first, remember, not the press."

She exhaled heavily and glanced at her watch. "All right. If you think it's really necessary, we'll talk to him. I have to head off to the museum now. How about if I call you again when my work's done? With any luck, I might have a free day tomorrow. Maybe we can get this out of the way before Lindsay arrives."

"Sounds good. Meantime, I'll let Urquhart know we're willing to meet with him. And Mariah?"

"Mmm?"

"As far as Renata's concerned? I know you and your mom and sister got a raw deal when Ben took off to Paris with her like he did. But Renata didn't last long, did she? He tired of her pretty fast. People who know her say she never got over him, though."

"Gee, that's really tough."

"Yeah, I don't feel too much pity for her, either. Your mom always believed Ben was going to come back to you guys, only he died before he could make it. But whatever happened over there, one thing is sure: in the end, Renata lost. Remember that if you see her, honey."

"No, Chap," Mariah said wearily. "We *all* lost."

Chapter
Four

Frank Tucker sat in his windowless office, feet on his desk, reading files that were mildewed and yellow with age. He'd been at it three hours, and his eyes felt scoured. His nose had long since blocked in protest over the barrage of mold spores, and his head ached from lack of sleep and the concentrated effort of reading the musty Russian documents. But his brain was racing.

He set down the file in his hand. As he stretched, the worn, cloth-covered swivel chair under him shrieked in protest at the shift of his great frame. Hands clasped behind his head, he stared at the random punctures on the ceiling's gray acoustic tiles, pondering again how it was that he, personally, had been selected to receive this carefully selected record of KGB mischief and misdeeds.

History is a moth-eaten fabric, full of holes—a vast tapestry of change whose underlying pattern is obscured by official secrecy and necessary lies. A thousand untimely ends and unaccountable triumphs are doomed to remain mysteries forever, their solutions locked away in the memories of shadowy operators who die unconfessed.

Some clues lie buried in the dusty files of the world's great clandestine agencies, where the harsh light of public scrutiny never falls. But as each regime gives way to the next, furnaces are lit and burn bags are consumed by flame—incriminating evidence lost forever.

Most, but not all, Tucker thought, glancing at the tattered files around him.

Of all the secret agencies, none hid more mysteries than the yellow and gray stone walls of the KGB's old Moscow headquarters. It was from behind the heavy steel doors of Lubyanka that a message had originated in late June, marked for delivery to one semi-burned-out official of the American CIA. It was that message, delivered late one night, a week earlier, that had sparked Tucker's quick, clandestine trip to the Russian capital.

He'd been driving home by a circuitous route along quiet back roads. It was nearly midnight, but day and night tended to lose meaning in his underground office, where not much happened and few people dropped by. Tucker spent his time these days poring over old agency files, responding to Freedom of Information requests from historians, journalists and the generally curious. He culled cover names, sources and other sensitive data from the files, deciding which could safely be declassified and released, and which had to remain closed to protect ongoing operations.

He had no clock to punch, no strenuous deadlines to meet. He simply worked alone until his eyes grew too bleary to read any longer. Then he returned to his empty house and prayed for sleep. Taking the longest possible route was his way of decompressing, releasing tension like a ball of string unwinding on the road behind him.

On that particular cool, starlit June night, the suburban back roads of Virginia were deserted when Tucker brought his Ford Explorer to a stop at an intersection in McLean, just a couple of miles from the agency. As he waited for the light to change from red to green, a dark sedan materialized out of nowhere, pulling alongside him. The driver got out and knocked at his passenger-side window.

Instantly on alert, Tucker sized him up—medium height and build, sandy hair. Fit-looking under his dark windbreaker. Young—thirty, tops, he decided.

Tucker pressed a button on his armrest to lower the opposite window. With his other hand, he reached down between the seats and came up with a nine-millimeter surprise. If the stranger was a cop or a fed, Tucker could produce a carry permit for the gun. If this was a hit, the guy might as well know right off Tucker wasn't going down without a fight.

The blue eyes in the window widened. "I mean you no harm, Mr. Tucker," he said. His tongue was tripping on the words in his rush to get them out. The vowels were clipped, the consonants weighted with a heavy Slavic burr.

"You know my name," Tucker said. "I should know yours."

"It is not important."

"That's a matter of opinion."

"I am only a courier."

"What can I do for you?"

"I have a message for you. Please?" The man raised a brown manila envelope in his trembling hand.

"Who's it from?"

"I cannot say. You take it, please?" He started to pass the envelope through the window, but Tucker raised the gun until it was aimed right between the young man's eyes.

"Hold it right there," he said. "I don't want that."

Obviously, this wasn't the anticipated response. "But... but, it is for you!" the courier sputtered.

"Do I look like I was born yesterday?"

"No."

"Then you'll believe me when I say I know a blackmail play when I see one. Where's the camera?" Tucker glanced around. The road was dark and quiet as death. If there were professional watchers out there, they were good. Still, the whole thing stank to high heaven. If he accepted the envelope, he was damn sure the next visit he got would be from this fellow's friends, threatening to expose him as a double agent. Then, another wary thought occurred to him. His own side? Could CIA security or the FBI be looking to jam him up for some reason?

"There is no camera. I swear it," the messenger said fervently.

"Just the same, I don't want that thing."

"It is important. I am instructed to give it to no one but you."

"You know where I work?"

"I am guessing you are employed at the C-I-A in Lan-ge-ley, Virginia," the stranger said with heavily accented precision. "Am I correct?"

"Deliver it to me there, then."

"Are you mad? I cannot walk into that place!"

Tucker considered the situation, then nodded toward the intersection. The light had changed from red to green, then back again. "There's a 7-Eleven store up ahead. Follow me, and you can hand it over inside." In front of a witness, he thought, and the store security cameras.

The courier shook his head. "If I do that, I am a dead man."

"I'm not going to hurt you."

The other man sniffed, as if such a threat was beneath his dignity to ponder now that he'd recovered from the initial shock of having the gun thrust in his face. "It is not you I am worried about, Mr. Tucker, nor your colleagues. My own people are another matter."

Tucker frowned. "Your own people? Oh, I see. You want to defect, is that it? Or are you just in sales?"

"I am a patriot!" the other man said indignantly. "It is why I do this. But perhaps my colleagues are mistaken. Perhaps you are not the man they take you for. In which case, Mr. Tucker, I will bid you good-night."

"Hold it right there."

Tucker studied him for a moment, as well as the thin envelope. Then, he reached into his pocket, withdrew a penknife, pausing to wipe the handle on his shirtsleeve before handing the knife over by the key ring attached to one end.

"Open this and use the blade to lift the flap. But do it carefully, hear? You're going to reseal the envelope afterward."

"I must not open it."

"Why? Some danger in that?"

"No, but—"

"Do it."

The young man hesitated, then sighed heavily. Opening the

penknife, he inserted the blade under the flap, separating it gingerly, leaving just enough gum in place to allow it to be closed once more.

"Now, spread the edges and show me what's inside," Tucker said.

No money. No fat wad of smuggled documents. Just a single sheet of paper that seemed to be covered with handwriting.

Tucker nodded. "Okay. Seal it back up again."

The other man licked the flap and pressed it shut. "You will take it now?"

"I want my knife back first."

The courier handed it through the window. Tucker took it with his handkerchief, transferring both to his left hand. Then, as the Russian started to pass in the envelope, Tucker's right hand clamped around his wrist.

"What are you doing?" the courier protested.

Tucker jabbed the other man's thumb with the tip of the knife. Not much—a pinprick, really, just enough to draw blood. Hardly enough to justify the stream of Russian obscenities that exploded from the other man's mouth. Yanking the man's arm downward, Tucker pressed the bloody thumb firmly against the flap, making a seal across the reclosed edges. Then, he released him.

The Russian jammed his thumb into his mouth. "What the hell you are doing that for?" he cried, grammar failing him in his fury.

Tucker closed the knife carefully, wrapped it in the handkerchief and dropped them both into the door pocket beside him. Only then did he take the envelope. "Sorry," he said. "Personal insurance. Now I have your fingerprints on my knife and your DNA on the envelope."

"If my people find out—"

"As long as you don't try playing games with me, your people will never know. You have my word on that. Now, what else? Do I need to get in touch with you again?"

"No, I have done my part. The next step is up to you."

"Meaning...?"

"Read the letter. You will know what you are to do. Good evening, Mr. Tucker."

With that, the Russian turned away in a huff, still nursing his injured thumb, climbed back in his car, jumped a red light and sped away through the empty intersection. Tucker took note of the red diplomatic plates as the car disappeared into the night. Curiouser and curiouser.

His eyes dropped to the blank brown envelope. He turned it around in his hand, then laid it on the seat beside him, keeping the blood-smeared flap on top, away from the upholstery.

As the light at the intersection changed from red to green once more, Tucker punched in a number on his console-mounted cell phone, picked it up and made a U-turn, heading back toward Langley.

A fingerprint on the knife allowed them to identify the courier from visa files. His name was Gennady Yefimov, a recently arrived third secretary at the Russian embassy in Washington—a junior flunky, albeit one already suspected of being part of the embassy's intelligence *Rezidentura*. His late-night rendezvous with Tucker pretty much confirmed it.

The source of the message was another kettle of fish altogether. The note was in Russian, but the signature was a single English word: "Navigator." It was a taunt, this use of the secret code name given to the Russian spymaster by his own adversaries in tribute to the man's ability to navigate Moscow's treacherous political waters. Even after the fall of communism, the Navigator had remained in place, thriving, by all accounts, when so many others had foundered and sunk.

That he knew and used his own Western code name was a galling reminder of the mole the Navigator had run for years inside Langley, a disgruntled petty functionary in the counterintelligence division. The mole had finally been caught, but not before his betrayals had cost the lives of dozens of Company assets in Russia.

Tucker had never seen the Navigator's face, except in one grainy, long-range surveillance photograph, nor had he ever heard the man's voice. Just the same, he knew his real name as well as he knew his own. For as long as Tucker had been in the business, Georgi Deriabin, aka the Navigator, had been the dream target of the entire Western intelligence alliance. As head of the KGB—later FSB—First Chief Directorate, he'd held overall responsibility, both before and after the Soviet breakup, for every aspect of Moscow's intelligence activities abroad. Compared to other sources of information on Russian agents, operations and long-term strategies, Deriabin was the frigging motherlode.

Or would have been, until recently. He'd be in his late seventies now, and rumors of ill health had begun to surface. Recently, the CIA's Moscow Station had floated the possibility that the Navigator had finally been shuffled out. Like J. Edgar Hoover in his day, however, the Navigator was said to possess incriminating files on everyone who might be a threat to him. When rumors began to spread of his eclipse at long last, there were those in Moscow Station who suspected he'd been arrested, possibly even executed. But if the Navigator really *was* the source of the note delivered to Tucker by the nervous courier, it had obviously been a mistake to write the man off too early.

The note said Deriabin wanted to meet with Tucker in Moscow—nobody *but* Frank Tucker—and it said he would make the meeting well worth the trouble. And so, after a small committee had vetted the plan and decided there was little to lose—except, Tucker knew they were calculating, one jaded officer whose best years seemed behind him—he'd flown to Moscow. If the operation had blown up in his face, they'd have simply written him off, issued some plausible cover story and saved the price of his pension.

But Tucker had come back, alive, well and carrying a crate of files whose contents remained to be determined. Not to mention the reason why the Navigator had decided to hand them over in the first place.

Chapter
Five

Mariah had her hotel-room key card in one hand and the other on the door handle, ready to leave. She was wearing her serviceable, goes-anywhere-but-a-gala-opening black Donna Karan suit. Her plan was to run over to the Arlen Hunter Museum, get the lay of the land and meet with the rest of the security contingent for the Romanov opening, chase back, change into the Chinese-mandarin silk number, then return in time for the 6:00 p.m. ribbon-cutting and reception.

But she hesitated at the door, her conversation with Chap Korman spinning through her mind. The bizarre allegation that her father had been murdered was patent, provable nonsense. But what about the claim that the manuscript she'd found had been stolen?

From whom? And why would Ben steal someone else's work? Writer's block? Not likely. In the nine short years before his death at the age of twenty-eight, her father had produced five novels, dozens of short stories and countless poems, not to mention several volumes of personal journals. You couldn't have shut the man up if you'd tried.

So why was this Professor Urquhart claiming the manuscript she'd found in the storage locker, the one Ben had titled

Man in the Middle, was stolen? And, more to the point, Mariah thought, why did she *know* that it couldn't be?

Something niggled at the back of her brain, telling her the manuscript had to be Ben's work. She just couldn't think what it was. The harder she tried to zero in on it, the more elusive it became, like trying to pick up mercury.

This was ridiculous. She had no time for this nonsense. God knew she had more pressing problems to think about. A teenage daughter on the verge of rebellion. This awkward role she'd been cast in, playing temptress to lure a possible double agent. The prospect of meeting her father's former lover.

Just the same, Urquhart's claims would drive her crazy until she knew the basis for them.

She did a quick mental calculation, cutting her afternoon turnaround times even tighter. Spinning on her heel, she rushed back into the room, tossed her purse and key card on the bed, then rummaged in drawers and closets until she found a Los Angeles telephone book. After a quick call to Courier Express, she pulled out her personal address book, picked up the phone and dialed out again.

It took three tries before she located someone at Langley who could tell her where Frank Tucker was hanging his hat these days. Every time she looked, he seemed to have retreated farther and farther away from the mainstream of agency operations. She was relieved to finally hear his gruff voice pick up.

"Tucker."

"Frank! You're there! I thought I was going to have to send out a search party."

"Mariah? Where are you? Lindsay said you'd gone to L.A."

"I did. I am—there, I mean. That's where I am. In Los Angeles." She paused to quell the fluster that had suddenly turned her into a stammering fool, then started again. "You've been talking to Lindsay?"

"A little while ago. I called to let Carol know I was back."

"Back from where?"

"I was away for a couple of days."

A non-answer if ever she'd heard one. It was like pulling

teeth, talking to him sometimes. "You've changed offices again. What's going on?"

"They needed my cubbyhole upstairs for some summer intern, so they gave me a broom closet down in the basement."

"The basement? Good Lord! Why do you let them do that to you? With your service—"

"I've got no complaints. Suits me fine."

Mariah slumped down onto a chair and leaned forward, elbow on the round glass table next to the bed, forehead in the palm of her hand. "Frank," she said wearily, "it's time."

"Time for what?"

"To come out from that rock you've been hiding under."

He said nothing for a moment, and she sensed she'd crossed an invisible line. She had known this man for eighteen years, ever since he'd first recruited her. There was no question they were bound to one another by something beyond mentoring, beyond professionalism, beyond friendship. They'd been through good times together, and sad. She'd known his wife; he'd known her husband. Once, she might have been able to talk to Frank about anything. Now, there was that invisible line.

Beyond this point there be dragons.

When he finally did respond, it was only to change the subject. "What's this about you covering the Zakharov visit? How did you get dragged into that?"

"Oh, no you don't," she said. Why should he always get to define the placement of the line? "You first. This trip of yours—where did you go?"

"That's a long story."

"I see. Holding out on me? You didn't happen to go to Florida by any chance, did you?" she asked playfully, trying to draw him out of the tight, defensive corner in which he seemed to live full-time these days.

"No," he said curtly.

Oops. She'd hit a nerve. Not surprising. Patty Bonelli had been at his side a long time, after all, and without her now, he seemed totally adrift, his last tether cut. It wasn't right or fair. He was solid, hardworking, capable. A good man, who looked as though he could carry the weight of the world on those broad shoulders of his—and had, professionally and personally, for years and without complaint. She was one of the few who knew the full price Frank had paid for that blind, stoic fidelity. Now he seemed to have closed himself off completely, to her, and maybe to everyone else, too.

"I'm sorry," she said. "I didn't mean to pry."

The line fell silent, but when Frank spoke again, she was relieved to hear a little of her old friend in his voice. "It's okay. The trip was business. That other, with Patty—it's just not happening, that's all."

"Have you spoken to her lately?"

"A couple of weeks ago. She called to say hi."

"How's she doing?"

"Seems happy enough down there. Got a cocker spaniel, apparently."

Poor Frank, Mariah thought. Replaced by a dog.

"Now tell me," he said, "what are you doing out there? I thought you and Lindsay were supposed to be on vacation."

"Day after tomorrow."

"Uh-huh. And explain to me why you, of all people, got dragged into covering the Zakharov visit?"

"That, too, is a long story, if you know what I mean."

"All right, not on the phone," he conceded. "Just tell me this—whose idea was it?"

"Hmm...well, remember Wanetta's old buddy?" Wanetta Walker had been a secretary in Frank's old Soviet section, rescued by him from the clutches of a certain Jack Geist from Operations, who'd been making her life miserable.

"He sent you? Son of a bitch." Tucker muttered. "You don't work for him, Mariah. You should have said no."

"I tried, but he pulled an end run on me. By the time he called me up to his office, he'd cleared it six ways to Sunday and it was pretty much a fait accompli. Anyway, not to worry. Job's just a twenty-four-hour deal. I'm heading out shortly, in fact. But, Frank? On an altogether different matter, I need a favor."

"What's that?"

"It's kind of a hassle. It involves running over to the Courier Express distribution center in Falls Church. If you don't have time for this, I want you to tell me, okay?"

"No problem. What's the deal?"

"They tried to deliver a letter to my house this morning, but I'd already left for the airport. Apparently, it had to be signed for, so they couldn't leave it. I called Courier Express and they said I could sign a release allowing a third party to collect it. There's an office just down the street from my hotel. I was going to stop in on my way out of here and do the paperwork. I wanted to give them your name, if that's okay."

"Sure," he said. "What's this about?"

"It's from my father's old agent, Chap Korman."

"Korman," he repeated, and Mariah had the impression he was writing down the name. "You want me to hold the letter till you get back, or ship it to you out there?"

"I was going to ask you to send it with Lindsay, but now that I think about it, I'd rather you open the envelope as soon as you get it. I want to know what the hell's inside."

"Why? What's going on?"

She exhaled heavily. "Chap Korman sent me a copy of a letter he received from some professor at UCLA who's working on a biography of my father. Apparently, this guy's come up with some kind of cockamamy theory that this manuscript I found—" She paused. "Maybe you didn't hear about that? I came upon an unpublished novel and some other personal papers of my father's a couple of months ago."

"Yeah, I read about it in the paper."

Mariah felt a tremor of guilt at the thought of Frank getting his news of her out of the newspaper. And seeing her photographed on Paul Chaney's arm. Damn. "Right," she said. "Anyway, this professor is apparently of the view that the manuscript was something my father stole. And it gets weirder. He's also suggesting Ben was murdered."

She expected derision or blunt dismissal of such an obviously stupid claim. A few pointed questions, at least. But all Frank said was, "I'll check it out."

"I just want to know where he's coming from before I see him while I'm out here. I'm sorry to be such a nuisance."

"You're not. I'm glad you called."

She'd called because there was no one else she trusted more, Mariah thought, struck by the realization of how much she'd missed Frank these past months. The line went quiet again, but this time it was one of those comfortable silences between kindred spirits, like an easy hand on the shoulder—more like the way things used to be before everything had gone so sour for them both.

She wished he weren't so far away and she weren't so pressed for time. Now that they'd reconnected, she wanted to talk—about a lot of things, including the worst part of this assignment Jack Geist had dumped in her lap—the possibility that it would bring her face-to-face with her father's old lover. But that, too, was a long story, and she had to get going to the museum. It was enough for now to know Frank was there.

"Thanks for doing this," she said. "I knew I could count on you."

His reply was almost inaudible. "Always."

Chap Korman had a fourteen-carat heart and a steel-trap mind, even at the ripe old age of seventy-seven. But his knees seemed made of pure chalk, screeching when he hoisted himself unsteadily to his feet. Wincing, he leaned against the low brick wall between his front courtyard and his neighbor's, and he waited for the pain to pass.

Since Mariah's call, he'd been busy planting a border of colorful impatiens along the wall. Thick, green gardener's pads Velcro-strapped over his khaki trousers helped a little to relieve the agony of working on his knees, but getting up again was another matter. There was no escaping that gravity works, and that his old joints just didn't support the weight of his body as well as they once had.

When he could finally move again, he knocked his trowel against the brick wall to dislodge clumps of loam, then slapped the dirt off his hands, viewing his handiwork with satisfaction. It was worth a few aches and pains. Emma's garden was looking good again. He'd never really appreciated how much work it took to keep it up.

Seventeen years ago, when they'd first moved out from New York, it was the location of this property that had appealed to them. The two-story clapboard house fronted on Newport Harbor, with only a pedestrian walkway between the front yard and the boat slips opposite running the length of the peninsula. The view was of anchored sailboats, Balboa

Island and the rolling hills of mainland Orange County beyond, rising above the masts.

Automobile access for the houses was via a nondescript lane at the back, a canyon of ugly garages at street level. But even that side of the house had had its secret potential—a spacious flat roof over the garage with a pristine and uninterrupted view west toward the Pacific Ocean, only a couple of blocks away. Just the place to add a deck to sit on in the evening and watch the setting sun.

The house had been run-down after years of hard use by summer renters, the front courtyard an arid wasteland of dead plants and broken flagstones. Chap and Emma had had the interior remodeled, consolidating two of the four bedrooms to provide a large library/office for Chap's wheeling and dealing on behalf of his clients. They'd also had a spa and gazebo added to the new back deck off the master bedroom.

Em, meantime, had single-handedly transformed the courtyard into a lush and brilliant oasis. It had been her greatest pleasure, a work-in-progress right to the end of her life. Chap, a night owl, would wake each day at midmorning to the soothing sound of her off-key humming under the window and know she'd been at it since sunup. In the end, it was the wilting garden, not the doctors, that told him how sick she really was.

At first, after she died, he'd let the yard go. When weeds threatened to overtake her beloved roses, and the blue Cape plumbago grew so leggy it started pushing over the low picket fence along the front walkway, he hired somebody to bring it under control and keep it tidy. But the day he came home to find Emma's roses butchered, Chap fired the gardener, dragged Em's tools out of the garage and took over the job himself. Lately, he was enjoying it more and more, despite his arthritic knees. He even found himself humming Sinatra as he worked, just as Em had done—although he liked to flatter himself that his pitch was better.

"Hey, Chap! Looking good," a voice behind him called.

Chap turned to see his neighbor being dragged out his front gate by a fat basset hound. At the other end of the leash, Kermit's big feet scrabbled under his saggy, low-slung body, tripping over his necktie ears, following his massive nose in headlong pursuit of whatever thrilling quarry it was he'd scented this time.

Chap grinned as he lifted the trowel in a wave. "'lo, Doug! See Kermit's taking you for your daily constitutional."

Doug Porter grimaced. "No kidding." He paused to wipe a fine sheen of sweat that was already forming on his bare scalp, close-shorn on the sides, bullet-smooth on top. "Listen, Chap, I'm glad I caught you out here. I was going to ask if your roses could be pruned back where they're coming through the fence."

Chap peered over. Sure enough, the climbers were beginning to wend their way into his yard. "Sorry about that. I never even noticed it," he said, reaching for the pruning shears hooked over his back pocket. "I'll cut 'em back right now."

"I hate to be a nuisance—"

"It's no trouble."

Chap started to reach over, but the hound rammed the gate and snorted his way through with a happy, basso profundo "Woof!" Chap turned and gave Kermit's tricolor head a pat, while Porter strained to keep him from climbing up the old man's frame. In his mid-forties, Porter was tanned and extremely fit, but the basset's powerful leg muscles and low center of gravity made the daily contest between them an uneven match that the dog inevitably won.

"Your friends arrive yet?" Porter asked breathlessly. He was dressed in his habitual black silk shirt and black pants— his signature look, Chap thought, though it seemed a ridiculous outfit for dog-walking on a hot day.

"Mariah did. She's up in L.A. Her daughter's coming behind. They should both be here tomorrow."

"So, what do you think? Would they like to come along and watch the fireworks from offshore?"

Porter had moved in a couple of months earlier, and this was the third or fourth time he'd held out an invitation to join him on his sloop, anchored in the harbor. Up to now, Chap had always found reasons to decline. Felt guilty about it, though. He had a sneaking suspicion his single neighbor was gay, and while his personal philosophy was a liberal live-and-let-live, a little knee-jerk anxiety always kicked in at the prospect of finding himself alone on a boat with the guy. But what did he think? That an overweight, arthritic senior citizen was in danger of being cast as a boy-toy du jour?

Porter seemed like a good guy, a gregarious architect who entertained all kinds of interesting people, from what Chap had seen. It would probably be a nice evening out there on the water, and Lindsay might get a real kick out of seeing the fireworks from that vantage point.

"I haven't had a chance to put it to them yet," he said. "I just talked to Mariah a while ago, but to be honest, I forgot to mention it. I hate to keep you on hold."

"It's no problem. I have to confess, I'd really love to meet them. I'm a huge Ben Bolt fan."

Chap paused, momentarily taken aback at that bit of news. A curious offshoot of the Ben Bolt legacy was the almost cultlike following inside the gay community, despite Ben's solid reputation as a ladies' man. Sounded like Porter was one of those devotees.

"I have to tell you," Chap said, "Mariah's not—a fan, I mean. She was only seven years old when Ben walked out on the family. Doesn't make for a lot of warm fuzzy memories on her part."

The dog had turned back toward the gate, and his claws scratched the sidewalk in his anxiety to move on. "Kermit, sit, dammit!" Porter commanded.

A waste of breath if ever there was. The dog seemed deaf as well as single-minded. The tug-of-war continued.

"Incorrigible mutt. Thanks for the warning, Chap. I'd have spent the whole evening blathering on like some starstruck teenager if you hadn't told me. I'd still love to have you all on board, though."

"It sounds like something they might enjoy," Chap admitted. "Can I ask them and get back to you?"

"You bet." The other man finally conceded defeat and gave the scrabbling mutt his head. "Catch you later!" he called over his shoulder, breaking into a loping jog.

Chap waved after them, grinning, then turned back to the roses and started pruning the few that were encroaching on the Zen-like tidiness of Porter's courtyard. He grunted as his short arms reached over the top of the pickets. If he had any brains, he'd walk around to the other side of the fence to do this, but he was tired, and he wanted to pack it in.

"Ouch! Damn!" he bellowed, nearly losing his balance as his bare fingers closed on a stem full of thorns. Now he knew why Em had always worn gardening gloves. He'd always thought it was just to protect her manicure.

When he'd finally cut back the last of the stragglers, he dumped them in the green waste recycling bin he'd rolled out to the courtyard, then gathered up the rest of the garden tools. His body was a mass of aching joints and muscles. He could do with a nap, he decided, dragging the bin and tools back to the side of the house. Then he had another thought—a wee drink, a nice soak in the Jacuzzi to ease his weary bones and *then* a nap.

He parked the bin in the narrow, shady passage between his house and Porter's, then entered the garage through the side door. Brilliant light assaulted his eyes, bouncing off the concrete lane and gleaming white stucco of his neighbors' high walls across the way.

Idiot. You left the garage door open.

He berated his absentmindedness. The neighborhood was virtually crime-free most of the year, but summer always brought a spate of burglaries—opportunistic crimes, petty thieves slipping through unlocked back doors, stealing wallets and purses while residents sat in their waterfront courtyards.

Chap walked out, glancing up and down the lane. Not a soul in sight. With its astronomical real estate prices and postage-stamp yards, the area attracted mostly professional singles and empty nesters, so there were no kids out riding bikes. Nor, with its narrow sidewalk and blinding, foliage-free glare, did the lane encourage strolling.

Satisfied the coast was clear, he went back in, rounding his old, silver-gray Jaguar to Emma's worktable. He wiped down the tools with an old rag, then gave them a coat of oil, just as she'd always been careful to do, and replaced them in her red wicker gardening basket. He unstrapped the Velcro knee-pads and hung them on their pegboard hook, then traded his old, mud-spattered Topsiders for the soft kid slippers he'd left by the inside door. His hand hit the button to close the garage door as he walked into the house.

Next item on the agenda: two or three fingers of scotch.

He carried the glass and bottle upstairs, setting the bottle on the nightstand. After a couple of sips from the glass, he set it on the rim of the spa and hit the controls to turn on the jets. He stripped out of his clothes on his way back across the bedroom to the bathroom, then showered off the garden dirt.

He was wrapping a towel around his waist when he heard a click. A door latch?

Chap stepped cautiously into the bedroom. Nothing. He padded out to the hall. His office next door was cluttered, as always, with manuscripts waiting to be read. He slid open the closet door. The space inside had been fitted with shelves to hold some of the overflow. There, on the bottom shelf, sat the cardboard box containing the trove of Ben Bolt papers Mariah had sent him.

Not for the first time, it occurred to him that he really needed an office safe. There wasn't much of irreplaceable value in the room, but those papers were one of a kind. There were people who'd give a pretty penny to get their hands on an unpublished Bolt manuscript or his private journals.

No more procrastinating, Korman. Right after the Fourth, you call a contractor and get a safe installed.

Another noise interrupted his resolution-making. He stepped back into the hall, peering over the banister to the open area below. Mr. Rochester, the old black tomcat Em had adopted from the local animal shelter, was sprawled in a sunbeam on Emma's favorite blue chintz chair, one rear leg raised high as he washed himself.

"Keep the noise down, will ya?" Chap grumbled.

Rochester peered up, blinked disdainfully, then went back to licking his rear end. The cat had stopped coming upstairs altogether. Too bloody fat to make the climb, Chap decided. During the months Em was sick, though, the animal never left her bedside except to eat or use the litter box. After she died, the cat had walked around the house yowling plaintively for days. Now, man and feline cohabited like some interspecies Odd Couple. Rochester lived on Em's chair, ignoring Chap entirely except at mealtimes. Even then, the Fancy Feast got a suspicious sniff before he deigned to bolt it down.

"Stupid cat," Chap muttered, returning through his room to the deck. He'd overdone it in the garden. His joints felt as if they were swelling. He should take a pill, but he was too damn tired to walk back to the bathroom cabinet.

Instead, he dropped his towel and climbed naked into the churning spa, as he habitually did now that Em was no longer there to fret about peeping Toms with binoculars. The nearest building high enough to see down onto his second-story deck had to be half a mile away. Odds were, nobody out there was looking, but if they were, his round, sagging, hairy-ape body made for pretty poor voyeuristic pickings. Anybody that hard up was welcome to the thrill.

Reaching for his drink, he took another long sip, then set it back on the edge of the tub and leaned into the molded seat and cushioned neck rest. Soothing amber comfort slid down to his center core. Chap closed his eyes, one hand lazily raking his matted chest. The warmth of the scotch, the sun and the Jacuzzi melted his aches and lulled him. This was as close to perfect as it got, he thought, lacking only Em to share it.

Suddenly, he felt a distinct vibration under his butt, like the tread of a nearby foot. His eyes opened to the brilliant blue sky, and he looked around. Em's red geraniums swayed in the breeze, potted in the old whiskey cask she'd transformed into a dual-purpose planter and base for the green market umbrella that shaded their his-and-hers rattan lounge chairs. Except for chirping birds and the dull rumble of distant beach traffic, the afternoon was sunny, hot and blessedly silent.

Had he locked all the downstairs doors before coming up? The garage he'd closed—that much he knew. But the side door? And the front, leading to the courtyard and the walkway beyond? Must have. He hadn't lived in New York for nearly sixty years without acquiring a few security tics, after all.

He strained to mentally retrace his steps. Hadn't even used the front door today, he realized. Mariah had called just as he was getting ready to put the impatiens in the front bed. He'd taken the call in the kitchen, then gone out through the garage to collect the tools, the flat of plants and the recycling bin.

The side door of the garage was on a spring. Had he reset the lock?

He took another sip of his drink and settled back into the gently pulsing water. Check it later. He was a New Yorker. A onetime amateur boxer with a 17–0 record. Never lived timidly before. Wasn't about to start now. Too tired to sweat it, anyway.

The churning of the Jacuzzi lulled him like rolling waves. Like being on a boat, he thought, drifting. Porter's boat. Mariah. And Lindsay...fifteen, already! Last time he'd seen her? Her dad's funeral. A heartbreaker even then. Like her mother. Grandmother, too. Incredible Ben would abandon his pretty wife, Andrea, for a man-eater like Renata Hunter. Human nature, Chap thought...no accounting for it.

He reached for his drink. Misjudged the distance. His perspective was all wonky, he realized idly. Fingers only brushed the glass. It tumbled in slow motion to the deck, each amber drop distinct as it splashed on the wooden planks.

Chap felt his butt slide a little on the smooth plastic bottom. So tired. His head lolled on the cushioned rest. He looked back toward the bedroom. Squinted, then frowned. Was that someone in the doorway?

"Hey, you," he called. Thought he did.

Did he?

Figure in the doorway never moved. Half hidden in shadow. Just a grim smile. Teeth gleaming like a goddam Pepsodent commercial.

Well, let him stand there, Chap thought grumpily. Guy wasn't going to make the effort to be sociable, neither would he.

He lay back and closed his eyes. So comfortable.

He felt himself slipping a little more. Opened his eyes. Guy in the doorway still watching him. Why? he wanted to ask, but he felt a little dizzy. Short of air. Inhaled deeply and slipped again on the slick plastic, his body pivoting. Almost on his side now, shoulders underwater.

Be up in a minute, Em. Just gonna grab forty winks here, okay?

So sleepy. A deep sigh. Another long slip on the smooth bottom, his head bumping on the hard plastic edge as Chap Korman sank beneath the churning bubbles.

Chapter
Six

The quiet was beginning to get on Tucker's nerves. When
he started hearing the building breathe, he knew he was losing
it.

Logically, he knew the deep thrum permeating his office
walls was the reverberation of massive air conditioners. Their
primary function was to cool—not people but a vast array of
supercomputers, satellite receivers and transmission devices—sensitive equipment that bristled day and night, pro-
cessing the agency's sensory input and outgoing commands.

Once aware of the pulsing rhythm, though, Tucker couldn't
shake the sense he'd been swallowed alive by some huge
beast of prey.

He glanced at his watch, wondering if he had time to run
out and pick up Mariah's letter from the Courier Express distribution center in Falls Church. The place was open till
10:00 p.m. He had plenty of time. What he didn't have was
patience. Geist's secretary had phoned down over four hours
ago to tell him to stand by to be summoned upstairs for a
debriefing on his Moscow trip. Now he was itching to walk
out.

It would have been premature to tell Mariah this Urquhart
character might not be as far off base as she thought. Better

to find out what the professor knew, then decide what to do about it. This should have been ancient history by now, Tucker thought grimly. She had enough on her plate. Damn them all to hell, anyway.

One file sat on his desk a little apart from the others he'd pulled from the Navigator's crate. He'd stumbled across it not long after talking to Mariah. Finally, the pieces were falling together. His late-night message from the courier. His cryptic conversation with the Navigator in Moscow. And the reason why he, in particular, had been chosen to receive this loaded gift.

Tucker had met with Georgi Deriabin late at night in a modest *dacha* on the outskirts of Moscow—although recognizing the infamous Navigator had required a leap of imagination on his part.

Deriabin was tall and skeletally thin, with weathered skin the color of mustard. His wispy white hair was shorn to a stubble, leaving his head almost as smooth as Tucker's own. On closer examination, Tucker saw the ravages of chemotherapy. When the old man reached out to shake hands, Tucker was afraid he'd crush those birdlike bones.

"I'm glad you could come, Mr. Tucker."

"Hard to turn down such an intriguing invitation."

The wizened figure just smiled and shuffled ahead of him into the cottage. Most of the ground floor seemed to consist of a small sitting and dining room. A cloth-covered table had been set for two, a bottle of vodka nestled in an ice bucket alongside.

Since Tucker's arrival that morning, he'd spent the entire day at the Intourist Hotel, waiting, as directed, for further instructions. The smell of onions, sausage and other good things now was a painful reminder he'd eaten nothing all day except a protein bar he'd taken from the emergency-rations stock of the Company plane that had flown him in.

"You will join me for dinner, yes?" Deriabin said.

Tucker considered refusing for about a millisecond, then nodded.

As soon as they sat down, a portly woman he took to be the housekeeper started carrying in food, generous platters of herring, black bread, sausages and sauerkraut, blinis and *piroshki.* Hearty but simple fare.

Tucker glanced around. The cottage, too, was comfortable but modest, with white plastered walls, exposed rough beams and sturdy country furnishings. A KGB safe house? he wondered. Or a sign of the Navigator's reduced fortunes? Yet how diminished could Deriabin's position be when he'd been able to arrange not only to get a message out, but also for the CIA plane to over-fly and land in Russian territory?

The old man poured a glass of vodka for each of them. The toast, the first of many that night, was perfunctory enough, if ironic.

"To your good health, Mr. Tucker."

Tucker considered reciprocating, but in the other man's case, the wish seemed a little belated and beside the point. He lifted his glass and nodded, then followed the old man as he threw it back.

They directed their attention to the food, but Deriabin ate little, picking at it for a few minutes before setting his fork aside and lighting a cigarette. "You will excuse me, please. The food, I assure you, is excellent. And perfectly safe," he added, reading Tucker's mind. "Unfortunately, my appetites are no longer what they once were. Liver cancer, my doctors tell me. I gather I have a few weeks. Three months, at best. But we must live for the moment, no?" He refilled their glasses, raised his briefly, then downed it in one gulp.

Over the next few hours, Tucker watched the bottle slowly drain, doing his part to keep up with the old man. Deriabin seemed coherent, despite his obvious illness and the amount of drink he'd consumed. Like most men with unfettered power, he seemed to have lost the art of two-way conversation, requiring only an audience. Tucker was content to give him one, and Deriabin rambled on about myriad subjects both philosophical and trivial without ever zeroing in on the heart of the matter—why he had made contact. Tucker decided to let the hand play itself out. Having taken up the dare and come, he was at the old man's disposition. All he had to do was keep his cool and see where things went.

When the dishes had been cleared away, they sat alone and uninterrupted. For a while, a television droned in another room, where, it seemed, the housekeeper and driver were watching a dubbed version of *Jurassic Park*. Pretty appropriate, Tucker thought as he listened to the dinosaur across the table from him rehash the good old days, when the struggle between the Soviet and American empires had dominated the international landscape.

The bottle was nearly empty when Deriabin threw out what seemed at first to be no more than a drunkard's complaint. "Women!" he grumbled. "Why is it so impossible to put a good mind and a good ass in one package, eh? Tell me that."

No reply was expected. Tucker let the man rant.

"Every woman with half a brain they ever sent up to me had a face like a potato and legs like tree stumps! And the decent-looking ones? The mental capacity of pickled herring—although," Deriabin added, arching a grizzled eyebrow, "there's good eating in that, just the same, eh?"

He chuckled at his own humor, but it quickly turned into a strangled cough. His yellowed skin grew darker as he gasped and pulled a handkerchief from his sleeve. He was wearing a heavy hand-knit sweater, despite the warmth of the summer night. Tucker averted his gaze as he spit into the phlegm-stained square.

When he finally recovered, Deriabin squinted at him through a blue haze of smoke. "Anyway, this has been my problem. But you," he said, waggling a bent, tobacco-stained finger, "you have been very lucky, eh, you sly wolf? How did you manage this?"

"Manage what?"

"To keep that woman at your side all those years. What was her name?"

Tucker frowned. Patty? Why would he—

"You know," Deriabin insisted, "the blonde. Small, very attractive, from the pictures I saw. Clever, too, I'm told." He snapped his fingers impatiently, struggling for a name. "The lovely widow."

Tucker's blood froze. Mariah. He forced his gaze to remain steady on the old man. "Can't think which one you mean. Got a few good-looking ones kicking around the place," he added wryly, tilting his glass.

The Navigator's jaundiced eyes narrowed. Then he tipped

back his own glass. Tucker watched it drain. How a man with a diseased liver could consume that much vodka defied all logic.

The tumbler dropped back to the table. "It only proves my point," Deriabin rasped. "You get more beautiful women than you can even *remember,* while my people never send me one who doesn't look like she was suckled on lemons instead of mother's milk."

Nothing more was said on the subject as they worked their way through what remained of the bottle and the night. At 2:00 a.m. the driver knocked on the door to let them know it was time to leave for the uncharted airstrip on the outskirts of Moscow where the Company plane had been cleared to land and wait for Tucker's predawn departure.

Deriabin went along for the ride. As soon as they pulled onto the tarmac, the driver jumped out, but the Navigator remained in place behind the car's opaque tinted windows. Tucker felt the rear of the car dip and rise as the driver opened the trunk and removed something. His guard went up, but when the lid of the trunk slammed, he saw through the rear window that the driver had only unloaded a wooden crate.

"I am giving you some files for safekeeping," the Navigator said.

The driver opened the back door of the car on Tucker's side and lifted the lid of the box for inspection.

"What's in them?" Tucker asked.

"Not a bomb, if that's what you're thinking."

"Wasn't worried about that," he replied truthfully. The aircraft crew would pass the crate through metal and chemical scanners before they would agree to load it. He could see them through Deriabin's window, watching the car. Wondering what the hell was going on, obviously.

"At least, not a bomb of the traditional variety," Deriabin added, striking a match and cupping his hands to light another cigarette. He straightened creakily, inhaling the smoke deeply, as if the predawn breeze coming in through Tucker's open door was too rich a mixture for his compromised system to handle. "You will find they make interesting reading." He nodded to the driver, who closed the crate and walked over to the plane, handing it off to one of the American crewmen.

"Why are you turning these papers over to us?" Tucker asked.

"Not 'us,' Mr. Tucker. I am turning them over to *you*."

"Fine. Me. Why?"

"Because you have time to give them the attention they deserve. You are underused these days, I'm told."

"If you know that, then you know they could easily be taken off my hands the minute I get back."

"That would be a great pity and a great mistake. Take my word on this, my friend, even if you are disinclined to believe most of what I say. No one else will have as much interest in these files as you. No one else will ensure that what they contain is properly handled."

Deriabin extended his emaciated hand. Again, Tucker worried about crushing the brittle bones under that transparent skin, but the old man's grip was firm.

"This will be goodbye for me," Deriabin said. "Only remember this, my friend—no man on earth desires as passionately as a Russian. Beware the one who desires too much."

On the flight back, Tucker had been too exhausted and too drunk to give that or anything else much thought. It was only the next day, picking through the files, that he recalled the Navigator's words. Who was "the one who desires too much"? he wondered.

Foreign Minister Zakharov, he presumed now. It seemed clear from the content of the files that Deriabin was determined for some reason to derail the man's ambition by any means necessary—even treason. Zakharov's rise to power had been nearly as ruthless as Deriabin's own, but Tucker was aware of no evidence the two men had ever been rivals before now. So what had changed?

Then there was the old man's apparently drunken commentary on women. His pointed reference to Mariah had been anything but haphazard, Tucker knew. It was to demonstrate the man knew where Tucker was most vulnerable. That, however debilitated the Navigator might seem, he had no compunction about manipulating that vulnerability for his own purposes. And that he was confident Tucker would act on the information in the files.

Well, maybe, Tucker thought grimly. But not necessarily

in the way Deriabin expected. Because the linchpin in the Navigator's scheming, he now knew, was the death in Paris nearly thirty years earlier of an impoverished American author. And if it were up to Tucker, that episode could bloody well remain shrouded in lies.

But it wasn't up to him.

After Mariah's call from Los Angeles, he realized the decision might already be out of his hands. Although fame had eluded Ben Bolt in life, it had grown exponentially in the years since his death, pretty much guaranteeing that someone, sooner or later, would stumble on the truth. If not this Urquhart character, then someone else.

Now it was time for damage control.

Still shaken by the eerie timeliness of Mariah's call, and by hearing her voice for the first time in weeks, Tucker gathered the musty folders abruptly and got to his feet. If they hadn't called him upstairs by now, to hell with them. He'd go and collect her letter.

Or not.

A rap sounded on his door and the Operations deputy strode in without waiting for a response. "Hey there, Frank," Jack Geist said breezily.

Tucker nodded. "Jack."

"Don't get up on my account." Geist dropped his lanky frame into a chair on the other side of the desk, giving the cramped office a smug once-over as his legs sprawled out in front of him. "See you got back safe and sound from your trip. Would've called you up first thing, but things have been a little wild today."

"I figured."

"You heard about this Kurdish business?"

Tucker nodded and sat down again. He was out of the loop, but he wasn't brain-dead. He'd been in the game long enough to know that any situation making headlines would have the front office running to stay ahead of the breaking-news wave. The morning papers said the Turkish crisis had heated up overnight, with rebel Kurds massing for imminent confrontation with government forces.

"I gather the Russians have sent forces southward through Armenia," he said.

The deputy grimaced. "Bastards just can't resist mixing into it, can they?"

"They'll say they're looking to protect the country's soft underbelly in case the situation spills across borders."

"That's what they're saying, all right. Situation's turning into a bloody circus. The Russians, Iran, Iraq, Greece, Cyprus—all getting their knickers in a twist. And, of course, the usual charges that *we're* behind everything, orchestrating the situation for our own nefarious ends."

Tucker nodded. The truth was less tidy than anybody's simplistic explanations would have it, but it didn't change the fact that once again, policy wonks like Geist here had gotten themselves caught on the horns of their own shortsightedness. It had probably seemed like a good idea after the Gulf War to enforce a no-fly zone to protect Saddam Hussein's Kurdish opponents in northern Iraq. Except now that they no longer had Baghdad to worry about, the Iraqi Kurds were free to come to the aid of their unhappy brethren living across the border in Turkey, launching a full-scale assault on the weakest link in the NATO chain.

"Kind of makes you long for the good old black hat–white hat days of the cold war, doesn't it, Jack?"

"No kidding. Look, I gotta get back upstairs real quick. National Security Council's meeting this afternoon, and we're trying to come up with a position that doesn't absolve the bloody Turks, who are anything but blameless, but doesn't piss them off so much they take their ball and go home." Geist laced his fingers across his flat belly and tipped his chair back on two legs. "So where are we on this Navigator business? Learn anything useful over there?"

He fixed Tucker with the dramatic, piercing stare that was infamous inside the agency for setting younger, less experienced operatives off on uncontrollable fits of stammering. The effect was lost on Tucker, who could outglower anyone— although he did consider pointing out that the furniture in this crummy office was strictly ancient government surplus and probably not up to the physics of two-legged rocking.

He decided against it. Geist was an ambitious hotshot looking for quick glory, the first to claim credit when an operation went right, and to distance himself when one went sour. If he ended up ass-over-teakettle, it'd be nice payback for the open cynicism he'd shown when he heard that a has-been like Tucker had been handed a personal message from the Navigator.

It was no surprise that, rather than call a meeting of the small committee that had vetted Tucker's trip to meet the Navigator, Geist had nominated himself to drop in alone for a debriefing. He was hedging his bets—still downplaying the business internally, but determined to stay on top of things in case there was any chance of a major payoff.

"We've got about fifteen hundred pages' worth of what looks to be the genuine article," Tucker said carefully. "Originals, not copies. I can do the initial examination myself. Eventually, I'll need a couple of computer people, Russian-language capable, to log it all in and create a secure database I can cross-reference and run against our own files."

One of Geist's eyebrows rose. "That all? Sure you don't want us to take one of the Crays offline and dedicate it to this little assignment?"

Tucker ignored the sarcasm. "I could do it manually, but it would take time. I get the sense we don't have that long. There's a reason the Navigator chose to give us these particular documents out of all the millions inside Moscow Center. Sooner we know what all's in them, sooner we'll know why."

"Did he give any hint where they're coming down on support to Iraq or the Kurds?"

Bloody Geist, right on schedule, Tucker thought. Man suffered from chronic, extreme tunnel vision, never seeing past his immediate interests.

"He never mentioned the Kurds," he said evenly, walking a fine line between overplaying or underplaying his hand. He didn't want anyone he couldn't control looking over his shoulder until he knew how much damaging information was in the files.

The key, he realized as he studied the deputy's rumpled shirt and the bags under his sleep-deprived eyes, was to reinforce the notion there was nothing here that bore on Geist's current problem. Once Geist was satisfied of that, he'd be out the door, hurrying to put himself back at the center of the high-profile crisis du jour. Jack Geist wasn't the type to let a little thing like a door opening into an old enemy's inner sanctum distract him from those areas in which he felt he could shine.

Still balancing on the chair's rear legs, Geist two-fingered the mottled yellow manila file Tucker had set apart from the others. It was a nice fake from a guy who, Tucker happened to know, didn't read a word of Russian. A good thing, too, since the name spelled out on the spine, albeit phonetically and in Cyrillic script, was "Benjamin Bolt."

"Have you got the slightest reason to believe there's anything important here?" Geist inquired, flipping disdainfully through the pages.

Tucker suppressed the urge to yank the file out of his hands, but there was little chance Geist would recognize what he was looking at. Geist had come up the ranks through a series of mostly Middle East–station assignments. The Soviet collapse, combined with the recent agitation of tin-pot dictatorships like Iran, Iraq, Syria and Libya, had fallen on his career like manna from heaven.

"I've done a preliminary flip-through," he said. "It's a mixed bag of old KGB operations—external agents, a few internal dissidents who were 'disappeared' into the Gulag."

"Sounds like ancient history. KGB's dead."

"Not dead. Not even dying. Regimes come and go in Russia, but the security service is forever. New guys come to power, think they've lopped off its head, but it just grows two more. Been that way for centuries. The Navigator, more than anyone, knows that. That's how he managed to survive as long as he did."

"No doubt. But I think we've got the situation pretty much in hand these days, Frank. There've been a lot of changes since you were on the old Soviet desk—operations you're not aware of, new sources we're running over there. Hell, we've even got some cooperative bilateral programs going with our new Russian friends."

Watching the deputy's smug self-assurance, Tucker's thoughts flashed on the Navigator sitting across from him, the dwindling bottle of vodka between them. Lifting his glass at one point, Deriabin had offered a raspy toast. "To friendship between nations. Of course," he added, "there are no friendly intelligence agencies, are there, my friend? After all, where would we be without our enemies?"

Geist closed the manila folder. "You say these are old ops?"

"Pretty much. Doesn't mean some of the players aren't still in place."

"You saying he gave us *active* sources? Now, why the hell would he do that?" The deputy's voice dripped disbelief, and he pushed the file away. "I'm having a lot of trouble buying that this isn't some whopping disinformation ploy designed to waste our time. What do you want to bet this Navigator character wants us looking the other way while his people are busy on some new scheme?"

"No argument."

"You agree?" Geist sounded surprised.

"That this could be nothing but a bunch of irrelevant junk, manufactured to distract us for God knows what purpose? It's possible. Unlikely, though."

"Why unlikely?"

"Because of the source."

"The source is Georgi goddamn Deriabin. Right? You *did* meet him? He's not dead, like Moscow Station was thinking?"

"Met him face-to-face for five hours."

"Guy's got cheek, I'll give him that," Geist said, shaking his head and leaning back on his precarious perch again. "Forty years he's worked against us, now I'm supposed to believe he wants to make nice? Give me a break."

"I'm just telling you how I read it."

"How *you* read it?"

Tucker found himself once more the object of that practiced, thousand-yard stare. Seconds ticked by, the silence broken only by the drumming of the deputy's fingers. He had the impression he was supposed to be quaking in his boots, worrying about whether his own loyalty was suspect.

He waited it out, knowing that if Geist sniffed any hint of anxiety, he'd take the files away and either bury them or pass them over to someone else. Tucker couldn't let that happen.

He needed to maintain control. Impress Geist with the files' potential so he'd get the time he needed, but not get him so worked up that he'd panic and set up some kind of task force.

"So, what's the deal?" Geist said finally. "Deriabin looking to walk? Cold war glory days are over, so now he wants us to set him up in a Miami Beach mansion?"

"Nope."

"Then what?"

What, indeed? Tucker frowned, wishing he had an easy answer. "He wants to leave a legacy, I think. I don't know exactly what, but I can tell you this—he's dying."

The chair legs finally dropped to the floor. "Say what? He tell you that?"

"Yeah, but even if he hadn't, I would've known. His skin's the color of that folder there."

The deputy's eyes strayed back to the mottled yellow file on the desk. "No kidding."

"Liver cancer, apparently. He says they've given him three months, max."

Geist's right hand rotated in an impatient, forward-rolling notion. "And so—?"

"I think he's looking to settle a score before he kicks off."

"And he wants us to help him to do it?"

"That's my guess."

"So, what's in it for us?"

Tucker hesitated. This was the tricky part. He was pretty sure part of the Navigator's plan was to undermine the presidential ambitions of Foreign Minister Zakharov. But who stood to benefit from that? Russia? America? International peace and stability? Some unknown protégé to whom the dying old man was preparing to hand his torch of secret power?

Tucker didn't know. He only knew who had the most to lose if this wasn't handled carefully. But how could he tell the deputy director of the CIA that he'd burn these files and the evidence they contained before he'd let any harm from them rain down on the woman whose name the bloody Navigator had known would be the key to forcing his cooperation?

"Just give me a little more time, Jack. I'll do you up a full report."

"How much time are we talking?"

"Twenty-four hours."

"Done," Geist said abruptly. He got to his feet.

Tucker watched him head for the door. He knew he should leave well enough alone, but he couldn't. "One more thing," he said. "Why was Mariah Bolt assigned to cover the Zakharov visit?"

Geist paused at the door, frowning. "That's pretty much 'need to know,' buddy. She doesn't work for you anymore."

"I know that."

"And so? You got some proprietary interest there? That'd be tough, since I hear she's seeing that hotshot TV anchorman...what's his name?"

"Paul Chaney."

"Right, Chaney. So...?"

Tucker shrugged. "I'm just curious why an analyst gets sent out in the field."

"I had a little job needed doing, and she was the best person for it. Anyway," the deputy said briskly, pulling open the door, "this is awesome work, Frank, getting your hands on this stuff. Truly awesome. I'll need that memorandum on my desk soon as possible, though. You'll get right on it, won't you, big guy?"

He winked and pointed his finger in a stagy "you-the-man!" gesture, then was gone before Tucker had a chance to respond with the contempt the performance deserved.

Chapter
Seven

So, how exactly did one go about luring a man into betraying his country? Mariah wondered. Bat her eyelashes? Show a little leg? Offer to meet him at the Casbah?

Really. This was hardly her area. As femmes fatales went, she felt about as lethal as a librarian.

One thing was certain. Even if the DDO's sources were right and Yuri Belenko was carrying some sort of torch for her—something she highly doubted, since their previous meetings had been pretty innocuous as far as she was concerned—she would *not* sleep with the man. Once again, she cursed herself for not having turned Geist down flat.

She hovered at the edge of an upper-level courtyard of the Arlen Hunter Museum, her second visit of the afternoon. By the time she'd arrived earlier, after stopping at Courier Express to arrange for Frank to collect Chap Korman's package in Virginia, the security detail had already finished their sweep of the site. She'd had just enough time to show her credentials, walk around and get the lay of the land, and run over the program for the Romanov opening, before heading back to the hotel to change into what she was coming to think of as her Tokyo Rose dress.

Now, after all her scrambling, the guests of honor were

running late. Typical Murphy's Law. It was already after six, and the early-evening sun was casting a magical, luminescent glow over the restless crowd waiting for Secretary of State Kidd and his Russian counterpart to show up.

It was nearly twenty years since she'd last set foot in California, and she'd forgotten this strange quality of the light, Mariah realized—the way it cast a magical glow on everything it touched, lulling with seductive promises it had no intention of keeping. Like a smiling thief, the place could rip out your heart in an instant and leave you too stunned to do anything but offer up your soul as well.

A warm Pacific breeze wafted over the balcony walls, and potted palms and crimson hibiscus rustled softly. The air was thick with expensive perfume and the ripe, masculine scent of the cigars in which one or two of the guests were indulging while they waited to see the Russian imperial treasures.

The irony was not lost on Mariah that the *Last Days of the Romanov Dynasty* tour should kick off here in the capital of American glitz and materialism. On display were the lavish worldly possessions of that family whose bloody murder had set in motion decades of deadly struggle between Moscow and the West, bringing the planet several times to the brink of a nuclear catastrophe unimaginable in the Romanovs' day. But eighty years after their massacre at the hands of the Bolsheviks—shot, stabbed, their bodies acid-drenched, burned, then dumped down a mineshaft in an orgy of overkill—the last czar and his family were finally going to be buried in a St. Petersburg royal crypt with appropriate, if tardy, pomp and circumstance. The niceties taken care of, Russia's cash-strapped regime could get on with the profitable business of exploiting the luckless royals in a manner that would have seemed hypocritical coming from previous communist governments. America, for its part, seemed willing to let bygones be bygones.

Looking over the list of dignitaries expected at the opening, Mariah's heart had sunk to discover Renata Hunter Carr's name near the top, just as she'd feared. Well, no matter. The woman was ancient history, and she herself was a long way from the confused little girl whose daddy had run off with the rich man's daughter.

Sure she was.

She glanced up, feeling dwarfed by the eight-foot-high letters of Arlen Hunter's name deeply carved into the pearl-gray marble walls of this monument he'd built to himself on Santa Monica Boulevard. So why did suborning treason feel like a piece of cake compared to the prospect of meeting the late magnate's home wrecker of a daughter?

Were her masters at Langley even aware of the grudge she bore Renata? she wondered. Did Geist know? Doubtful. It was conceivable that the woman's name was lodged somewhere in her personnel record, a gossipy detail on her famous, philandering parent, noted in passing, then filed away by whatever spit-polished security specialist had done her recruitment background check—an insignificant detail by now, surely, after eighteen spotless years of service. If Jack Geist had realized how much that bit of personal history still rankled, though, he might have thought twice about sending her out on this ridiculous assignment. Then again, knowing Geist, maybe not.

She patted her hair self-consciously. It felt too fluffy. She'd amped up her cosmetics for the occasion, too, and her skin felt plaster-coated. An extra coat of mascara had her feeling as though she was peering out at the world from under lacy awnings.

Ah, well, she thought wryly, the spy, to be truly effective, must be an expert at camouflage, possessed of that subtle capacity to seem neither out of place nor conspicuous. With the bevy of California beauties gracing the arms of the assembled rich and powerful here, her own overdone look no doubt blended right in.

Several well-known figures dotted the patio. The mayor of Los Angeles had already arrived, as well as both of California's senators and several politically connected Hollywood types. The guest list also included representatives of foreign governments who maintained consulates in Los Angeles, and business people dutifully networking on behalf of their multinational corporations.

Mariah sighed. And then there were the bureaucrats. A considerable number of them, from the State Department, FBI and Secret Service, plus at least one representative of the

CIA—though, for all she knew, Geist could have sent others. All attempting, with greater or lesser success, to blend into the party scene. The Secret Service agents were hopeless at it, conspicuous by their stern expressions, coiled collar wires, and plastic earpieces carrying a subaudible stream of clipped commands and sitreps—situation reports—on the movements of and potential threats to Secretary of State Kidd and Russian Foreign Minister Zakharov. Dressed in almost identical dark suits, they also had a distracting tendency to mutter, Dick Tracy–style, into their shirt cuffs.

A flutter of wings sounded behind her as two doves landed nearby on the half wall lining two sides of the terrace. A third dove settled a little apart from the pair, cooing plaintively, keeping a lonely watch. Gossamer violet feathers shimmered as the bird craned her head this way and that.

"Where's your fella, pretty girl?" Mariah murmured.

Black pearl eyes cast a baleful glance her way. Mourning doves were monogamous, she recalled, mating for life, slow to accept a new partner at the death of a mate. This one's mate must have fallen prey to some urban catastrophe, dooming her to follow behind the other pairs in the flock, permitted to observe but never join their comfortable circle.

Mariah felt her own loss thrum like an arrhythmia of the heart, a dull, aching reminder of David's absence and the permanent empty spaces his death had created inside and around her. The sense of isolation. She felt like someone stuck at the top of a broken Ferris wheel—rocking and waiting, looking at the world from a distance. Half the time, she ached for the wheel to start turning again. The rest of the time, she lived in terror of the next, inevitable downward plunge.

The melancholy cooing of the doves sounded a counterpoint to the hum of traffic moving up and down Santa Monica Boulevard. Long shadows drifted like pale purple gauze across the courtyard walls. She glanced once more at her watch. Six-fifteen. Nine-fifteen, back in Virginia. Lindsay would be up for a while yet. Like most teenagers, she prowled late at the best of times, and it would only get worse now that she was on summer vacation. If she got back to the hotel in the next couple of hours, Mariah calculated, she could still call without disturbing anyone at Carol's house.

Then she had another thought. Frank. Before this afternoon, she hadn't heard his voice in weeks. Now, the prospect of hearing it again brought a smile to her lips.

She leaned over the balcony's edge to see if the VIPs were in sight. The solitary dove followed her gaze, peering down at the steady stream of cars still pulling up, disgorging high-powered passengers into the building's maw. A small crowd had gathered on either side of the entryway. In Los Angeles, apparently, all it took to assemble an audience was to string a barrier, roll out a red carpet and wait for the celebrity-seekers to materialize like ants at a picnic.

Suddenly, the doves scattered on a flutter of wings as a strong hand gripped Mariah's elbow. In her ear, a low voice murmured, "Don't jump!"

She swung around to find a pair of crystal-blue eyes grinning down at her. "Paul! What are you doing here?"

Chaney kissed her cheek, as eyes had turned in their direction. Paul tended to have that effect on crowded rooms. So much for blending.

"Thought I'd surprise you," he said. "You look gorgeous."

"Thank you. I *am* surprised, but I'm confused, too. How—?"

"I got an invitation to this shindig weeks ago. I wasn't going to come until you mentioned yesterday that you were. Decided I'd deliver your keys in person."

Based in Washington, Paul had friends everywhere he'd ever stood in front of a camera. The only reason Mariah had called to tell him she'd be in L.A. early was that the beach cottage near Chap Korman's house where she and Lindsay were planning to spend their vacation belonged to some friend of Paul's. He'd been making arrangements to get the keys to her that week.

His appearance always set off mixed reactions in her, but right now, it was mostly dismay Mariah felt. "You shouldn't have come all this way," she said, meaning it.

"I know, but I wanted to. I thought it might be a little

tricky for you tonight, what with Renata Hunter Carr being here and all. I came to offer moral support.''

Oh, Lord, Mariah thought, I am an ungrateful wretch.

"I was running late, though. Thought I'd miss the whole shebang,'' Paul said, glancing around. "I gather Zakharov's plane was late arriving?''

Mariah nodded.

He settled on the low balcony wall, long legs crossing at the ankles. His charcoal suit—Armani, no doubt—draped his athletic body with an elegant ease that most mere mortals could only envy. He had also been blessed with the even, agreeable bone structure camera lenses favored. He was fair-haired, with just a little gray and white intermingling at the temples. His face, classically good-looking, was also slightly weathered, adding a patina of maturity to an appearance that might otherwise have been too boyish to carry the weight of the award-winning television newsmagazine he anchored.

"Have you seen her yet?'' he asked.

"No. Apparently, she's part of the ribbon-cutting detail, so I imagine she'll make her entrance with Zakharov and Kidd.''

"How are you holding up?''

"Just fine,'' she lied. "It was sweet of you to do this, Paul, but it's really not that big a deal. I've seen her picture in the paper dozens of times. I'm hardly going to have a nervous breakdown just because we happen to be in the same room.''

"What if you have to talk to her?''

"No reason I should. She doesn't know me, and I'm obviously not going to go out of my way to introduce myself.''

Chaney studied her for a moment, then turned back to the crowd. "There's Nolan,'' he said.

"Nolan?''

"Nolan Carr, her son. The young Robert Redford clone over there with Mayor Riordan and the senators.''

Mariah followed his gaze across the courtyard to where an attractive, self-assured young man was locked in close conversation with the three politicians.

"Looks like he's lobbying,'' Paul said.

"For what?''

He shrugged. "Who knows? Rumor has it his mother's got political ambitions for her only child.''

Mariah studied the would-be politician. "He looks barely old enough to be out of school."

"He's pushing thirty, I think. As for school, he attended Princeton for a while, his late father's alma mater. I don't think he ever graduated from anywhere except Playboy U, though. Like I said, politics seems to be his mother's idea."

"His father was Jacob Carr, the former state attorney general, right?"

"Mmm... Plus, of course, Mrs. Hunter Carr's a major contributor in her own right. When the time comes, I'm sure Nolan will have the backing he needs."

Mariah gave Paul a curious look. "How do you know all this?"

"I interviewed Arlen Hunter not long before he died," Paul said. "I met both Renata and Nolan, though he was just a kid at the time. Pretty rambunctious, at that. I've run into the mother once or twice since."

"You never told me that," Mariah said, frowning.

"Well, I knew it was a touchy subject. Frankly, there's never really been a time before now when I thought it needed to be mentioned."

"Hmm...." Mariah said. How very politically correct of him.

The director of the Arlen Hunter Museum, who'd been pointed out to Mariah when she'd passed through that afternoon, walked over and whispered something in Nolan Carr's ear. Carr smiled and nodded without missing a beat, then shook hands with Mayor Riordan and the senators and headed off for the elevators. Along the way, he stopped and shook a few more hands, ever the dutiful host in his grandfather's establishment. Preternaturally adept at the glad-handing game, Mariah thought. Clearly, the boy had a future.

"So, what exactly does he do for a living?" she asked Paul. "Not that he has to worry about where his next meal is coming from, I suppose."

"Hard to say, exactly. He's on the board of the various Hunter corporations and trusts. Dabbles in a little land development, I think. Skis. Sails. The usual."

"Nice work if you can get it."

"*N'est-ce pas?*" Paul said wryly.

A sudden change in the pitch of street noises set off a murmur on the terrace, and people began to gravitate toward the edge of the balcony. The distinct growl of high-powered, armor-encased motors and the deep, throaty whine of motor-cycle outriders announced the arrival of the official cavalcade at the front of the building.

Chaney peeked over the edge, then got to his feet. As he took her arm, Mariah felt his fingertips lightly brushing the sensitive place at the inside of her elbow. "Here we go," he said. "Ready?"

She glanced around, but jaded gazes used to celebrity-spotting had already shifted away from them, anticipating the arrival of bigger fish. "Paul, I don't know how to put this delicately," she murmured, "but I'm *working* here."

He slipped his hand out of her arm. "Oops, sorry." He knew what she did for a living. He'd been David's friend first, but when he'd decided to investigate the suspicious car accident that had led up to David's death, Paul's and her professional paths had tangled. "I'll stay out of your way," he said. "But it had occurred to me, even if you were tied up for the evening, there's always a window of opportunity between sunset and sunrise." He flicked an imaginary cigar, his eyebrows doing a mischievous Groucho Marx bounce.

In spite of herself, Mariah smiled. "Where are you stay-ing?"

His expression shifted to sheepish, and he fingered the al-most imperceptible scar on his chin, an old hockey injury. Mariah had been drawn on more than one occasion to slowly trace that small, welcome imperfection. "With you?" he sug-gested.

"Oh, I don't know about that. I have no idea what time I'll be done tonight, and—"

"I have a confession to make. My bag's already in your room."

"What? How did you get into my hotel room?"

"I know the manager at the Beverly Wilshire. Stayed there a dozen times. I know it's presumptuous, but you and I get so few opportunities to be together, I didn't want to let this one pass. I told the manager we needed to keep it real low-key. In this town, believe me, it's not the strangest request he's ever had. He's totally discreet, I swear."

She studied those wide-open features, wondering how many times Paul had relied on that discretion in the past. Wondering, too, how thrilled the DDO would be to find out they were sharing quarters here. But there wasn't time to argue the point now. In any case, when the chips were down, Paul had proven more loyal than the CIA brass. There were plenty of reasons for their relationship to go slow, but at this point, she couldn't care less what Jack Geist thought about it.

The elevators pinged, doors opening on a rush of air. Several Secret Service men stepped off first, taking up positions at either side of the opening. Three or four of their beefy Russian security counterparts followed. Multiple pairs of dark glasses panned the room as they, too, fanned out, the Russians forming an inner cordon, the Security Service, like tugs around an ocean liner, keeping the dignitaries and Zakharov's bodyguards in a containment pattern as they moved forward.

"All right," she conceded. "I'll catch up to you later. But right now—"

"I'm outta here. I'll leave you to your spying, Janey Bond."

She scolded softly, "I'm State Department here, buster, and don't you forget it."

Chaney grinned and walked off. She watched as he made his way to the front of the room. At least a hundred and fifty people separated him from the red velvet ribbon strung before the main gallery, but Paul Chaney was one of those people with a God-given gift for putting himself at the center of the action. As he threaded his way forward, faces in the crowd glanced up at him, temporarily distracted from the main attraction. Then, like the Red Sea at the approach of Moses, they parted to let him pass.

Turning back toward the elevator, Mariah recognized the cropped, silvery head of the secretary of state. Next to him was a short, chunky man in an expensive suit, the top of whose head barely cleared Shelby Kidd's shoulder. Zakharov's golden cuff links glittered as he lifted his hands to smooth the sides of his thick, snow-white hair. He looked almost cherubic, Mariah thought—Santa Claus in Savile Row—but Zakharov had been a KGB colonel with a reputation for unparalleled ruthlessness before making the transition to politician. She doubted the old leopard had changed his spots at this late date.

Why was it that the most ferocious characters were so often such stumpy little men? she wondered. There had to be a psychology thesis in there somewhere.

As the two ministers started toward the gallery, accompanied by their translators, Mariah spotted Yuri Belenko, Zakharov's right-hand man and her main reason for being here. Belenko's back was to her as he paused at the elevator threshold, reaching back to offer his arm to the last occupant, hidden till now.

Almost against her will, Mariah craned to see, but caught only the briefest glimpse of blond hair and a flash of earring before the small figure of a woman disappeared in the thicket of sturdy, protective bodies sweeping en masse toward the red velvet rope.

Suddenly, an awful memory flooded over her: her mother crying on the sofa, one arm curled protectively around the curve of her belly.

"Mommy? Where's Daddy?"

"He's gone."

"Gone where? When's he coming home?"

"I don't know, sweetheart. I don't know."

Damn it to hell, Mariah thought, swallowing hard. She circled the wall, settling in a nook off to the side of the main gallery entrance, where her view was relatively unobstructed.

And there she was.

Heiress and culture maven Renata Hunter Carr was busy introducing the two ministers to her son and to the museum director. The woman obviously gloried in being the center of attraction—and in her triumph. Both the Smithsonian and the Metropolitan Museum of Art had vied to host the inaugural stop on the Russian imperial treasures tour, but with deft lobbying in two capitals, Renata had done a run up the middle and scored the coup for the Los Angeles–based institute founded by her father.

Oil magnate Arlen Hunter had made the first of many fortunes in the early twenties, trading with a famine-stricken, postrevolutionary Russia whose Bolshevik government knew what it needed and scarcely valued what it had—furs for Ford trucks, priceless icons for U.S. wheat. For the rest of his life, Arlen Hunter acted as a self-appointed American trade and cultural ambassador to every Soviet leader from Lenin to Gorbachev, reaping huge profits for himself in the bargain. It was a measure of continuing Russian appreciation for the departed mogul that Moscow hadn't hesitated to grant the opening of the Romanov exhibit to the museum that still bore his name, carved in those eight-foot-high letters on the marble walls.

Hence, Renata's role in the opening ceremonies. Hence, too, Mariah's own predicament, struggling to maintain some sort of professional detachment when she felt seven years old all over again.

She tried to keep her attention fixed on Zakharov and Belenko, who had yet to notice her, but her gaze kept wandering to that other unnerving presence. She'd wanted to see a wizened and stooped harpy. She'd wanted to find the woman Chap Korman had described—someone crushed by disappointment, still, after all these years, mourning the loss of the man she'd stolen. She saw nothing of the kind.

Renata was animated and vibrant, possessed of the kind of understated elegance that knows it needn't strive to impress, and is all the more impressive for that careless confidence. Her oyster-blond hair was expertly razored to chin-length. A deceptively simple black dress draped her trim figure like ermine, her only jewelry a pair of discreet pearl and diamond earrings with a matching collier. Mariah knew the two of them were a full generation apart, but Renata could almost have passed for a contemporary, with that smooth complexion and those bluesteel eyes. Only a light crepiness around the neck betrayed her.

This woman was my father's lover. For her, he left us.

As the museum director stepped up to the microphone and began introducing the guests of honor, Mariah felt detached, floating. She was vaguely aware of the secretary of state and Foreign Minister Zakharov taking their turns at delivering platitudes, but their voices seemed a long way off, part of a scene viewed through the wrong end of a telescope.

Eventually, someone extended a pair of gleaming silver shears, and Renata stepped up to the ribbon and opened them around the crimson velvet, then she paused, turning toward a bank of photographers standing at Mariah's left, waiting while they took their formal opening shots.

It was at that moment the two women made eye contact.

Renata's pupils dilated almost imperceptibly, and a tiny crease appeared at the corner of her mouth. The whole re-action lasted a split second, at most—so brief that Mariah doubted anyone else on the terrace had registered it. Then, the moment passed, and the older woman's self-confident gaze traveled over the crowd once more.

Mariah was taken aback. Somehow, against all odds, Ren-ata had recognized her. She was certain of it. Given that Ma-riah been seven years old the last time their paths had crossed, and then, only briefly, the woman's memory seemed extraor-dinary.

Or maybe, she thought grimly, it was simply the power of a guilty conscience.

Chapter Eight

Twenty-four hours. One day, Tucker calculated. Maybe two, if he was lucky.

Geist would be too distracted by Turks, Kurds and presidential briefing opportunities to notice immediately that the report on the Navigator's files hadn't shown up on his desk as promised. But the man was a micromanager, a human vacuum for information that he monopolized and doled out as his own agenda dictated—a tried-and-true route to personal advancement. Sooner or later, the DDO's thoughts would turn again to the files in the basement. At that moment, Tucker knew, people would start looking for him.

He stood awkwardly outside a Dutch door on the third floor of the agency's main building, waiting for the lone occupant of the large, open room on the other side to notice him, still wrestling with the morality of what he was about to do.

The door was divided horizontally, the top and bottom halves operating independently of one another. It was an architectural throwback to old farmhouses and barns, allowing air and conversation to circulate over the top while holding back unwanted intruders like chickens and dogs—or old bosses seeking special favors.

Wanetta Walker was working alone in the document pro-cessing unit, reams of paper piled high on her corner desk. All those requests for bulk printing, copying, collating, labeling, uploading and downloading onto computer disks would no doubt require urgent attention from her staff tomorrow, but Tucker was relieved to see that everyone else had left for the day. Just what he'd been hoping to find.

When Wanetta finally did glance up, she started, then her wide face erupted in a broad smile. Her half glasses dropped to her not-insubstantial bosom where they dangled by a beaded chain slung around her neck.

"Well, well, well! If it isn't the long lost Mr. Frank Tucker!"

"Hey there, Wanetta. What are you doing hanging around at this late hour?"

She got to her feet and ambled to the door. "Tryin' to get a little ahead of the game here. I wouldn't mind taking a long Fourth of July holiday weekend, but it's not looking real promising at the moment."

"Management not all it's cracked up to be?"

"Oh, I don't know about that," she said, leaning amiably on the half door. "I like givin' orders a *whole* lot better than I liked gettin' 'em."

She was a big woman, standing nearly eye-to-eye with him. Probably close to his own age, Tucker estimated, though he'd always been too much of a gentleman to ask. She kept herself more up to date than he did, though. Row on row of tiny braids divided her peppered hair today, each braid ending in black and amber beads that tinkled gently when she moved. Her deep mahogany skin gleamed against the brilliant orange African-inspired print of the flowing, knee-length robe she wore over black slacks.

"Where you been hiding, anyway?" she asked.

"Oh, they gave me a little corner 'bout two miles underground and left at West Virginia."

"You don't belong down there," she said indignantly. "When you gonna get back in the swing of things, stop whippin' yourself like some mad monk?"

He shrugged. "It's not so bad, you know. No committee meetings. No deadlines. No stupid requests from seventh-floor executive assistants who graduated from kindergarten day before yesterday.''

"Yeah, sure. And where'd you be if you couldn't chew up at least one snot-nosed E.A. a day?"

"Right where I am, I guess. Listen, Wanetta," he said, lifting the folder of carefully selected documents he'd brought up from his office, "I was wondering if you could put these on a disk for me."

She slipped her glasses back on her nose and looked askance at the thick pile. "*All* of it?"

"You can do that, right?"

"While you wait, no doubt." One of Wanetta's eyebrows arched high as skeptical brown eyes peered at him over the top of her glasses, letting the absurdity of that proposition sink in for a moment.

"If you wouldn't mind. I'm kind of in a rush."

"You'n everybody else." Her head gave a rueful shake, the beads on her braids clacking softly.

"I like the hairdo, Wanetta. Looks real nice."

"You just get along with your flattery, now, Frank Tucker," she scolded in her deep, melodious lilt. She held out the flat of her hand. "Give me that. What is it, anyway?"

Tucker gave her the file. When she opened it, her nose wrinkled at the mildewy smell of the loose, yellowed papers. She frowned at the Cyrillic lettering.

"How *old* is this stuff? Isn't even in English."

"They're part of an old Russian archive," he said. "Thing is, I'm supposed to be putting together an itemized proposal for the resources I need to analyze the whole bunch. It's basically a stalling tactic from the front office. A bureaucratic way of telling me to get stuffed."

She glanced up sharply. "Frank Tucker! You want to jump to the front of the queue here, and you haven't even got a budget authorization number for me, do you?"

"No, ma'am, I don't."

"Do you know how much I get hammered by the comptroller if I don't account for every minute of time we spend and every last piece of paper that moves in and outta here?"

"I've got a pretty good idea."

"Well, then," she said, using the elaborately patient tone

normally reserved for the intellectually challenged and seventh-floor executive assistants, "why don't you just go on over to whoever it is ordered this project and ask him to assign an interim authorization number to get you started?"

"Because it's Jack Geist."

He might as well have said it was Jack the Ripper, the way Wanetta's playful expression vanished. She gripped the door latch and stepped back as it swung open. "Come on in and set a spell, honey," she said grimly. Her flowing robe billowed as she swung around, file clutched in her hand, and headed to a bank of machines against the far wall.

Tucker trudged behind her, feeling guilty. What he had in mind could get Wanetta fired if her assistance was discovered, not to mention the probability of five-to-ten in the Allenwood federal pen that he was pulling down on his own head. He didn't care much about the risk to himself, but she was an old friend.

But, he reasoned, her minor role need never come to light. He could plausibly argue that he'd copied the documents to disk himself. Only Patty, who knew the level of his computer skills, would see through the patent lie, but she wasn't around. Even if she were, she'd never betray Wanetta. If Wanetta could do the job now, with no staff around to see her doing it, they'd be home free.

At the thought of her staff, Tucker couldn't suppress a small grin.

He'd spent more than a quarter of a century in the CIA, and in that time, he'd seen a revolutionary change in the way the agency's day-to-day business was conducted. These days, every officer worked with a desktop computer terminal linked to all sections of Langley and to CIA stations around the world. Those with the proper security and operational clearances had instant access to a vast archive of intelligence assessments and operations, past and present. The systems software also contained idiot-proof document formats that even a technological Neanderthal like himself could learn to work. Nowadays, a basic knowledge of that software was about all it took, mechanically speaking, to create the intelligence assessments that were the Company's bread and butter—the product that kept the administration and Congress informed on threats to American security and justified the billions of dollars allocated annually to keep the intelligence program and the nation in a state of watchful readiness.

But in the old, pre-desktop era, the only computers at Langley had been clunky, room-size Univacs dedicated almost exclusively to the arcane work of cryptology, the code breakers' tool for deciphering messages intercepted from the opposition. As for the agency's massive paper product, the essential cog in that wheel had been an army of security-cleared typists drawn from the old central steno pool.

Wanetta Walker had had the bad luck to join the steno pool about fifteen years earlier, as the wheel of technology was beginning to turn, creating new opportunities in some areas but rendering other skills obsolete, just as weavers of old had been replaced by mechanical looms and auto welders by computerized robots. Many women in the steno pool had been selected for computer retraining, but when the budget crunch of buying new systems hit, many others were scheduled for layoff, since officers themselves would henceforth do their own drafting and revising online.

At the time, Jack Geist had been doing a brief tour of duty in administration, a strategic career move designed to bolster his trajectory into management's upper echelons. Downsizing the steno pool had fallen under his jurisdiction. His approach was a rigid last hired–first fired arrangement—though it didn't take long before people began to notice that exceptions were being made for a few perky young things, for whom "admin trainee" positions suddenly seemed to materialize.

Wanetta Walker had been a recent hire with only basic typing skills, a widow with two sons to raise. It had counted for nothing in Geist's scheme that what she lacked in experience, she made up for in hard work, her family situation sufficient motivation that she ran rings around the "perky brigade."

Fortunately, when the proverbial hit the fan, Wanetta had already worked a temporary replacement stint in Tucker's Soviet unit, which kept its own small group of secretaries to handle material too sensitive for the steno pool. When Patty found out Wanetta was scheduled for layoff, Tucker requested an additional position for his unit, then stared down Geist until he agreed to let Wanetta fill it. She'd been inordinately grateful for his intervention, and Tucker had never let on that he knew about the humiliation she'd suffered when the job she so desperately needed was threatened—and that Jack Geist had cornered her alone one evening and propositioned her, telling her "a little brown sugar" would go a long way toward sweetening his disposition. Geist, the ass, had bragged about it himself, figuring a good ol' boy like Frank Tucker would surely appreciate the humor.

Wanetta stood at the document scanner now, feeding through the papers Tucker had spent the last hour and a half selecting from among all those in the Navigator's crate.

"I had a postcard from Patty," she said over the hum of the machine. Then she glanced up, wincing. "Oops! Sorry. Am I allowed to mention that?"

"Sure, it's okay," Tucker said. "I talked to her a couple of weeks ago myself. She tell you she got a dog?"

"No kidding. That's nice. So you guys—?"

"It was an amicable parting," Tucker assured her.

"That's good." She smiled at him and went back to feeding paper. When she was done, she moved to a computer station, inserted a new floppy disk, then linked up to the scanner and started downloading the documents she'd just fed into digital storage.

Tucker watched her work, impressed as always by her amazing efficiency. She'd only lasted about a year in his section before the personnel wheels had turned again. Jack Geist had moved on to a station chief position abroad, while Wanetta's obvious competence marked her for one promotion after another.

Now, here she was, running one of the technological units for which she'd once been considered too unqualified even to apply. She'd remarried a few years back, too, and was a grandparent, just like him.

"What about Mariah?" she suddenly asked over her shoulder.

Tucker looked up sharply. Damn! She didn't miss a thing. "What about her?"

"She still seeing Mr. Blow-Dry?"

He stifled a grin. "Not nice, Wanetta."

She downloaded the final document, then popped the floppy disk out of the drive, closed the scanner link and swiveled in her chair, handing the disk over to him. "Nice guys finish last," she said. "Here you go."

Tucker studied the computer screen. "This isn't still in the system, is it?"

"Nope. I deleted it. You've got the only copy. And here," she said, getting to her feet and gathering the Navigator's papers back into the file folder, "are your originals. I'm guessing the line is, 'You were never here,' right?"

"No, ma'am, I was not."

"Got it. But in future, you don't be a stranger, hear?"

"You bet. I owe you."

"Been a while since we've tasted your Chicken Marbella."

Tucker smiled. He had a bit of a reputation, mostly overblown, as a gourmet cook, although you couldn't prove it by the way his clothes hung loose on him these days. "You got it. I'll give you guys a call. And thanks again for this."

"No problem at all. You just make sure you *do* call. And Frank?" she said, walking back to the door and holding it open for him. "Don't give up on her. She's a smart lady. Mr. Blow-Dry won't last, mark my words."

Tucker shook a finger at her. "You are a wicked, wicked woman, Wanetta."

She grinned. "But in the nicest possible way. Now, git!"

He returned to his office just long enough to use the shredder. Page by page, the Navigator's files were transformed into mulched confetti.

Then he sat down in his chair, placed Wanetta's disk against the inside of his right calf and secured it with two heavy rubber bands. He winced pulling his sock up to cover them, suddenly acquiring a new appreciation for the female ritual of leg waxing. Grabbing his sport coat and briefcase, he locked his office door and headed back up the elevator.

At the building's exit, the security guard gave the inside of his briefcase a bored once-over. Then he waved Tucker out the door.

Chapter Nine

The cold flicker of Renata's bluesteel eyes had stunned Mariah into brief immobility, unleashing a flood of images that ripped through her calm.

A little girl, seven years old, alone in the dark. Petrified. Something has woken her from a troubled sleep, but the drafty house is silent now. Eerie quiet. Then, she hears it again. A terrible, keening sound. Her mother, in the next room, weeping. The little girl pulls her knees up into her chest, wrapping herself into a tight ball. Wishing she could disappear the way she made him disappear. Rocking. Whispering, "I'm sorry I made him go, Mommy. I'm sorry I made him mad."

The museum crowd stirred around her like a living breeze. When Mariah looked up, Renata and the ministers had disappeared into the gallery.

She sloughed off the guilty memory like a dank old shroud. *It wasn't you who made him leave,* the adult in her reminded the child. *It was that ogress in pearls. You stumbled across the two of them together, and that was what precipitated Ben's last temper tantrum before he finally stormed out for good. But it wasn't your fault.*

Right. So why had she never been able to believe that? Mariah wondered grimly.

Inside the windowless galleries, the lighting was subdued, the gray marble decked out for the occasion in royal-blue silk damask draperies, swagged and tied with heavy gold tassels. Plush, mushroom-colored carpeting muffled the sound of footsteps, but in her chest, Mariah felt the deep, tympanic reverberations of Rimsky-Korsakov flowing from concealed speakers, the majestic symphony reducing voices to a reverent hush.

It was like being in church, except the object of worship here was material excess—glass-enclosed treasures illuminated by the heavenly touch of strategically aimed ceiling spots. Bejeweled Fabergé Easter eggs. Gilt icons and priceless religious relics. The czar's coronation uniform, adorned with gold braid and gleaming military medals. Gem-encrusted tiaras, necklaces and gowns that had been worn by the czarina and her four pretty daughters.

And then there were the personal items—the elaborate wicker and filigreed wrought-iron carriage in which the tragically hemophiliac young son had been wheeled about. The little boy's toy soldiers. His sisters' careful embroidery samplers. And hundreds of photographs, letters and wistful pages from the journals of the obliviously doomed Nicholas and Alexandra.

Mariah watched two hyper-thin beauties sigh over the royal love letters, written in English to deflect prying palace eyes. An older woman shed an obligatory tear over photos of the murdered children.

It was voyeurism at its Hollywood best, offering equal measures of glamour and pathos. Those old Bolsheviks were no dummies, she reflected. They'd had no use for their monarchs in the flesh, but they must have sensed a surefire commercial gimmick when they'd squirreled away this treasure trove of regal memorabilia rather than condemn it to the same ash pit where they'd dumped its owners.

She'd already taken a quick look at the artifacts that afternoon after the Secret Service and FBI contingents had done their security sweep for bombs and booby traps. Now she was on the lookout for Yuri Belenko, determined to make contact sooner rather than later, try to gauge where his interests lay, and if it seemed worthwhile, arrange a meeting on quieter turf. Then she could in good conscience blow this pop stand.

She was at a disadvantage, though. The crowd was dense and, typically, she was one of the shortest people there. Unless she stood on one of the marble benches, there was no way to see above the mass of shoulders and heads around her. She wove from room to room, watching for her target. Nervous at every turn about running into Renata.

Then, inspiration struck. There was a glass-enclosed atrium at the center of the building where the post-opening reception was to take place. If she slipped ahead of the wave of people, she could position herself strategically to spot Belenko when he came in, and look for an opportunity for their paths to cross casually—and, at the same time, stay out of the way of that other person.

She short-circuited the box-shaped route through the exhibit and cut straight across to the atrium, catching a brief glimpse of Shelby Kidd's silver head bent over a case of ceremonial weapons. Foreign Minister Zhakarov was standing next to the secretary, engaged in a spirited explanation of some sort. The translator at Kidd's elbow was frantically trying to keep up with the Russian's scattershot lecture. But before Mariah could see if Yuri Belenko was still with his minister, the crowd closed in, and her view was blocked.

She pushed against the heavy glass doors leading into the atrium, and was immediately greeted by a fragrant welcome. Long, blue-draped tables held sparkling, leaded-crystal glasses. Copious amounts of champagne and vodka stood chilling on ice. Ivory porcelain plates, stamped in gold with Arlen Hunter's curlicued initials, were stacked at either end of a groaning buffet table. Blue flames flickered under steaming silver chafing dishes of hot canapés, while seemingly endless varieties of cold ones covered every other available inch of blue tablecloth.

In the center of the buffet, a massive ice sculpture rose out of the biggest platter of beluga caviar Mariah had ever seen. The crystalline beast, a two-headed eagle, wings unfurled, clutched a scepter in one claw, an orb in the other, and the Romanov imperial crest between its great wings. It towered a good six feet above the spread, its fierce heads gazing east and west, as if still keeping watch over the vast expanse of the Russian empire.

A few other guests had already fast-tracked through the galleries and were getting a jump start on the free-flowing champagne. Mariah waved off a white-coated waiter and took up a position against a pillar with an open view of the doorway from the last room in the exhibit, determined to take command of the field.

She hadn't counted on a sneak attack from the rear. When a voice sounded next to her, she nearly jumped out of her skin.

"You didn't enjoy the exhibit?"

Mariah swung around, then recoiled. Renata Hunter Carr stood next to her, perfectly plucked eyebrows arched in question.

Up close, the woman looked older, she was gratified to see. Even unnaturally tight skin turned translucent and blue-veined with age, it seemed, and bright blue eyes, too, took on an opaque density with the years. Eternal youth was apparently harder to come by than the cosmetics industry would have us believe.

"I beg your pardon?" Mariah said.

"I was asking if you found the exhibit not to your liking."

"It's very impressive."

"You didn't spend much time inside." It sounded like a reproach, as if her social graces had been examined and found to fall a little short of civilized. But before Mariah could reply, the other woman added, "It's Mariah, isn't it?"

She nodded slowly.

"I knew it. I excused myself with Shelby and Minister Zakharov and went to search out Paul Chaney, just to be sure. But I knew I couldn't be mistaken."

"Ah, yes. Paul," Mariah said. "I hadn't realized the two of you were acquainted."

"Our paths have crossed a few times. He really is quite adorable, isn't he?"

Mariah ignored the best-girlfriends-sharing-secrets smile. Only the woman's thin, liver-spotted fingers, playing with heavy gold rings, betrayed any sign that she was less than utterly confident here. Mariah leaned back against the pillar and decided to let silence work for her. Refusing to be on the defensive.

"I would have thought you'd be at least a little interested in the Romanovs," Renata said.

"They're a source of perennial fascination, I'm sure. I had a quick look at everything when I came through with the security contingent."

"Security? Did you think I was in the habit of setting traps for my guests?"

Still shaken at having been cornered, Mariah thought immediately of black widow spiders, but she resisted the temptation of sarcasm. "Some people would find Secretary Kidd or Minister Zakharov tempting targets."

"That's certainly true. But what does it have to do with you?"

Mariah shrugged. "Goes with the territory. Everyone in the secretary's delegation needs to be security-conscious."

"You're here with Shelby Kidd's entourage? But I thought..." Renata frowned, glancing back at the galleries. "Well, never mind. You *are* here. It's all that matters."

A waiter stepped up with a tray. "Mrs. Carr? Champagne?"

"No, I'll wait. But, Mariah, please, you go ahead," she said, waving a hand at the glasses.

Mariah shook her head. When the waiter moved on, she had an overwhelming desire to follow him. "Excuse me," she said, "I should really—"

The other woman grabbed her arm with fingers like talons. Mariah stared at the hand, then the woman, until the grip loosened and the hand slithered off.

"What can I do for you, Mrs. Carr?"

"I think it's more a question of what I can do for you, Mariah."

"What do you mean?"

"I've been wanting to talk to you. I've been keeping tabs on you for some time, you know."

"I beg your pardon? Tabs?"

"And so I happen to know," Renata said quietly, leaning close with another of those conspiratorial grins, "that you are not employed by the State Department, my dear." She winked and touched a forefinger to her lips. Then her hands fluttered through the air, their little secret banished to the winds.

Mariah said nothing. Neither confirm nor deny—the unofficial agency motto.

The older woman seemed to need no confirmation, in any case. A line marred her unnaturally smooth forehead. "I'm also told your husband, David, passed away not too long ago. I'm sorry for your loss, dear. It can't be easy, losing him so young, having to finish raising Lindsay all alone."

The sympathy sounded rote. And there was something obscene, Mariah thought, about hearing David's and Lindsay's names come out of this woman's mouth. Not to mention a little surreal. Renata offering sympathy? How about an apology, instead, for a ruined childhood? Or a little sympathy for that other woman she herself had turned into a struggling single mother?

"But I did want to meet you," Renata went on, oblivious to the irony. "We might have picked a less awkward moment, mind you, but it's become rather pressing, so the sooner the better, I suppose."

"'Awkward' doesn't begin to describe this situation, Mrs. Carr. And frankly, I can't imagine we have much to say to each other."

"Oh, but we do, Mariah, we really do. We have something in common, after all."

"And what would that be?"

"Your father. We both loved him." Renata's lips pursed, and she gave the impression she'd picked up a whiff of something disagreeable. "But all this dredging into the past. Releasing his private papers and draft manuscripts. You don't want to be doing that."

Mariah felt her spine stiffen as she pushed off from the pillar. At her height, there weren't many people she could look down on, but Renata, luckily, was one of the few who fell into that category. She was grateful for small mercies. Anything to gain some advantage in a situation that was taking a truly bizarre turn.

"You presume a lot," she said. "In the first place, I don't really remember my father with love. In the second, even if

I did, you are without a doubt the last person on earth with whom I would stand around sharing warm fuzzy memories of him.''

''We did share him, though.''

''We didn't share him! You stole him. You ripped him out of our lives, mine and my mother's. I was seven years old. She was his wife, and pregnant besides. Did you know that? Did you care?''

''That's all very long ago, and—''

''Ancient history to you, no doubt. But painfully fresh in my mind, I can assure you. We never saw him again. In her entire, short life, my little sister never once set eyes on our father, nor he on her. Tell me, Mrs. Carr, what kind of 'sharing' was that?''

''I realize it must have seemed hurtful at the time.''

''How *very* insightful of you.''

The older woman finally had the grace to blush.

''And as for his papers,'' Mariah went on, ''that really is none of your business. I control them. I'll do with them as I see fit.'' Enough was enough. She glanced around, looking for the nearest exit.

But the room was beginning to fill, most of the crowd giving the two women a wide but curious berth. In the midst of it, however, she spotted one figure whose gaze was locked on them. When he realized he'd been made, Nolan Carr walked over.

''Excuse me for interrupting, ladies. Mother, I came to fetch you. Minister Zakharov was wondering where you've gotten to.''

Something flashed in those blue eyes. Impatience? Renata Hunter Carr, Mariah imagined, was not in the habit of being ''fetched.''

''Tell him I'll be along shortly,'' Renata said.

''Shelby wants to hear about the Nova Krimsky project. We don't want to neglect our guests of honor, do we?'' Nolan said reasonably. Then he turned to Mariah and held out his hand. ''I don't think we've met. Nolan Carr.''

''This is Mariah Tardiff,'' Renata said hastily. ''Mariah, my son, Nolan Carr.'' Her eyes locked onto Mariah's.

A warning? A plea? Mariah wondered, curious that Renata

would introduce her by the married name she rarely heard except from Lindsay's teachers and friends. If she'd been checking up on her, as she said, she'd known Mariah had continued to use Bolt professionally after her marriage, as much to keep her personal life out of her workplace as anything else.

But what did the Bolt name mean to Nolan? Surely he had to know about his mother's affair with Ben? It was hardly a secret, since it was mentioned in virtually every Ben Bolt biography ever written. Renata hadn't been Ben's only extra-marital fling, but she did have the dubious distinction of being the last and most fateful. His final flight to Europe with Arlen Hunter's headstrong daughter was part of the standard Bolt lore—as well as the fact that she'd dumped him there, so that when he fell ill, he was doomed to die alone and penniless on foreign turf. At the end of his life, it seemed, Ben finally met his female match.

But what about Nolan? Was his mother's wild past a source of embarrassment to him? He didn't look remotely embarrassed now, Mariah thought. He'd folded her hand between both of his and fixed her with a warm smile.

"Mariah? That's a really great name. It's nice to meet you."

"You, too, Nolan." What else was she going to say? It wasn't his fault his mother was horrible. His father, Jacob Carr, had apparently been a decent man, a well-respected California attorney general before his career was cut short by a fatal heart attack. One out of two wasn't bad in the parental lottery odds. She ought to know.

"I really am sorry to drag my mother away," Nolan added, "but you know how it is. Duty calls."

She nodded understandingly. "Don't let me hold you up. We're all done here, anyway. You wouldn't want to keep the minister waiting," she added to Renata.

"No, I suppose not. We'll continue our conversation another time." To Mariah's utter astonishment, Renata leaned over and embraced her stiffened shoulders, planting an air kiss on her cheek. Hissing softly in her ear, *"You're being very stupid!"* Then she pulled back, wearing a smile to charm the gods. "It was *such* a pleasure to see you again, dear."

She looped a hand through her son's arm and gave him a brisk nod. As they headed back into the gallery, the crack of Renata's stiletto heels echoed like pistol shots off the atrium's polished marble floor.

Mariah spotted Paul, standing near the two-headed ice sculpture with Mayor Riordan and some other people she didn't recognize. He'd obviously seen her talking to Renata, because his furrowed brow telegraphed a question. She tried to send back a reassuring smile, but an arm reached across her field of vision, deftly rescuing two glasses from a passing tray.

Yuri Belenko handed one to her. "My dear Mariah! At last I catch you alone!" He took her free hand and lifted it to his lips.

"Yuri, there you are! I was just looking for you."

"Ah, we are great minds to think so much alike, are we not? I spotted you back on the terrace. I have been looking for you ever since."

"How have you been?"

"You know what they say—every day above ground is a good one."

She smiled. "Well, I'm glad you're having a good one."

He clinked his glass against hers, grinning. "It just got much better."

"It's good to see you, too," Mariah said. And it was, she decided, taking a grateful sip of the drink she sorely needed by now. How could anyone not warm to a fellow with such corny lines and the ingratiating habit of kissing a lady's hand? The most charming thing about him was that he seemed perfectly aware how hokey it all was. If international intrigue was still "the great game," Yuri Belenko played it with self-mocking humor and style.

His heavy-lidded brown eyes fixed her with a warm smile. "Bedroom eyes," some would call them. Forty-three and divorced, according to his CIA file, he was a substantial physical presence, a six-footer, his barrel-chested girth imposing. Not fat, precisely, but with the well-nourished look of a man who denies himself few pleasures and submits to few exertions. His lips were sensual and port-colored, hinting at a decadence that might or might not be illusory. His hair was thick, dark and shining, parted off center and on the long side—unusually Byronic for a political hack—and he had a distracting tendency to rake it back languidly with one hand as he spoke.

"The world is a small place, after all," he said. "I was hoping to see you here, but I wasn't sure your State Department masters would let you out to play."

"Oh, I rattled my cage when I heard you were coming with your minister," Mariah said. This, too, was part of the game. Each of them knew the other's true affiliation. *Knew* they knew, but pretended not to.

"What did you think of the exhibit?" he asked.

"Very Hollywood. Glamour, romance, murder—all the ingredients of a blockbuster movie, wouldn't you say?"

"A piece of our history. A little glorious, a little shameful. Can you say your country's history has no shameful chapters of its own?"

"We who burned witches and practiced slavery? Who've assassinated a few leaders of our own, and are still shooting at each other on a daily basis?" She shook her head. "I don't think I'll bother trying to claim the moral high ground today, Yuri. I didn't mean to offend."

"You could never offend, dear Mariah. And you're right about the exhibit. It really is a little ghoulish, in some respects. History as entertainment. Inevitable, I suppose. No doubt the struggles of our own generation will also become the *divertissements* of the next."

"I'm too tired to struggle today, Yuri. What do you say we deny the next generation its entertainment and just lead dull, boring lives?"

"Eat, drink and be merry, for tomorrow we die!" he said, nodding and tapping her glass once more. "It works for me."

"Speaking of which," Mariah said, "shall we check out that buffet? Something smells incredible and it's making me very hungry."

Belenko glanced over. "The line is very long. I think my minister is holding things up."

Zakharov had been moving along the table, Mariah noted, loading a plate held for him by one of his bodyguards, but he had stopped midway. He was apparently delivering another long explanation to Shelby Kidd. The secretary, tall, rail-thin, patrician, was nodding with interest, while Renata and her son, Nolan, listened intently.

"Minister Zakharov seems very animated this evening."

"Oh, yes, he's in fine form," Belenko agreed. "We just received word from Moscow that Premier Tolkachev has resigned."

She pivoted toward him, surprised. "Tolkachev resigned? Has it been announced?"

"It will be shortly."

"Oh, my. Doesn't sound like you're in for dull or boring times, after all."

Premier Constantin Tolkachev was the third beleaguered head of government to fall victim in the last eighteen months to economic and political turmoil inside the Russian Federation. His departure cleared the way for another push forward by Zakharov and the powerful coalition of former Communists and rabid nationalists he led. Zakharov's longtime rival, the ailing Russian president was running out of ways to avoid naming him to the premiership, which would bring the feisty foreign minister one step closer to his ultimate goal—the presidency itself.

Which explained Zakharov's late arrival at the reception, Mariah thought. No doubt the next set of intercepts from the agency's satellites would confirm the old bear had been talking with his political allies back in Moscow, looking to cement his position.

She studied the normally dour minister once more. "Think he'll cut short his visit here and head back early? Seems to me he'd want to be home, getting his ducks in a row."

Belenko gave her a puzzled look. "Ducks in a row?"

"Like a mother duckling? It means lining up resources. In the case of your minister, so he can make a bid for the prime minister's job."

"Ah, I see! Ducks in a row...I must remember that one." She could almost hear mental machinery clicking as Belenko filed away another cliché for his collection. "It's hard to say if he will want to return too soon to Moscow. We will have a major trade deal on the table at the Pacific Rim conference."

"I suppose a high-profile meeting right now could do him good back home, especially if the trade package goes through."

"Well," Belenko said, watching his boss, "Minister Zakharov is certainly determined to be seen as the solution to our country's problems."

To be *seen* as the solution? That was an odd choice of words, Mariah thought, especially from a man who prided himself on his skills as a wordsmith. Did Belenko doubt the minister really was the solution? Where did his loyalties lie, if push came to shove?

Or was she reading too much into this? He was Zakharov's executive assistant, after all. If he played his cards well, Belenko could end up at the right hand of a new Russian leader—one who, she reminded herself, had also risen out of the ranks of the old KGB. Since the days of the earliest czars, control of the secret police had been an essential requirement for attaining and holding power in Russia. Zakharov and Belenko would both know that anyone planning to occupy the top of that shaky political apex needed a loyal and efficient dark arts specialist close at hand.

She, too, watched the minister's entourage. Young Nolan had the floor now. Good for him, Mariah thought. If he was forceful enough to get Valery Zhakarov to shut up and listen for a change, the boy obviously had a future.

"Yuri? I didn't realize Arlen Hunter's grandson was involved in the Nova Krimsky project," she said.

Mariah's colleagues had taken to calling Nova Krimsky the "Las Vegas in the Crimea." The resort area around Yalta was being redeveloped into a massive casino and entertainment center that some thought would rival Monte Carlo for the business of the European gambling set.

Belenko waved a hand around him. "As a matter of fact, it was Arlen Hunter who first proposed it, many years ago. A very grand scheme, but ahead of its time, then. Too much capitalist decadence for the old regime, you see."

"And now that it's going to fly, Arlen's daughter and grandson are involved?"

"Among others. A joint venture that large will draw many international partners. Anyway," Belenko said, taking her arm and drawing her away, "enough business and politics, dear Mariah. Eat, drink and be merry—isn't that our new golden rule?"

"Right," she agreed.

"Good. And since it does not look like they are going to leave anything for us at that table, and it's much too crowded in here, anyway, why don't you join me for dinner?"

"What—somewhere else, you mean?"

"Can you get away from your Secretary Kidd for a few hours?"

"I suppose," she said, "but won't your minister be needing you?"

"Not for much longer. He is running on Moscow time. He likes to retire early when he travels."

"What about you? You must be feeling the effects of jet lag, too."

"Not really. In fact," he said, taking her hand to his lips once more, "I am curiously revived. So, what do you say? Do you dare have dinner with a big bad Russian?" The brown eyes reflected amusement, like a challenge laid down. Or, who knew? Maybe it was an attempt at seduction. For someone who'd been dangled as a lure here, Mariah thought, she was proving to be no great shakes at reading the signs. Years of happily married status had dulled that part of her radar.

Then she remembered Paul. She glanced across the room, looking for him, suddenly recalling, too, that his bag was back in her room at the Beverly Wilshire. Lord, but life was complicated! Should she find a way to talk to him first? No, she decided. It had been his choice to follow her out to L.A. He knew she was here on business. He had no need to know that contacting Yuri Belenko was the business she'd been sent to take care of. In any case, whatever her relationship with Paul was, it wasn't proprietary. She didn't want that, and he'd never pressed for it.

And, anyway, she told herself, this was just dinner.

"Yuri," she said, "you're on."

Wednesday,
July 3

Chapter
Ten

It was 1:00 a.m. by the time Mariah finally called it a night—
4:00 a.m. in Virginia, she thought, exhausted.

Yuri Belenko had dropped her back at her hotel a little
before midnight. Dodging his bid by the front door to keep
the evening going over drinks in her room, she'd waited out
of sight in the lobby until his car had pulled away. When she
was sure he was gone, she'd walked out once more and
flagged a cab. If the doorman was intrigued by her revolving
entrances and exits, he was too well trained to show it. Paul
Chaney was right—they were a discreet bunch at the Beverly
Wilshire.

Paul. He was probably upstairs waiting. A potent mixture
of irritation, anticipation and guilt accompanied the thought.
Why hadn't she come right out and told him how annoyed
she was by his conniving with his hotel manager buddy to
move into her room?

Because, she answered her own question, even if his behavior was presumptuous, he'd made the effort to come out
of concern for her, and she hadn't wanted to offend him by
appearing ungrateful.

And therein, of course, lay the real crux of the problem in
their relationship—her reluctance to go forward, her hesita-

tion to go back. Was it simple fear of being alone that made her so irresolute? How pathetic was that?

Whatever the case, she couldn't do anything about it right then. Paul—and the whole issue of Paul—would have to wait.

She had the cab drive her to the Federal Building on Wilshire Boulevard, a few blocks west of the hotel. Under a full moon, the rooftop of the high-rise tower bristled with a vast array of antennae. In its underground comcenter, a massive bank of highly encrypted computers hummed, providing a secure twenty-four-hour link to the entire federal government, including the CIA's vast communications net.

The duty officer seemed a little nonplussed to find a woman in a blue silk cocktail number flashing a CIA identity card on the other side of the bullet-proof glass, but Mariah was determined to get her contact report into the system as soon as possible, before she lost her nerve.

She and Belenko had slipped away from the reception at the Arlen Hunter Museum as soon as their respective ministers had left. The Russian foreign minister, as Belenko had predicted, wanted only his bed. The two of them had then made their way to a downtown seafood restaurant. With no reservations, they'd been obliged to hang out in the bar of the Water Grill for nearly an hour until a table came open.

But as unwelcome assignments went, Mariah thought, this one had been a romp. Belenko was a terrible gossip, and his wicked mimicry of colleagues and public figures was dead-on. It had been a long time since she'd laughed so freely. The man was a tonic.

Which only made this business of courting treachery all the more bizarre. It was hardly a simple matter of raising a glass and saying, "Cheers, Yuri! And by the way, could I interest you in betraying your country and becoming a double agent so we can keep tabs on that lunatic you work for?"

All Geist had asked her to do was feel Belenko out. *"Note I said 'out,' not 'up,' Mariah—har-har-har!"* See where his sympathies lay, then leave the rest to Operations.

Fair enough. She'd taken him at his word. Between Belenko's comic banter and constant flirtation, she'd managed to probe his serious side just enough to have something to file in her report. As for the Russian, if he'd had an agenda of his own, it hadn't been obvious. Even the after-dinner seduction bid had been typical of the man—playful and low-key. As if he knew it was expected, but knew, too, that it was a long shot. When she'd demurred, he'd conceded the round with good humor.

And now, her contact report was in the system, for better or worse.

Subject is both sophisticated and pragmatic. Has a remarkably clear-eyed appreciation of strengths and failings of Minister Zakharov. Notes minister's continuing hard-line association with rump Communist party seeking to regain control of Russian government at national and local levels. Expresses doubt that "old, collectivist solutions" will work any better now than in past. Also expresses dismay over virulent xenophobia (esp. anti-Americanism and anti-Semitism) of minister's nationalist associates—and minister himself, subject confesses. At same time, subject sees need for strong, centralized authority to counter growing power and influence of Russian mafia and resulting corruption and violence becoming endemic throughout country. Notes that economic reforms demanded by Washington as condition of economic aid will be difficult to realize in current state of internal political turmoil.

The bottom line, Mariah added, was that Yuri Belenko was a Russian patriot, but also pragmatic and personally ambitious—the kind of man who enjoyed occupying a position near the apex of power and managed to arrange his ideals so that they dovetailed nicely with his self-interest. She could think of more than a few fellow Americans with the same talent.

Her report would be on Geist's desk first thing in the morning. As far as she was concerned, her work here was done. If Operations wanted to initiate follow-up action, the ball was in their court. She only hoped the deputy would see it that way.

When she stepped out of the cab under the brightly lit canopy of the Beverly Wilshire Hotel for the second time that night, the doorman was there to hold open the car door and extend a hand to her. The *same* doorman.

"Good evening again, madam," he said, smiling.

"Hi there," she said. Smoothing her dress, she tried not to think what conclusions he must be drawing about her nocturnal comings and goings.

He rushed ahead to open the big brass and glass doors, but at the threshold, Mariah paused.

"Are we staying this time?" he asked.

"Yes," she said vaguely. "I just thought..."

Spine tingling, she turned back to the street. The semicircular driveway in front of the hotel was empty. Traffic on the Wilshire-Rodeo corner was light, but at the curb near the bottom of the drive, a black sedan stood half in, half out of the no-parking zone. It had tinted side windows, but under the yellow glow of sodium vapor streetlights, she could just make out the dim figure of a man through the windshield, sitting at the wheel.

Surveillance, for sure. But whose? The car's license plate was hidden in shadow, but it didn't look dark enough in color to be diplomatic or federal. Still, who said watchers from either side wouldn't drive an unmarked vehicle?

She gave the doorman a weak smile and passed into the lobby, recalling Geist's report on how Belenko had followed her back to her hotel in Paris that past spring. Had Yuri or one of his apparatchiks spotted her leaving again after he'd dropped her off earlier? If so, he would know she'd gone to the Federal Building, and it wouldn't take much for him to figure out why. And so? What of it? It would come as no great surprise to a veteran like Belenko. For all she knew, he was at the Russian consulate this very moment, filing his own contact report on her.

On the other hand, she thought, crossing to the elevator banks, the watcher outside could just as easily be one of Geist's people. And at the restaurant? She tried to remember if anyone there had been paying particularly close attention to her and the Russian. The place had been crowded. Anyone could have been observing them. For that matter, by the time their table had been readied for them, who knew what extra equipment could have been laid on with the cutlery and salt shakers? If Ops could bug Yuri's dinner with his brother in Moscow, how much easier would it be for them to do the same in Los Angeles?

The elevator dinged softly and the doors slid open. Was that how Geist's people would approach Yuri? she wondered as she stepped on and pressed the button for her floor. Show him tapes and photos of himself in obviously friendly contact with a known American intelligence official? She pictured all the possibilities: their heads bent close as Yuri whispered a particularly juicy bit of gossip. His hand casually on hers. A light embrace and a harmless kiss on saying good-night. Of course, it was all as innocent or incriminating as a viewer was prepared to believe—even without getting into the possibilities offered by photographic doctoring or the creative use of body doubles.

So what did that make her? she asked herself. A practitioner of the world's second-oldest profession, spying, dabbling in the oldest?

Hunting in her purse for her key card, she cocked an ear at the door of her room, listening for sounds of movement inside. No light escaped the crack at the bottom. Her hand found the key, but still, she wavered. Suddenly, she was Garbo. She wanted to be alone.

Her life, however, seemed determined to transform itself into a fishbowl. There was the very public Paul Chaney. Geist and his murky operatives. Belenko and his. Media interest in her father's newly discovered papers.

And then, she remembered grimly, there was Renata Hunter Carr. The woman had said she'd been keeping tabs on her. How? A private investigator? How else would she know about David and Lindsay? More to the point, why did she care? And what did she want?

Mariah's gaze passed down the crenellated wall, each door set into a deep alcove where a person could easily conceal himself while he waited and watched. Baffled walls and thick carpeting muted all sound except the low, rhythmic hum of the air-control system and an insistent TV laugh track seeping from under one door a little way beyond her own. At the end of the hall, elevators droned softly, rising and falling, always seeming to bypass her floor. Still, her nerve endings fairly bristled.

This is paranoia, girl. Get over it.

She slipped her key card into the slot, determined to resist the generalized anxiety that was coming down on her like a bad drug reaction. As she stepped into the suite, the door swung shut on its pneumatic hinge. One small lamp was on in the outer room, but the bedroom was dark, except for the dim glow of a night-light in the bathroom. Through the open bathroom door, she saw her flowered makeup bag sitting on the edge of the sink. Next to it stood a battered leather shaving kit.

She closed her eyes briefly, then turned to the walk-in closet, sliding the door open as softly as possible. She stepped in and put her purse on the high shelf, then slipped her feet out of her heels, burying her toes gratefully into the carpet's deep pile.

As she backed again, drawing the door closed, a pair of arms circled her from behind. Paul's voice sounded low in her ear, sending a reactive tremor right down through her very center. "I thought you'd never get here."

"You idiot," she said, trying to hold on to a little pride. "You scared me to death. Why are you skulking around in the dark?"

"Sorry. I stretched out to wait, and next thing I knew, you were coming through the door." He kissed her neck. "God, you smell good! I wanted to ravish you at the museum."

"Thank goodness for the Secret Service," she said dryly. Her mind cried at having him there when all she really wanted was to soak in a hot tub and then sleep. But as his lips moved unerringly to the spot beneath her ear that he knew was a hot button, her body, which had been running on little more than nervous energy all day, started to betray her.

She sighed and settled against him. "How was the rest of the reception?"

"All right," he murmured. Slipping the top buttons of her dress open, he spread the mandarin collar wide. His mouth moved down her neck to the soft concave where it joined her shoulder. "My mind wasn't on it."

"What was it on?"

"Diplomacy."

"How so?"

His fingers descended the front of her dress, and small, black pearl buttons surrendered, one by one. Opening the dress, he pulled her even closer, his hands cupping her breasts. "I was trying to think of a diplomatic way to warn that Russian hotshot to keep his hands and eyes off my girl. Or is there something I should know?"

"Like what?" Mariah asked, her mind registering the possessiveness of his words, puzzling over it. Wanting to protest, but letting it go.

"How about a line on the hanky-panky going on inside the American and Russian delegations between that slippery Russian and a certain lady from Langley who shall go nameless?"

"Wouldn't you like to know?" she answered in her best woman-of-mystery voice.

"Yes. I would, as a matter of fact. Where did you two get to?"

She frowned, turning to face him. "We went for dinner. Paul, I'm sorry, but I told you I'd be working tonight."

"Going off alone with that oily guy is work?"

"It's a dirty job, but somebody's got to do it," she said lightly. He didn't seem to be amused. "Yuri's all right. In fact, you'd probably like him. Don't be mad. It was just work."

He sighed. "I'm not. And I did speak with him for a few minutes, actually, just before you guys disappeared. He's okay, I suppose. I asked him about an interview with his boss, Wacky Zacky, the mad Russian."

"Aha, so this is a business trip, after all."

"No, I came to be here with you, like I said, only you dumped me for another guy. Wait'll I see him again," he added, his irritation gone as suddenly as it had appeared. "I may have to challenge him to a duel."

"I wouldn't do that if I were you. You'd probably lose."

"Is that so? So what are you telling me? That this Belenko's a KGB thug like his boss?"

"It's FSB now, and let's just say you shouldn't say anything around Yuri that you wouldn't want ending up in a file in Dzerzhinsky Square.''

"I see. So, you guys go for dinner—a couple of old spooks trading secrets, is that it? Meanwhile I sit here all alone, pining away.''

"You? Pining away? Why am I finding this difficult to picture?''

"Because you have a naturally suspicious mind?''

The shadow of a grin outlined his perfect mouth. The curtains were open, only diaphanous sheers covering the arched windows on the far wall, running floor to ceiling. Below them, Rodeo Drive and the Santa Monica hills beyond sparkled like a piece of the celestial firmament that had accidentally fallen to earth. In its pale light, Paul's blue eyes seemed luminescent.

"No, because I know you," she said. "Did you manage to get some dinner while you were pining away so pathetically?''

"Just what I ate at the reception. I'm starving, now that you mention it.''

Mariah grinned. "Oh, you are a sad case." Her arms encircled his waist, ready to give in to anything at this point. Only one small, critical piece of her still held back, appalled by her surrender. Where was her will? "Do you want me to call room service and order something for you?" she asked.

His hands reached inside her dress once more, lightly skimming bare skin as he reached up and slipped the dress off her shoulders. The silk wafted soundlessly to the carpet at her feet.

"Later," he said, stepping backward, drawing her into the room and easing her down onto the bed. "Much later.''

Mariah lay on her side with her head cradled in her bent arm, her gaze tracing the smooth, sculpted outline of Paul's features as he slept. His profile was backlit by the diffuse pink glow of dawn breaking. City lights still sparkled, but the morning haze rolling in off the ocean rendered the scene gauzy and ethereal. Against such a mystical backdrop, it wasn't much of a leap to envisage him as some minor deity in repose, with that high, broad forehead and fine Saxon nose.

The mouth both firm and sensuous. The strong chin, slightly cleft.

He *was* gorgeous, Mariah thought wistfully. But how was she going to end this?

Rumpled bedsheets, yanked down in haste, were tucked around them now that their passions were spent, their bodies cooled by the relentless air-conditioning. Paul had held her close after they made love, his attentiveness meant to convey reassurance, she supposed, that she meant more to him than just a quick lay. Instinctively, she believed that, without quite understanding what the attraction was. For months now, her vague uncertainties and very real grief over David had kept Paul at arm's length, emotionally if not always physically. Yet still, he was coming around. It must mean something.

Even the most considerate lover had his limits, though. With a final kiss and a stifled yawn, Paul had eventually rolled onto his back, and his breathing had slowed until it settled into a deep, steady rhythm. Exhausted as Mariah had been, it had taken her a lot longer to fall asleep.

Now, much too early, she was wide-awake again. She closed her eyes and tried to drift back off, but her buzzing thoughts made it hopeless.

She glanced at Paul once more. If she spooned herself into him, it wouldn't take long before he stirred, and they would end up making love again. Then she might sleep a little more. But she couldn't bring herself to move. She felt utterly alone, and what had felt right—or good, at least—in the night felt all wrong now, with a new day dawning.

What was she doing here, playing Mata Hari, bouncing from dinner with one man to bed with another, instead of being where she belonged—at home with the daughter she and David had raised together? Half raised. Then he'd gone and died, leaving her to finish the job and face the future alone.

She felt a cold stab of fear as she thought of Lindsay. *I'm blowing it.* Nothing else she did in her life would mean a thing if she messed up her child. Until she'd lost David, she'd felt reasonably up to the task of raising a happy and productive human being. Even after, for a while, she'd thought she was managing not too badly. After all, she, more than anyone, knew what Lindsay was dealing with and what was at stake. She remembered all too clearly what it had been like to lose a much-loved father, then watch her mother sink into an endless cycle of overwork, fatigue, mourning and self-recrimination. Those memories had inevitably carried over into adulthood, coloring every aspect of Mariah's life. She'd sworn her child would be spared that kind of scarring, but now, Lindsay seemed angry more often than not, and Mariah couldn't seem to get through to her.

She watched Paul sleep. What was she doing with a man who dwelt so far outside the basic, inescapable reality of her life? He was a charming man, who led a charmed existence, but he seemed oblivious half the time to the things that preoccupied her. And even if she were prepared to take their relationship to the next level, as Paul seemed to expect, Lindsay, she was beginning to realize, would never accept him.

This aversion to Paul—when had that started? Mariah wondered. She thought about the day the *Washington Post* article had appeared with the photo of her and Paul at the press awards banquet. The next day, when she'd gone to throw out the papers, she'd found the picture defaced—Paul's head sporting nasty eyebrows, a beard, and a devil's horns and pointed ears. He'd once counted among Lindsay's heroes, his link to their family the envy of her school friends, but no more. This new resistance, Mariah suspected, sprang from nothing more than the simple fact that nothing could turn Paul into that other man they'd loved and lost.

And what was in it for him, anyway? He could have any woman who caught his steady, blue-eyed gaze. Why was he bothering? Couldn't he see where this was going to end up? As far as Mariah was concerned, if it came to a choice between Paul and her daughter, it was no contest. So why were they forestalling the inevitable?

Nerves thrumming, too restless to lie still, she slipped out of bed. Since pacing the floor wasn't an option, she padded into the bathroom. There was a telephone extension in there, she recalled, although why anyone needed a phone in the bathroom was beyond her. It seemed to be a phenomenon of power-city hotels. It was too early to call Lindsay, but there was a pool downstairs. She could call and see if it was open yet. When all else failed, swimming laps always helped clear her head and chase away the anxiety gremlins.

By the time she was done, maybe Paul would be awake and they could order breakfast. They'd never gotten around to ordering room service the night before. She was starving, and unlike him, *she'd* had dinner. And maybe they could talk.

When she went into the bathroom, she found the phone's message light blinking. Mariah frowned and peered back into the bedroom. Paul's shirt was draped over the extension in there. No wonder she hadn't noticed the indicator flashing when she'd come in last night.

Shivering, naked on the cold bathroom tile, she pulled a thick, terry hotel robe off a wall hook and shrugged into it, then searched the base of the phone for instructions on how to retrieve messages. When she punched in the number, an electronic voice said she had one message, recorded at six-twenty the previous evening. Then, she heard Frank Tucker's deep voice.

"Mariah? I've got the stuff you wanted. Let's talk."

Good old get-to-the point Frank, she thought. Leaves a typically blunt message that reveals precisely nothing. He could be so irritating at times. God, how she missed him.

She turned to the mirror, yanking the belt tight on the robe, combing her fingers through her hair as her mind pondered how to liberate her Speedo from the zippered garment bag in the closet without disturbing Paul.

Then, she paused. A woman with smoky eyes, tousled hair and bruised-looking lips was staring back at her from the glass. Well, look at you, Mariah thought grimly. Who are you? Mata Hari? Incompetent parent? Some babe who got lucky?

Or fortune's fool?

Chapter
Eleven

Newport Beach homicide detective Jim Scheiber got the call-out a little after 7:00 a.m. He wasn't due into the office for another couple of hours. When the phone pealed, he was at home in bed with his bride of eleven days.

He groaned into the pillows. "Oh, Christ! Not *now*."

It wasn't fair. Everything about Liz was velvety, ripe and warm. The last thing he wanted was a distraction. He was tempted to rip the phone cord out of the wall.

Too late. Liz had already slipped out from under him and was making a grab for the infernal machine. She lifted the cordless receiver out of the cradle. At the same time, her other hand whipped her nightgown up from the floor, deftly one-arming it over her head, successfully maneuvering the phone through the gauzy material and slinky straps. Pretty amazing gymnastics for so early in the morning, he thought with admiration.

The reason for her scramble announced itself in the next room. Scheiber heard a thump, followed a split second later by small, bare feet pummeling down the hall at breakneck speed. By that time, Liz had already managed to get the gown pulled down. When the bedroom door banged back against the frame, she was leaning against the headboard with the receiver cradled between her chin and shoulder.

"Hello?" she said, looking and sounding as calm and composed as if she'd been up for hours.

Scheiber just stared in wonder. How did mothers do that— react to what their kids were going to do before they even did it? He'd seen the phenomenon a thousand times, and it never ceased to amaze him. It was like hanging out with some Marvel Comics character. *Stay tuned for the next adventure of Supermom! Sees the future! Knows all!*

He yanked up the sheet in a belated reflex of modesty and self-preservation as her six-year-old hurtled himself onto the bed. The kid landed, the mattress bounced and Scheiber's skull caught the headboard on the rebound.

"Ow! Damnation!" Liz shot him a cautionary look and raised a warning finger in Lucas's direction. Scheiber gave the boy a grim smile, the best he could muster under the circumstances. "Hey, bud," he murmured, probing his bruised cranium. "Phone wake you?"

"Yeah. What's for breakfast?"

He spit the "s" both times, so that Scheiber had to wipe a couple of wet spots off his cheek. He tried not to take it personally. The kid was missing his two front teeth and probably couldn't help it. With that dental deficit, plus his sleep-shocked hair and rumpled Joe Boxers, he looked like a midget fighter past his prime.

"How about some cereal?" Scheiber proposed. "I bet you could get that all on your own, huh? I think there's some of that Choco-stuff left. The one with the marshmallows your mom gave us so much grief about buying? Want to go down, check it out? Maybe watch some cartoons while you're at it?"

The small, tawny head shook vehemently. "Uh-uh. I want waffles. Waf-fles! Waf-fles!" He got to his feet and started bouncing up and down on the bed.

Scheiber winced as a small foot slammed into his shin. He tried not to take that personally, either. He and the boy had been making real progress over the past few months, but it was probably inevitable that his and Liz's kid-free honeymoon would set things back some. Now it was payback time.

"Lucas, cut it out," his mother said. "Guess who," she added, handing the phone to Scheiber.

He grunted.

The voice on the other end of the line was annoyingly cheerful. "Hey there, Romeo! Rise and shine!"

"This better be good, Eckert."

"Hey, you don't want us thinking we can get along without you, do you? You been back two whole days. Yesterday was too quiet—call it a wedding gift from the good folks of Newport. But it's time you got back in the saddle, pardner."

"Yeah, sure," Scheiber said, rubbing his face wearily. "So what have you got?"

"Floater in a hot tub. Old guy. Looks like rigor's already set in, so he's probably been curled up there since yesterday. Coroner's gonna have a hell of a time getting him out and onto a gurney. They aren't careful, he's gonna roll off and bounce off down the street like an old tire."

"Cute, Dave. What's the address?" He sent an apologetic grimace in Liz's direction.

"Come on, Lucas," she whispered. "We better go see about breakfast."

The boy sprang off the bed, whooping, "Waf-fles! Waf-fles!" He charged down the hall, doing his best impression of an elephant herd.

"Whoa! What was *that?*" Eckert asked.

"That noise? It's something new," Scheiber said. "Revolutionary technology. It's called sonic birth control."

Liz slapped his arm, grinning. She started untangling her feet from the blankets, but Scheiber reached out and grabbed her by the waist, pulling her back to nuzzle her neck. Her skin smelled of sleep, musk and grass, and her shoulder-length auburn hair was smoky from the barbecue they'd had the night before.

"Yeah, well, you can have it," Eckert said. "Think I'll stick with the old-fashioned methods. Anyway, this house with the floater? It's on Edgewater, near Medina. You'll see the black-and-whites. I'm there now."

"You're an eager beaver this morning."

"Went in early to use the darkroom. Call came just as I walked in the door."

"Okay. I'll be there in half an hour or so," Scheiber said, as Liz slipped out of his grip. He leaned back against the headboard, admiring the view as she climbed out of bed and let her nightgown fall over the best pair of legs in Orange County. A onetime professional dancer, she'd wasted three years keeping house for Lucas's father, a minor Hollywood honcho who kept promising to make an honest woman out of her right up to the day he married somebody else. To support herself and her son after that, Liz had taken up teaching jazz and ballet to little girls in pink leotards, one of whom had been Scheiber's own daughter from his first marriage.

"This guy's not going anywhere," Eckert said. "Take your time."

"Gee, thanks, Dave. *Now* you tell me. I'll see you in a while."

Scheiber hung up the phone as Liz perched on the edge of the mattress. "I'll go put some coffee on while you shower. You want some waffles, too, before you go? Or eggs?"

"How about a two-fer in the shower, instead?"

She smiled and smoothed his mustache, then ran a hand around his sandpaper chin. "You look like the Frito Bandito. You better shave if you're going out to face the public. But hold that shower thought, okay? Maybe tonight?"

"Tonight?" he said. "Come on, I'm *dying* here." It was a pitiful bid for sympathy, he knew. But damn, the day had been off to such a great start until a few minutes ago.

"Poor baby," she crooned. Her glance shifted to the phone. "Was that a murder Dave was calling about?"

"Doesn't sound like it. Some old guy overdid the hot-tub routine and blew out his ticker, that's all. We treat it as questionable until we rule out foul play, but believe me, honey, I really could spare a few minutes here."

"A few minutes, huh? So, what are you saying? Less than two weeks into the marriage and it's already 'Wham, bam, thank you ma'am'?"

"Oh, no, ma'am, certainly not. I just meant—"

She grinned and kissed him, ruffling his hair. He patted it down again, hoping she wasn't noticing how thin it was going on top. Still finding it hard to believe she'd said yes to a tired old piece of work like him. It had taken a while, mind you.

They'd run into each other by accident after his divorce—long after his daughter, Julie, had gone to live in Portland, Oregon, with Scheiber's ex and her new husband. He and Liz had been magic from the get-go, but she knew his case-obsessed behavior had already torpedoed one marriage, and she'd been burned in the relationship department herself. It wasn't until he walked away from LAPD Robbery-Homicide and took the less demanding Newport job that she realized how serious he was about changing his ways.

"I'd love to step into the shower and get all slicked up and slippery with you," she said, "but if I don't go put food into that son of mine, we'll never get any peace. Will you forgive me?"

"Yeah, I guess," he said, playing the martyr now. But as she got to her feet and lifted her bathrobe off the end of the bed, he added soberly, "Liz? I'm sorry about this. I knew the Fourth of July weekend was going to be a zoo, but I didn't think it would get crazy so soon."

The television downstairs suddenly came to life with a roar. She winced, but stayed put. "You don't have to apologize."

"It's not going to be like before, I promise. You won't have to go through what—" He caught himself. But she knew.

"I married a cop," she said.

"One who's learned his lesson. The caseload down here's not the same, Liz, I swear."

"I know, my love. And I know you did this for me—and Lucas." A frown creased her forehead as she stroked his arm. "But are you sure you won't miss it? You gave up something that was your life—"

"I want you, not the chase. I mean it."

She nodded. "Okay. But I'm not Allison, either. I signed up with my eyes wide open. So, just do what you have to do, and don't worry, okay?"

He nodded. "Okay. I love you."

She kissed him warmly. "Me, too. Big time. Now, I'd better go turn down that TV before the neighbors take up a petition against the new people on the block." She slid her feet into slippers and headed for the door.

"I was thinking I'd stop at the hardware store on the way

home and buy a lock for the bedroom door," Scheiber said. "Think ol' Lucas'll be emotionally scarred for life if I do?"

"It's probably a good idea."

"Beats walking in as the wicked old stepfather's ravaging his darling mommy, huh?"

"You're not a wicked old stepfather. He's crazy about you. And I," she added, vamping over one satin-robed shoulder, "am crazy about being ravaged. Did I mention, by the way, that Lucas has a play date this afternoon at his new buddy Aaron's, down the block?"

"Oh, lady! If that isn't an incentive to come home early, I don't know what is. You just made yourself a date."

She smiled on her way out the door, and Schreiber got up and headed for the shower, whistling. Suddenly, the day was looking bright once more.

When he drove up the alleyway behind the Newport Beach address Eckert had given him, he found the house cordoned off and the narrow lane crowded with looky-loos. Death comes to Paradise, he thought. Always a crowd pleaser.

He parked behind a haphazard row of black-and-whites and got out, squinting in spite of his dark glasses. The sun was already high in the sky. It was going to be a scorcher. Heat shimmered over red tile roofs, and glare bounced off white garage doors and stucco courtyard walls packed together in an unbroken line of blinding glare.

It was close quarters for homes in the million-dollar-and-up range, but like the real estate guys said—location, location, location. The Balboa peninsula was probably only a dozen or so miles as the crow files from Scheiber's own new home in suburban Laguna Hills, but each time he drove out onto this long spit, with the Pacific Ocean on one side and Newport Harbor on the other, he felt the subtle change in the air that came from moving from one distinct ecological zone to another.

The smell of the salt water and the lazy heat had him yearning for his Baja honeymoon. One sweet week in Rosarita—not nearly long enough. But after agreeing to keep Lucas for two weeks, the boy's father had announced at the last minute that the bimbo he'd married had surprised him with tickets to

Venice. And no, it wouldn't be convenient to change their plans. Lucas had ended up staying with Liz's mother, but she was sixty-five, and there was a limit to how long she could cope with his high-energy needs.

They'd cut the honeymoon in half. Back on the job only two days now, Scheiber felt as if he'd never left.

As always when a rare call like a 929–D, discovery of a dead body, went out, every cop on the shift had contrived to show up and take a gander. Anything to relieve the tedium of cruising quiet, tidy streets, reassuring the good Newport citizens that their exorbitant tax dollars were hard at work. A surplus half-dozen cops were milling around by the victim's garage. Scheiber spotted a couple more on the roof overhead, enjoying the novelty of the situation. On his own first LAPD beat, he recalled, he'd stopped counting corpses after his first month.

At the yellow perimeter tape, he nodded to an officer standing guard over the scene. The black-uniformed cop nodded back, but when Scheiber ducked to pass under, a beefy arm blocked his path.

"Ah, excuse me? You can't go in there."

Scheiber sighed. Fair enough. He was dressed in street clothes—a sport coat and open-necked shirt—and although he was a one-man Homicide Division, he hadn't been on the job long enough to have met every single one of the uniforms, or for them all to recognize him. His ride was also unmarked. On the other hand, who but a cop ever drove a Chevy Caprice?

"Scheiber," he said, pulling out his badge.

"Oops. Sorry about that, Detective." The young cop lifted the tape to let him through.

"No problem." Scheiber glanced at the acetate name badge on the lapel of the man's short-sleeved shirt. "Cathcart?"

"Ken Cathcart, yeah."

"Good to meet you. Were you first on the scene?"

"No, that'd be Sergeant Livermore. He's upstairs."

"Who called it in?"

"I think it was a neighbor. Livermore would know for sure."

"Okay. See if you can get some of these other guys to block off both ends of the alley, would you? Residents with ID only in and out. The coroner's people will be showing up eventually, and they'll need to get their van in." Scheiber glanced at the craning heads on the other side of the tape. "Let's try to move this bunch back, too. Any of 'em see anything?"

"What? Like, pertaining to the DOA?"

"Yeah. Anybody talk to 'em?"

"No, I don't think so. Livermore said the old guy croaked in the hot tub. He figured it was a heart attack, so—"

"Yeah, well, let's get a couple of guys talking to these folks, anyway, just in case. Find out if anybody noticed anything out of the ordinary recently."

"I'll get right on it."

"Thanks very much. I'll check back after I've had a look around inside. What's the best way in?"

"Side door of the garage is open. Spa's on the deck, up on the roof above us here. Just off the master bedroom."

"Got it."

Scheiber pulled off his shades as he entered the dim garage, pausing briefly to admire the silver-gray Jaguar parked inside. It was an older model, from before the Ford buyout of the company—notoriously unreliable, but sleek as an Arabian thoroughbred. The new models were thoroughbreds crossed with good American quarter-horse stock—solid and steady, but lacking in allure.

After his divorce, Scheiber had bought himself an old Corvette. His enthusiasm for the two-seater, his ex had announced, was a symptom of complete reversion to juvenile irresponsibility. She'd also noted the male preoccupation with speed and power as a substitute for virility. Scheiber regretted every penny he'd spent on tuition so she could finish that psychology degree of hers.

The door into the house was cracked open. From force of habit, he elbowed his way into a laundry room, taking care not to touch anything. He passed through into a kitchen that was small but well appointed, with stainless-steel appliances, buttery maple cabinets and buff-colored granite countertops.

The house looked at least thirty years old, so this was obviously a renovation job, he decided, and expensively done, at that. Blue and yellow accessories—hand-painted dishes mounted on plate holders, a collection of cobalt-blue bottles in glass-fronted cabinets—indicated a woman's hand in the decoration. But the faint smell of cigars and the clutter on the counter—junk mail, keys and a mound of spare change—suggested a bachelor life-style. A pile of newspapers was spilling off one of the bar stools. The *New York Times.* Guy was not a local. But then, few people were.

A patrolman rounded a corner from the next room. This guy Scheiber knew. Alan Livermore, carrot-topped, freckled, young for the sergeant's stripes on his black sleeve. Cocky. Determined to make detective, and still pissed that an outsider had been parachuted into the department's sole, coveted homicide position.

A fat, shining black tomcat was following closely at the sergeant's heels, but when he saw Scheiber, the cat hesitated, looking from one man to the other. The animal's experience to date with Livermore must have made up his mind, because he ran to Scheiber, yowling and circling his legs, looking for sympathy.

"Hey, puss. What's up?" Scheiber bent to scratch his ears, but the cat pulled back, holding himself just out of reach. Whatever he was after, it wasn't affection.

"He's hungry," Livermore said. "Complaining to anyone who'll listen. That's what alerted the neighbor."

"The one who called in the body?"

"Uh-huh. Lives next door. Went out around six to walk his dog, says he heard the cat yowling. When he came back from his walk, cat was still at it. Something about it didn't feel right, he said, so he came to the patio door to have a look. Apparently the cat was going crazy inside."

Scheiber had pulled a notebook out of his pocket. "Did he come in?"

"Yeah. Said he saw Korman working in the yard yesterday and he wasn't looking too hot. Got worried when he saw the old guy wasn't doing anything about the cat."

"Korman. That's the dead guy?"

Livermore pulled out a notebook of his own and consulted

it. "Albert Jacob Korman. Seventy-seven, according to the driver's license I found in his wallet."

"And the neighbor?" Scheiber said.

"Porter. Douglas Porter." Livermore lifted a hand and let it flop limp-wristed. "A real thweetie, you know? Thaid he was terribly, *terribly* contherned about the poor old fellow."

Scheiber ignored the exaggerated lisp. "So how did Porter get in?"

"He said he knocked at the patio door and rang the bell. When nobody answered, he walked around to the side yard, found the garage door open."

"Was it actually open, or just unlocked?"

Livermore hesitated, looking defensive. "He said 'open.'"

The cat was becoming really irksome, crying and insinuating himself around and between Scheiber's legs. "Let's see what we can do about feeding this guy."

He pulled a pair of latex gloves from the pocket of his sport coat. As he made a quick circuit of the kitchen, the cat stuck close by him, meowing at every step. A pantry next to the refrigerator yielded a tall stack of cat-food tins. Scheiber handed one to Livermore, nodding to the empty dish on the floor mat next to a water bowl.

"Could you do this?"

Livermore took the tin with a grimace. As he popped the top and shook the food out into the dish, Scheiber opened the fridge. Sparsely stocked—a little cheese, a couple of pots of yogurt, a carton of orange juice. No tidy, Tupperware-stored leftovers. Several bottles of Heineken and Guinness on the door, plus some soda and tonic water. Two shriveled limes in the crisper. An unopened package of bacon and some loosely wrapped cold cuts in the meat compartment.

The kitchen was well-appointed, but the fridge belonged to someone who wasn't much of a cook. Scheiber closed the door and moved on. There was a six-burner gas cooktop set into the granite counter, but the range hood over it held a good week's worth of dust. A single coffee mug and a water-spotted blue plate sat on the sink board, probably rinsed fast and left to drain. The dishwasher was empty.

Livermore dropped the food dish back on the mat, and the

cat dived at it. "Jesus! You'd think he hadn't been fed in a month."

"Only if you've never lived with cats," Scheiber said, remembering his daughter's twin calicos and their chronic short-term memory deficit where their last meal was concerned. "They've got a special talent for embarrassing their owners with this pathetic neglected routine. This guy could have been fed two hours or two days ago."

Livermore's foot was poised over the pedal on the trash can.

"Better leave the tin on the counter for now," Scheiber said. "We may have to go through there."

"Through his garbage? What for? The guy had a heart attack. Or stroked out, maybe. There's no sign of foul play."

"Yeah, well, until we know for sure, we treat it like a crime scene. If the side door was open, somebody could've slipped in. Wouldn't be the first time a homeowner had been done in by a burglar surprised in the act."

"Uh-uh," Livermore said, frizzled red head shaking. "I found his wallet in a dresser drawer upstairs. Nearly two hundred bucks in it."

"Yeah, well—or not," Scheiber conceded. "Still, until we've got a firm cause of death, best not to muck up a scene." It was meant as a reminder to Livermore that his job was to secure the site, not paw over evidence. "I'm going to take a look upstairs. Where's the neighbor now?"

Livermore cocked a thumb over his shoulder. "I sent him home. Told him somebody would be over later to talk to him. Not me, if you don't mind. Guy hovers just a little too close for my taste, you know?"

His shudder was overdone. Scheiber was pretty sure Allison's psychology textbooks would have had something to say about the latent tendencies of your average rabid homophobe.

"The guys outside are supposed to be moving the looky-loos back and clearing the street for the coroner," he told Livermore. "We also need to find out if anyone noticed anything unusual going on the last day or so."

The cat-food tin clattered on the granite counter as the young sergeant made a beeline for the garage. "I'll get that organized," he said, obviously eager to be at a task more suited to his management skills.

"You do that, thanks."

Watching Livermore straight-arm the door, Scheiber winced, but he held his tongue. He was the new man in the department, and he wasn't going to earn any allies by throwing his weight around just yet. He made a mental note, however, to watch out for contaminating prints if they ended up having to dust the place.

He headed for the front of the house. It, too, looked as if it had undergone extensive remodeling. The bar that defined the boundary of the kitchen overlooked a dining area, which flowed into a large living room. The far side of the room was entirely lined with French doors. The interior plan was airy and modern—almond walls, open-beam ceilings and polished hardwood floors scattered with expensive-looking Persian carpets and good furniture.

Scheiber walked over to the French doors. The sun was streaming in through the small-paned windows. The bricked courtyard outside was filled with flowers in pots and planters. Beyond the walkway on the other side of the low, white picket fence, sailboats anchored in Newport Harbor bobbed on the morning tide, their masts oscillating like upturned pendulums.

"Hey! Jimbo! What's keeping you, man?"

Scheiber turned back to the circular wooden staircase in the center of the house. It rose to an overhead loft area, and Dave Eckert was grinning down at him from the long balustrade that lined it.

"I saw your car pull up ten minutes ago. Waddya been doing?" Eckert was dressed in a black polo shirt and khakis, his thirty-five millimeter Nikon slung around his neck, the department's Polaroid in his hand.

Scheiber started up the twisting stairs, feeling every one of his forty-four years with each step. "Oh, you know, getting a feel for the place and the victim. Feeding the damn cat. The guy lived alone, I gather?"

"Yeah. Apparently he was a widower."

Scheiber paused at the top of the stairs.

"You out of breath there, old fella?" Eckert asked, grinning. "Honeymoon really wore you out, did it?"

Scheiber scowled. "I'll 'old fella' you. And turn that damn
cap around, will you? You look like some gangsta-rapping
homey."

He flicked Eckert's black NBPD cap, which he was wearing backward, as always. It rarely left his head. A civilian
member of the force, Eckert had been a professional photog-
rapher before falling into a second career as a crime-scene
investigator. He was a tad insecure, Scheiber suspected, about
not being part of the police academy brotherhood. Or, who
knew? Maybe the cap was a fashion statement—a bid to camouflage the male pattern baldness that aged him beyond his
thirty-odd years.

"It's functional," Eckert said. "Brim gets in the way of
the camera and screws up my light meter."

"Yeah, right. Screws up that case of terminal coolness
you're workin' on, too."

Eckert grinned. "Eat your heart out, old-timer. Come on.
The body's through here."

Scheiber followed him down the hall, pausing briefly at the
door of what looked to be a large office. The walls were lined
with heavily loaded walnut bookcases, and a large desk in
the center of the room was covered with papers and thick
documents.

"Livermore told me this guy was seventy-seven years
old," he said. "Aren't most guys retired by then?"

"I sure plan to be."

"So what was this Korman doing here?"

"I think the neighbor said he was an agent of some kind."

"Agent. Like, a Hollywood agent?" Scheiber wondered,
stepping into the office. "So, would these be movie scripts,
then?" His latex-covered fingers turned around the top sheet
from one of the fat piles. *"A Time for Every Purpose,"* he
read, *"A Novel by P. K. Lester."*

"A book agent?" Eckert ventured.

"Yeah, must be." Scheiber turned the page back the way
he'd found it.

The wall around the windows, the one wall of the room
not covered in floor-to-ceiling shelves, featured dozens of

framed photographs of people in various sizes of groups and various kinds of settings, most of them involving raised glasses. One man appeared more often than anyone else, someone's arms invariably draping his shoulders, or his theirs, as they beamed at the camera. Must be Korman, Scheiber decided, maybe with some of his more famous clients. Not that he recognized anyone. Unlike movie stars, writers seemed to be a pretty anonymous-looking bunch.

He turned back to Eckert. "Okay, lead on, Macduff."

They headed back down the hall toward the master bedroom. The room was nicely decorated in creams and yellows and blues, but, like the downstairs, it was a little cluttered, a little dusty. If he had to guess, Scheiber would bet Mr. Korman had a cleaner in every other week. Often enough that things didn't get too out of hand, but not so often for someone to get underfoot. By the look of things, the place was due for another visit any day now.

The covers of the bed had been pulled up in a halfhearted effort, but reading material overflowed the night tables. Several items of clothing had missed the laundry hamper in the corner and lay scattered across the deep blue carpeted floor. On one of the night tables, next to a water jug and glass, he spotted a brown plastic vial.

"The label says Dalmane," Eckert said, following his gaze. "Do you have any idea what that is?"

"Sleeping pills, I think."

"Uh-oh!" Eckert lined himself up in front of the table and took a couple of close-up shots of the vial, once with the Polaroid, once with the Nikon. "Maybe our guy didn't have a heart attack, after all. He was drinking, too."

Scheiber noticed the half-empty bottle of Glenlivet on another table. He peered closer at the pills. "It's a good theory, but I don't know about it in this case. The container looks pretty full. Most suicides who go the pills-and-booze route don't leave anything to chance. They down 'em all. Could be grounds for an accidental mishap ruling though, if he took one or two, and then fell asleep in the tub. We'll have to make sure the lab does a thorough tox screening."

He turned and walked out to the deck, Eckert trailing close behind. Squinting in the brilliant sunshine, Scheiber nodded at the officers standing guard over the redwood spa and pulled his sunglasses out of his pocket.

"The jets on the spa were still running when I got here," Eckert said. "I took a couple of shots and then turned 'em off so we could see the body better."

Scheiber peered over the edge of the tub. The old man lay on his side, curled up in a ball, just as Eckert had said on the phone. The lower elbow was bent, the arm tucked back under his head. Eyes closed, he looked as if he was asleep on the molded gray plastic floor. His hair was very sparse, clipped short around the ears but long on top, so it floated like white seaweed around his face. His scalp was shiny and bare. Must have worn a comb-over. Resist that option when the time comes, Scheiber reminded himself. Whatever anyone's vanity might say, it fooled no one.

"You said the jets were on?" he asked Eckert. "Aren't these things on timers?"

"It is. That's the switch right there on the back. I don't know, maybe it was malfunctioning."

Scheiber frowned. A heavy glass lay on its side on the deck next to the tub, all but a drop or two of the contents spilled out. "You got a picture of this?" When Eckert nodded, he picked up the glass and sniffed. "Smells like the Glenlivet, all right. Got a couple of evidence bags?"

Eckert walked over to a case by the door and pulled out a Ziploc and a paper bag. Scheiber nodded appreciatively, slipping the glass inside the plastic bag, taking care to seal in the few remaining drops of liquid. He then took a few scrapings off the deck where the glass had spilled and put those in the paper bag. He labeled the bags and set them aside.

"Better take the towel, too," he told Eckert, nodding to one of the wicker lounge chairs. A white terry bath sheet lay across the striped padded seat.

Walking around the deck a couple of times, then zeroing in on the tub once more, Scheiber looked for any sign that there might have been a struggle. Like maybe someone had overpowered the guy and held him under until he drowned in order to—what?

Livermore had said there was two hundred dollars in Korman's wallet. There was an expensive-looking stereo system downstairs, and at least three televisions that Scheiber had seen—one downstairs, one in the den, one in the bedroom. The art on the walls was all original, decent quality from what he could tell. Albert Jacob Korman was obviously no pauper. Who knew what else of value was in the place?

But there was no sign anything had been taken. No sign anything had happened here except the guy decided to have a drink, soak his old bones and take a nap on the bottom of the tub.

"Okay, enough is enough," Scheiber said. "I want to get a better look at the body. Let's call in the coroner so we can haul the guy out of there."

"You thinking—?" Eckert ventured.

"I'm thinking it's too nice a day to stand around here any longer than we have to," Scheiber said. *And I'm thinking I'm missing something.*

Chapter
Twelve

Sleeping with the wrong man isn't all that difficult, Mariah thought. The lonely fog of night masks a lot of doubt, and need has a way of strangling resolve. Waking up with the wrong man is another matter. The cold glare of morning is pretty unforgiving.

She studied Paul over the rim of her coffee cup. He was reclined on his side, one elbow sinking into the mattress. When the room-service waiter had knocked on the door, Paul had slung the loose top sheet around his waist. Lean and well-muscled, he had not an ounce of fat on him. The sheet looked like a toga at half-mast. The waiter had cast sidelong glances as he set down the breakfast tray. Mariah was reasonably certain Paul had been recognized, but he seemed completely unselfconscious.

She lay opposite him now, also propped on one elbow, the remains of breakfast on the tray between them. A couple of Romans at an orgy.

No toga for her, though. The thick hotel robe was wrapped around her, her wet Speedo hung out to dry on the shower rail. Sixty laps in the downstairs pool had gone some way toward easing the nervous thrum in her spine, but she still couldn't shake the feeling she had no business being there.

She wanted to call Lindsay. And Frank. But not with Paul around.

This was only the third time since she and Paul had been seeing each other that they'd been able to spend an entire night together. Normally, she ended up having to rush home to Lindsay. The unfamiliarity of it all—was that why she was still waking to morning-after regrets? Or was there a deeper message here about their compatibility—or lack thereof?

Or was it just that being with Paul reminded her of David— and the attack on her husband and daughter that had been meant for her? If it hadn't been for Paul's investigation, she might never have learned the truth. Was that it? Deep down, did she resent Paul for dredging up those memories and the guilt she still felt over David's death?

"What are your plans for today?" Paul asked.

"I have to check my morning mail packet over at the Federal Building," she said vaguely, praying there'd be no follow-up messages from DDO. "And I have a few calls to make. What about you?"

"I'll be over at the network doing my homework. Your friend Belenko said there was a window this afternoon. If the Zakharov interview looks like a go, I have to make sure we'll be ready to roll."

"I'm impressed. You do work fast. This will be quite a coup if you land this just as Zakharov's named to the premier's post."

"Just a lucky break. I happened to be in the right place at the right time. First thing Belenko wanted to know was whether the interview would air right away. It'll get picked up by satellite, so I imagine their people will make sure it gets rebroadcast over there. Probably figure it'll help raise Zacky's profile while he's making his bid for the job. I'm sure that's the only reason they're agreeing so quickly."

"He's using you, you know."

"Oh, no, Mariah! You think so?" He clutched his chest with one hand, backhanding the other to his forehead. "I feel so *dirty!*"

"Oh, you cheap slut, you," she said dryly.

He grinned and wedged himself into the pillows, back against the headboard, lacing his hands over his washboard stomach. "It won't be a love fest, believe me. Zakharov is reputed to have carried out some pretty ugly maneuvers to clear his way to the top. I'm in no great rush to help a thug like that cement his hold on power. By the time I'm through with him, his people may want to jam that satellite signal."

"Sounds like your plate's full today."

"Uh-huh. But I'm still planning to pick up the beach-house keys later. How about if we meet for dinner?"

Well, that answered one question, she thought. It didn't sound as though he had any plans to fly home today. "Let's see how the day goes," she said.

A frown creased his forehead. The man was an expert interviewer, and he knew a stall when he heard one. "You had a call from Frank Tucker, I noticed."

"You listened to it?"

He shrugged. "The voice-mail light was flashing when I got in last night. I thought it might be my producer getting back on this interview. When I realized the message was for you, I left it on the system." He started pushing toast crumbs around his empty plate. "What does he want?"

She hesitated, loath to bring up the business of Chap Korman and the UCLA prof's bizarre allegations about Ben. Paul was a little too enthusiastic for comfort on the subject of her father. If it hadn't been for his and Lindsay's horror at the idea, she might have given in to her first instinct and thrown out those moldy papers when she'd found them in her flooded storage locker. She wished she had. Look what a headache they were turning out to be.

"It's just a work thing," she said.

"I thought he was out of the picture."

"Who? Frank? What do you mean, out of the picture?"

"I thought you two weren't working together anymore."

"We're not. It doesn't mean our paths never cross. He was doing some research for me yesterday."

"I see," Paul said. The way he said it, it was hard to tell just what it was that he saw. "So how is old Frank these days?"

"Doing a little better. A long way from being back in the swing of things, though. I worry about him. He took his son's death awfully hard, and he doesn't really have anyone to share his grief—except Carol, I suppose, but she's busy with her new baby and a toddler. Frank being Frank, he wouldn't want to burden her, anyway. Steven was her twin brother, after all. She's got her own mourning to deal with. She says Frank comes around for the occasional dinner and puts up a good front, but he still looks like a guy who's been hit by a freight train. It's the same thing at work. He's just going through the paces. Disengaged."

"Have you been seeing a lot of him?"

"At work, you mean?"

He shrugged. "There, or on your own time."

"Not really."

"Not really? So you *have* been seeing him?"

"What's that supposed to mean?"

"Well, it's just that *I* don't seem to see you that often, and..." He looked away for a moment. "Look, I know it's nobody's fault that we so rarely seem to be able to find time to be together. My schedule's crazy, and you're busy, too, between your work and Lindsay."

"That's right. So what does it have to do with Frank?"

"His girlfriend walked out on him, right? He's on his own now?"

"So?"

"Come on, Mariah! It's pretty obvious, isn't it? I've seen the way Tucker looks at you when he thinks no one's watching. And I can't help wondering sometimes whether you're looking back."

"Why would you say a thing like that?"

"Why are you so defensive?"

"I'm not!"

"Yes, you are. Your hackles went up the minute I mentioned his name."

"Because he's my oldest and dearest friend. You know that. You've known it right from the start."

"Yes, I guess I have," he said. Then he exhaled heavily. "Look, I'm sorry. I don't mean to sound like I'm doubting you. But as for Frank—well, it was one thing when he was still with Patty. I've got to believe she finally figured out the lay of the land, though. That's probably why she left him, don't you think? And if he's starting to come around now, Mariah, it's obviously for one reason only.''

''That's ridiculous. I was the one who got in touch with him. I told you, he was doing some research for me. There was something I needed done, and he was the best person to do it. So would you just lay off him?'' She felt annoyed and protective. But why? Frank was a big boy, and hardly needed protecting from the likes of Paul Chaney.

His long, tapered fingers drummed the mattress. ''I'm sorry,'' he said finally.

''Why are you acting like this?''

''I don't know. Insecurity, I guess.''

''Hmmph!'' She doubted he'd ever had an insecure minute in his life. His clear blue eyes crinkled at the corners as a small smile—sheepish? apologetic?—crept over his face. She was meant to do something here, Mariah supposed. Lean over and kiss him? Brush away his worries, tell him they were groundless? *Oh, Paul, how could anyone take your place?*

Instead, she tightened her robe. ''Anyway, I'll follow up with Frank later. The first thing I want to do this morning is phone Lindsay.'' She slid off the bed and reached back for the breakfast tray. Time to get this show on the road.

''She called,'' Paul said.

''What? Lindsay called? When?''

''Last night, around nine.''

''Why didn't you tell me?''

''I just remembered. It was too late for you to call her back by the time you got in, anyway.''

She put the tray on the table. ''Her message isn't on the system anymore. What did it say?''

''There was no message. The call came just as I walked in the door. I talked to her.''

Mariah stared at him, icy dread slicing through her middle. *Oh, hell!* Lindsay knew he was here.

''Like I said,'' Paul said quickly, ''I was fielding calls from my producer and researcher. When the phone rang, I thought it was one of them, so I picked up.''

''How did she sound?'' Mariah asked. Stupid question. She could just imagine how Lindsay would react to finding Paul sharing the room after she'd gotten thumbs-down on her own bid to come.

"A little surprised," he said.

The understatement of the year. Mariah slumped down onto a chair. "No kidding. Damn!"

"I guess we should have warned her I might be here?"

"Well, yes, perhaps we should have, but I could hardly do that, could I, since I didn't know myself. Oh, hell, Paul! She's going to be furious. She wanted to come with me and I said no. Now she's going to think it was only because of you."

"Only me." Again with the improbable insecurity.

"You know what I mean."

"Actually, no, Mariah, I don't. Why is this so awful? Surely she's figured out by now that you and I are more than just casual acquaintances. Or has she? I mean, do you talk to her about me? About us?"

"Us? Paul, *I'm* not even sure about us. I told you after David died that I needed to go slow."

"Could we possibly be going any slower? Do you hear me complaining about the fact that I'm lucky if I see you a couple of times a month?"

"You can't only blame me for that. You said yourself, your schedule is even busier than mine."

"I know that," he conceded. "But even when we are together, I'm never sure you aren't wishing you were somewhere else. Like when I showed up at the museum last night. That was more than surprise I saw on your face, Mariah. You were annoyed. You didn't want me there."

She puffed up her cheeks and exhaled heavily. "That's not exactly true. I really appreciate that you came to offer moral support, knowing I'd probably be running into Renata. But I was distracted. Nervous about Renata. Watching for a Russian I was supposed to be chatting up, worried about how that was going to go."

"Yuri Belenko? The guy you left the museum with?"

"We left separately," she said, frowning at him.

"Yeah, but I saw you over the balcony, getting into a car with him downstairs."

"Score one for the investigative reporter. Just tell me you're not going to start feeling insecure about that, too."

"I'll overlook it. I know it was business."

"Well, thank you for that. And do me a favor—don't be repeating what you saw, okay? Not that it's a national secret or anything. Both his people and mine knew we had dinner. Members of opposite delegations do it all the time, picking each other's brains. That's all that was going on there."

Paul saluted. "Yes, ma'am."

"Thank you. So, anyway, last night at the museum—I was nervous about Renata and Belenko, and still worrying about a fight Lindsay and I had had before I left home. When you showed up out of the blue like that, it sent me into sensory overload, that's all." Mariah frowned. "But I have to tell you, Paul, this is a major complication, the fact that she found you here."

"To be honest, she didn't sound too happy about it," he admitted. "It's not the first time I've noticed it, either. I don't get it. I thought she and I were buds, but I sure don't seem to be in her good books these days. I can't figure out what I did wrong."

Mariah sighed and moved over to sit beside him on the bed. When he reached out, she hesitated, then tucked reluctantly into his arms. This was an altogether new phenomenon for him, she realized. There couldn't be many people in Paul Chaney's life—especially females—who resisted his charm.

A person could almost hate him. Ambitious and intensely social, he had a relaxed self-confidence and benevolence that probably came from never having been seriously thwarted. His childhood, by all accounts, had been a comfortable, middle-class affair, nurtured by intelligent, loving parents who'd managed to avoid the excesses of both overindulgence and hyperdiscipline. His passage through life seemed to have been largely painless, the few bumps in his road smoothed out by his own hard work and basic decency. It was as if Paul Chaney lived in some easygoing parallel universe most poor fools could only dream of, Mariah thought. All very far from her own experience—which might explain why she found it impossible to relax around him. It was hard to let down your guard when you were conditioned to expect the Bird of Paradise to dump on your shoulder as it swooped in to land on the next guy's.

"It's not you personally," she said. "It's David's memory she's trying to protect. She'd probably resent anyone she thought was moving in to replace him. If she's unhappy with anyone, in fact, it's me."

Paul was stroking her hair, but she tried not to be lulled. She needed to think clearly, decide how she was going to deal with this new complication before she called Lindsay back.

"Maybe this vacation will help," he said.

"I hope so. We really appreciate your lining up the house for us, Paul. Both of us. I mean that."

"Anything to up my approval rating. To tell you the truth, I was hoping to sneak away for a little beach time with the two of you."

Yikes. Mariah winced and pulled away from him. Beware Greek gods bearing gifts. "Are you telling me you want to join us?"

"Only if that's okay. Just for a couple of days, maybe? Doesn't have to be this week, if that's a problem, especially after the phone blooper. I could fly back out here next weekend. Or the weekend after?"

"Oh, Paul...I'm not sure. Lindsay's been going through a really rough time these past few months. I need some time to figure out what's going on in her head."

"Alone, you mean."

"I think so. I'm really sorry. If that makes a difference in terms of us using your friend's house, I'll understand, but—"

He shook his head firmly. "No, it doesn't. And I understand, really."

Did he? she wondered.

"Don't give it another thought. Can we still try for dinner tonight, though? Assuming," he added, "that I get done with Zakharov in time and you have no more Russian Joes to court."

"Let's try to talk this afternoon," she said. "Call back here when you get a free minute. I should know by then whether or not I'm done working. If I'm not, I'll leave a message for you. We'll try to work it out."

"I'll settle for that—for now." He stretched langorously,

and then his hand fell casually to her thigh and began to stroke it. "Do we have time for one more—"

"No, Paul, it's late," she protested. "You need to get moving and so do I."

His blue eyes twinkled. "I was going to say one more *coffee.*"

"Sure you were."

"I was. Come on. Just one." He reached to the bedside table for his cup.

Mariah slid off the bed to retrieve the coffee carafe, reluctant to hang around but loath to give him the bum's rush after he'd been so understanding.

"I noticed you and Renata had a chance to talk last night," he said. "I debated coming over, but you seemed okay. She even kissed you when she was leaving."

Mariah grimaced as she filled his cup. "Air-kissed. Not exactly the embrace of long-lost soul mates."

"What did you talk about?"

How to describe that strange encounter? "Not much," she said, "and not for long. Son Nolan came and said she was neglecting her guests—the *important* ones, I presume he meant—and dragged her off. Just as well. He's a smooth operator, isn't he, for such a young man? Quite the wheeler-dealer. Yuri Belenko said he's one of the partners in a scheme to turn the Crimea into a Russian Monte Carlo."

"Is that right? I heard about that Nova Krimsky thing, but I didn't know he was in on it."

"Yuri said the idea started way back with Arlen Hunter. I'd heard about the project, of course, but I never knew about that connection."

Paul nodded. "Sounds like something old Arlen would think of. And the Russians have a long track record of co-operation with Hunter businesses, so it makes sense that Nolan has an entrée into the project now that it's finally getting off the ground. He had quite a reputation as a party animal for a while there, but I guess he's starting to straighten up and fly right. What do you mean, 'just as well' he dragged Renata off?"

Mariah dampened the tip of her finger and lifted a crumbly

flake of croissant off her saucer. "I think she's had a private investigator snooping into my life."

"Why would she do that?"

"I have no idea. Nolan showed up before I could get her to explain herself. One thing is clear, though. She's very upset at the prospect of those papers of Ben's being released to the public."

"She's probably in good company. Some people think a writer's unpublished work should die with him. That if he didn't see fit to release it in his lifetime, releasing it after he dies is an invasion of his privacy."

"You don't, though, do you? Weren't you the one who suggested I send them off to Chap Korman?"

"From the little you showed me, I thought it was work your dad would have been proud of. Who knows why he never got around to submitting it himself."

"Sheer disorganization?"

The journals, poems and draft novel she'd found in that soggy box had been carefully stowed away by her mother years earlier. Some looked to have been written not long before his death, but Mariah had had no idea how they'd ended up with her mother when so many other of his papers only showed up years later in the run-down Parisian flat where he'd died.

But Mariah did remember that her mother, with her usual unwarranted optimism where Ben was concerned, always thought he was coming home. Right up until the day she found out he was dead, she had kept a watch out for him.

Maybe this week, Mariah. I've got a really good feeling. I bet you're going to walk in that door after school any day now and find your daddy at the dining-room table, working away, just like before.

Of course, it had never happened. What Mariah did come home to find one day was her mother sitting on the seat-sprung couch in the living room, nursing Katie and crying. Someone had called that afternoon to tell her Ben was dead.

Now all Mariah could presume was that he'd mailed the papers before he got sick. Who knew why?

"I suspect I know what's worrying Renata," she said, putting her coffee cup aside. "With all this momentum building toward Ben's sixtieth birthday, people are digging around for something new to write about him. What do you want to bet she's worried about the journals? The woman's been dining out for years on stories of her *affaire scandaleuse* with the late, great Ben Bolt. If it turns out he dissed her in his private journals, she could end up looking pretty stupid.''

''She probably deserves to worry a little,'' Paul said, ''although to be fair, Mariah, it was a long time ago, and they were both pretty young.''

''In their late twenties. Old enough to consider how their selfish behavior was affecting other people,'' she said stubbornly. ''You know what the funny thing is, though? If Ben *did* write anything about Renata, good, bad or indifferent, I've never run across it. Chap hasn't mentioned it, either. Still, let her sweat, that's what I say.''

''Aren't you at least a little curious?''

''About what?''

''What she can tell you about your father? What happened that last year? How he died?''

''I know how he died. Of hepatitis and neglect, all alone. He was living in a grotty room on the top floor of a run-down house in Gentilly, outside Paris. I saw the place.''

''The house itself?''

''Uh-huh. When Lindsay and I were in Paris this past March. Her idea. We were doing the 'Ben Bolt Memorial Tour.' She wanted to retrace his steps, see some of the places he'd hung out. It had never really meant much to her before, being related to him, but this year, between studying Ben's work and—''

''And dealing with losing David,'' Paul said, completing the thought.

Mariah nodded. ''I guess she's thinking about family and heritage, and where she fits in the grand scheme of things. Anyway, as far as Ben's last days are concerned, I don't think Renata's got much to tell me that I haven't already figured out for myself. My father, it would seem, was your basic idiot savant. A brilliant wordsmith, but a complete moron when it came to personal relationships. By the way he died, I'd say he wasn't much better at taking care of himself than of the people close to him. Renata probably had ample justification for dumping him in Paris.''

''That sounds suspiciously like sympathy for the woman.''

She shook her head. ''I would not go that far. But after the two of them ran off, Renata and Ben stayed in an apartment near the Champs Élysées that belonged to her father. A nice arrangement, until Renata caught Ben stepping out on her— conveniently forgetting that this was, after all, his track record. Why else would he have been there with her when he had a wife and kid—make that *two* kids by then—back here in California?'' Mariah reached for her cup again, took a sip of cold coffee, winced and put it back on the table. ''Ben cheated on Renata, Renata dumped him, he got sick and died. End of story. At least, that's the version I've managed to piece together.''

Her mother's version had a slightly different twist, Mariah recalled. In it, Ben was a martyr. *None of us was good enough for him, baby. He needed us, but we let him down.*

Yeah, well, not me, Mom. I didn't let him down.

Mariah felt a flicker of anger, just as always when she thought of her mother and the excuses she'd made for Ben's abysmal behavior. What did the shrinks call it? Enabling? It might sound like blaming the victim, but that was the role her mother had played. Even after his death, she'd continued to protect his memory, denying even to herself the full enormity of his selfishness.

Paul sank back into the pillows, his long legs stretching the length of the bed. ''Did you and Lindsay visit his grave over there?''

''Yes, another regulation stop on the tour. She wanted pictures for her English class.''

Mariah recalled the thudding shock of seeing her father's face, never really forgotten, in the photograph embedded under glass in his marble marker. Over the years, many people had noted her resemblance to him, but until that day in Paris, she'd never given it much thought. It had been a bizarre experience, seeing her own deep-set gray eyes staring at her from the grave.

''I always thought it odd he ended up in Père Lachaise Cemetery,'' she said. ''That's got to be high-end real estate, as Parisian graveyards go. My mother could never have paid for that plot, much less the ostentatious marble marker.''

Paul arched an eyebrow. ''A pretty obvious conclusion to be drawn, wouldn't you say?''

''That Renata paid for it?'' Mariah nodded. ''She must have. There was no one else.''

She thought again of the day she'd found her mother crying on the couch after getting word Ben was dead. Somehow, through the tears, the poor woman had managed to dredge up a smile.

They're putting up a monument to your daddy, sweetheart. In Paris, France. Imagine! Real marble, in a nice place, like a park. He'd like that, wouldn't he? One day, the three of us will go and see it.

It had taken thirty years, but Mariah finally had seen it. Not her mother, though. Not her sister, Katie, either, who'd drowned accidentally at age twelve.

''I visited his grave myself once,'' Paul was saying, ''years ago, when I was doing my own version of the famous writers' tour—bookstalls on the Seine, sidewalk cafés, Les Deux Magots and all that. Père Lachaise, of course. Ben ended up in illustrious company, as I recall, about midway between Proust and Oscar Wilde.''

Mariah took his empty cup and set it aside, nodding. ''And listed right after Balzac and Sarah Bernhardt on those tour maps they hand out at the gate—*Benjamin Bolt, auteur américain.* Of course, my father would have deemed that only fitting. He never suffered from any doubt as to his rightful place in the cultural pantheon, as I recall.''

''What did Lindsay think?''

''She was thrilled, of course. It's like having a rock star in the family. As a matter of fact, we counted as many admirers' tributes on his grave as we saw on Jim Morrison's.''

The drug-addled former lead singer of The Doors was also buried in that Parisian mecca to culture junkies. Obviously, Mariah reflected, a screwed-up personal life was no barrier to the undying devotion of fans. Lindsay had spent over an hour examining not only fresh flowers on her grandfather's grave, but also locks of hair, heartfelt letters and tear-stained poems in several languages—all for a man who'd been dead nearly three decades.

Paul's thoughts, meantime, had gone down another track. "Don't you think it would be worthwhile to talk to Renata while you're out here, anyway, Mariah? She may be a pushy old broad, but she's probably finding this as awkward as you are. Maybe it's kismet, your being assigned to cover an event at her father's museum. Maybe you were fated to meet, so you can both get past that shared history of yours."

Mariah shot him a skeptical glance. "Kismet? Funny, you don't look like a superstitious guy." She unfolded her legs and got up off the bed. "I don't think so, fella. My father's my father, and I'm trying to come to terms with him, for Lindsay's sake, if nothing else. But Renata's a whole other matter. It's not just me. It's what she did to my mother and sister I can't forgive. Just talking to her felt like an act of disloyalty, as if I were betraying their memories. Until last night, that woman lived only in distant memory—and a rotten place it was, too. That's where she should have stayed."

Chapter Thirteen

A knack for judging character, even of a man he'd never met—that was the Navigator's real genius, Tucker decided. The key to the old villain's viselike grip on secret power. Of all possible candidates in the western alliance, Deriabin had chosen *him* to receive the dubious gift of those secret files. It made sense. Pick a man with little to lose but a lot to protect. If push came to shove, there was no telling what such a man would be capable of.

Tucker rounded the corner of his daughter's street in Alexandria, just a couple of miles from his own. He'd spent the morning paying bills and arranging to have his newspaper deliveries discontinued, his mail held. Picking up laundry. Packing a small bag. Withdrawing cash from the bank and visiting his safe-deposit box. Making plane and car-rental reservations with a credit card he'd taken from the safe-deposit box along with sundry other pieces of identification—all of them bearing the name Grant M. Lewis. It was an alias he hadn't used since his Operations days. For twenty-five years, he'd kept it current, unbeknownst to anyone. Just in case. Old habits die hard.

The air had been dense all morning with oppressive heat and humidity, but as noon rolled around, the sun disappeared behind a high black and purple thunderhead. The temperature was dropping fast, and wind was gusting strong enough to rock the Explorer as he passed a strip-mall parking lot. The hairs on his arm, resting on the rolled-down window, prickled with the static warning of the oncoming storm.

He was no man's puppet, he told himself. Well, all right. The Navigator *had* correctly calculated that he'd react to the information dumped on him. But that didn't mean he had to follow the script the old man had written. By destroying most of Deriabin's files and stealing the rest, he'd already started rewriting it.

Of course, he'd also committed a couple of indictable offenses in the process. And he wasn't done yet.

By the time he reached the bottom of Carol's driveway, the rain was starting to come down in huge balloon droplets. Her house was a small postwar bungalow, its garage detached and set to the side and well back on the lot. When Tucker pulled up to it, he spotted her red minivan inside.

"Damn," he muttered.

He'd phoned ahead, but had gotten the machine. Perfect, he'd thought. If Carol and Lindsay were out with the kids, he could use his key to get into her house, get what he wanted and leave without having to explain himself. Or implicate anyone else.

As he killed the ignition on the Explorer, his peripheral vision caught a movement in the backyard. Carol, dressed in a long, cotton shirt and an old pair of shorts, was getting wet as she struggled to yank whipping sheets and towels off the clothesline. Lindsay was out there, too, a hood pulled over her head as she scrambled to pick up a fleet of brightly colored Tonka trucks scattered across the lawn.

Tucker jumped out of his car and ran toward them. Scooping a couple of trucks Lindsay had missed, he lobbed them with satisfying accuracy into a red plastic toy bin on the back porch, then crossed the lawn to help Carol get the washing down.

"Hi!" she called, straining to be heard above the whip of the sheets on the line. "Good timing!"

She took down the last sheet and grabbed two corners of it, trying to wrestle it into a fold, but her light brown hair was blowing into her eyes and the sheet kept getting away on her. Tucker grabbed the flapping bottom. While he held it, she folded the sheet in half, then end over end. He jammed it on top of the laundry hamper.

"What are you doing hanging wash when there's a thunderstorm coming?" he bellowed.

"Didn't hear the forecast. No matter. Everything's dry, anyway. We just have to get it inside. Grab the basket, Dad, and take it in quick before it gets wet. I'll get the last few towels."

Hooking the hamper under one arm, Tucker ripped a couple of towels off the line and ducked under it, heading for the cedar deck by the back door. Lindsay had already gone in with the toys. The rain was starting to come down in earnest now, but at the steps, he paused for a second, raising his face to the sky. Cool rain pelted him, and he remembered another day, another storm. Long ago it was, certainly before the twins were born—a summer day that had started out hot, like today.

He and his wife were alone at her parents' cottage on the Susquehanna, sunning themselves. Suddenly, the wooden dock beneath them vibrated with a deep roll of thunder. Within minutes, the skies darkened, then opened.

What happened next was the kind of stunt kids pull when there's no one around to remind them they really aren't immortal. Instead of running for cover as they should have, he and Joanne had lifted their faces to the sky, drinking in the rain. Tiny droplets had clung like prisms to her long lashes. She was so young, and healthy in a way she wouldn't be for much longer, although the babies would be born before leukemia fully reared its ugly head. Had the disease been at work even then, Tucker wondered, massing deep in her bone marrow, rallying white cells for the deadly insurrection they would mount against her?

Her lips had parted, her tongue reaching to taste raindrops, and he hadn't been able to resist kissing her. It had been stupid to stay out in the storm like that, but pretty damn thrilling, too, to strip out of their suits and slide off the dock, making love in the silky water as the storm whirled and crashed around them like some Wagnerian opera.

Not long before Joanne died, he was sitting next to her hospital bed one afternoon, watching her gaunt body struggle to breathe. She'd been only semiconscious for days, but when a crack of thunder shook the walls, a sudden smile dawned on her parched lips. She opened her eyes briefly, and her tube-laden hand reached out to touch his—sharing the moment one last time.

The memory weighed on Tucker, sweet and heavy, as he yanked open the screen door and walked into their daughter's kitchen. Lindsay was crouched on the floor, sorting his grandson's toys. She'd kicked off her sandals by the door, but wet blades of grass stuck to her bare feet. Her water-spotted, hooded green shirt was short-sleeved, and when he noticed her wrists and hands, he was taken aback.

Tattoos? A chuff of relief passed his lips. No, not tattoos. She'd just drawn on herself, doodles and curlicues in multiple colors of ink. But what the hell for?

His tread on the linoleum made her turn her head, and she gave him a shy smile. Damp copper curls peeked out from under the hood, sticking to her small, oval face like little tongues of flame. Her eyes, huge, dark and always beautiful, looked gaunt and slightly sunken now. She was wearing makeup she didn't need, and it had gotten smeared by the rain. It had only been a couple of months since he'd last seen her, Tucker reflected, at his grandson's second birthday party. What had happened to that pretty young girl?

Easy there, mister, he told himself. Kids mature in fits and starts. This hard-edged look was just some phase she was going through. It'd pass. He remembered Steven at this age, full of anger and raging hormones and senseless rebellion. Why couldn't he have tried harder to understand what the boy was going through? Steven had lost his mother, for Christ sake. But had Frank Tucker cut him any slack? Oh, no. *Knuckle down, boy! Quit whining! Be a man!*

Stupid fool. Now his son was gone, and it was too late to tell him how sorry he was. Even if Stephen's death had been officially labeled a suicide, Tucker would go to his grave knowing that his own insensitivity to that mixed-up boy had, for all intents and purposes, pulled the trigger.

"Some storm, hey?" Lindsay said.

"Pretty wild," he agreed. A tiny rivulet streamed down his head, dripping onto the shoulders of his black knit polo shirt. He set the basket on the floor and used one of the towels he'd rescued from the line to wipe himself dry. "How are you doing?"

She shrugged self-consciously and went back to sorting the toys, putting cars and trucks in one plastic basket, small people figures in another. "Okay. I was out for a bike ride when the sky went black. I barely made it back ahead of the rain."

He averted his eyes, focusing on wiping his damp shoes on the doormat. It was too hard to look at her sometimes. Inevitably, his thoughts turned to her mother, and from there, went places they shouldn't. Dwelling on things that would never be.

Pushing the screen door, he cast his gaze back across the yard. "Where did Carol get to?" he wondered aloud. Then he caught a glimpse of his daughter's white blouse at the garage window, moving around inside. He closed the door and turned back to Lindsay. "Where are the babies?"

"Still napping, I guess. Alex went down early. He's got the sniffles."

"He okay?"

"Carol says it's just a summer cold. I guess the medicine makes him pretty sleepy, though. We gave him an early lunch, but the poor little guy fell asleep in his high chair, facedown in his noodles."

Tucker felt the ache in his chest start up again. She had a great smile. Nothing like her mother in looks, apart from the fine bone structure. Lindsay had to be at least a full head taller, to start with. Then there was the matter of those dark eyes, the wild flame of hair and the stubborn determination that seemed to go with it.

In the car wreck she and David had been in, Lindsay's leg had been crushed. Mariah said she still limped when she was tired, but she swam on her high-school swim team and played right wing in a mixed hockey league—the latter a passion picked up from David, an amateur player himself. She was one tough kid.

The porch steps creaked, and he reached back to open the

door. Carol blew in on a gust, carrying the last of the towels from the line. "Phew! Thanks," she said gratefully.

"What took you? You're half soaked."

"Alex's tricycle was on the grass. I went to put it in the garage and discovered tennis balls all over the floor."

"Oops! My fault, sorry," Lindsay said. "I was teaching him how to do a slap shot this morning. We were using the badminton net for a goal. I strung it up between the work bench and the motorcycle."

Carol smiled and nodded. "Thought I'd better pick it up. I had visions of Michael coming in from work after dark and getting himself hung up like a fly in a spiderweb." Her husband was a patrolman doing twelve-hour shifts with the Fairfax County Police. She turned to her father. "What brings you out in the middle of the day? How come you're not at work?"

"I had some stuff to do at home. I was wondering if you still had your brother's laptop computer."

"His laptop? Sure, it's here. Do you need it?"

"I wouldn't mind borrowing it for a few days."

"It's in the den, I think. We haven't used it much. Take it for as long as you need it. What's wrong with your PC?"

"Nothing, but I have to go back out on the road. I thought I could use the laptop to catch up on some paperwork." He felt a guilty twinge at lying to her.

"I guess I'm not supposed to ask where you're going, as usual?"

He shrugged. "You know how it is."

"I'll get it for you," Carol said, shaking her head. "Want some coffee? I just brewed a fresh pot."

He hesitated, shifting the basket. "Maybe just a quick cup. Where should I put this laundry?"

"I'll take it with me," Carol said. "I need to run up and change into dry clothes."

"I'll get the laptop," Lindsay said. "It's on the bookcase in the den, next to the sofa bed. I saw it there last night."

"I'll get it on my way back," Carol told her. "You guys stay and visit."

After she left, Lindsay turned back to Frank and caught him looking at her arms. She stuffed her hands deep into the pockets of her shorts. He stood back by the door, shuffling self-consciously.

"So," he said finally, "your mom's went to the opening of the Romanov treasures."

"Yeah. At least, that's the official story."

Tucker heard the scathing tone, the kind of rampant disdain only a teenager can muster. "You're not buying it?"

"Awfully convenient Paul Chaney just happens to be out there, too, wouldn't you say?"

Tucker felt his gut contract, but he kept his tone neutral. "It's a pretty big deal, this show. The Russian foreign minister came over to open it. That's the kind of thing Chaney would normally cover. I'm not surprised he's there."

"Well, maybe, except I know what he's *really* covering."

"Listen, Lindsay—"

"They think I'm stupid, you know? She let me go with her to Paris. I wanted to go this time, too, but she said no way, she'd be too busy. Yeah, right. Busy entertaining Paul in her hotel room."

Tucker's response was immediate. "That's no way to talk," he said sternly.

"But it's true! I tried to call her at her hotel last night, and guess who picked up, like he owned the place?"

"Doesn't matter. She's your mother, and I don't think it's right for you to talk about her that way."

Lindsay fell silent, finally offering a grudging, "Sorry. But they make me so mad, you know?"

He knew exactly, but it wasn't his place to commiserate with her. If Chaney made Mariah happy, so be it. "I thought you liked him," he said.

"Ha!"

"Your friends probably think it's a big deal you know him."

"Oh, sure they do," Lindsay said disdainfully. "They always want to know if he's going to be over at our house so they can just happen to drop by. People who'd never even talked to me before started getting all friendly after the paper ran that picture of Mom with Paul the night he got that press award. And, of course," she added, "wouldn't you just know that Paul would tell the reporter who Mom was, and who her father was—like, that's the only reason a big shot like him would be hanging around with her. Now the popular people are always saying hi to me in the hall, when before, I was just another nerdy insect under their feet.''

Tucker tried not to smile. So, she had a temper as well to go with that red hair, did she? ''Kind of makes you wonder who your real friends are, huh?''

''Oh, I know who *my* friends are,'' she said firmly. ''I'm not sure my mom does, though.''

Carol came back into the kitchen wearing dry clothes, her wet hair brushed. She tiptoed to the cupboard for coffee mugs, looking reluctant to interrupt their conversation. By the expression on her face, Tucker knew she and Lindsay had already had this conversation. Well, good. Unlike Steven, at least Lindsay had someone she could talk to about things that were bothering her. He was glad for that.

On the other hand, things couldn't be too easy for Mariah these days, either. ''Paul was a help to your mom when your dad passed away,'' he reminded Lindsay.

''Fine. He was Dad's friend. That doesn't mean he should be dating his wife. And you know what? If she weren't Ben Bolt's daughter, I bet you he wouldn't be, either.''

The girl was bright, no doubt about that. Secretly, Tucker had always harbored the same suspicion about Chaney, though he wasn't about to tell Lindsay. He had no business interfering in Mariah's life. He wanted what was right for her—for her own sake, and not because of her father, whose books he'd never read and whose reputation he didn't think much of.

''How about that coffee?'' Carol said, the fingers of one hand looped through three mug handles, the other hand reaching for the pot.

Lindsay's hands came out of her pockets and she scrambled to help. ''Here, let me get those.''

''They're kind of tangled,'' Carol said. ''I'd better—''

She froze, and when Tucker followed the direction of her stunned look, he realized why.

''Lindsay, your hair!'' Carol exclaimed.

The hood of the girl's shirt had slipped off her head, and

the thick mass of hair Tucker had thought was jammed inside wasn't there. All that was left was a crop of short, spiky curls.

He was taken aback. "You cut it all off," he said in a deft mastery of the obvious.

Lindsay touched it self-consciously. "I've been thinking about doing it for a while. When I rode past the Supercuts place up at the corner just now, there were no other customers inside. So, I figured, what the heck? Just do it, right?" She said it a little too brightly.

"Oh, my," Carol said.

Lindsay's face fell. "Is it really awful?"

"No, no," Carol said quickly, "it's not. Honestly. It looks really cute, as a matter of fact. It's just a shock, that's all."

"Uncle Frank? What do you think."

"I suppose."

Her dark eyes glistened. "You hate it."

"No, I don't hate it. It looks nice. It's just...well...*why?*"

"Because it was hot and heavy, and it gets in the way when I'm swimming, and..." The tears started to overflow. "Oh, God, I shouldn't have done it, should I? I look horrible. I feel so stupid."

Carol set aside the coffee pot and put down the mugs. "You have no reason to feel stupid," she said, wrapping the girl in her arms. "I love it, Lins. I *really* do. It's a change, that's all. We've all been used to seeing you with long hair ever since you were a little girl, so naturally it takes some getting used to. But you look gorgeous. Very sophisticated."

Lindsay pulled away enough to look her in the eye. "Honest? You really think so?"

"Absolutely." Carol smiled and wiped the tears off the girl's cheeks, then passed a hand over the short, coppery crop. "It's so soft! It's going to be a lot easier to take care of, too. You'll love that. Anyway, the beauty of hair is that if you change your mind, it grows back. But how are you going to know what you like if you never try anything new?"

Lindsay nodded. "That's true. And my friends won't see it until I get back from California, so I should be used to it by then."

"There you go," Carol said encouragingly.

"Does your mother know you were planning to do this?" Tucker asked.

Lindsay's dark eyes flashed. "No. I wanted to tell her last night that I was thinking about getting it done before I left, but she wasn't in, was she? And I sure as heck wasn't going to ask Paul Chaney for permission."

"Is she going to be okay with it?" Tucker pressed.

Carol shot him a warning look that said, *Back off, Dad. Don't make a federal case out of this.*

Lindsay folded her decorated arms across her chest. "It's *my* hair. Anyway, she never said I couldn't. Better to do it when she wasn't around. Every time I mentioned it, she got all teary, like, 'Oh, no! My baby! Don't cut your beautiful hair!'" Her voice had pitched itself up into a high, mocking defensiveness. Fearful, defiant, yet needing reassurance.

Carol laughed and nudged her—seeking to break the tension, Tucker knew, and to remind him to stop mixing in where he had no business. "You *are* her baby, Lins," she said, retrieving the coffee pot. "Might as well face it. That's never going to change. I guarantee, when Charlotte gets to be your age, I'm going to be a totally neurotic old nag. She's going to hate me."

Lindsay got the mugs and put them on the table, then draped an arm around Carol's shoulders. "Nah, you'll be way cool. And my mom won't care," she added to Tucker. "Not much, anyway. Like Carol said, it's just hair. It grows back."

"Speak for yourself," he said, smoothing a hand over his own head. Lindsay grinned.

"Sit down, you two," Carol said.

He settled onto an oak chair that was padded in ruffled blue gingham. Lindsay folded her long legs onto another one opposite him and leaned her elbows on the table, chin resting in her hands as she studied him.

"How come you never let your hair grow out?" she asked.

Carol passed behind him with the coffee pot, patting his head with her free hand. "Bald as a baby's butt."

Tucker shrugged. "Don't know. Habit."

"Have you always shaved it?"

He nodded. "Since I was in the navy."

"Dad was a frogman," Carol said, returning the carafe to

the counter and settling on a chair beside him. "Mr. Demolition Man."

"That why you started?" Lindsay asked.

He nodded. "More practical for underwater work."

Carol poked him in the ribs. "Liar. It was sheer vanity. I'll show you his high-school graduation picture, Lindsay. His hairline was receding even then. Inherited the fringe-over-the-ears look from a long line of Scottish bookkeeper ancestors, so he shaved it all off to look tough and get the babes. Right, Dad?"

He shook his head and scowled into his coffee mug.

Lindsay closed one eye and cupped an inverted hand, peering through it. "I'm trying to picture you with hair. Black, like your eyebrows, I guess?"

"That's the Lakota Sioux," Carol said. "His great-great-grandfather was a Plains warrior in South Dakota. Did you know that?"

"Like *Dances with Wolves?* Cool."

"Ancient history," Tucker said, secretly flattered to be the object of all this attention. "Anyway, it's probably more gray than black by now."

"Think an aging Bozo the Clown," Carol suggested.

He gave her a playful tap on the jaw. "You watch your step, little girl."

The two young women smiled.

For the next half hour thunder rumbled outside, and rain beat a steady tattoo on the roof, but inside Carol's cheerful blue and yellow kitchen, the three of them sat companionably, drinking their coffee.

At one point, a hollow-sounding snuffle echoed though the room, like water coming down a long copper tube. Carol paused to listen to the two baby monitors on the counter, her face set in that look of intense concentration that is the private domain of young mothers. Watching her, Tucker saw Joanne, standing outside the nursery door, listening intently as their twin babies slept in their matching blue- and pink-canopied cribs.

Carol was the daughter of his first great love, he reflected. And across the table, that lovely, copper-haired girl on the brink of becoming a woman was the daughter of his other.

He'd have liked to try to be a father to her, too, now that she needed one. He could never be anything more than an also-ran after David, he knew, but maybe he could help her through these rocky years. He like to think he could do better than he had with Carol and Steven. What was the point of getting older, after all, if you didn't get a little smarter, learn from your painful lessons?

He held his cup between his big palms, his gaze moving between Lindsay and Carol, who were still talking about ancestors. The company of women was a gratifying thing, he decided, thinking of not only these two, but their mothers, and Patty and Wanetta. Most of his male friends had been colleagues, and when his career had stumbled, those friendships had, too. After Steven had died, he'd had a few visits from guys who felt duty-bound to offer condolences. But they always looked relieved when the time came to go, backslapping him on the way out, making keep-in-touch promises they both knew would never be kept. The fraying of another man's life made them nervous, like a disease that might be communicable. In the space of a few short weeks, most of his male friends had drifted away.

The phone rang, and at a nod from Carol, Lindsay got up to answer.

"I've been getting a preview of life with a teenager," Carol told her father. "The phone's hardly stopped ringing since Lindsay got here, but it's never for me."

"Ha!" he chortled. "Nice to see you put up with it for a change instead of your old man. I called earlier, by the way."

"I heard the ring," she said, nodding. "Lindsay was out on the bike and I was nursing the baby, so I let the machine get it."

"Hello?" Lindsay said. Then she grimaced at the two of them. "Hi, Mom."

Tucker's mind flashed on the computer diskette in his back pocket and Chap Korman's package out in his car. He caught Lindsay's eye and mimed a phone at his own ear.

She nodded. "Uncle Frank's here," she told her mother. "He wants to talk to you." She slumped back down into her chair. "Me? Not much. Except—well, I got my hair cut." She glanced at Carol and rolled her eyes melodramatically.

"A little while ago. I went out for a bike ride, and it was really hot. I went by the Supercuts near here and decided to go ahead and do it.... Pretty short.... Carol likes it. You can ask Uncle Frank yourself. So, are you having fun out there?" she asked, abruptly changing the subject. Her finger traced a pattern on the tabletop, and her mouth tightened into a grim line. "Yes, Mother, it certainly *was* a surprise. You could've warned me, you know. I felt like an idiot.... Look, it doesn't matter. I don't *care,* all right?"

From the tears welling in her eyes again, Tucker guessed she did care, very much.

Lindsay listened for a while. "I just wonder when you were going to get around to telling me he was there. Or were you not going to mention it? You know, Mom, it would've been nice if you'd been honest and told me that's the real reason you didn't want me to go with you."

She rocked back in the chair, wedging the phone between her ear and shoulder while her arms crossed defiantly. Tucker glanced at Carol, who was getting to her feet.

"I forgot the laptop," she mouthed, pointing down the hall toward the den.

"Whatever," Lindsay was saying. "Look, Mom, you do what you want. I've gotta go. I'm putting Uncle Frank on the line now."

She straight-armed the phone to Tucker, then got up and walked over to the counter. Opening the dishwasher, she put her cup in, then closed it and stood with her back to him, staring out the window.

He watched her for a moment, then took a deep breath. "Hi, Mariah."

"I guess this means I'm out of the running for Mother of the Year, huh?" she asked.

"Don't ask me."

"Do you know what she's mad about?"

He debated lying, but what for? "Yeah, she mentioned it."

He heard the depth of her sigh. "I had no idea Paul was going to show up at this Romanov thing," she said.

That didn't explain how Chaney came to be in her room, of course, but at a certain point, Tucker thought, the details really didn't matter. "Oh," was all he said. What else could he say?

"So, I hear Lins cut her hair. How does it look?"

"It looks good," he said, relieved at the change of subject, "once you get over the shock."

"Shock? How short *is* it?"

"How short is it," he repeated thoughtfully. "Good question. Lindsay, what's the name of that Irish girl singer with the razor buzz? The one who went on TV that time and tore up the pope's picture?"

Lindsay turned to him, eyebrows raised over her sparkling, red-rimmed eyes. "Sinéad O'Connor?"

"That's the one. Like Sinéad O'Connor," he said into the phone.

"Get outta here," Mariah exclaimed. "She didn't."

"Well, yeah. Had to, you know."

"Why?"

"How else was anyone going to appreciate the tattoo?"

"The *what?*"

"Tattoo. You know—ink and needles? On her neck? What do you call that pattern, Lins? Kind of a barbed-wire-choker affair, isn't it?"

Lindsay shook her head, grinning at him. Carol had just come back into the room with the laptop, and she'd heard enough to walk over and smack his arm. "Stop that," she chided, her eyes laughing.

He leaned back and nodded. "Yup. Barbed wire. That's it."

"Frank?" Mariah said.

"Uh-huh?"

"Get stuffed, would you?"

He grinned, giving Lindsay a thumbs-up sign. She leaned across the table and high-fived him. "I made that Falls Church run you asked me to," he said, turning back to the phone.

"So I heard. Thank you. You're a wise guy, but I forgive you everything. What did the letter say?"

"Um...this is not a good time."

Mariah was silent for a moment, then she said, "You know

what? I don't care if Lins and Carol hear. I'm sick of family secrets.''

''No. Not on the phone.''

''Well, can you give me a hint at least? Does this Urquhart person really say my father was murdered?''

''Uh-huh,'' Tucker confirmed.

''And? Do you buy it? You don't think it might just be some kind of shakedown to cash in on Ben's rep, what with all these sixtieth-birthday tributes looking to get so much press?''

Tucker glanced at Carol and Lindsay, who were clearly riveted to his half of the conversation. He exhaled heavily. ''I might,'' he said, ''except I got something from another source that tells me he could be on to something.''

''What other source?''

''Remember the Navigator?''

''Sure.''

''My trip?'' he hinted.

There was a stunned silence at the other end of the line, and then Mariah breathed, ''You're kidding! *That's* where you were?''

''At his request. I can't go into it on the phone, except—''

She interrupted, her voice urgent. ''Frank, the Navigator's dead.''

Tucker sat up straight in his chair. *''What?''*

''I'm in the Federal Building comcenter right now. I came over to check my messages, and it was in this morning's cable traffic out of Moscow Station. Weren't you copied on it?''

He ran his hand over his head. ''I didn't go in to work today. Anyway, I'm so far out of the day-to-day loop, they probably wouldn't have copied me.''

''But if you were just there over on business...?''

''Station wasn't informed—deliberately. Strict 'need to know' rules. They had no need. When was this supposed to have happened?''

''They said he was found at his *dacha* yesterday. That he'd been ill, but his death had been unexpectedly sudden, to the point of being suspicious. The papers over there are saying the police want to question a foreigner who reportedly visited

him a couple of days ago. Oh, Jesus, Frank! *When* did you
see him?''

''Day before yesterday.''

The line fell silent. The rain on the cedar deck outside beat
a nervous rattle that matched his own rising anxiety. He was
one of the last people to see the Navigator alive. Maybe the
very last, outside of the man's driver. *He* knew he'd left the
old man alive, but who'd believe him? Not the Russian authorities, that was for sure. And the American crew of his
aircraft hadn't actually laid eyes on the man, who'd stayed
behind tinted windows the whole time the limo was on the
tarmac.

Once again, Tucker had the sinking feeling there was a
script playing itself out here and he had a central part in it—
except someone had forgotten to give him his lines. Was turning him into a hunted man part of the Navigator's Machiavellian plot? For what purpose? Might Deriabin have committed suicide, speeding up the inevitable? Or had his enemies
finally caught up to him?

Tucker recalled the old man's mustard-brown skin, wheezy
cough and stick-thin body. Death is the surest cure for all
disease, but few people take it willingly. Somehow, he
couldn't see Deriabin as a suicide. He hadn't been fooled by
that deceptive frailty. Behind the bright, fevered eyes, Tucker
had seen the self-obsessed glitter of the true sociopath. Deriabin had destroyed colleagues, friends—even, it was said,
lovers—over the fifty years he'd spent clawing his way up
and then clinging to covert power. Despite his weakened
physical condition, he'd obviously still had the power to send
secretly for Tucker, then arrange for him and his Company
aircraft and crew to enter, move around and leave Moscow
at his personal will and whim. The man Tucker had met
would never relinquish control willingly, and the disease
looked like it had a way to go before doing him in. He had
to have been murdered.

''Frank?'' Mariah said finally.

''What?''

''You said the Navigator had something to say about my
father?''

''Sort of. Look, I'll show you what I've got very soon, but

in the meantime, you need to sit tight on this. How did you leave things with the literary agent?''

"We were going to try to meet with Professor Urquhart before Lindsay gets here tomorrow—except now, I'm going to try to change her flight so she can leave tonight. I made a big mistake not bringing her with me right off the bat. She's still my first priority. If I let this misunderstanding drag on for another day, it's just going to fester.''

"Fine. Do that, but hold on the other business. I've got some things to look into.''

"Frank, I don't want you taking time away from your own work for this.''

He snorted. "It's not like I've got anything too urgent going on at the moment. Anyhow, I've become a self-contained research unit.''

"What does that mean?''

"Nothing. Look, you just carry on, and I'll get back to you as soon as I can.''

When he hung up the phone a moment later, Carol and Lindsay were sitting back in their chairs, arms crossed in identical poses of expectation.

"What?'' he said.

"You don't really imagine we're going to let you walk out of here without telling us what's going on, do you?'' Carol said.

"Is my mom in danger?'' Lindsay asked.

"Why do you say that?''

"Because you look worried,'' she said. "Don't tell me you're not. I'm not a child, and I'm not stupid. What's going on?''

"Nothing's going to happen to her, I promise. In fact, she's trying to change your ticket so you can fly out tonight instead of tomorrow. You'll see for yourself, she's just fine. She misses you.'' Then he pushed his chair away from the table. "I better get going.'' He scooped up the laptop, then hesitated, frowning.

"What?'' Carol asked.

He picked up the phone once more. "Nothing. I just need to check my messages.''

All things considered, he wasn't too surprised to hear an

irritated message from Jack Geist on his office voice mail, only vaguely shrouded in the deputy's phony bonhomie.

"Frankie! Jack. Where'd you get to? We need to talk, buddy. We've had a disturbing message about our sick friend. I've already fielded a call from the Russian embassy. I'm sure you don't know any more about this than we do, but there's also the matter of those files. We opened up your file cabinet, but we can't seem to find them. And, funny thing—your shredder basket is full of musty old confetti. I'm *very* curious, to say the least. Minute you get this message, big guy, I want to see you in my office. Understand?"

Yeah, right, Tucker thought, grimacing as he hung up the phone.

"Dad?" Carol pressed.

He leaned over, giving her a buss on the head. "Thanks for the coffee, kiddo. Gotta run."

He turned and ducked out into the rain before either Carol or Lindsay could finish protesting.

Chapter
Fourteen

It was something you had to see to believe.

This wasn't the first time Scheiber had witnessed a body being pulled out of very warm water, so he was prepared for what was about to happen. But after making a casual inquiry, he learned it was a first for Dave Eckert and a couple of the younger NBPD cops hovering on the late Mr. Korman's rooftop.

He could warn them, Scheiber supposed. But where was the fun in that?

Instead, he stood slightly to one side to watch their reactions. The coroner's deputy gave the nod and they hoisted the naked, curled and nearly rigid body out of the hot tub and lay it on its side on the wooden planking. Sure enough, the others were taken aback, to say the least.

"Son of a bitch," Eckert exclaimed, his voice breaking like a choirboy who'd sat in the loft past his musical best-before date. He glanced around self-consciously, but he wasn't the only one caught out by surprise. At least one of the young officers had gone deathly pale.

"You okay, Miller?" Scheiber asked. "Maybe you should go sit down, drop your head between your legs for a couple of minutes?"

"No, I'm fine," Miller said sheepishly. "I just didn't expect...jeez Louise! What the hell's happening?"

Everyone—Scheiber, Eckert, the cops and the coroner's deputies—looked back down at the body, which was going through a transformation right before their eyes, from pinkish-gray to pale gray and white, marbling and streaking in a way only a Hollywood special-effects man could have dreamed up. Within a few minutes, it looked like something Rodin might have carved out of a heavily veined piece of alabaster.

"The way it was explained to me," Scheiber said, "it's got something to do with the postmortem growth of microbes. Dave, what's the temperature of the water?"

Eckert lifted out a bobbing thermometer attached to the wall of the spa by a rope. "Hundred and four Fahrenheit. I already checked out the heater," he added. "Thermostat's set high, and with the timer jammed like it was, he's been cookin' all night. Maybe he meant to keep it on all the time, but why would you waste the gas and power when these things heat up in ten, twenty minutes?"

Scheiber frowned. "I can't imagine. Seems to me you'd blow the system before long."

"Yeah, me, too. Anyway, I guess water that warm would make those little microbe buggers multiply fast."

"There you go," Scheiber said, nodding. He turned to Miller, whose own color was slowly returning to normal. "But the oxygen supply is restricted as long as the body's underwater, right? Keeps the bacteria in check. Prevents them from working like they're supposed to, which is to break down the body tissue. It's like the troops are all massed but the charge is delayed. Minute the body hits air, though, decomposition starts instantaneously, marching double-quick time."

"Looks like a speeded-up time-lapse sequence," Eckert said, recovered enough from his initial shock to kick in with a familiar photographic analogy of his own.

"That's about it. I don't understand all the details, I just know it happens. I'm sure Iris here has a more technical explanation."

Iris Klassen was crouched by the body, opening a multi-tiered crime-scene case and withdrawing a pair of latex gloves. Her white knit polo shirt said CORONER in crumpled block letters across the back. "It's a matter of aerobic versus anaerobic action—with and without oxygen," she said, snapping on the gloves. "You explained it just fine, actually."

Scheiber hovered over her shoulder now as she went to work, looking for signs of violence or anything else unusual on the body.

Eckert, meantime, was snapping pictures. "What do you think, Iris?" he asked. "Heart attack?"

"Give me a minute. I'm good, but I'm not Wonder Woman." She took the body temperature and noted it on her clipboard. "Anyway, if it was an MI, we'll only know for sure after the autopsy."

"What's the temp?" Scheiber asked.

"Ninety-nine point four, but that's just the hot tub talking. Rigor says this fellow's been dead awhile. He'd have cooled way down by now if he hadn't spent the night stewing in his own juices."

She examined the corpse inch by inch, up one side, down the other. Scheiber and a couple of the others standing around helped her turn it over. No small task, given the fact that the body was in a state of solid rigor mortis, a sure sign death had occurred at least eight or ten hours earlier, even allowing for the fact that the heat of the water would have speeded up the process. There was nothing unusual to be seen on the other side.

"He took a bump on the temple," Klassen noted, kneeling low and probing the victim's head gently with a latex-tipped finger. "Not too much bruising, but it definitely happened before he was dead." Her fingers explored the rest of the scalp, separating the old man's sparse white hair. There were no other signs of trauma that Scheiber could see.

"Brought down by a sharp blow to the head?" Eckert wondered aloud.

Scheiber mimed a striking motion on his partner, switching hands and angles, trying to hit the spot at the ridge of the brow where the body was bruised. "I don't know. It's kind of an awkward action, unless he was lying flat on his back at the time." He glanced at the spa, with its hard plastic sides, then the body once more, his eye traveling down. He pointed to the right leg. "There are bruises on the shins, too, but they look older. Maybe he banged the edge of the tub with his head as he slipped in.''

Klassen studied the shins and nodded. ''These are older bruises.'' She leaned close and sniffed the body. ''Mostly chlorine,'' she said, ''but I'm getting a boozy note, too. Any evidence he was drinking?''

''Funny you should mention it,'' Eckert said. ''We recovered a glass by the side of the tub. Contents spilled, but it smelled like Highland single malt. We bagged it and some scrapings off the deck, but I betcha the lab report back says it's pure Glenlivet.''

She arched an eyebrow. ''Whoa! You're good!''

''Wasn't hard to figure out,'' he admitted, lifting his shoulders in an aw-shucks heft, ''since the bottle's sitting on a table right there in the bedroom.''

Klassen grinned, then shifted aside a little. ''Here, you want to get a shot of the bruises, just in case?''

''Thanks,'' Eckert said, moving in for a close-up.

Scheiber watched them curiously. Had they been this helpful and chatty on other cases they'd worked recently? Or had something gone down while he was off on his honeymoon?

Most people would probably think it a strange place for courtship, but more than one off-duty romance had bloomed over a homicide case—not that there was any evidence they were dealing with a homicide here. So far, it was looking like natural causes, maybe compounded by an accidental mishap, like a slip in the tub.

He tried to recall the last few crime scenes they'd worked with Klassen. Had she and Eckert been making googly eyes those other times? Well, why not? They were both single, healthy and heterosexual.

And come to think of it, Scheiber noted wryly, Iris was unusually well behaved today. When he'd first met her, he'd been a little put off by her overt flirting and slightly ribald humor. He didn't like it when women in law enforcement thought they had to outjock the jocks.

But he'd quickly decided to cut Iris some slack after learning about her husband, a rookie Santa Ana cop who'd taken a gunshot to the head from a gangbanger less than six months into the job. She'd nursed him herself for two years, until a fatal embolism finally did the poor guy in. It was after he died that she'd taken her nursing background and put it to work in the coroner's office, determined to be on the front lines of crime solving.

Dave Eckert's own wife had left him for the orthopedic surgeon who'd pinned the leg he broke in a ski accident. Eckert would probably think Klassen's loyalty qualified her for sainthood.

"His hands are really scratched up," Klassen said, turning them over and peering at them. "Here, look, Jim." Scheiber crouched at her other side. "It's hard to see after they've been soaking all night, but there are a lot of cuts and scratches there."

"Neighbor said he was working in the garden yesterday," Eckert pointed out. "I saw roses there."

"So what was he doing? Ripping them out by hand?" Scheiber said skeptically. The burglar scenario kept playing in his head like an old newsreel on a continuous-feed loop. "Iris, those wouldn't be defensive cuts? Like maybe he was fighting off somebody with a knife?"

She shook her head. "Doubt it. These slices look too short to have been made by a blade. Some of them are just little punctures. I think Dave could be right about the roses."

"Yeah," Scheiber agreed, looking closer. "Anyway, you'd expect to see defensive cuts on the palms, not in the creases of the fingers, like these are."

"Nails are clean as a whistle," Klassen added, "but a long soak'll do that." She went over the rest of the body, then nodded at her assistant, who rolled a gurney over.

Scheiber's knees protested audibly as he got to his feet. "I'll be anxious to see the tox-screen results."

"Why? You find anything to suggest suicide?" Klassen asked, also rising.

"Not sure. There are sleeping pills on the night table— Dalmane, the label says."

She made a note of it on her clipboard.

"And some Prozac in the bathroom medicine cabinet," Scheiber added. "Except I did a count, and there's only eleven sleeping pills missing out of a prescription for sixty.

Only half a dozen of the Prozac pills left, but the prescription is nearly a year old.''

"Somebody said his wife died last summer?''

"I think we got that from the neighbor, yeah,'' Scheiber said. "I need to verify it. So maybe he was down in the dumps and was prescribed the Prozac. But the label says he had two more refills coming. Unless he was switching bottles, it doesn't look like he ever filled them. Same thing with the sleeping pills. I'll check with the pharmacy, but it doesn't look like Mr. Korman here was a big pill popper.''

"Okay. You guys,'' Klassen said to the officers on the side, "want to give us a hand loading him on the stretcher? We're going to have to dispense with the body bag, the way he's locked up. We'll just lie him on the gurney sideways, like he is now, and strap him down.''

The two coroner's deputies, Scheiber, Eckert and two of the officers surrounded the body.

"On my count,'' Klassen said. "One, two, three!''

A collective grunt sounded as they lifted the unwieldy form onto the gurney. When it was finally strapped in place, Klassen and her assistant draped a heavy sheet over it and secured that, as well. Still, the corpse's knees and one elbow hung over the edge of the stretcher. Klassen took a black vinyl body bag and opened it out flat, stretching that around to help camouflage the shape.

"Don't want to be giving any little kids nightmares,'' she said. She made a few more notes on her clipboard. "Did you see any other prescription medications around?'' she asked, finishing up her site report.

"An empty tetracycline container, some Tagamet,'' Scheiber said. "That's about it. For an old guy, he seems to have been remarkably healthy.''

She made a note of it. "Anyone else live here?''

"Doesn't look like it.''

"Do we know who his next of kin might be?''

"Not yet. I'll have to let you know on that,'' Scheiber told her.

"We're going to have to seal the premises,'' Klassen said. "You going to do it, or you want me to?''

"No," he said. "I'll do it. I'm keeping this one active until we've got a confirmed cause of death."

Klassen nodded. "Okay. I'll call you as soon as the autopsy's scheduled. Probably won't be till day after tomorrow, though. Morgue's down to a skeleton staff for the holiday."

Scheiber winced. "Oh, Iris! Bad pun."

"You think that's bad? You don't want to be around me at Halloween," she said, grinning. "We could use a little help getting this gurney down that circular staircase," she added, shifting her gaze to Eckert.

"You got it," he said, scrambling to set his cameras on one of the lounge chairs.

Scheiber walked over to the deck railing. The crowd below, if anything, had gotten thicker, although it was being held away from the house now by a line of yellow tape. He turned back to Eckert. "Hold on a sec, Dave. Bring your Nikon."

Eckert picked up the thirty-five millimeter once more and walked over. "What?"

"Did you get a shot of the looky-loos?"

"Couple." He raised the camera and snapped off a few more. "You don't really think we got a killer hanging around out there, do you?"

"Wouldn't be the first time, but to be honest? I doubt it. Old guy probably did overdo the tub and struck out. Still, better to be safe than sorry."

Eckert was zooming the telephoto lens up and down the alley. Suddenly, he snorted and dropped the camera back to his chest. "Jeez! Would you check out that ass Livermore?"

Klassen had moved beside them, and she joined Scheiber in looking over. "Ah, yes," she said, "God's gift to the female sex."

Livermore was strutting up and down the line, looking very serious, pausing now and again to take a few ostentatious notes. A couple of pretty young things with short shorts and halter tops were leaning across the yellow tape. One of them said something to him, and the other giggled. Livermore sauntered over, adjusting his black wraparound sunglasses as he went.

"Look at him. He's checking out their cleavage," Klassen said.

"The man-in-uniform phenomenon," Scheiber said. "Works like a charm every time." Eckert looked irritated, but there wasn't a cop in the land—himself included, Scheiber reflected—who hadn't milked it now and again.

"Yeah, well, maybe," Klassen said, "but personally, Livermore leaves me cold."

Eckert looked relieved.

Just then, a phone rang inside the house. Scheiber and Eckert glanced at each other. "Take it?" Eckert asked as they headed for the bedroom.

"Hang on. Let's see if a machine kicks in." Scheiber's latex-gloved hand picked up a portable from beside the bed, but as it rang a second time, he headed out into the hall, leaning over the balustrade to the open area below. At the third ring, he spotted the answering machine on the bar dividing the kitchen from the open dining–living room, and reminded himself to check it before he left. The machine clicked on, and a recorded voice, male, drifted to the high, oak-beamed ceiling above.

"You've reached the Korman Literary Agency. Leave a message. I want to hear from you."

Strong, blunt, accented. No hint that the speaker was a senior citizen, Scheiber thought. A New Yorker, for sure. They grew 'em tough back there.

After the beep came a woman's voice, her accent hard to place. Not a New Yorker, though.

"Hi, Chap, it's Mariah. I was hoping to catch you before you lined up that meeting with Professor Urquhart. I'm thinking maybe we should hold off until we've had a chance to discuss this a little more. The more I think about it, the idea of plagiarism doesn't hold much water—never mind the murder theory."

Eckert and Scheiber exchanged lifted eyebrows. Murder? Eckert mouthed.

"You knew my father. Whatever he was lacking in moral fiber, Ben Bolt never seemed short on ideas to write about, did he? So why do I keep thinking this Urquhart character is trying to shake us down?"

A long sigh whistled down the line.

"I realize now I should have read those unpublished pa-

pers more carefully before dumping them on you. I'm sorry about that, Chap. But before I see this Louis Urquhart, I do want to read them, so I can at least gauge where the man is coming from. Like it or not, I guess that's how I'm going to have to spend my vacation. Then, we'll decide what to do about the professor, if that's all right with you. I'll get the papers back when we see you. I was hoping I'd be free today, but the powers that be, curse them, are not ready to cut me loose yet. We'll probably drive down there sometime tomorrow, but if you need to reach me in the meantime, just leave a message at the Beverly Wilshire, okay? Otherwise, I'll see you tomorrow. Bye!"

Scheiber and Eckert stood in silence for a long moment. "Okay," Scheiber said finally, "now, I'm officially intrigued. Nobody—and I mean nobody—comes in here without my permission until we find out what *that* was all about."

"She called him 'Chap'?" Eckert said. "You figure that's a nickname?"

"Must be. A book thing, maybe? Like, short for 'Chapter?' Who knows?"

A gurney wheel squeaked behind them. "What's up, guys?" Iris Klassen was leading the stretcher into the hall. Her driver and a couple of the NBPD uniforms were struggling to tuck in the edges of the vinyl body bag so it would squeeze through the bedroom door. Twice they got stuck, slamming what had to be the victim's knees into the doorframe, and had to back up and try again. It was such an undignified business being dead in the presence of strangers, Scheiber thought, wincing at this assault on the late Mr. Korman's old bones.

Klassen must have been thinking the same thing. "Hey, guys! What do you say we try to get the son of a bitch to the morgue in one piece, hey?" She turned back to Scheiber and Eckert. "What was that about the woman's father?"

"It sounds like it was Benjamin Bolt's daughter calling," Eckert said. "You know—the writer? Korman was a literary agent, so I guess Bolt must have been one of his clients."

Scheiber frowned. "He's pretty famous, isn't he?"

"Well, du-uh, Jim—of course he's famous," Eckert said.

"Like, practically on a par with Ernest frigging Hemingway?"

"That was his *daughter* on the phone?" Klassen asked.

Scheiber nodded. "She was supposed to meet with Korman. Must be from out of state. She's staying at the Beverly Wilshire."

"La-di-da."

Scheiber pursed his lips and tapped his pencil against his notepad. "So, if Mr. Korman here had unpublished Ben Bolt papers in his possession, they'd be pretty valuable, wouldn't they?"

"I imagine they would," Eckert said.

"Hmm..."

"What?"

"Nothing," Scheiber said. "You guys go ahead and get the body loaded up in the van. I'm just going to take another look around here before I seal the place up and go have a chat with the neighbor."

As the others wrestled the clumsy gurney down the winding staircase, Scheiber went back into the book-lined office. Settling in the buttoned leather armchair behind the big desk, he sifted through the enormous piles of papers and manuscripts scattered across the top. After he finished with them, he began opening drawers and digging through their contents. When Dave Eckert returned, Scheiber was in a closet, rummaging through boxes and running his hands over the walls.

"What are you looking for?"

"A safe. It looks like this used to be two small bedrooms, only they knocked out a wall to make a bigger office. One of the closets got gutted for bookshelves, over there. I thought maybe Korman would have put a safe in this one, but I can't find it. You didn't notice one anywhere else in the house, did you?"

"No, but I'll do another go-round, see if I can see one. Behind pictures, maybe? There's not much free wall space in here, but some of the larger works downstairs would be the right size to cover one."

"I agree. Let's go look."

They went through every room in the house, down and up, ending back in the office.

"No safe," Eckert said.

"No safe."

"So what does it mean?"

"It means, if the lady on the phone is to be believed, that Mr. Korman had some very valuable documents lying unsecured somewhere in his house. Not in here, though. I've looked and looked, and I can't find them."

"Like, how valuable, do you figure?" Eckert asked.

"Well, let's put it this way—if somebody had an unpublished Ernest Hemingway novel sitting in his bottom drawer, or maybe the guy's personal diaries, how much would they be worth?"

"Jeez. A fortune."

"There you go," Scheiber said. He held out his arms. "But they don't seem to be here, do they?"

"Uh-oh," Eckert said ominously. "Motive."

Scheiber nodded. "Motive." Just then, something he hadn't noticed before caught his eye. He walked to the open closet, eyeing the row of shelves, and crouched next to the bottom one. "Hey, Dave, get a picture of this, would you?"

"What? An empty shelf?"

"Empty," Scheiber said, nodding. "Strange, no? Since all the others are overflowing? But it wasn't always empty. See? Korman was no great shakes as a housekeeper. There was something sitting here until very recently. Look, the center of the shelf is mostly clean. But here, see the dust? A distinct outline of a large, rectangular object."

Eckert took a light reading and lined up the shot. "More books? Or manuscripts?"

"Nope. Too big. A box, I'd say. Not exactly lightweight, either. See the drag marks?" He sat back on his haunches while the camera clicked.

"So, what was in the box?"

"And where did it go?" Scheiber added. "And, more to the point, who removed it, and when?"

Chapter
Fifteen

Nothing is ever simple, and no good deed goes unpunished. Those were life's elemental truths, Mariah thought with a sigh. The DDO's terse reply to her contact report burned into the glass of the computer screen in front of her.

Prospect looks promising. You are to attend state luncheon. Look for sideline opportunity to raise prospect of mutually beneficial cooperation with subject. Report back.

Her stint on the front lines wasn't over yet. Jack Geist wanted her to go and watch Shelby Kidd and Valery Zakharov spar with each other over an interminable rubber-chicken lunch—and, while she was at it, corner Yuri Belenko and ask him if he'd care to become a double agent.

"Great," she muttered. "Just bloody great."

Other keyboards pattered around the gray padded cubicle she occupied in the federal comcenter. The place was a hive of computer workstations, each terminal linked to the most secret parts of the federal net, where machines spoke to each other in heavily encrypted digital code said to be uncrackable. Designed primarily for civil-emergency situations, the comcenter's reinforced walls and ceilings reputedly were strong enough to withstand any natural or man-made disaster short of a direct hit by a ballistic missile.

The facilities were open for use to visiting officials like herself, but with the long Fourth of July weekend about to get under way, the place was as empty today as it had been last night at midnight, when she'd dropped by to file her report on her contact with Belenko. Mariah glanced around, but the few faces she saw were strangers. No surprise there, given the mammoth size of the federal bureaucracy.

She grimaced at the deputy's message. Other people might be pursuing holiday plans, but Jack Geist clearly thrived on different pleasures. The originator code on the e-mail said he'd sent it from Langley at 5:37 a.m. EDT, only an hour or so after she'd sent her report winging eastward. Did the man have a home? Did he sleep?

The last thing she wanted was to attend a state luncheon, but he'd left her no room to opt out. Fine. The assignment had turned into a two-day affair, after all. She'd attend the luncheon. Then she was out of the picture. And, please, she thought, offering a fervent mental prayer, don't let Renata be at this damn function. It was one more problem she didn't need today, worried as she already was about a daughter on the brink of rebellion. Lindsay had been left behind, unhappy and resentful, only to discover that her supposedly hardworking mother was shacking up in an L.A. hotel room with Paul Chaney. A man, Mariah was beginning to realize, she wasn't in love with and probably never would be. What on earth was she doing?

Picking up the phone next to her, she called to confirm the rental car she'd reserved and to say she would pick it up later that afternoon. But changing Lindsay's plane ticket was another matter. In the end, the best she could manage on the eve of a busy holiday was a flight due into LAX at midnight—a gain of only a few hours, but preferable to the alternative of leaving Lindsay back in Alexandria spitting nails for one more day.

When she called Carol's house again to give her the revised flight information, Lindsay seemed less than thrilled. "I don't know why you bothered."

"Because I want us to be together," Mariah said, "and sooner rather than later."

"What about Paul?"

"He's getting the keys to the beach house today. We could go straight there, but it'll be so late by the time you get in, it probably makes more sense to stay at the hotel tonight and run down first thing in the morning."

"Is he going to be staying at the beach with us?"

"Paul? No, he's not," Mariah said firmly. Though it had been a close call on that score. She was still irritated by Paul's blithe assumption he could invite himself along. "But while you're busy being grumpy about him," Mariah added, "you might remember that he's the one who went out of his way to get this beach house for us. It's a little ungrateful to treat him like Public Enemy Number One."

"Yeah, well, you slept with him, Mom, so I guess he got the thanks he was after."

Mariah felt the blood drain from her face. She counted mentally to ten before allowing herself to reply, and when she did, her voice was low, even and dangerously controlled. "Lindsay, I have never, ever struck you in your entire life, but you're lucky you weren't standing beside me just then. So, listen to me carefully. If you ever say anything like that to me again, or use that tone with me, there will be serious consequences. Do you understand?"

The line was silent.

"*Do* you?"

The response was the correct one, but as grudging as it could be. "Yes, ma'am."

"Look," Mariah said, "I know you were taken by surprise last night. I'm sorry about that. If I'd known Paul was going to be out here, I'd have told you, but it was as much a surprise to me as it was to you. I'm making allowances for your behavior this time only, though. There's a limit to how far even you, my love, can go with insulting me or sticking your nose into certain private matters. Are we clear on this?"

"He was Dad's friend, Mom! He's got no business trying to take his place!"

Mariah sat back in the rolling desk chair and closed her eyes, putting a hand to her forehead. "Oh, Lindsay, he couldn't possibly. No one could."

"Then why does he keep hanging around?"

"He's trying to be a friend. If you'll recall, you were the

one who thought he was so great at the beginning, when I kept trying to get rid of him. And now...'' She twisted the phone cord in her hand. ''I don't know how this got so out of hand, Lins. Believe it or not, we mothers are not all-knowing or infallible, despite our propaganda to the contrary. I'd be lying if I said I knew what to do about Paul—or much else, for that matter. The only thing I am certain of these days is that you're the most important person in the world to me. So could we *please* call a truce for a while and try to have a nice vacation?''

She sensed Lindsay might be crying, or on the verge, but the line was quiet. If her daughter was affected by what she'd heard, she wasn't about to give her mother the satisfaction of letting her know it. Nor, obviously, was she prepared to let her off the hook just yet.

''I'll see you tonight,'' Lindsay said abruptly. And then Mariah found herself listening to dial tone.

Brilliant sunshine blinded her as Mariah left the federal comcenter. She paused for a moment at the door to let her eyes adjust and rifled through her purse for her sunglasses. The air was warm and desert dry, typical of all the southern California days she could remember from the time she'd spent growing up here. Logic told her there must have been some rainy days, but she couldn't recall one—as if her subconscious, like some kindly charity lady, was trying to compensate for the bleakness of the past by offering candied recollections of nonstop sunshine and balmy breezes. Nothing but gorgeous days like this.

Dark glasses found, she slipped them on and started across the wide esplanade in front of the Federal Building, heading for the parking lot. She'd called a cab to take her to the restaurant where Shelby Kidd was hosting the luncheon in honor of the visiting Russian foreign minister.

The government complex was the sole occupant of a large square block of prime Los Angeles real estate, the high-rise set well back from surrounding streets. Around the perimeter of the block, concrete posts stood closely ranged like stout little soldiers, a first line of defense against the prospect of a fanatic with a truck bomb. A row of needle-nosed Italian cypress trees posed like backup sentries against the white tower. The esplanade was crowded with civil servants taking outdoor smoke breaks and a steady stream of visitors coming and going to the passport and immigration offices and other federal agencies warehoused in the big building.

At one end of the wide plaza, a row of folding tables had been set up, covered with potted greenery. A hand-painted wooden sandwich board propped in front advertised herbs and houseplants for sale, grown by the rehab patients of the Veterans Administration hospital across the street. Two men were working the tables, dressed in casual pants and sport shirts. A third, sitting on a stone bench behind them, caught Mariah's eye as she approached. He was a big, bearded bear of a fellow, with a long, graying ponytail and rimless glasses. Attractive in the rumpled, unselfconscious style of some old folksinger or poet, he was feeding bread from a bag to sparrows dancing around his feet, looking up occasionally to check on his two friends.

Mariah had just about decided he must be a social worker or psychologist from the VA hospital, sent to supervise, when one of the others said something to him. The big man slowly put down his bag of bread crumbs and picked up a green tin sprinkler can. Rising laboriously, he shuffled along the row of plants, muttering under his breath as he watered.

She was taken aback. Human beings had a million cruel and capricious ways of wounding one another and themselves. What was his story? she wondered. He was too old to be a Gulf War veteran. A holdover from Vietnam, still, after all these years? Poor man. How many people who'd loved him had had their dreams shattered by whatever accident of fate had befallen him?

Her taxi was nowhere in sight yet, so she paused at the table, looking over the plants, lifting a pot of basil to inhale its sweet fragrance, the scent prying an image out of some forgotten corner of her mind: her mother at the kitchen stove. An odd memory, since her mother had never been much of a cook. Homemade spaghetti sauce had been one of the few recipes in her limited repertoire, and every once in a while, Mariah recalled, guilt over serving too many meals from tins would send her mother into a frenzy of production that she'd divvy up into margarine pots and freeze, resolving to serve healthier meals in future. But with the long hours she worked to support herself and two young daughters, they soon slipped back into old habits.

Suddenly, the rumpled man let out a bellow. "Incoming!" His shoulder slammed into Mariah, knocking her sideways, and the potted basil went flying. She grabbed the table's edge to steady herself. "Incoming! Duck!" he yelled again. His watering can clattered to the sidewalk, sending water splashing over her shoes as he threw his arms out in a protective reflex.

"What the—?" Mariah cried.

The man shouldered her back as a helmeted bike rider connected with one of his big, outstretched arms. The cyclist wobbled in place, sunlight glinting off his opaque black wraparound glasses. The two of them locked in a brief wrestling match, and then, as the big man let out a cry, the cyclist shook him off. He stood high in his stirrups and bore down on the pedals, weaving between shouting pedestrians as he streaked away, bumping down the half-dozen steps to the driveway. The last Mariah saw of him, he was careening off to the left and disappearing down a side street like some mad messenger from hell.

"Martin!" one of the other plant sellers cried, running around the table as the big man dropped to his knees.

"Incoming," he gasped, weakly this time, wrapping his arms around himself, tucking his hands under his arms.

"No, just some idiot on a bike," his friend said. He turned to Mariah, grasping her elbow to steady her. "Are you all right?"

Her purse had fallen to the ground. She gathered it up and hooked the strap over her shoulder. "I'm fine. Where did that bike come from?"

"God knows. Just appeared out of nowhere."

"What about him?" she asked. The man was almost prostrate now, covering his head with his arm. "He was trying to shield me." She crouched beside him and reached for his hand, but he recoiled from her touch, pulling into himself into a tight ball. "His hand's bleeding," she said, looking up anxiously.

His friend squatted beside them. "Must have scraped it on the can. Martin," he said quietly, "it's okay. It was just some nut on a bike. Let me see your hand. You've cut yourself." The man called Martin lifted his head. His glasses were askew, and he peered around, owl-like and skittish. "It was just a guy on a bike," his friend repeated.

"Are you all right?" Mariah asked.

The big man's darting gaze settled on her for a split second. "Enemy incoming," he said, his voice vibrating like double-bass strings. He wavered for a moment, then his eyes flickered, and he crumpled to his side on the pavement.

"Oh, shit," his friend said, studying him closely. He looked up at the other man at the table. "Better call the clinic, John, and tell them to get over here. I think Martin's on something."

"Can I do anything?" Mariah asked.

"No, we'll handle it. He's got a bit of a problem." The man crouched lower, raising his voice a little. "Martin? What are you on, buddy? Where'd you get it? Come on. I can't help you if you don't tell me what you took. What was it?"

The big man's bleeding hand rose to cover his face, hiding from the insistent questions. The other man pulled his hands away. Martin resisted for a moment, then slumped onto his back, eyes rolling up into his head so that only the whites showed.

The other man at the table had a cell phone. He snapped it shut and slipped it into his pocket. "The ambulance is on its way," he said. He shook his head sadly. "Oh, jeez, Marty! What do you want to be doing this for?"

"Are you sure there's nothing I can do?" Mariah asked. "He looks so pale."

"'Fraid not. He's gotten his hands on some drugs. I don't know how—or why. He was doing so well in rehab."

"I really think he was trying to protect me from that crazy biker," she said.

The guy on the ground nodded. "That'd be just like Marty. He'll save everyone but himself. Look, ma'am, there's really no reason for you to feel you have to hang around here. The ambulance is on the way, and we'll take good care of him."

"You're sure?" Mariah said. Down in the driveway, she

noticed, a cab had pulled up to the walkway, and the driver was looking around impatiently. She glanced at her watch. She was running late. The last thing she needed was to lose her cab, hard as they were to get in this city. "If you're certain there's nothing I can do...?"

"Yeah, I'm sure. We've been here before, believe me."

"Well, when he's better," she said, "could you tell him I said thank you?"

"I'll do that."

Mariah got to her feet and watched a moment longer, reluctant to walk away when her erstwhile protector was lying prostrate on the ground. The man seemed to be slipping into a drugged stupor, his arms lying limply at his sides now, his legs sprawled at bent angles. She heard the sound of an approaching siren as she turned reluctantly and headed for the taxi. Selflessness and self-destructiveness, she thought, reflecting on what his friend had said. What a tragic and lethal combination that was.

And then it hit her. Maybe it was because she'd been thinking about her mother just before being knocked out of the cyclist's way, but as Mariah started down toward the waiting taxi, a realization slammed into her like a Mack truck seen coming but impossible to avoid—the real source of the rage that had simmered inside her for as long as she could remember. Something her mind had never allowed itself to admit.

Neglect is easier to forgive than self-sacrifice.

It wasn't just her father, she realized—how being abandoned by him at seven had screwed up her head, leaving her slow to trust and quick to anticipate betrayal. It was her mother, too, and that blind, stupid, selfless loyalty of hers. The way she'd handed over her life to Ben, then watched him throw it away—throw them *all* away—like it meant nothing. The way she'd allowed him to steal her youth and her light, easy laughter. And then, to cap it all off, her refusal to ever, even once, allow a bad word to be said about him in her presence.

You got a raw deal, Mom! Where was your pride? Where was the anger? Why did you always have to defend him?

Even as she thought it, a wave of guilt washed over her. How could she blame the poor woman? Andrea Larson had been eighteen, only a couple of years older than Lindsay, when she'd met Ben at a coffeehouse on the University of Chicago campus. Dazzled by his glib charm, she'd dropped out of her freshman year of college and run off with him a week later, to the horror of her staid parents. For the next eight years, she'd supported him while he produced the bulk of the work for which his adoring fans remembered him to this day—only to find herself ultimately abandoned and left to raise two young children alone.

For all her belief in Ben's talent, Mariah realized, her mother had never lived long enough to see the extent to which he would be lionized by the world. Never knew how his work would stand the test of time, so that now, thirty years after his death, he was more read than ever, while she, who'd made it all possible, was utterly forgotten, except by her one remaining child. And even then, Mariah thought, her memories were mixed with frustration as much as love. Nothing about it was remotely fair.

Her mother had been a lovely woman. Other men had come courting after Ben left, but she was like some rare orchid that needed just the right conditions to thrive. The removal of Ben from her life caused her to wither away, as if deprived of some essential nutrient. Even if the official cause of her mother's death was ovarian cancer, her spirit had died long before that final insult to her body.

Mariah flagged the cab, and the crunch of its tires kicked up loose stones on the roadway as it pulled forward to meet her.

Why now, after all these years, did the thought of that self-sacrifice make her so angry? Blinking away tears, she looked up at the stunning azure blue of a sky unmarred by a single cloud. How could anyone have a bad thought, let alone a bad day, under a sky so beautiful?

The past was past, she resolved. She couldn't change her parents' lives. She could only move forward, paying close attention to the foundation she, in turn, was laying for Lindsay's life. Her father's behavior had run true to what he'd probably learned growing up, abandoned by his own parents, shuffled between dour, demanding relatives. Maybe that was what her mother had responded to—the sad little boy inside the brilliant writer. The world always made allowances for genius. So, apparently, had her mother. For her sake, Mariah just hoped Ben had been worth it.

She climbed into the car and gave the driver directions to the restaurant. He moved out into traffic just as the VA ambulance entered the lot, screeching to a halt at the entry to the plaza. Mariah glanced back as white-coated attendants jumped out and headed for the ambulance's rear doors to pull out a stretcher.

And then she saw the dark sedan again—the same one, she thought, that had been outside her hotel the night before, its windows tinted black. It pulled up close behind the taxi, too close for her to see its plates. When the cab turned down Wilshire Boulevard, it was still following close behind.

Chapter Sixteen

"Mr. Lewis? Can I offer you some champagne before lunch?"

Frank Tucker tore his gaze away from the rounded green slopes of the Appalachian Mountains, thirty thousand feet below the aircraft. The big Rolls-Royce engines had throttled back to a cruising drone. From the galley at the rear of the cabin, warming food smells were already wafting forward. A blond, ponytailed flight attendant stood over him, holding a tall glass flute. He caught a hint of grassy perfume as she bent lower to show him the label on the opaque black bottle resting in the palm of her other hand. Her fingers cradled its neck, her thumb expertly hooked in the deep, concave depression at its base.

He nodded. "Why not?" The man named Frank Tucker would probably be in handcuffs and leg irons for the return flight, squeezed into a seat way back in Economy with a couple of federal marshals on either side of him. But Grant M. Lewis was an executive who flew first-class in wide leather seats more suited to his oversize frame. Might as well enjoy this fictive life while it lasted.

"Are you heading to Los Angeles on business or pleasure

today?'' the attendant asked as bubbles cascaded into the goblet.

"Business, mostly."

She handed him the glass. "Business, hmm? Let me guess. I'm usually pretty good at this."

She leaned an elbow on the seat back ahead of him, a crease of a frown appearing above her pert nose as she checked him out. She'd taken his sport jacket and hung it in the closet at the front of the cabin when he'd boarded. Tucker, feeling self-conscious under her intense, blue-eyed scrutiny, was grateful that his black knit shirt was new—a birthday gift from Carol, who kept trying to counter the effects of her old man's self-neglect. And middle-aged hulk though he might be, living alone these past months had dropped his weight closer to Navy trim than he'd been in years. Some people were intimidated by his size and black-eyed looks, he knew, but this young woman didn't seem remotely nervous.

"Entertainment?" she guessed. "An agent? No, wait...you don't look like somebody who'd be happy stuck behind a desk. Something more active." A pink-tipped finger tapped her chin as she thought about it. Then her face lit up. "I know! A stunt coordinator! Explosions and car chases and stuff. Am I close?"

Amused, he debated how to reply. She was wrong, but not totally off-base. Although the circumstances of his family life, and his wife's long illness in particular, had arranged things so that he'd ended up stuck behind a desk for most of his career, his restless nature had never really been content there. And he had certainly set off a few explosions during his time in the service.

On the other hand, he reminded himself, that was Frank Tucker's reality. Who was Grant Lewis today? "I've pulled a few stunts in my time," he told her, "but I'm more into headhunting right how."

"Aha! A talent scout. Well, just the same, it was a pretty close guess, wasn't it?"

He nodded, letting her continue to draw her own conclusions.

"I told you I was pretty good at this," she said happily. "I've been flying for six years. You meet all kinds of people.

After a while, you get to the point where you can just tell what line of work someone's in, you know?''

"Uncanny.''

"Isn't it? So,'' she asked, settling companionably on the arm of the empty seat ahead of him, draping her arm over the back, "are you with one of the big studios?''

There were only a couple of other passengers in the first class cabin on the L.A.-bound flight, and none of them seemed to require her ministrations at the moment. Or warrant her undivided attention, Tucker noted, bemused. It was a rare day when he got to enjoy the company of so many pretty young women. First Carol and Lindsay, now this nice girl.

"I'm more of a free agent,'' he said.

"That must be nice, running your own business. My boyfriend wants to do that, too. He's a software developer with Microsoft right now, but he'd like to start up his own company. Do you like working for yourself?''

He shrugged. "Well, I'm not real good at taking orders, I guess.''

A soft beep sounded overhead, and she grimaced, glancing at the cockpit and rising with a reluctant sigh. "I hear you there,'' she said. "Duty calls. Can I get you anything else before I go? Maybe a video player? We've got a good selection of movies on board.''

"No, thanks.'' Tucker nodded at the briefcase on the empty seat beside him. "I've got some work to do. Is it okay to use the laptop?''

"Sure, no problem. You should be fine until we start our final approach into LAX.'' Her smile enveloped him once more. "I'll check in on you later, Mr. Lewis. We'll be serving dinner soon, but if you need anything, just let me know, okay?''

"Thanks, I'll do that.''

Her hand rested briefly on his shoulder, and then she left to answer the summons from the front of the plane. Tucker closed his eyes, basking in the residual warmth of her touch, hardly able to put a name to the longing it stirred deep inside him. It had nothing to do with that young woman in particular, and it was far greater than a simple desire for sex. The need to connect and belong somewhere had him operating on instincts so primal he hardly knew what he would do next. He sensed only that he was moving in the direction he needed to be going. He also felt more alive than he had in years.

He took a long swallow of the champagne, then set the glass on the wide armrest beside him and reached for the briefcase. When he snapped the locks and lifted the lid, Mariah's Courier Express package slid across the laptop's hard plastic case. He hesitated, then picked it up, turning it sideways. Three sheets of onionskin paper covered in spiky, densely packed handwriting tumbled out. A handwritten letter was a rare thing these days, he reflected, unfolding the pages to reread it. Either Professor Urquhart was a technology-resistant Luddite like himself, or the man hadn't dared to trust what he had to say to a computer's memory.

A yellow Post-It note from Korman, the literary agent, was stuck to one corner of Urquhart's letter.

Mariah:
This letter came in response to the press stories about your father's papers. The allegations are news to me, but we're going to have to decide what to do about them before we make a decision on publishing the novel. We'll talk about this when you get here.

Chap

The attached letter was written on university stationery with the professor's name and title embossed at the top: "Louis B. Urquhart, Professor of American Literature and Society, University of California at Los Angeles."

Dear Mr. Korman,
Lynn Barnard, editor in chief of Workman-Brown, Benjamin Bolt's publisher, was kind enough to give me your address. She may have told you that I am currently in the process of writing an in-depth retrospective of Bolt's life and work. You may also know that I received a Pulitzer Prize for my biography of Jack Kerouac. I mention this only to underline the seriousness of my credentials.
I understand from Ms. Barnard that you are in regular

contact with Bolt's daughter and sole heir, Mariah. I know she has refused interview requests in the past, but I am hoping you will agree to put me in touch with her. Obviously, I am eager to interview her for recollections of her late father. But at the same time, I feel certain she would wish to be apprised of new information I recently uncovered concerning his final days. Please assure her I am not looking to create scandal. Rather, it is my admiration for Benjamin Bolt and his work that makes it quite impossible for me to remain silent.

Let me put what I am about to say in context:

As you know, the early sixties, when Bolt produced the bulk of the writing for which he is remembered, was a period of intense political activism at home and tension abroad: the idealism of the Kennedy Administration, the Civil Rights movement, the cold war, the Cuban Missile Crisis and the beginnings of American involvement in Vietnam. There is little doubt these events influenced Bolt's thinking and his work. None of his other biographies, however, make mention of a chance event shortly before his death.

I am not even sure whether you, as his agent, were aware of his brief involvement with an organization called Writers for Peace. This international association of poets and authors was considered by many at the time to be a Communist-front organization financed by Moscow. While this has never been proven definitively, my research suggests that the Soviet leadership did, at the very least, consider WFP open to manipulation—an "innocents club," to borrow a term from Soviet propagandists: liberal-minded intellectuals through whom a sympathetic view of the USSR could be channeled to the West.

In June 1964, a WFP conference was held in Paris, attended by some sixty writers from various countries. President Kennedy had been assassinated a few months earlier. With this country slipping into the quagmire of Vietnam, and the Civil Rights movement turning violent in the South, the WFP conference showed every sign of turning into a strident anti-American event.

Hoping to capitalize on that mood, and as a gesture of its alleged openness, Moscow took the unusual step of allowing a famous Russian writer, Anatoly Orlov, to attend the conference. A hero of World War II and officially lionized in the Soviet Union, Orlov had been little heard from since the end of the war. There were rumors his later writings had offended the Communist leadership. Some said he was living under virtual house arrest. That he received an exit visa to attend the WFP conference is probably the best evidence we have that Moscow felt it could control the agenda. Perhaps the Kremlin also calculated that, at seventy-two, Orlov was too old to stir up trouble, and his attendance would be a risk-free move.

Few of the conference participants are alive today, but I managed to locate one source who reported that Anatoly Orlov and Benjamin Bolt not only met, but seemed to bond. A rumor even began to circulate that the two were planning a collaboration of some sort. But then, Orlov collapsed and was rushed back to Moscow. Three months later, his death was announced in Pravda. *Orlov was given a state funeral attended by the entire Politburo. Thousands of ordinary Russians filed past his coffin where it lay in state in the Kremlin. To this day, however, not a single Orlov work written after 1945 has ever been published.*

Bolt, meantime, disappeared from view. This same source I interviewed said Bolt told friends he was working on a new novel, but he was vague about details, and few people saw him again after the WFP conference.

Benjamin Bolt died in Paris on September 4, 1964—the same day Orlov's death was announced in Moscow. I think this is no coincidence. I believe Bolt was murdered—as, I am certain, was Orlov.

Mr. Korman, I have no desire to cause undue distress to Mr. Bolt's daughter. For this reason, I have not told anyone, including his editor, what I believe to be the case: that the manuscript she reportedly discovered among papers he mailed from Paris just days before his death is not his work at all, but an English translation of a samizdat *novel by Anatoly Orlov, smuggled out of the Soviet Union at the time of the WFP conference. My presumption is that Orlov entrusted it to Bolt for delivery to a publisher in the West.*

Sooner or later, the truth is bound to surface, especially with the fall of communism in Russia and the gradual opening of secret files there. If you allow the novel to be published under Bolt's name, it will inevitably bring embarrassment to his family and an undeserved stain on the man's excellent literary reputation.

I think it is imperative that we meet very soon to discuss the best way to proceed on this matter. In the meantime, I strongly advise you to put the publication of the novel on hold.

Yours sincerely,
Louis B. Urquhart

Tucker folded the letter slowly and put it back in the envelope.

Chap Korman may not have known about Ben Bolt's involvement with Writers for Peace, but the CIA had. Like most groups suspected of Communist sympathies at the time, WFP had been infiltrated by agency operatives, who had dutifully recorded the names of those "innocents" the Kremlin hoped to manipulate. The 1964 conference was a minor blip on the radar of the long, tense history of the cold war, but fifteen years later, it had surfaced again, in the course of Mariah's recruitment into the CIA. It was then that her father's flirtation with the WFP was uncovered during a routine security-clearance check.

As the person most responsible for godfathering her into the Company, Frank Tucker had taken it upon himself to look more closely into the matter. In doing so, he'd come to the same conclusion as Louis Urquhart—that Ben Bolt may very well have been murdered by KGB agents sent to retrieve the manuscript Orlov was rumored to have smuggled out of the USSR. The Soviets had done a good job of burying the evidence—literally, it seemed, given the number of other witnesses who happened to pass away in the months after the WFP conference. Urquhart was right. Few witnesses of the

Bolt-Orlov meeting survived. It didn't take a rocket scientist to figure out there was more than coincidence to so many nearly simultaneous deaths.

Tucker had told no one about his suspicions, however. Not then, not ever. Because, in the course of investigating her as a possible recruit, he had acquired something more than professional interest in Mariah Bolt. The more he'd gotten to know about her and her past, the more her well-being had become a matter of personal interest to him. Her father had disappeared when she was only seven. She was estranged from his memory and contemptuous of his legacy. She had worked hard to overcome the handicaps of growing up poor and abandoned, suffering one family tragedy after another— first losing her father, then her younger sister, and then her mother. In spite of that, she'd soldiered on, acquired a good education and expertise the agency could use.

Bottom line: Mariah had wanted the job, and Tucker had wanted her working with him. Except the security file stood in the way.

In the normal course of things, no one whose parent's allegiance was even remotely suspect would be allowed near classified work. Given her father's involvement with the Soviet-funded group, Mariah's application should have been dead in the water. But why, Tucker had reasoned, should Ben Bolt's actions be allowed to forever cast a shadow across her life? It was ancient history, so he had set about to change it.

The Navigator's files weren't the only CIA property Frank Tucker had destroyed in the course of his career. Rather than allow it to damage Mariah's prospects, he had systematically expunged from her security file all record of her father's brief association with Writers for Peace before anyone else in the agency had had a chance to know about it.

Now, the past was coming back to haunt him—and Mariah. Before Urquhart, no one else had put the pieces of the puzzle together. But the truth was finally seeping out, and the results could be devastating. Tucker cared little about suffering the consequences himself of what he'd done eighteen years earlier. But Mariah—and Lindsay, too, he reflected—were another matter.

It was time for damage control.

Chapter
Seventeen

The roses in Mr. Korman's sunny front courtyard were in bloom, a riot of pink and yellow and peach. Two thickly padded lounge chairs, similar to the ones on the deck upstairs, were well placed to catch their sweet, heady scent. The midday temperature was already pushing into the nineties. If this had been his place, Scheiber thought, he'd have been tempted to pop a cold one and settle into one of those puffy, blue-striped cushions for the duration. Hell, he was tempted to do it, anyway—except he didn't drink anymore, so the cold one would have to be a soda.

Both the choice of beverage and the urge to take it easy were measures of how far he'd come since leaving the LAPD. Here he was with a suspicious death on his hands—slightly suspicious, anyway, after that odd message from the daughter of the dead man's client—and he felt none of the adrenaline rush that had come with every new call-out during his eight years in the Robbery-Homicide Division.

He stood in the courtyard, smoothing down his mustache, working up the enthusiasm to go and interview the next-door neighbor. He didn't feel the rush, but he remembered it. It was the kind of high junkies talked about, and when you were hooked, you needed that fix on a regular basis. The very first time was always the best, though. Like the addict's first hit, the experience of a first big murder case was so intense you spent the rest of your days trying to recapture the headiness of it. It was a sucker's game, though. You couldn't do it with the job any more than with the needle. You got excitement and variety, because you never knew what you were going to find at a homicide scene. But you were never going to find that same pure adrenaline charge again.

For as long as he was with the LAPD, he'd kept trying for it, anyway. He told himself he put in the time because he was a good cop, conscientious, attentive to detail. But his wife had seen right through him.

She was back at school then, working on the psychology degree. God, how he'd hated when she practiced on him.

"The job allows you to avoid emotional commitment. And you do it well, so it rewards you by validating the way you live. Gives you that sense of being indispensable. And, my vain darling, you even love the press scrums—your steely eyes and silver hair reassuring the City of Angels it can sleep soundly because Jim Scheiber, guardian angel, is watching over it."

He shook his head. "This is such garbage. You can psychoanalyze me all you want, Allison, but this is just my job."

"No, it's not your job. It's your life."

Scheiber had hated the fact that she was probably right. He hadn't planned to be a lousy husband and father. He'd loved his wife. He was pretty sure of that, at least at the beginning. Later, after one too many arguments and one too many silences, it got harder to know what was love and what was just the memory of love. As for his daughter, there was no question. He'd die for Julie. But even on those nights he'd managed to circle home to sit for a while and have supper with her, his mind had still been working the cases, anticipating that next raw thrill of discovery.

These days, their times together were few and far between. At thirteen, Julie's life was getting busier and she was reluctant to leave her friends in Portland to come down here. She had also refused so far to say what she thought about him marrying her former dance teacher. She was always friendly enough to Liz, but her visits had started getting shorter right about the time he and Liz had begun dating. One of these times, he feared, she was going to call and say she couldn't make it at all. He'd lost his daughter to the job, for all intents and purposes, Scheiber reflected, and he hadn't felt the professional rush in a long time, either. Maybe there was a connection.

He glanced back at the clapboard and bougainvillea-covered house on the harbor. Some rich old guy had croaked in his hot tub. Not even the fact that it might have been other than accidental was enough to ignite the old fire. He was thinking about his lost daughter and his new wife, and how soon he could go home. He wasn't thinking about the hunt, or about playing the hero in the war on crime. But that didn't change that Albert Jacob Korman—apparently called "Chap" by his friends—was on his way to the Orange County morgue. His house on the Balboa peninsula was locked and sealed with yellow plastic crime-scene tape. And, like it or not, his death needed to be investigated.

The neighborhood, now that the commotion had died down, seemed determined to carry on with the summer day as if nothing had happened. The looky-loos had dispersed, and out on the water, boat boys were swabbing decks in anticipation of boat owners showing up for the extended holiday weekend.

Overhead, a seagull squealed, drawing Scheiber's gaze upward. The bird dived toward the water, just skimming the surface, then veered and came up to a perfect two-point landing on a striped channel marker. The marker bobbed gently under the sudden weight. Scheiber exhaled heavily. "Man! It's a hell of a lousy day to die, isn't it?"

"Are there any good ones?" Eckert asked.

Scheiber glanced over at his partner, whose gaze was locked on a departing sailboat. On the forward deck, two women in tiny thong bikinis were lounging in low deck chairs, taking turns slathering each other's backs with sunscreen. One of them had untied the neck straps on her bikini top, and the miniscule yellow triangles of fabric looked in serious danger of slipping off their precarious perches. You wish, Scheiber thought, grinning at Eckert's rapt, open-mouthed anticipation. The woman squeezed a dollop of white cream onto her hands, slicking lotion across her breasts with languid, circular strokes.

"Jeez," Eckert said, head shaking, "I don't think I'm living right."

"I know what you mean."

"Ha," Eckert said, reluctantly wrenching his gaze away as the woman on deck retied her top strings, dashing his hopes. "You've got nothing to complain about. A week on the beach with the beauteous Liz couldn't have been any too shabby."

"It was pretty great," Scheiber agreed. "We could've used a couple more, mind you. Would have made it at least two if Lucas's father hadn't up and buggered off at the last minute."

"Guy sounds like a real jerk. Didn't he say he'd keep the boy while you were away?"

"Yeah, but I think it's the wife who rules the roost there. This surprise trip to Italy was just the latest stunt. She's got a real talent for coming up with reasons why they can't take Lucas half the weekends he's supposed to be there. Like, they're getting ready for a big dinner party. Or the floors have just been refinished and the varnish is still wet. Or the maid took the weekend off to visit her sick mama in Tijuana and there's nobody to cook."

"Isn't that why God invented Pizza Hut?"

Scheiber unlatched the low picket gate and stepped out onto the walkway. "Guess the good news hasn't reached Beverly Hills," he said.

Eckert followed him through. "So, how are you finding fatherhood?"

"I've been doing fatherhood for thirteen years. I'd like it fine if I could see Julie more often. As for young Lucas..." He shrugged resignedly. "That's going to take some time. Right now, we're still jockeying to see who gets to be alpha dog around the house. He's had his mom all to himself up to now. I'd hate me, too, under the circumstances. Anyway," Scheiber added, "never mind my domestic arrangements. What's with you and the lovely Mrs. Klassen? Haven't I ever told you you're not supposed to drool on the job, Dave? Mucks up the DNA evidence something wicked."

"Get outta here."

"Are we blushing?"

"Chuck you, Farley," Eckert said, plucking his shades from the pocket of his shirt and slipping them on.

Scheiber grinned, but the smile faded as they reached Korman's neighbor's courtyard. "Well," he said dryly, "this is certainly different."

Where the Korman house was all shingles and shutters and white picket fences, the place next door was a stark arrangement of concrete boxes in muted desert colors, set on top of one another at odd angles and irregularly pierced through by opaque glass bricks. A line of polished wooden ties ran all the way around the courtyard, except on the one side where Korman's incongruous picket fence stood. The pickets had gotten there first, Scheiber figured, but they must have irritated the bejesus out of whoever had designed this place. An effort had obviously been made to camouflage them with a fountain that ran nearly the full length of that side of the property, a long, low wall of slate with water sliding over the top. Identical, mocha-colored slate squares covered the courtyard ground. Nature would have been too intimidated to dare throw up a shoot of grass between them.

"Looks like Hiroshima the morning after," Scheiber said.

The only furniture on the patio was a couple of low, complicated wooden chairs that looked uncomfortable as hell. A flat-topped stone boulder between them had probably been put there on purpose to do double duty as a table, although a person might almost believe it had rolled down the San Gabriel Mountains in the last major earthquake, coming to rest just a few feet shy of the building-block house. A regrettable miss, some might say.

"I don't know," Eckert said. "It's kind of interesting,"

Scheiber gave him a skeptical glance. "Yeah, you would think so." There were days when he thought Eckert saw himself as the cultural dean of the NBPD. "Anyway," he added, "we were discussing Iris and your love life. Spill your guts, buddy. And don't tell me you don't know what I'm talking about. That woman had her eye on you from the moment she showed up here. Between your panting and her eyelash batting, I thought I was going to have to throw the both of you under a cold shower."

Eckert stopped at the edge of the slate patio. "We went out to hear some jazz on the weekend, that's all."

"Jazz, huh?"

"Yeah. She happens to like jazz, as a matter of fact."

"That so? You take her home and show her your collection? Let her touch your Bang & Olufsen? Huh, Dave? Didja?"

"You are a sick, sick puppy, you know that?"

Scheiber grinned. He'd been in Eckert's Costa Mesa apartment once, and it was as meticulous as the Korman place had been disordered. His European stereo system was to die for, and all his records, tapes and CDs—more than three hundred, Eckert said—were tidily shelved in alphabetical order, from Louis Armstrong through Lester Young, each artist's albums arranged in chronological sequence from earliest works to most recent. His darkroom looked the same—chemicals neatly labeled, bottles stored in a straight, gleaming row, bamboo tongs lined up in a holder like a well-tended, leafless little forest. Even the prints and negatives Eckert hung to dry were always evenly spaced to the last millimeter. For a guy who couldn't manage to put his hat on the right way around, he was a bit of a neat freak, Scheiber reflected. Iris Klassen, on the other hand, gave no indication she even owned an iron. Must be a classic case of opposites attracting.

"Iris is good people," he said, relenting. Poor Dave could use a little disorder in his life.

As they crossed the brown slate patio, a shadow stirred at ground level behind the opaque glass block windows next to the door. Scheiber depressed a lighted glass button and a muted gong replied from inside like something out of a "National Geographic" special on Tibetan monasteries. At the same time, the shadow at the bottom of the window went crazy. A deep, frenzied baying accompanied the scrabbling of claws on metal. The door, painted the color of dried blood, seemed to be made of solid steel.

A muffled voice from behind the door cried, "Down, Kermit! Get down! Away from the door!"

As the claw-on-metal scrape continued, Scheiber winced, imagining what the paint job on the other side of the door must look like. As far as struggles for alpha dog status went, Korman's neighbor had obviously lost that battle.

"Just a moment!" the man sang through the closed door. "I need to tie up the dog."

"Newport Beach Police," Scheiber called back. "We'll wait." He rolled his eyes, then pulled out his notebook, flipping back a few pages to the name Livermore had given him. "Porter," he said quietly to Eckert. "Douglas Porter."

"We know what Mr. Porter does for a living?"

Scheiber cocked his thumb at the spartan, rock-faced courtyard. "Monk?" he suggested. "Quarryman? No, wait, I've got it. Fred Flintstone. Changed his name after his series went off the air and retired to Newport to get away from the fans."

"Cool. I always thought Wilma was hot stuff."

"I'm more of a Betty Rubble guy myself, but Livermore figured Fred here was more likely to be shacking up with Barney."

"Is that right? Man, am I disillusioned," Eckert said. "These Hollywood types are so phony, you know?"

The door finally opened. Porter was tall and bullet-headed under a rapidly receding hairline. He seemed only slightly flustered after his struggle with the dog, now baying from another room upstairs. "Hi! Sorry about that. He's friendly, but he slobbers."

"No problem," Scheiber said. He introduced himself and his partner. "We'd like to ask you a few questions about your neighbor—Mr. Korman. I understand you found the body?"

Porter leaned on the doorjamb, folding his silk-shirted arms, his expression shifting to suitably stricken. Dressed all in black as he was, he looked like a professional mourner. "Yes, I did. It was very upsetting, I can tell you. I told the officer who arrived first that I was out walking Kermit—that's my basset hound—when I noticed Chap's cat going crazy inside those French doors off his living room. He's a fat old thing and he hardly ever moves off his chair, so I thought he was behaving a little strangely."

"There's no one home in the house on the other side of Mr. Korman's, I noticed."

"Oh, no. That house is owned by some Iranians who live

in Paris most of the year. That's what Chap said, anyway. Personally, I've never seen anyone in the place.''

"How long have you been living here yourself?''

"I moved in April first.''

"But you've gotten to know Mr. Korman pretty well?''

"Actually, fairly well, yes. We both had home offices, for one thing. Poor old Chap was a literary agent, you know.'' Scheiber nodded. Porter went on, "Myself, I'm an architect. We'd see each other nearly every day. You have to take a break and just get out sometimes, you know, even if it's just to walk around the block or go for coffee or something. People think it must be great not to have to commute to an office every day, and it is, but it's also very isolating. And then, of course, there's the problem that you're never really away from the office. You can't close the door and go home, because you're already there, and the work is, too, looking at you all day, making you feel guilty.''

Scheiber nodded. "I guess that would be a problem. So, you spoke to Mr. Korman regularly?''

"Yes, pretty much every day, like I said. He'd strike you as a crusty old guy when you first met him, but he was really very sweet. I think he was pretty lonely. His wife died just last year. Fifty years they'd been married. Imagine!''

"Did they have any children? The coroner has responsibility to notify the next of kin, but we're still trying to determine who that might be.''

Porter nodded. "He has two sons back in New York. One teaches at Columbia, and one's a stockbroker. Their names escape me at the moment,'' he said, frowning. Then he brightened. "But I know how you can find them. I noticed Chap had their numbers listed on the AutoDial pad on his phone.''

Scheiber made a note of it. "That's helpful, thanks.'' As his pen skipped on the notebook, he shook it, then looked up at Porter. "Do you think we could come in, Mr. Porter? I have a few more questions, and I'm not real good at taking notes standing up.''

"Oh, I'm sorry!'' Porter said, flustered. "Well, yes, sure, I suppose.'' He stepped back from the door. "The place is a bit of a mess, I'm afraid. I'm in the middle of a big project and I just received a load of material samples yesterday. I haven't had time to unpack them all.''

They followed him down a long narrow hall into a large, open room. Its walls were painted in a mottled, muted gray, and, like the patio outside, it was minimally furnished in hypermodern pieces that looked a little hard and unyielding. He'd take his La-Z-Boy over this stuff anytime, Scheiber thought. On the other hand, it was probably right up Eckert's alley. His partner, he noted, had taken off his sunglasses and hooked them on the collar of his shirt, and he was busy examining the artwork on the walls.

Despite Porter's modest protestations, the place looked neat enough to Scheiber, although there were several packing crates stacked against one wall. As they walked into the sitting room, he noticed a large blueprint and an architectural rendering of a building tacked to a wall next to a drafting table angled across one corner of the room.

Porter followed his gaze. "It's a project I'm working on right now. Those blueprints and the front elevations were just delivered yesterday along with the material samples. I stuck them up last night to study them before I went to bed. I find it helps when I try to visualize a problem just before I go to sleep, don't you? Then I let my subconscious go to work overnight.''

"Did you design this building?'' Scheiber asked. The multilevel complex looked like something out of Shangri-la—or Las Vegas, come to think of it. Or something a wedding-cake maker on acid might whip up. The artist's rendering featured lush greenery and fountains and a couple of Rolls-Royces pulled up along the complex's long, winding drive. Another wall held aerial photos of what looked to be the project site.

"No, unfortunately, I'm just a subcontractor,'' Porter said. "I'm working some of the interior structures, like the main ballroom and some of the larger hotel suites.''

"What is this? Another Las Vegas casino?''

Porter shook his head. "A casino-resort complex, but not Las Vegas. It's an overseas project. I'm involved with a large international consortium that does projects around the world. Why don't you sit over here?'' he added, clearing some space at a low, lacquered black table shaped like the amoebas Scheiber remembered from his high-school biology textbook. "Can I get you something? Coffee? Iced tea, maybe?"

"Not for me, thanks," Scheiber said. Eckert also shook his head, and they settled onto a low, electric-blue settee. "We don't want to hold you up any longer than we have to, Mr. Porter. I wonder if you could tell me what happened after you went back to Mr. Korman's this morning?"

Porter settled his lanky frame onto a stool by the drafting table and picked up a pencil. "The cat was yowling, like I said. I couldn't understand why Chap wasn't doing anything about it. He wasn't crazy about that cat, but he'd never abuse or neglect it. Mr. Rochester—that's the cat—belonged to Emma, Chap's wife, so he would never let it go hungry or anything. I thought maybe Chap had gone out, but it was only about six-thirty, and Chap was not a morning person, believe me. I know he said he was going to go out today for groceries for the company he had coming tomorrow, but nothing much would be open at that hour. And, anyway, he would have fed the cat first. So, process of elimination," Porter added, "the only remaining possibility I could think of was that he was sick or hurt."

"When was the last time you'd seen him?"

"Working in his garden late yesterday afternoon. I was taking Kermit for a walk—again," he said, rolling his eyes. "You must think I do nothing but walk my dog and snoop on my neighbors."

"No, not at all," Scheiber assured him.

"I try to be a responsible pet owner. Anyway, this morning, I knocked and rang the bell and called out, and then I finally tried the doors when there was no answer. The patio doors were locked, but I found the side door into the garage open, so I went in through the kitchen."

"When you say it was open, do you mean ajar, or just unlocked?"

Porter frowned and thought about it for a moment as he doodled on a sketch pad in that awkward, hand-bent way left-handers had. "Neither, as a matter of fact. Seems to me that when I tried the handle, it didn't turn, like it was locked. But when I pushed against it, the door opened right away. Like, maybe Chap meant to lock it, but the latch didn't catch? So, anyway, his car was there, so I knew he had to be home. Wasn't much of a walker. I tried to get him to come with Kermit and me a couple of times. Frankly, he could have used the exercise. He'd let himself get a little paunchy, you know? But Chap said he was allergic to exercise. To be fair, I think his knees were pretty arthritic, but really, even so. There's always something you can do, you know, so your body doesn't deteriorate like that, isn't there?'' He shuddered. ''I don't mean to sound catty, but I don't know why someone would want to do that to himself. Why grow old before your time?''

For seventy-seven, Scheiber thought, Korman was doing pretty well for himself to still be working as he'd been. But there was no mileage to be gained by disagreeing with a co-operative witness. ''So you went inside...?'' he prodded.

''That's about it. I called Chap's name, but he never answered. Couldn't, of course, poor old thing. Went upstairs, and there he was.''

''You said he was expecting company tomorrow?'' Eckert asked.

''Yes, an old friend and her daughter. The woman's the daughter of Ben Bolt—the author, you know? Chap had been Bolt's agent. I had actually invited them and Chap out to watch the fireworks tomorrow night. On my sailboat,'' Porter added, nodding to a silver-framed photo on the lacquered table. It showed him, shirtless, at the helm of a sloop. The name across the bow said *Wright Think'r*.

''Wright as in Frank Lloyd Wright, the architect?'' Eckert asked.

''That's right! Very good, Officer,'' Porter said, nodding appreciatively, seeming to notice Eckert for the first time.

''I'm not an officer, I'm a crime-scene investigator,'' Eckert said, frowning down at his notebook. Guess he didn't want to be appreciated, Scheiber thought, suppressing a grin.

''Oh, well, good thinking, anyway,'' Porter said, still directing his attention to Eckert, whom he'd obviously decided was no Philistine.

And so cute, Scheiber thought mischievously, tempted to pinch Eckert's pudgy cheek. But Eckert was beginning to squirm under the attention, so Scheiber decided to save him.

"Have you met this writer's daughter—what's her name?" he asked Porter.

"Mariah Bolt," Porter said. "No, I haven't, but I was really looking forward to it. I'm a huge Ben Bolt fan. I've read everything he ever wrote and pretty much everything that's ever been written about him. He was such an interesting man, and I just adore his writing, don't you?"

"I can't say that I've ever read it," Scheiber confessed, "though I gather he's supposed to be pretty good. Was she planning to stay with Mr. Korman while she was here?"

"No, Chap said she and her daughter had a beach house close by they were going to be using while they were in town. God! I guess this is going to come as a real shock to her, isn't it?"

"Did Mr. Korman ever mention anything about new work he might be handling?"

"Not really, though I know he did take on new clients from time to time."

"No, not a new client. I meant new work by Benjamin Bolt?"

"By Bolt? How would that be possible? He died years ago." Porter took his top lip between his teeth and frowned, head shaking. "No, not that I heard of." Then he glanced at his watch. "I'm sorry, gentlemen. I'm going to have to wrap this up pretty soon, if you don't mind. I've got some calls to Europe I need to make before they go to bed over there."

"Sure, we understand. Just one more thing," Scheiber said. "Besides his arthritis, did Mr. Korman have any other health problems that you're aware of?"

Porter wrung his hands and looked very sad indeed. "He was seventy-seven years old, Detective. I'd be amazed if he didn't, but he never discussed them with me. I thought he looked a little peaked yesterday. It did occur to me to wonder if his heart was in good enough shape to be handling strenuous work like that. Between you and me, and I'm not a medical expert, mind you, I'm sure the poor old dear just overexerted himself."

"I'm sure you're right," Scheiber said, ignoring eighteen years of experience that were telling his gut otherwise.

Chapter Eighteen

Being an object of curiosity was the pits. Was now, always had been. Mariah found herself second-guessing every step she took, feeling more and more paranoid in the process. Wondering who was watching, and what they knew—or thought they knew—about her. It wasn't the first time she'd stepped through the looking glass into covert operations, but given past experience, she should have known better than to agree to this latest bit of skulduggery.

It was a nasty fact of life that when you started poking your nose into private places, your own privacy went up for grabs. She knew she was being followed. She'd first noticed the tail the night before outside the hotel, and presumed it was related to her assignment to recruit Belenko—although after learning Renata had been making inquiries about her, she couldn't even be sure of that. At this point, there was no telling the players without a scorecard. Now she'd picked up a tail again.

Were Jack Geist's people keeping watch as she tried to carry out his orders, or was it the Russians she sensed dogging her heels? And if the Russians, which faction? Those loyal to the presidential ambitions of Valery Zakharov, the bellicose foreign minister, or those opposed to him? Yuri Belenko's easy association with an agent from the other camp would play right into the hands of anyone looking to weaken his boss. She didn't so much mind the prospect of Zakharov being undercut, but she liked Yuri well enough to feel a flicker of concern over his prospects. He was an old hand at these games, and could no doubt take care of himself, but what if Zakharov himself had doubts about the loyalties of his aide? The man was reputed to be suspicious of everyone, even those closest to him, and his opponents had an unfortunate tendency to meet untimely ends.

As a matter of fact, Belenko already looked as if he had one foot in the grave when Mariah met up with him at Ziggurat, the Grand Avenue restaurant where Secretary of State Kidd was hosting his luncheon for Zakharov. She found Belenko next to the bar in the private dining room reserved for the event, a glass of what looked like unadulterated soda water at his elbow.

"Yuri, are you all right?" Mariah asked, her concern real. His dark hair, usually lush and flowing, was plastered to his forehead by tiny beads of perspiration. His skin was the color of parchment, and even his lips, normally plummy and full, looked bleached out.

He straightened and brushed his pin-striped suit in a half-hearted effort to spiff himself up a little, always maintaining appearances. "Mariah, good, you made it! They said you were coming." He took her hand as always and put it to his lips, but the gesture lacked his usual panache. His pseudo rep tie was loosened and slightly askew, and when she looked closer, Mariah noticed that the top button of his sleek dress shirt had been unfastened.

"You don't look long for this world," she said. "Are you ill?" Or hung over? she wondered. It was late in the day to still be suffering the effects of a hangover. In any case, he hadn't drunk all that much in the time she'd been with him the night before, and his capacity for alcohol was prodigious. At a dinner in Paris that past spring, she'd seen him put away the better part of two bottles of wine all on his own, having already downed several predinner cocktails, and he'd shown no ill effects at all, then or the next day. She had no idea how much he'd drunk at the Arlen Hunter reception, but afterward, when they'd gone for dinner, he'd done no more than match her sedate pace.

"Death would be welcome compared to living through another night and morning like I've just gone through," Belenko said miserably. He gave up trying to be gallant and slumped against the zinc bar once more.

The restaurant was the kind of clubby, wood-paneled place where Mariah would have expected a conservative establishment figure like Shelby Kidd to host a function. It was reputed to be a favorite hangout for that part of Los Angeles society that liked to fancy itself the old-money crowd—although the concept was entirely relative in a place that had counted more cows than people only a century earlier. The Ziggurat smelled of well-roasted beef, stiffly starched linen and fine Napoleon brandy. The wine-red carpets were plush, lending a sedate hush to the atmosphere, but the place was crawling with Secret Service agents. As she'd run the gamut of guards and metal detectors at the entryway, she'd noticed several well-dressed matrons grumbling about the tight security.

Poor old Yuri Belenko, however, looked as if he would have welcomed a bomb right about now to put him out of his misery. "What's the problem?" she asked, resisting the impulse to reach out and feel his forehead. Maternal instinct dies hard. "Is it the flu, do you think?"

"No," he said wearily. "It seems I have no—what do they call it? No sea legs."

"Sea legs? We're on dry land, Yuri."

"I am only just, and my stomach has not yet caught up with me. I don't dare get too close to the ministers right now." He waved at the opposite side of the room where Zakharov and Kidd were having preluncheon drinks.

"I don't understand. Have you been out sailing this morning?"

He sighed the martyred sigh of the much-put-upon. "My minister," he said, "insists we be on board the *Aleksandr Pushkin* at all times while we are here, except during official functions. We slept there—although 'slept' is a very loose use of the term—and then spent the morning on board, briefing him in preparation for his meetings. I tell you, dear lady, I have never been so happy to attend a tedious luncheon. Oh, forgive me," he added quickly. "No offense intended. But I think you will agree that they are tedious, these affairs."

She nodded. "They are at that. Why does he want to stay aboard the *Pushkin?*" It was a rusting hulk of a Russian oceanographic research vessel, commissioned decades ago and presently berthed off the Port of Los Angeles. Frank Tucker had once told her that the *Pushkin*'s silhouette was one of the first ships U.S. sailors were trained to recognize on sight, since its "research" tended to be of the covert variety as often as not. "I thought your delegation was being put up at the Russian consul's residence. Didn't anyone tell him it's a beautiful place?"

"Oh, he knows. I would much rather have stayed there, and believe me, I tried very hard indeed to convince him. Unfortunately, my minister is a product of the cold war. He trusts *no one.*" Belenko dropped his voice and folded his face into a dark glower, a bang-on imitation of his boss's peevish demeanor. "Those people at the consulate, bah! How long have they been in this den of corruption? How do we know they haven't been perverted and compromised?" He rolled his eyes heavenward. "I think he expected his room to be gassed, his bodyguards overpowered and a naked woman...no, wait...a naked *man* to slip into his bed and start doing terrible things to him before the flashing cameras of CIA blackmailers."

"Oh, Yuri," she chided playfully, "would my countrymen do a thing like that?"

He leaned toward her, a sparkle of humor reanimating his sultry brown eyes, half-lidded with exhaustion though they were. "Frankly, dear lady, I wouldn't care if they did. I'd much rather share my nice, wide, comfortable feather bed at the residence with one clean, naked gigolo than spend the night as I did, on a hard iron bunk with fifteen sweaty Russian sailors snoring all around me. And then, the rocking and swaying! All night long! *Oi!*" he groaned. "The little sleep I did get, I kept dreaming my country was being overrun by the Mongol hordes again. Wave after wave after wave of them." He closed his eyes and sighed.

Mariah shook her head, grinning. "So, the consulate's people are not to be trusted, but the *Pushkin*'s sailors are safe?"

As always, Belenko was being scandalously indiscreet—although his indiscretions, she'd noted, were carefully selected for maximum impact and minimum revelation. It was hardly a national secret that Valery Zakharov suffered from paranoia that probably bordered on the certifiably psychotic. It only made sense that he'd feel safer in an isolated environment controlled by his covert colleagues.

"The *Pushkin*'s sailors are never allowed off the ship, except briefly, two by two, and always in the company of, shall we say, a very careful colleague?" Belenko said. He took a sip of his soda, and waved the barman over. "But enough of my troubles. What will you have?"

"The same as you," she said. "Looks like soda?" He nodded and the bartender produced the glass, popping a wedge of lime on the rim. Ice tinkled as she raised her glass. "Here's to more trust between nations so you can get a better night's sleep next time you visit."

"Hear, hear."

She settled in next to him, back against the bar, one foot on the brass rail, debating whether to broach the subject of what Jack Geist's message had called "a mutually beneficial relationship." The timing wasn't ideal, given the state he was in, but the other members of their respective delegations were all fluttering around the ministers, and there was no telling if they'd find another opportunity to speak privately.

Before she could launch into the pitch, though, Shelby Kidd glanced in her direction. When he spotted her, he waved her over. "Hmm," she said. "Looks like duty calls. Could you excuse me for a minute, Yuri?"

"Yes, yes, you go ahead. Just don't forget about me, will you, Mariah? I'll be waiting here on my deathbed, composing my last will and testament."

"You poor thing," she said, setting down her glass.

Kidd turned with an affable smile at her approach. "Mariah, glad you could join us!"

"Glad to be here," she replied, as if she had any choice in the matter. But what was he so chipper about? This was the first time the secretary had ever addressed her by her given name—or any other, for that matter, as far as she could remember. Spook-averse as he was, Kidd seemed to do his best to forget she was there on these rare occasions when she found herself attached to one of his delegations. But he took her by the elbow now and turned back to his Moscow counterpart. "Minister Zakharov, I'm told you're a connoisseur of the literary works of the American author Benjamin Bolt. It happens his daughter is a member of my delegation. Let me introduce Mariah Bolt, one of my very capable aides."

Zakharov was listening to the Russian-language explanation of who she was, examining her suspiciously as he took her outstretched hand. What did he imagine? Mariah wondered. That Kidd was offering her up for his personal pleasure? But when the interpreter relayed her parental connection, Zakharov's beady eyes flickered. Whatever Kidd's sources might have told him, it wasn't quite the gushing reaction of the average Ben Bolt enthusiast she was used to. But then, powerful men were hard to impress. Given that Zakharov was still fighting a rearguard campaign to revive the cold war in the hope his side would come out on top this time around, he'd also be loath to convey the impression he was starstuck over any American.

"Ms. Bolt, a pleasure," he said, nodding soberly.

"The pleasure is mine." She shifted into Russian to bypass the clumsiness of simultaneous interpretation. "I had no idea you were interested in twentieth-century American authors." Her tongue felt creaky, and her face grew warm before the suddenly curious crowd of aides and onlookers. The problem of having ridden a desk all these years was that her comprehension of the language was fluent, but she had few opportunities to let her spoken Russian out for an airing.

From the corner of her eye, she noticed Shelby Kidd regarding her with newfound interest. For once in her life, she knew it wasn't just because she was related to Ben Bolt. Her father's name had come up, in fact, the first time she'd met Kidd, at the last U.N. General Assembly session, but from the way he'd raised, then quickly moved past the subject on that occasion, she knew he'd been briefed on her family connection but was not himself a Bolt afficionado. Not surprising, given his age. Ben's work tended to appeal to younger, less conservative readers. Nor was it any skin off her nose. She'd never sought to play cheerleader or fan club president for her father. Whatever his personal tastes in literature, though, Kidd obviously wasn't above exploiting any advantage in the name of diplomacy.

"Your father's poetry is much read in my country," Zakharov said. Neutral and noncommittal.

"So I've been told," Mariah replied. "But, of course, the Russian love of poetry is well-known."

"That is true," he said, his lower lip jutting as he nodded. "Our culture runs deep. You must know this, since you have made the effort to study our language. It takes more than Hollywood glitter or rock and roll to excite us. We prefer the deeper complexity of the classics—Tolstoy, Turgenev." Zakharov shifted his stocky frame and handed off his glass to one of his ever-present bodyguards so he could cross his arms across his barrel chest. It was a stretch. "But, of course, my nation is over a thousand years old. America," he sniffed, "has yet to demonstrate whether it can produce anything of lasting value. And you, Ms. Bolt? Do you also write?"

She shook her head. "Oh, no. No talent whatever in that department, I'm afraid."

"I see. And your father? Is he well?"

Mariah hesitated. "Well...no, actually, he's not." What kind of connoisseur didn't know that the object of his supposed study, if not adulation, had been dead thirty years? "He passed away some time ago," she said as tactfully as she could.

Zakharov seemed oblivious to the blunder. "I am sorry for your loss. It is difficult to lose a parent."

"I was a child when he died. I have very little recollection of him, actually."

"I see." The minister retrieved his drink. "So! A famous writer's daughter." He scrutinized her a moment longer. Then, apparently lacking any more astute commentary on the subject, he bowed briefly and turned his attention back to Shelby Kidd. She was dismissed. The writer's daughter had been examined and found uninteresting.

The strange audience over, Mariah slipped tactfully away from the two ministers, but didn't get far before Belenko appeared at her side once more. "Can I get you a refill?" he asked. He was looking a little recovered. The color was back in his cheeks, and he'd refastened his shirt and straightened his tie.

"No, thanks, Yuri," she said, glancing back. "From the looks of things, I'd say the ministers are getting ready to sit down to lunch."

"You and I are neighbors at the table."

"Really? How did that happen? I expected to be in social Siberia, way down at the end."

"Perhaps you might have, had Secretary Kidd not learned of my minister's interest in the celebrity in our midst."

"Hardly a celebrity," she said. "But who, pray tell, told him your minister was a fan of Ben Bolt's work?"

"Oh, I may have planted that little bug in his ear." Belenko smiled coyly. "What did my minister have to say to you?"

"Not a whole lot. If you say he reads my father's work, Yuri, I'll take your word for it. Frankly, I got the impression he wouldn't know Ben Bolt from Charles Dickens."

Belenko chuckled. "You are very astute, as always, Mariah." He bent closer and his voice dropped to a confidential level. "The minister is something of a barbarian, to be honest, but he likes to think he can fake a certain cultural *je ne sais quoi.* He would have you believe he is the consummate cosmopolitan Commie."

Mariah felt her eyebrows rise involuntarily. There was a time when Belenko could have landed himself in the Gulag with a remark like that. "You sound less than fully enthusiastic about your minister," she said.

He shrugged. "I am a realist."

"You do have a refreshingly frank take on things." She glanced around, but they were alone in the crowd. "You know," she said quietly, "there are people who would be very interested in your views."

"But not you?" he asked pitiably.

"I mean besides myself."

The smile never left his lips, but there was calculation behind the sparkle in those brown eyes. She felt his hand on her elbow as he, too, glanced around to ensure no one was listening. "My dear Mariah," he murmured, "are you making a little recruitment speech here?"

"I think you know your present situation gives you a

unique perspective on certain matters of interest, Yuri. I also think you're smart enough to take advantage of that."

"*My* advantage?"

She shrugged. "Those who aid the greater good aid themselves. What is of advantage to others can certainly be of advantage to you, as well."

"And these others? What do they offer in exchange for this unique perspective of mine?"

"That would be up for discussion. But there is a generally accepted principle in my country that superior talent should be well compensated. Don't you agree?"

The pinging sound of silver on glass drew their attention toward the table, where, at center position, Shelby Kidd was tapping a fork against a goblet to announce it was time to sit down.

"Can I say you're interested in conversation?" Mariah asked quietly. She wished she could look him levelly in the eye to try to gauge how he was taking this, but of course, looking anyone over twelve years old in the eye was always problematic for someone of her stature. Glad as she was that Belenko was feeling recovered, at the moment she would have preferred him still slumped on the bar, closer to her level.

"Can I give it some thought and get back to you? Would that be all right?" Belenko asked, glancing over at the others. "Right now, our presence is required."

"That would be fine," she said. As they headed for their places near the head of the table, she changed the subject. "So, tell me, that business of convincing Kidd your minister was a connoisseur of my father's work, were you just being mischievous?"

"I confess, I was. But it worked, didn't it? Now we get to enjoy each other's company over lunch."

"You're a devious man, Yuri Belenko."

"What about Secretary Kidd? Is he a Ben Bolt afficio-nado?"

"I don't think so. I suspect he prefers literature of an older, more sedate vintage. Doesn't earn me any Brownie points, being related to Ben."

"Brownie points?" Belenko repeated, intrigued.

Another cliché for his collection. Mariah tried to decide how to explain about Brownies. "They're like Young Pioneers," she ventured, "only all girls, and with brown neckerchiefs instead of red."

Belenko's broad forehead rose with enlightenment. "Ah, I see! Like Boy Scouts, only female. Scoutlettes."

Mariah nodded. "There you go."

"Brownie points," Belenko said happily, filing it away for future reference.

The murmuring voices increased in volume as the two chief envoys sat down, the rest of their respective retinues falling dutifully behind. Mariah found herself seated next to Belenko and diagonal to his minister, and directly opposite a fellow who seemed to be the main bodyguard. And food taster? she wondered, noting with amusement how the bruiser—a Mr. Lermontov, his place card said—scrutinized every plate set down in front of his master. Lermontov was built like a brick wall, his white-blond hair cropped in a buzz, like a dense, round carpet of needles. The buttons of his suit jacket strained dangerously across his chest as he propped one trunklike forearm on the table, the other on the back of his chair. Had she not been afraid of losing a hand, Mariah might have been tempted to reach over and unbutton them, just to relieve the tension of waiting for them to pop spontaneously—which they were bound to do, sooner or later.

"Olympic wrestling team of '84," Belenko whispered in her ear as Lermontov's disapproving gaze swept up and down the room in a searchlight arc of vigilance. "Undefeated then or since."

Mariah turned to face his ever-present grin. "Why am I not surprised?" she murmured. "Remind me not to try out my half nelson on the man."

"It would be a big mistake. Old Boris there was part of the great steroid experiments. It left him lacking in mental subtlety and totally devoid of any sense of humor."

The soup course was served, and Mariah turned her attention to it and away from the wrestler-turned-bodyguard, keeping one ear dutifully cocked to the official conversation at the center of the table. When the main course came, however, she noticed Belenko regarding her closely. "What?" she asked. "Have I got spinach on my teeth?"

"No. I was just wondering."

"What?"

"Well, my little joke with the secretary about my minister being a fan of your father—I hope it was not out of place? I never hear you speak of him yourself."

Mariah trotted out her stock answer, usually sufficient to blow off the subject. "No offense taken. He moved out when I was very young, that's all. I scarcely remember him."

"What about his work? Do you like it?"

She thought about that for a moment. It was an interesting question, one no one had ever thought to ask her before. *Did* she like her father's work? "It's hard for me to read it with detachment," she said finally. "I see the power in the writing, but I can't help thinking about what was going on in his life— in *our* lives—as he was producing it. When he writes about a woman, for example, I can't help wondering what woman he was thinking of."

"Your mother, perhaps?"

"In some cases, yes. But it's no great secret that my father had a few lovers along the way. When I read a description of a woman who's obviously not my mother, I wonder who she was. And since my mother always proofread his work before he sent it out, I also can't help thinking it must have hurt her."

"It's not easy to live with an artist," Belenko said, nodding. "But perhaps he was more attached to your mother than you know."

Mariah broke a piece of bread and watched the crumbs spill onto her plate. "I think my father believed in marriage and family," she said, "but only in the abstract. He never had a real family life as a child, so he never quite got the idea that a family is a kind of social contract. A bargain with the future. You give up a small piece of your freedom in exchange for the good of the whole, especially children. Ben wasn't prepared to sacrifice his own needs, though. They always came first."

"Perhaps the demands of family life interfered with his art?"

Mariah was dubious. "My mother made it possible for him to write. After he left her, he produced very little, and he didn't even live all that long. By all accounts, his self-indulgence was what killed him."

"He destroyed his family for his art," Belenko said quietly. "Sad, but interesting. In my country, for a very long time, it was the other way around. Artists strangled their creativity so they and their families could survive in the climate of censorship." He frowned into his plate. He seemed genuinely troubled, and Mariah sensed it was the first time she'd ever caught a glimpse beneath the playfulness that underscored all their conversations. But then, like a passing cloud, the moment passed. Belenko looked up and gave her one of his disarming smiles. As she returned it, she noticed that there was only one other person besides themselves not hanging on the ministers' every word.

Belenko raised his glass. "To better times, Mariah."

"Better times," she answered.

At the clink of their goblets, Lermontov, the bodyguard, scowled.

Chapter Nineteen

By late afternoon, the low, gray concrete headquarters of the Newport Beach Police Department were virtually deserted. Everyone who wasn't actually out on patrol had snuck away to get a head start on the long holiday weekend, but the uniforms would all be back tomorrow night and out on the street in full force. Two-thirds of the city's annual arrest numbers would be racked up on the Fourth of July blowout, as dozens of party animals landed in the department's tiny lockup for various misdemeanors, mostly of the drunk and disorderly or disturbing the peace variety. In the meantime, anyone who could sneak in a little advance beach time was doing it.

Not Scheiber, though. Liz had called to say Lucas's play date had shifted to their house when the other mother pleaded a sick younger child. So much for afternoon delight. "Okay, look," he said, coward that he was, "I'm going to stick around here for a while and do the paperwork on this old guy we found this morning."

"Ha! You just don't want to land in the middle of this mayhem," Liz said. In the background, he heard the annoying shriek of the toy laser guns Lucas's stepmother had thoughtfully bought for his birthday, then refused to allow him to keep at their house for the rare weekends she actually let him stay.

"No, it's not that," he lied.

"Relax, I'm kidding. Although believe me, I'm envious. I wouldn't want to be here, either. I just wish I'd remembered to hide those guns. Aaron's staying for dinner, so don't feel like you have to rush home. We can have a quiet dinner later, after Lucas goes to bed."

"To be honest," he confessed, "I was half thinking I should run up to L.A., anyway."

"No problem from my end. What for?"

"There's a lady I'd like to talk to about the guy we found in the spa this morning. She's staying at the Beverly Wilshire, but just for one more day, by the sound of it. If I don't catch her there, I'm not sure I'll be able to track her down."

"Did the man have a heart attack, like you thought?"

"Probably, but we won't know for sure until the autopsy. Meantime, though, I'm worried there might have been a theft from his house. If there was, and it turns out the guy's death was from something other than natural causes, it's a whole new ball game."

"And this lady at the Beverly Wilshire?"

"She's the daughter of Benjamin Bolt—the writer? The dead guy was Bolt's literary agent. Apparently, he had some papers I'm guessing would have been pretty valuable, but when I went to look for them, I couldn't find them anywhere in the house. For all I know, the old guy put them in a safe-deposit box or somewhere for safekeeping. If the daughter can clear up the mystery, maybe Dave and I won't end up running around on a wild-goose chase. Speaking of Dave," Scheiber added, looking up, "here he is." As Eckert rounded the low wall of his cubicle, Scheiber held up a forefinger to let him know he'd be done shortly.

"Tell him I said hi," Liz said.

"Liz says hi."

"Hi, Liz!" Eckert called, dragging an extra chair into Scheiber's small cubbyhole and settling himself into it.

On the phone, the pulsating whine of a mock laser interrupted her answer. "Oh, Lord, I've gotta go, Jim," she said. "I think they're trying to fry the fish tank."

"Are you going to be okay?"

"Absolutely. If they get too rambunctious, I'm going to throw them both in the car and take them over to the swimming pool. Make the little buggers swim laps until they collapse from exhaustion."

He smiled. "Okay, I'll call you later."

"Love you. Rain check on fun and games?"

"You betcha. Me, too." He hung up and turned to Eckert, whose sneakers were tapping with the nervous energy of news just waiting to be spilled. "What's up?"

"You know how Porter said he loved Ben Bolt so much, read everything by and about the guy, but didn't know anything about those papers?"

"Yeah."

"I just did a quick Internet search on Ben Bolt, and guess what I found out? There's been a whole ream of articles in the past few months about some journals and an unpublished novel showing up in a box of junk of his that his daughter had had in storage for years—the daughter being that Mariah woman who called and left the message while we were at Korman's house. Kind of funny Porter didn't know anything about it, don't you think? Especially living right next door to Bolt's agent?"

"I don't know. I never heard anything about it, either, and I look at a newspaper most every day."

"Yeah, but you're not a Bolt fan, so you wouldn't necessarily pick up on it."

"Maybe Porter doesn't read anything but books and architectural journals."

"Yeah, I suppose that's possible," Eckert conceded, "assuming Korman never mentioned it to him, which seems like a pretty big assumption to me. What do I know? But that's not all. I also keyed Porter's name into the search engine, and that turned up a little morsel of interesting information, too. Turns out he was one of the subcontractors on the early stages of the new Getty Museum up in Malibu a few years back, only he was dismissed from the project under murky circumstances."

"Murky? Like, legal problems?"

Eckert pursed his lips and shrugged. "Not clear. The press

reports mentioned him and a couple of other people in connection with a possible diversion of project funds, but it looks like the whole thing was hushed up by the Getty Trust. At the time, the museum was going through major hassles with environmentalists who didn't think they should be bulldozing Malibu hillsides so the Gettys could beam their name across the city. The trust probably didn't want any more public relations problems than they already had.''

Scheiber propped his feet up on the desk and folded his hands across his stomach. "If Porter got smeared on a big project like that, it might explain why he works overseas now. I've got to believe that if people as powerful as the Gettys put your name on a blacklist, there aren't too many other developers in the country who will take a chance on you.'' He nodded. "Okay, let's run his name through the system, see what turns up. I was thinking we should be doing it, anyway, as a matter of course, since he was probably the last person to see Korman alive. I'd hate to have the M.E.'s report come in and find out the guy died of other than natural causes and we've lost valuable investigation time. And, speaking of the medical examiner, is there any chance you can prevail on your special relationship with the coroner's office, see if they can hurry up that autopsy?''

Eckert's color elevated, but he didn't protest, Scheiber noted. "Already talked to Iris, as a matter of fact.''

"Aha! Making plans for the weekend, are we?''

"Not that it's any of your business, but yeah, as a matter of fact, we're going to watch the fireworks down in Dana Point.''

"You sly dog. Did you give her the names of Korman's sons?'' Following up on Porter's information, they'd gone back into the house and found the names Michael and Philip at the top of Korman's telephone AutoDial list. Cross-checking against a Rolodex on Korman's desk, Scheiber had looked under the letter K and come up with New York home and work addresses and phone numbers for both a Michael Korman and a Philip Korman.

"I did,'' Eckert said. "She said thank you very much, we made her day much easier. She was going to give them a call right after she hung up from talking to me.''

"What did she say about the autopsy?"

"The M.E. wants to squeeze it in tomorrow morning. They're trying to clear the decks over there before they get backed up with the holiday surge of binge drinkers and road-kill."

It was sad but true that people tended to die in greater numbers on holiday weekends, mostly from drinking- and traffic-related accidents. "So much for my Fourth of July," Scheiber grumbled. Attending autopsies was his least favorite part of the job, but there was less chance of missing crucial evidence if he oversaw every step of the investigation, starting with any clues the body might turn up at autopsy. "What time?"

"Iris is going to call back to let me know, but probably midmorning."

Scheiber picked up a pencil and tapped it on his knee. "Didn't you do wedding pictures for somebody in the sheriff's crime lab?"

Eckert nodded. "Daughter of one of the examiners got married a couple of weeks ago. I just finished developing the pictures."

"Sure would be nice if we could get Korman's tox screen hustled through there. Why don't you hold off on delivering those pictures until the blood and tissue samples are ready?"

"You want me to hold their firstborn child for ransom, too?"

"Only if the wedding pics don't get us the speeded-up service we need. Meantime, let's see if there's any criminal history on either Korman or Porter. I'm going to run up to L.A. and try to track down this Mariah Bolt person. Who knows? Maybe she can tell me if there's any reason to suspect Korman might have been depressed enough over his dead wife to intentionally take a lethal cocktail before his dip in the spa."

Chapter
Twenty

Wanting something too much is a surefire guarantee of paying too high a price for it, Mariah thought as she sat on the
edge of her hotel-room bed, holding the beach-house keys in
her hand. She'd found them on the table when she came in,
along with a note from Paul saying he'd be at the network
studios all afternoon getting ready for his interview with Zakharov. She jangled the keys, feeling their heft. For a couple
of small bits of brass and an address tag on a ring, they
seemed awfully heavy. Must be the weight of all the guilt
that came along with them, she decided.

All she'd wanted was some quiet time to reconnect with a
daughter who was the center of her wobbly universe. Lindsay
had wanted a summer vacation in southern California, another
phase in her effort to retrace the footsteps of the grandfather
she'd only just begun to discover. Paul, ever the knight in
shining armor, had stepped in with a hassle-free answer to
both their prayers.

But in life, there's no free lunch, as Mariah was always
careful to remind herself. Paul had obviously been looking
for something in exchange for lining up the beach house. It
was a measure of his decency that he'd come through with

his end of the bargain even after she'd balked at paying the price he asked, which was to be included in their holiday.

The note he'd left included a phone number where he could be reached that afternoon. She settled back onto the bed, leaning against the headboard, and listened as her call was bounced forward from the main network switchboard to wherever he was. When they were finally connected, Paul sounded distracted and rushed.

"I won't keep you," she said. "I just wanted to let you know I'm back at the hotel and I found the keys. Thank you so much for doing this. Lindsay will be thrilled."

"You're welcome. I just hope you'll be okay with it." There was an undercurrent in his voice that, to a guilty conscience like hers, sounded a lot like resentment. But maybe he was just preoccupied. He did have other things to think about, after all.

"Are you sure *you're* okay about it?" she asked. "I feel a little awkward about exploiting your connections like this." And then expressly disinviting him to join them. She told herself it was for Lindsay's sake, but maybe that was a bum rap. What if Lindsay had been better disposed toward Paul? Would Mariah have been eager to share her vacation with him then? She didn't think so. Ever since David's death, she'd been running on sheer, empty inertia, worrying about Lindsay, giving little thought to where she herself was going— her life transformed to driftwood, its course directed only by the shifting tide of her child's needs. But the time was rapidly approaching when Lindsay would move on. College was just two years away, and at the moment, she seemed determined to choose one as far away as possible from the D.C. area. There wouldn't be many more chances for them to have time alone together. And when Lindsay was launched on her own life? Mariah thought. What would she herself do with the rest of her days?

"You're not exploiting my connections," Paul said, "but I want you to understand about this. When I said I wanted to be there with you—" He was interrupted by a muffled voice in the background, and Mariah waited while he excused himself to discuss camera angles with someone. Then he was back. "Sorry about that," he said. "Look, it's a little crowded in here. This is probably not the best time to talk."

"I know. And I do want us to talk, Paul, but you've got other things to worry about right now. I gather your interview with Zakharov is on?"

"We're just waiting for him to show up. His people called to say he would only talk to me if we taped the interview in a location near the port. They wouldn't say why, but I found out it's because he's staying on what's reputed to be a Russian spy ship while he's here in the city. Did you know that?"

Her response was noncommittal. She'd long since given up trying to figure out Paul's sources. There was very little he didn't find out sooner or later, as often as not before she did.

"Anyway," he went on, "we were going to do the taping in Burbank, but then we had to scramble to get a suite in a hotel near the port. That's where I am now. We're set up, finally, but it took all afternoon for the techs to get the equipment in, and they're still testing the feeds. We're cutting things a little close. How did the luncheon with Kidd go?"

"As well as could be expected," Mariah said. "The official communiqué's going to say that they had a 'full and frank' exchange of views."

"Ouch! That bad?"

She smiled. Paul had been covering international affairs long enough to know diplomatic shorthand by now. When an official communiqué reported a "full and frank" discussion, it meant the normally genteel language of diplomacy had been abandoned in favor of blunt talk. If the communiqué said someone had given a "frank assessment" of a situation, chances were, an ultimatum had been issued. And if the pinstriped suits announced that an "open exchange of views" had taken place, it meant the delegates had been in each others' faces like WWF pro wrestlers. "Let's just say that the translators had their work cut out for them," she said.

"And the financial aid Zakharov was looking for? Did he get it?"

"You know I can't be telling tales out of school, but it should come as no great surprise that anything he gets will have strings attached. The package has to go before Congress, and Zakharov's got to pass the terms by his own side, too, before any deal can be nailed down. You'd probably do well, though, to ask him what he knows about the routing of funds to the Kurdish and fundamentalist opposition to the Turkish government, and whether he's willing to risk food and fuel this coming winter by undermining Washington's efforts to mediate there.''

"Guns or butter, the eternal dilemma," Paul mused. "Some people might wonder why we'd even bother to consider an aid package now, when the timing can only help the ambitions of this thug who hates us. But," he said, answering his own argument, "I guess it's a case of better the devil you know than the one you don't. What about the Russian divisions massing in the south? Did Kidd demand they be rolled back?''

"That would be a logical *quid pro quo,* wouldn't it? And nobody's ever accused Shelby Kidd of being illogical.''

"Okay, thanks. That's helpful," Paul said, sounding as if he was taking notes. "Are the meetings over?''

"The bilateral ones. Both sides have retreated to their corners. Zakharov and Kidd are scheduled to be on the *Queen Mary* tomorrow evening for the opening of the Pacific Rim conference.''

"So where does that leave you?''

"Cooling my heels, for a pleasant change. I just filed my last report. As far as work's concerned, looks like I'm outta here.'' She'd returned to the Federal Building after the luncheon to let Geist know that the offer had been made, and that Belenko hadn't run screaming in panic from the room. But neither had Yuri jumped at the opportunity to become a traitor for hire. If Belenko contacted her again, she'd let Geist know. Otherwise, the ball was now in the DDO's court.

"Can I buy you dinner?" Mariah asked. She owed Paul that, at least, and probably some honesty, too, about why she'd turned him down. And why it might be time for them to consider cooling it.

"I was hoping you'd be free," he replied. "In fact, I already asked somebody here to make dinner reservations for me. I've got a table at Spago for eight o'clock. Is that going to be okay?''

"I suppose so.'' She would have preferred somewhere quieter, but the timing was good. Eight o'clock gave them enough time for a good talk before she had to leave for the airport to meet Lindsay's flight. "Last-minute tables at Spago," she added. "Pretty impressive. I guess that's one of the perks of being a big-time TV personality."

The tease fell flat on its face. Paul's response was distinctly irritated. "You've got plenty of name recognition of your own, Mariah, if you'd just lighten up about it. Your father couldn't have been all bad. Don't you think it's about time you cut him a little slack?"

She frowned. "Excuse me? Where did that come from?"

"Forget it. Look, I've got to go. We'll talk at dinner, all right?"

"That's fine," she said, adding a conciliatory note, "I really do appreciate your going to bat on the beach-house thing, Paul."

He exhaled heavily. "I'm just trying to help. That's all I've ever wanted to do."

"I know that. I'll see you at eight. Meantime, break a leg with Zakharov, okay?"

"See you later."

She hung up the phone and replaced it on the night table, then sat back, trying to decide what to do with the hours between now and then. There was the car to be picked up. And, come to think of it, she should probably call down to the front desk to make sure they knew she'd be staying one more—

"Oh, damn it all to hell!" She smacked her thigh angrily. She'd forgotten to tell Paul she'd changed Lindsay's flight, and that she was coming in tonight instead of tomorrow. Although, she thought grimly, maybe that was a conversation just as well had over dinner, too. But there was no way she was going to have Lindsay stay in a hotel room by herself while she and Paul spent another night together, especially after the way Lindsay had reacted to finding him there in the first place. Breaking that news to Paul was just going to be insult added to injury, though. The best thing to do was pack her things and call down to the front desk to line up a double room she and Lindsay could share tonight, and leave this room to Paul. Then, while the bellhop was moving her bags,

Mariah calculated, she could run out and pick up the rental car.

She slid off the bed and headed for the bathroom, and started stuffing her cosmetics and toothbrush into her flowered toiletry bag. She was on her way out with it when she stopped dead in her tracks. Frowning, she turned back to let her gaze wander slowly over the bathroom. It was spotless, not a thing interrupting the impeccable sheen of the marble countertop, except for the tray of bath samples and plastic-wrapped glasses that the maid had left when the room was cleaned. Her Speedo was still draped over the shower rod, where she'd left it after her morning swim. Mariah returned to the room and slid open the mirrored closet door. Her blue, rip-stop nylon dress bag hung from the rod next to the cobalt blue mandarin number she'd worn to the Arlen Hunter reception, plus another couple of backup dresses she'd brought along, just in case. On the floor were her shoes. The bigger suitcase she'd packed for the beach was on the luggage rack in the room.

There were no other personal items anywhere. No battered leather shaving kit in the bathroom. No size twelve men's Cole Haans on the closet floor. No monogrammed shirts in the pale blue Egyptian cotton that punched up the color of Paul's eyes when he sat before the cameras, seducing the country with that easy charm, making men trust him and women lust after him. All of his things were gone. He had done more than line up the beach-house keys while she was gone. He'd packed his bag and moved himself out, lock, stock and calfskin flight bag.

Mariah shut the closet door and sat down on the edge of the bed, stunned. Was this how a drifting affair ended? It was a nasty surprise, psyching herself up to back gracefully away from this arrangement of theirs, only to find out she'd been beaten to the punch.

Her relationship with Paul had been stormy at the outset, warmer later, but always vaguely unsettled, picking up intensity from time to time, only to drop off again as one or the other or both of them got too busy to tend to it properly. Relationships had to be nurtured if they were to grow strong. Otherwise, they just withered on the vine. But there had never seemed to be enough time to nurture theirs. Maybe not enough enthusiasm, either.

Now, evidently, the attraction between them had finally worn so thin it had reached the breaking point, the separate-vacations thing just the final rub. And, perhaps, that's what this dinner he'd planned was about—why it was going to happen in that most public of all Los Angeles restaurants. After all, if there was one thing Paul hated, it was noisy melodrama. Hadn't he once confided—only half-jokingly, now that she thought about it—that a crowded venue was the best place to terminate a relationship? He should know. Before she'd gotten involved with him, she'd seen Paul Chaney run through more than a few of the ambitious, self-sufficient women he seemed most attracted to—the kind who'd be loath to make public spectacles of themselves in high-profile places—so it was only to be expected that he'd have the art of the clean split mastered by now.

There you have it, she thought. Here she was, having second, third and fourth thoughts about what the hell she was doing, and all the while he was getting ready to dump her. Mariah sat in the quiet room, taking the pulse of her reaction. She was irritated, not so much that he'd moved himself out without telling her as by the sneakiness of his unilateral withdrawal. Although, to be honest, wasn't that what she'd just been planning herself? Yes, she thought indignantly, but only because of the Lindsay factor. She was sorry she'd hurt his feelings, but on the other hand, Paul should have asked whether it would be all right to barge in on her vacation, instead of simply presuming.

In any event, it was ending. Was she distressed? No, she decided, not really. She even felt a hint of exhilaration at her impending freedom. Now that she'd figured out what was going on, she could have done without the dinner date. Still, to be fair, he was preoccupied with work, and he *had* come through one last time for her. She could at least grant him this, if that was how he preferred to shut things down. They'd part on friendly terms, and she'd survive. And, on the plus side, she thought, at least she didn't have to worry now about lining up another hotel room.

She glanced at her watch. Three and a half hours till dinner.

It was too nerve-racking to sit in the hotel room and wait. She'd go and pick up the rental car. Then, if nothing else, she could always follow the time-honored tradition that when the going gets tough, the tough go shopping.

That was what she did. After picking up the car in Westwood—a fire-engine red Mustang convertible, she decided, making an impulsive last-minute switch from the staid, mid-size sedan she'd originally reserved—she drove to the Beverly Center and spent an hour and a half browsing luxury shops and trying on clothes. At Saks, she bought a new bathing suit for the beach, sandals and a straw hat. And then, on impulse, a short, sleeveless dress in a soft, turquoise silk that skimmed her body like a custom-made cocoon.

Eat your heart out, Media Man, she thought, taking perverse pleasure from the reflection in the dressing-room mirror. There was no need to don sackcloth and ashes for the occasion of being publicly dumped, and this was about as far from mourning garb as it was possible to get. The summery color set off the glow her skin had already acquired after only a day and a half of walking in and out of golden California sunshine. Her gray eyes took on the turquoise cast of the silk, and her hair had never seemed so blond. At the service desk, an obsequious sales associate pointed out a matching silk shawl in an abstract print of turquoise shot through with bits of silver.

"Good. Perfect for the disdainful fling over the shoulder," Mariah agreed, tossing it onto her pile of purchases. The saleswoman gave her a puzzled smile.

Returning to the hotel with just a half hour to spare, she left the red Mustang with the valet at the front door, ran upstairs, showered and dressed, taking a little extra time to punch up her makeup.

"Let him wait," she muttered.

The effect must have been what she was hoping for, because the white-haired doorman—the same one who'd watched her comings and goings the previous night—and the young valet tripped over each other in their competitive haste to hold open her car door and study her legs as she slipped behind the wheel. Not bad for the mother of a teenage daughter, Mariah thought, grinning at their flushed faces in the rearview mirror as she pulled away.

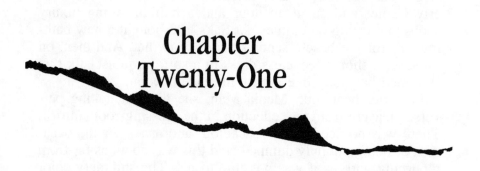

Chapter
Twenty-One

Jim Scheiber flipped open his ID at the front desk of the Beverly Wilshire Hotel. "I'm looking for one of your guests," he told the conservatively suited woman who'd approached him with a smile. "I know she's staying here, but I'm not certain what name she'd be registered under."

It was after eight-thirty. He'd planned to run up to L.A. earlier, but at the thought of holiday-weekend traffic, he'd decided to stop by his house to have supper with Liz and the boys, after all, and wait out the rush hour. Big mistake. By the time he got onto the 405 freeway, it was gridlocked from San Diego all the way up to Malibu with a series of major and minor accidents, the Fourth of July fracas off to a typically early start.

Diverting to alternate routes had turned out to be a slow, frustrating competition with a few million other savvy locals who'd had the same brilliant idea. The entire Southland freeway system had been transformed into a vast, red sea of brake lights that not even flashing lights and a siren could have navigated at anything over a snail's pace. Rather than fight it, Scheiber had opted to go with the flow, doing the only sensible thing he could, under the circumstances, which was to tune the car radio to the oldies station, groove to the Beach Boys and relive his misspent youth.

The woman behind the hotel's long wooden front desk studied his badge briefly, then looked up at him. She seemed puzzled, but her practiced smile barely fluttered. "You're looking for a guest, but you don't have a name?" The gold acetate badge on the lapel of her black suit said her name was B. Latham and that she was the hotel's Assistant Manager/Client Services. She was a streaky blonde, middle-aged and well tended, but without the surgical stiffness he so often saw in women whose self-confidence had been killed by the city's Barbie-doll culture.

Despite all his years on the LAPD, this was only the second time he'd ever ventured into the Beverly Wilshire Hotel. Built in the 1920s, it was a local landmark, with a reputation established on discreet but meticulous service, fabulous facilities and an illustrious clientele. Walking through the heavy front doors, Scheiber's shoes had sounded boorishly loud to him as he crossed the Italian-marble floor laid out in an intricate mosaic design. The hushed lobby was filled with fantastic floral displays, massive antique tables and overstuffed couches that a small child would disappear into. The smell of the place put him in mind of beautiful women, subtle colognes and thick billfolds.

"I know this woman's maiden name," he said. "I'm just not certain that's what she goes by. Or, for that matter, if she's even checked in under her own name. For all I know, she could be with here with a husband."

"Well, Detective, why don't we give the name you've got a shot, and then go from there?" Ms. Latham proposed, indulging him. Her fingers were poised over a computer keyboard. "What is it?"

"Mariah Bolt."

Her hands dropped. "Oh, well, that's an easy one. She's definitely a guest here."

"You're sure?"

"Oh, yes, absolutely. As a matter of fact, you're the second person in the last twenty minutes to ask for her. She's not in, though. If you'd like to leave a message, I'll be sure she gets it."

"You're sure she's not in, without even calling up?"

"Yes. I saw her leave about a half hour ago."

"You must have a lot of people here. You definitely know her to see her?"

"Let's say I made a point of knowing."

"Why is that?"

"It would be indiscreet for me to say, Detective." She shrugged mysteriously.

"Don't tell me," he said. "She's shacked up here with somebody."

"That is not a term I would use. Our guests' private lives are no concern of ours."

"But she is here with someone?" Scheiber asked. Latham nodded. "Okay, look," he said wearily, "I really don't care about that, either, but it's very important I talk to her."

"This is official police business, you said? You're not just some celebrity seeker?"

Scheiber grimaced "Hardly. I'm working a case."

"Well, all right, then. I suppose I could tell you what I know. I turned down the last fellow, mind you, so don't think we do this for everyone. We have a reputation to uphold, you know."

"I really appreciate it," Scheiber said.

"She checked in yesterday," the woman at the desk said. "She said she'd only be here for a night or two at most, but I presume she's staying on tonight, because she hasn't been in touch about checking out, although we know her roommate did leave with his bags this afternoon."

"He wasn't registered?"

"No. He arrived alone and left alone."

"So, just out of curiosity, how do you know he was staying with Mariah Bolt?"

"He's a high-profile person. For one thing, he was seen and recognized by the room-service waiter who delivered their breakfast this morning. The waiter's a young fellow and still a bit starstruck by some of our guests," she added. A little grimace of guilt crossed her face. "Actually, it turns out my manager let this man into Ms. Bolt's room when the gentleman said he wanted to surprise her. It's not something I would have done, myself, mind you. We pride ourselves on personal service here at the Beverly Wilshire, but opening a guest's room to someone else without her permission, no matter who that person may be, is a little beyond the pale, in my opinion.''

''So, I gather this gentleman friend is a powerful person?''

She shrugged. ''If you equate fame with power. Of course, in this city, most people do. When word spread that this fellow was in the hotel, everyone on staff was a little curious about his lady friend, so I'd say most of us know her by sight by now.''

''What?'' Scheiber asked, noticing her smile.

''Our doorman is convinced the lady is some kind of high-priced call girl. Seems before she even got to her guest upstairs, she was out with another man last night. Then after he dropped her off, she slipped out again for an hour or two. Arturo, the doorman, thought she'd gone to turn another trick. That was before I told him the lady was the daughter of Benjamin Bolt.''

''I see. But she's been pretty active, has she?''

''In and out.'' The assistant manager's shoulder rose and fell in a blasé, seen-it-all shrug. ''Maybe just a party animal. We get a lot of those here, as you can imagine—rich people's kids with more money than brains.''

''She strike you as that type?''

''I haven't really spoken to her at length, but just to look at her? Not really. For one thing, she's got to be in her late thirties, I would think. A little old for that circuit, but what do I know?''

''Hmm,'' Scheiber said. ''So, anyway, this high-profile person has left, and Ms. Bolt is not in her room right now?''

''As I said, I saw her leave about a half hour ago.''

''But she definitely hasn't checked out?''

''She was dressed to the nines when she left, and not carrying luggage. I have to presume her things are still in her room. When or whether she'll be back tonight, I couldn't say, but her suite is covered by a credit card, so if Ms. Bolt wants to pay for a suite she's not using...'' The assistant manager's go-figure expression said it all.

''Would you mind if I took a look at it?'' Scheiber asked.

''Why?''

"Just to satisfy myself that she's still around and will show up at some point. If so, I'll leave a message for her to contact me. I may even hang around and wait for her. But if she's not coming back and just hasn't gotten around to telling you, I'd rather know about it sooner than later. As I said, it's critical I talk to her about this case I'm working."

Latham glanced around the lobby, but the place seemed quiet at the moment, and there were at least two other people that Scheiber could see working the front desk. "I suppose I could take you up," she said, nodding. "Hang on while I get a passkey."

As they rode the elevator to the fifth floor, Scheiber asked, "You mentioned that someone else had been looking for her. Did he identify himself?"

"No, but offhand," Latham said, "I'd bet he was a fed of some sort."

"How do you know?"

"I've been in the hotel business twenty-two years, Detective. If you stand at a front desk that long, you get to the point where you can spot certain types at a glance. Like cops. Married people stepping out on their spouses. Hookers—which is why I would have known Ms. Bolt wasn't one, even if I hadn't found out who her father was. You know what I mean. You must do the same thing in your line of work. This way," she added, directing him to the left as the elevator door opened.

"And this caller who might have been a fed...?"

The assistant manager stopped at a door near the end of the hall, rapped twice, then slipped her pass card into the key slot. "Well, not FBI, for sure," she said as she depressed the latch and pushed. "I'd say he looked more like—"

Her words froze in midair and she gasped. Scheiber peered over her shoulder, his left hand preparing to shove her out of harm's way, his right reaching instinctively toward the holster at his back.

But Latham recovered quickly, and she merely shot him a grimace. "I'd describe the other man as looking exactly like this fellow here," she said.

Following her into the pastel-decorated suite, Scheiber saw a very solidly built, bald, middle-aged man standing before the open closet in the inner room, checking out the contents, which included a hanging garment bag and some dresses, from what Scheiber could see. The other man was casually attired, tieless in a sport coat over a black knit shirt. Even so, he looked like the type who might hear the phrase "Yes, sir" on a frequent basis. His smooth dome was certainly no trendy fashion statement. It was the kind of functional simplicity adopted by practitioners of certain hazardous professions with no margin of safety for distractions, like loose hair that flopped in their eyes or got snagged in tight spaces.

When the man looked over toward them, his dark eyes had a single-minded intensity that most people would probably find pretty intimidating. The assistant manager of the Beverly Wilshire Hotel, however, was undaunted.

"Would you mind telling me what you think you're doing?" she demanded, planting her hands on her hips. "And how you got in here?"

The man closed the closet, unhurried, then turned to face them full-on, seeming neither worried nor embarrassed to have been caught red-handed. Nor did Scheiber think he'd make a run for it—although the thought did cross his mind that stopping him would be no simple matter if the big fellow decided to steamroller over them and stroll off.

But finally, the other man deigned to reply. "I'm looking for Mariah Bolt." His voice was deep and gravelly, like a reluctant cement mixer starting up.

"And you thought you'd find her in the closet?" Latham asked dryly.

He liked her a lot, Scheiber decided. She had spunk. But he stepped around her, deciding it was time to take charge of the situation himself. "Who are you?" he asked.

The intruder's focus shifted, and he arched one black eyebrow. "Who am I?" he repeated. "Who are *you?*"

"Detective James Scheiber, Newport Beach P.D. Homicide."

"Homicide, huh?" The big man glanced around him. "No bodies here. Anyway, aren't you a little outside your jurisdiction?"

"A little," Scheiber agreed. "And you would be...?"

The big man hesitated—as if he was trying to decide who

he was today. Not a good sign. "Frank Tucker, Central Intelligence Agency," he said finally.

The assistant manager turned to Scheiber with an I-told-
you-so look. "See? Just what I was about to say."

"You're good," Scheiber agreed. That explained the hes-
itation, he supposed. "You've got some identification, I presume?"

The man scowled and reached into his back hip pocket,
withdrawing a laminated photo-ID card. It was the kind with
a metal clip for attaching to lapels, worn full-time in certain
high-security establishments. "You?" he asked.

Scheiber pulled out the leather folder with his NBPD
badge. They peered at each other's credentials while the
woman from the hotel stood by, arms crossed over her chest.
"Now that we've all been formally introduced," she said,
"would somebody mind explaining what the hell is going on
here? And you," she added to Tucker, "I still want to know
how you got in. I could have you arrested, you know."

"Not by him," Tucker said, cocking his thumb at Scheiber.
"He's off his turf."

"I don't suppose you'd wait while I call the LAPD?" she
asked.

"No, I'm about done here."

"Oh, good," she crooned, "I'm *so* glad to hear it. How
about you move along then?" She turned to Scheiber once
more. "And you, Detective? Have you seen enough?"

Scheiber did a quick survey of the place. In addition to the
dresses he'd spotted in the closet, there was a flowered cosmetics bag in the bathroom and tissue paper strewn on the
bed. A shopping bag from Saks Fifth Avenue sat on one of
the curved, upholstered chairs. He decided to restrain himself
from going through the drawers. Even if it hadn't been out
of his jurisdiction, as this Tucker character kept reminding
him, he had no business searching a room without a warrant.
At the moment, he felt the need to claim a little moral high
ground here.

He nodded to the assistant manager, and she extended one
arm toward the door. "Then, gentlemen, if you please?" She
glared at Tucker as he passed him into the hall. Riding the

elevator back down to the lobby, she looked from one to the other. "Is there anything else either of you will be needing?"

The two men glanced at each other. It occurred to Scheiber that he should leave a message for the Bolt woman to get in touch with him when she returned, but he didn't want Tucker getting away before he'd had a chance to ask him a few questions. He could leave the message afterward. Tucker was watching him, obviously going through some mental calculations of his own. In the end, the two turned simultaneously to Latham and shook their heads.

"Good. And I trust no one will be breaking into any more of my rooms tonight?" she added, glaring pointedly at Tucker. He nodded curtly as the elevator doors opened on the hotel's round, marble-tiled rotunda. "Then if you gentleman will excuse me, the exit is that way." One hand on her hip, she pointed across the lobby to the front door, standing guard until they walked through it.

Outside on Wilshire Boulevard, under one of the hotel's bright yellow, semicircular canopies, Tucker paused, waiting for Scheiber, then followed him a little way up the sidewalk toward Rodeo, out of earshot. The evening was warm and fragrant with the smell of the night jasmine dripping from the hotel's window boxes, and the air crackled now and again with the sound of illicit firecrackers as the holiday weekend kicked off early. LAPD Patrols would spend half their time over the next couple of nights chasing down reports of kids with Mexican cherry bombs, Scheiber mused.

"So, CIA, huh?" he said quietly, leaning against the hotel's gray brick walls. A couple of elderly German tourists in matching plaid shorts stood at the corner, trying to explain to a passerby how to use their complicated-looking camcorder.

"Guilty as charged," Tucker said. He turned his back to the video camera, Scheiber noted, dropping casually into deep shadow as the couple took up a pose under the Rodeo Drive street sign and smiled for the agreeable stranger they'd dragooned into service. Obviously, the man's instinct for camouflage was deeply ingrained.

"You work out of Langley?" Scheiber asked him.

"That's right. What about you? What are you doing up here, so far off your turf?"

"Not as far off as you are, but I'm here for the same reason. Looking for Mariah Bolt."

"Why?"

"I want to talk to her about a possible homicide."

"Who's the victim?"

Scheiber frowned. "What is this, Twenty Questions? Look, let's get one thing straight. This is not your field to control. I'm willing for the moment to overlook this little break-and-enter stunt you just pulled, instead of hauling your ass into the nearest LAPD division, like I should—"

"Like you could."

"Don't get into a pissing contest with me, Tucker. In the first place, I spent eighteen years on the LAPD, and I know this city like the back of my hand, not to mention every cop in it. No matter what the badge says, this is my turf. In the second place, I've been stuck in traffic nearly three hours. I've got a dead guy on my hands down in Newport, and it's looking more and more like my Fourth of July with my family is about to be shot to hell. All in all, I'm in a really lousy mood. So what do you say we extend a little professional courtesy both ways, huh?"

"Fine. Who's the victim?" Tucker repeated.

Scheiber sighed. "Guy by the name of Albert Jacob Korman, nickname Chap. Ever hear of him?"

The stony face finally broke and revealed some kind of reaction. "Korman's dead? How?"

"He was found this morning on the bottom of his hot tub."

"Murdered," Tucker said. It was a statement, not a question.

"You say that like you know it for a fact," Scheiber said, eyes narrowing. What did all this have to do with the frigging CIA?

"Wasn't he?" From the skeptical way he said it, there was little doubt he thought Korman *had* been murdered.

"It wasn't obvious from the body. We won't know for sure until the autopsy. What do you know about him?"

Tucker shrugged. "Never laid eyes on the man. I just know he was a literary agent."

"That's right, and he represented Mariah Bolt's father." The other man nodded. Scheiber asked, "And the CIA? Why are they so interested in this business that you'd break into Ms. Bolt's hotel room?''

"I didn't say the CIA was interested in her. I said *I* was looking for her. She's a friend,'' Tucker added quickly, just as Scheiber was getting ready to rip into him for yet another evasive answer. "I spoke to her this morning.''

"A close friend?''

"Yes.'' The man's monosyllabic answers said a lot more than the longer ones, Scheiber noted. He had a feeling that, however friendly Tucker and this Bolt woman were, maybe their relationship wasn't as close as the big guy would have wished.

"From what I hear, she seems to have a lot of friends,'' he said.

Sure enough, Tucker bristled. "What's that supposed to mean?'' And then something flickered across his face, the look gone before Scheiber could read it, and his expression went blank again. "Paul Chaney,'' he said. "He's staying with her.''

Aha! Scheiber thought. So that was the high-profile friend the starstruck waiter had delivered breakfast to. "I gather he checked out this afternoon,'' Scheiber said. "Ms. Bolt, meantime, apparently did a fair amount of coming and going last night. You know anything about that?''

"I doubt it's important. She's working here.''

That was the doorman's theory, too, Scheiber recalled wryly, but somehow he didn't think Tucker meant to suggest she was *that* kind of working girl. "What does she do?'' he asked. When the other man didn't answer, he groaned, "Oh, lordy. Don't tell me she's a spook, too?''

"I can't talk about that.''

"Yeah, right. Why am I not surprised? Well, in that case, try this. What can you tell me about her father's unpublished papers? Some journals and a novel, apparently?''

"What about them?''

"Where they are, for example? I gather Korman was supposed to be holding them, but if they're in his house, I couldn't find them.''

Tucker frowned. "Could he have given them back to Mariah?''

"She never got to see him before he died," Scheiber said, relaying what he'd learned from the woman's phone message and from Korman's next-door neighbor. "She doesn't even know he's dead, for that matter. That's one of the reasons I was trying to track her down. She mentioned someone named Urquhart when she called. My partner looked into it and found out there's a Louis Urquhart who's some kind of literary bigwig?"

Tucker nodded. "He's working on a biography of Mariah's father."

"Is there any chance Korman would have given the papers to him? Maybe to study?"

"Unlikely. But on the other hand," Tucker added, "if they are missing—"

"Those papers would have to be pretty valuable, I would think. Valuable enough to get Korman murdered?"

Tucker shifted restlessly. "I've got places to go," he said. Another non-reply.

"Where?" When he didn't answer, Scheiber guessed. "You're planning to pay a call on this Urquhart character, aren't you? Uh-uh, I don't think so. Not without me, anyway."

Tucker said nothing, but eighteen years of working the streets had taught Scheiber to recognize the early warning signs of a situation quickly going south—the cornered drug dealer getting ready to bolt, the gangbanger who didn't want to be frisked, the traffic stop that turned deadly. Tiny indications appeared, like the first flicker of muscle movement that precedes sudden action. Before the big man could actually move, Scheiber had already dropped back to steady his stance and simultaneously withdraw his gun from his waist holster, taking no chances. Tucker saw it and froze, his black eyes assessing and evidently calculating the odds. Scheiber flipped out his cell phone, too, and one-handedly hit the rapid dial button to his old division.

"I'm connecting to the LAPD area watch commander," he said. "You have mere seconds before they pick up, Tucker, so think carefully. You figure you can run and I won't try to stop you? Think again." His thumb flicked the safety off his nine millimeter. "And even if I miss, which is doubtful at this range, how far you think you can get in three minutes? Because that's the squad car response time in this neighborhood. Average. This place—" he cocked the phone back at the hotel "—this place they'd come a lot faster." He held up the cell phone, speaker toward Tucker as the first ring sounded.

"Scheiber, look—"

"No, *you* look. I still haven't heard a single word of explanation why my dead guy down there in Newport should be presumed murdered, but you seem to think he was. That makes you a material witness from where I'm standing. What are you doing here, anyway? Is this some kind of rogue Company operation? You guys think you're going to drop a murder down some black Ops hole where the light of day never shines? Well, think again, pardner. Not on my watch."

The line on the other end rang a second time.

The big man studied him closely, and Scheiber had the sense his measure was being taken. He steeled himself, anticipating the possibility of a head-on tackle. Hating the idea, knowing it would be like being run over by a refrigerator. The fact that the guy probably had a few years on him was small consolation.

"We're both getting too old for this macho shit, Tucker. What do you say you drop the Company tough-guy routine and we just cooperate, huh?"

As the phone on the other end of the connection rang again, Tucker seemed to make up his mind. "I'm not here in any official capacity," he admitted.

Scheiber broke the phone connection.

"The fact is," Tucker went on, "I'm so far off the agency clock you'd be doing them a favor by hauling me in. But if you do, Scheiber, I can pretty much guarantee you'll never get to the bottom of what really happened to Korman. There's people who'll make sure of it. And the worst of it is, I'm not sure it'll stop there."

"And you, out here looking for the Bolt woman? Is that against orders, too? Is she AWOL like you?"

Tucker didn't reply.

Scheiber raised the phone once more, finger poised over the rapid dial button. "Last chance," he said.

"It's personal," Tucker muttered. Once again, Scheiber imagined a world of detail in those turgid responses.

"Okay, here's the deal," he said. "You tell me what you know. If I think it's worthwhile—and if you can convince me you had nothing to do with Korman's death—we'll go together and pay a call on Professor Urquhart. Then we come back and wait for Ms. Bolt to return. I'm guessing she'll want to know that her father's agent has died, and I want to hear what she can tell me about him." When Tucker didn't immediately answer, Scheiber nodded at the cell phone. "The alternative is that I just haul your ass in. Did I mention, by the way, that the watch commander on duty tonight is a Lieutenant Al Green? He and I go back a long way. I'm godfather to his firstborn child, as a matter of fact. If I say you need to be booked, Green will arrest first, ask questions later. It's now—" Scheiber glanced at his watch "—9:03 p.m. on the eve of a Fourth of July holiday. How long do you suppose you'll have to sit in a jail cell before you get a bail hearing? What happens to your lady friend while you're cooling your heels in there? And what do you suppose are the chances your Company friends won't track you down in the meantime? In fact," Scheiber added, "I'm about ready to call them myself and ask what the hell a loose cannon like you is doing out here, messing up my day. So, what's it going to be?"

"Fine," Tucker grumbled. "We'll do it your way. Let's go see Urquhart."

In retrospect, it turned out to be one of the worst bargains he'd made in a while. But he'd stood in one place long enough, Tucker decided, and the best chance of moving forward with minimal fuss seemed to be to accept Scheiber's deal.

The Newport cop had already saved him some trouble by researching Urquhart's home address. But the UCLA campus was closer, Scheiber said, so they decided to try their luck there first. En route, Tucker gave him an extremely abbreviated account of his relationship to Mariah and what he knew about Korman and Urquhart. He certainly wasn't about to tell him about his trip to Moscow to meet the Navigator, nor the thirty-year old files that pointed to another set of murders that

Korman's death was probably designed to keep hidden. The question was, did Korman's killer know someone else had stumbled onto the truth about the death of Benjamin Bolt?

By the time they arrived near the center of the UCLA campus in Westwood, Scheiber seemed more confused and irritated than ever. Tucker found himself praying that Urquhart was off in Timbuktu or somewhere equally inaccessible, so he could lose the Newport detective and get on with his own business.

They found the way into the parking lot nearest Dickson Plaza, where Urquhart's office was apparently located, blocked by an LAPD cruiser parked at an angle across the drive. As Scheiber slowed his car, a uniformed officer walked toward them, hand raised, urging them back. Scheiber killed the air-conditioning, and as both he and Tucker rolled down their windows, a blast of dry heat blew across the front of the car. It wasn't awful for this time of year, Tucker thought. At least there was none of the dense, dripping humidity he'd left behind in Virginia.

"Hey, Stern, you old son of a gun," Scheiber called. "How you doing?"

The officer leaned down and peered into the window. "Detective Scheiber? That you? Well, hey! What brings you back to this neck of the woods?" he asked, reaching through the open window.

"Just couldn't stay away from the big-city lights," Scheiber said as they shook hands. The cop glanced across the front seat. "Frank Tucker," Scheiber added, cocking his thumb.

The young cop nodded briefly, then turned his attention back to the detective. "I hear you got married," he said.

"Yup. Just got back from the honeymoon in Rosarita."

"Tough life. How you liking it down in Newport?"

"Quieter than here, that's for sure. What's going on?" he added, nodding in the direction of the spinning red lights.

"Some professor croaked in his office. Campus cops were caught short-handed, what with the holiday, and all, so they called us in."

Scheiber glanced over, and Tucker knew they were both experiencing the same sinking premonition of having arrived too late. "This professor," Scheiber said, "his name wouldn't be Urquhart, by any chance, would it?"

"Yeah, how'd you know?" the cop asked, surprised.

Scheiber sighed heavily. "We were just on our way to look for the guy. Was he murdered?"

"Could be. Not obvious how, I gather, but they say a witness thinks something fishy went down here."

Tucker watched as Scheiber closed his eyes briefly. "Déjà vu all over again," the detective said, head shaking. "When did this happen?"

"Couple of hours ago," the patrol officer replied.

"Who's working the case?"

"Ripley and a guy named McEvoy from the U.C.L.A. P.D."

"You want to let me through?" Scheiber asked. "I think I'd better go have a talk with them. We might have some information they could use."

"Yeah, sure thing. Park in the lot up ahead, in front of my cruiser."

"Where's the professor's office?"

"Hertzberg Building, Dickson Plaza. Third floor. You'll see the guys when you get there. They can direct you."

"Okay, thanks. Good to see you."

"Yeah, you, too, Detective."

Scheiber parked the car. "Damn, it's hot," he complained, getting out of the car. "I think the bloody temperature rose instead of falling when the sun set."

"No kidding." Tucker nodded. "Okay if I leave my jacket in your car?"

"Yeah, sure," Scheiber said, waving distractedly.

Tucker slipped it off and dropped it on the seat. Scheiber locked the vehicle, and they headed up a tree-lined walkway to a broad plaza at the heart of the campus. Sodium vapor streetlights cast dappled yellow light across the pavement.

"I guess this lends some credence to your theory Korman was murdered, too," Scheiber said.

"I didn't actually say that," Tucker pointed out as they approached the wide front steps of a castlelike stone building. A brass plaque next to the carved oak double doors identified it as the Hertzberg Building of the Arts and Humanities. They made slow progress going up the steps. Scheiber, as advertised, seemed to know every LAPD cop on the beat, all of whom stopped to shake his hand, then wave him forward to the next in the gauntlet. Tucker sailed by in his wake, presumed, he knew, to be one of Scheiber's Newport police colleagues.

When they finally made it inside and up the stairs to the third floor, Scheiber explained again that they had information for the detectives in charge of the investigation. This time, although the cop standing guard outside the scene was friendly toward the detective, he frowned when he caught sight of Tucker. "Who's he?" he asked point-blank.

"Name's Frank Tucker."

"He work with you?"

"No, he's...um...a possible witness," Scheiber said.

The cop nodded slowly. "Okay, hang on. I'll go tell Detective Ripley you're here."

Tucker watched the officer head off down the brightly lit hall. *Now what was that all about?* The place smelled of disinfectant, he noted, the kind that brought back memories of a crusty old janitor and being detained after school for playing baseball too close to a window, which had paid the inevitable price for his grand slam home run. A custodial cleaning cart stood abandoned halfway down the hall. The speckled green linoleum on the floor was rippled from the tramping of thousands of pairs of feet over the many years since the old building had opened.

It was several minutes before a plainclothes detective emerged from an office toward the end of the hall and approached them. Detective Will Ripley backslapped Scheiber heartily, but his smile vanished as he nodded curtly at Tucker when Scheiber made introductions. Then Ripley took his former colleague aside. They were out of earshot, but by the way the LAPD detective glanced periodically over his shoulder, it was obvious he wanted a clear explanation who Tucker was and why he had suddenly appeared at his crime scene. Finally, after some intense discussion, the two detectives returned. Now Scheiber was frowning, too.

"CIA, huh?" Ripley said, studying Tucker closely. "What

do you know? You say you were acquainted with Professor Urquhart?''

"No, I didn't say that at all. I only heard his name yesterday for the first time,'' Tucker said, suddenly wondering whether coming along with Scheiber had been such a good idea, after all.

"How'd you hear about the professor?'' Ripley asked.

"It's a long story.''

"I see. Well, maybe you'll tell me about it later.'' Ripley turned to Scheiber once more. "Come on and have a look. You, too, Tucker,'' he added over his shoulder.

They followed Ripley down to the door from which he'd emerged. There, another young detective—McEvoy, from the U.C.L.A. police it seemed—came out, and was introduced over cryptic glances in Tucker's direction.

"I'll have to ask you to stay back here by the door so as not to muck up the scene while the guys do their thing,'' Ripley told them, "but feel free to take a look inside.'' He and McEvoy stood aside, watching while Scheiber and Tucker peered in.

The office was standard university fare, on the large side, as befit a senior professor, its stock institutional fittings supplemented by personal touches like framed photos and awards on the walls, plants, an Oriental carpet and a variety of tchotchkes on the shelves. All the dross and dreck of a long career. A couple of crime-scene investigators wearing white latex gloves were moving around the room, taking photographs and dusting for prints.

Directly opposite the door, a man—Louis Urquhart, Tucker presumed—was slumped in a high-backed leather chair, his head lying on the big oak desk in front of him. It rested sideways on one outstretched arm, next to an open book. He looked as if he'd paused for a catnap in the middle of reading. His hair was gray and thin on top. His outstretched right hand, bearing a heavy gold signet ring on one finger, lay extended, palm down. His left arm was folded beside his head. He wore a heavy watch of buffed gold, the thick leather strap well worn—the kind of watch handed down to sons and grandsons. Urquhart looked peaceful and relaxed, but despite the absence of any sign of violence, Tucker knew the man wasn't sleeping.

"Did he have any wounds?" he asked.

Ripley shook his head. "Nada, aside from what looks like a tiny paper cut on his right palm. Nothing missing that we can tell, either, although we'll have to have someone who knew the premises come in and help us make a thorough inventory. But that watch he's wearing is an old Rolex. The ring didn't come out of a Cracker Jack box, either. Whatever went down here, it wasn't about robbery."

"Any files missing?" Scheiber asked, peering behind the door at a bank of three steel-drawered cabinets.

Ripley arched an eyebrow. "I don't know. Should there be?"

The Newport detective shrugged. "You might want to talk to his secretary, find out whether he had a research assistant. He was apparently working on a biography of Benjamin Bolt—the author, you know?" Ripley nodded vaguely. "Anyway, if you can find anyone who's familiar with his research, it would be interesting to know if any of the stuff is missing, especially as it relates to Bolt."

McEvoy, the younger of the two LAPD detectives, looked skeptical. "We're not even sure we've got a homicide on our hands here, and you've already got a motive? Which is what? Professional rivalry? Somebody wanting to scoop the professor? How do you know?"

"I don't," Scheiber replied, "and I'm not even saying that's what it was. I'm just saying it's worth looking into." He turned back to Ripley. "I was talking to Stern out in the road. He said there was a witness who saw something suspicious go down?"

Ripley nodded. "An office cleaner. She'd finished in here, and had spoken to the professor while she was working. Said he seemed fine. Then, while she was doing next door, she heard what she thought was a cry, but she had the vacuum and a mariachi station on, so she wasn't sure. When she finished next door and went to move on down the hall a couple of minutes later, though, she saw a guy leaving Urquhart's office and heading for the stairs at a brisk clip."

"And Urquhart?" Scheiber asked.

"Unfortunately," Ripley said, "she didn't think to look in on him right then."

"Du-uh!" young McEvoy said, rolling his eyes.

"She thought the guy she'd seen leaving in a hurry was just some colleague of Urquhart's," Ripley added. "It was only when she'd finished cleaning the last office and was getting ready to leave that she finally got around to looking back in here. She found Urquhart just like this. Tried to wake him and realized he was dead. Dispatcher said she was hysterical when she called 911."

"She actually saw the killer?" Tucker said.

"And the killer didn't see her?" Scheiber added.

"Apparently not, luckily enough, or we'd probably be without an eyewitness," Ripley answered.

"Looks like a very professional hit," young McEvoy said sagely. "Guy worked fast. We know Urquhart was alive at a little after six, when the cleaner estimated she left his office, but dead by six forty-three, when the dispatcher took the call."

Tucker's gaze traveled up the office walls covered in framed photographs and diplomas. Several were hanging askew, as if an earthquake had recently shaken the place. Or maybe, he thought, someone had been looking behind them, searching for hiding places. It was the only sign of disorder in the place. It was a hit and it was very professional, as McEvoy said. Very KGB.

His eyes focused on the photos in the frames. There were about a dozen of them, mostly of the dead man, it seemed, in various locales and with various unrecognizable people. But one photo was of another man, alone—Mariah's father, Tucker realized with a start. It was one of the most famous pictures of Bolt, reproduced on the backs of his books and elsewhere. Mariah had told him once that her mother had taken the picture with an old Instamatic camera, near the cottage at Newport where Mariah had grown up. Her father stood on sand that seemed to stretch out behind him forever, waves crashing on a pristine shoreline. He'd been a fair-haired, good-looking guy. In the photo, he was wearing a simple white cotton shirt, his thumbs hooked in the pockets of his faded jeans. His bare feet sank in the sand. Brilliant light and shadow played on his even features, but his gray-eyed gaze was direct, his expression not so much serious as preoccupied, as if he'd been lost in thought a split second before being interrupted and asked to look at the camera. A portrait of the artist as a very young man—practically a kid, Tucker thought grimly—but a father, too, whose sober gray eyes he'd passed on to the little girl he'd abandoned.

He turned away from the photo with a shake of his head, and after one last glance at the dead man, stepped back into the hall—only to be startled by the sound of a piercing shriek. He swung around to find that Ripley had slipped away while he was staring at the pictures on Urquhart's wall, and now stood a couple of doors down, holding a middle-aged Hispanic woman by the elbow as she screamed, *"El es el asesino! El es el asesino!"*

The murderer she was hysterically pointing to was himself. Before he had time to react, Tucker found himself slammed up against a wall with his hands behind his back, held there by half a dozen uniformed officers who'd appeared out of nowhere. A pair of handcuffs clamped painfully onto his wrists.

"Scheiber!" he bellowed. "What the hell's going on here?"

"She says you're the one she saw in the hall," Scheiber replied. "When the officer on the stairs saw you come up with me, he thought her description fit you to a T."

"I didn't kill anybody! I was at LAX, just getting off a flight from Washington when this happened."

"She seems to think it was you," Ripley said.

"This is nuts. All you have to do is check with United Airlines. They'll confirm I was on the flight."

"Have you still got your boarding pass?" Scheiber asked him.

He thought about it. "No, I threw it out, I think. But I've got the ticket stub. It's in my rental car back at the Beverly Wilshire."

"We'll be looking into that," Detective Ripley said.

"No, *he* can check it out," Tucker said, nodding at the Newport detective. "Scheiber, the keys are in my jacket in your car. The rental's a dark blue Taurus. You can get the ticket out of the glove compartment—and that's *all* you can touch. As for you," he added, turning his head back toward Ripley, "you do not have my permission to go anywhere near my personal property. Are we clear on that?" He was thinking of the laptop and the diskette with the Navigator's information, locked in the trunk of the car. Scheiber was out of his jurisdiction and had no grounds to search. The LAPD detective would need a warrant incident to arrest to get into the car. With any luck, Scheiber would find the ticket and his innocence would be established long before Ripley could write up an affidavit and find a judge to approve the search warrant. At least, that was Tucker's fervent hope.

"Perfectly clear," Ripley said, "but in the meantime, you're going to have to come with us." He nodded to one of the uniforms, who patted him down for weapons.

"I'm not carrying," Tucker said wearily. "I just got off a plane, for God's sake." They pulled him off the wall and turned him around. "Scheiber, this is completely bogus. You can't let them arrest me. You know I didn't do this."

"I don't know that at all. All I know is that I found you rifling through a hotel room you'd broken into two hours after the professor was murdered. You had plenty of time to get from here to there."

"Why the hell would I have come over here with you if I had done this?"

"You didn't know the cleaning lady had seen you," young McEvoy said.

"It wasn't me she saw, dammit!" He turned back to Scheiber. "If you'll just check with the airline—" He paused.

"What?" Scheiber asked.

Tucker closed his eyes and shook his head, sighing heavily. This wasn't the way to win friends and influence people, but he had to confess. He didn't want to spend the weekend in jail. Scheiber, he knew, would insist on corroborating the ticket by checking it against the airline passenger manifest before he'd vouch for him with Ripley. But he wasn't going to find the name Frank Tucker on either the ticket or the manifest.

"I was travelling under an alias," he admitted. "I had good

operational reasons for it. The point is, I used a different set of ID.''

"How convenient," McEvoy said scathingly.

Tucker ignored him. "I'm telling you the truth, Scheiber. The name was Grant Lewis. The fake ID is also in the jacket I left in your car." He nodded at one of the crime-scene investigators. "Let this guy take a Polaroid of me. Then try to run down the crew of United's Washington–L.A. flight. It left Dulles at three fifty-five, local time. I was in the first class section, and I spoke with one of the flight attendants. I don't know her name, but she was thirty-ish, blond, good-looking—''

"Oh, yeah," McEvoy snorted. "Should be really easy to find. There can't be many like that."

Tucker ignored him. "She told me she had a real early return run tomorrow morning. That's United Airlines, Scheiber. Do it, will you, please?''

Scheiber still looked doubtful. "If you were going to operate undercover, why did you introduce yourself to me as Tucker? Is that even your real name?''

"It is. I gave it to you because I thought you might cut Frank Tucker of the CIA a little more professional slack than a Grant Lewis, anonymous businessman. Obviously, I was wrong."

"Yeah, well, I'm sure Detectives Ripley and McEvoy will follow up on the airline thing," Scheiber said.

"Right. While I stew in a cell all weekend. Come on, Scheiber!" Tucker said angrily. "What have you got to lose except the Korman case?''

"Who's Korman?" Ripley asked.

"Another case I'm working," Scheiber said, irritated. "That's what brought me up here in the first place. I needed to talk to a lady at the Beverly Wilshire, and that's where I ran into this guy." He stood for a moment, smoothing down his peppered mustache. "Godammit, there goes my weekend." Nodding at the CSI with the Polaroid, he asked Ripley, "Would you mind, Will? On the off chance this guy's telling the truth and there is a link between these two cases, we're going to have to coordinate, anyway. I might as well do a little of the legwork.''

"Hey, buddy," Ripley said to him, waving over the investigator with the camera, "you want to do my grunt work, it's okay by me. Personally, though, I think we're looking at an open and shut here."

"Open and shut," young McEvoy echoed, nodding enthusiastically.

Tucker was tempted to head-butt the little parrot right in his obnoxious beak.

Chapter
Twenty-Two

Mariah was twenty minutes late arriving at Spago. The trendy Beverly Hills establishment was more than a restaurant that prided itself on the quality of its menu and the celebrity quotient of its clientele. It was a cultural experience, a Tinseltown event.

It took several minutes for her to struggle her way through the crowd of hopeful diners in the lounge and bar, some with reservations, some foolishly without. Working to quell the nervous flutters in her stomach, she tried in vain to catch the ear of the maître d', while next to her, two young women from Georgia breathlessly recounted the famous people they'd already spotted in the hour and a half they'd been waiting—a group that ran the gamut, apparently, from several TV-sitcom stars and an actress who'd recently written a tell-all biography to a grandmotherly sex counselor who was a regular on the talk-show circuit. It was a clever businessman, Mariah thought wryly, who controlled his overhead by letting the paying customers serve as the floor show. On the other hand, the celebrities knew what they were getting into when they walked through the door. It was no doubt a mutually gratifying experience.

When she was finally able to get a word in edgewise with

a hostess and mention that she was there to meet Paul Chaney—news that brought wide-eyed gasps from the Georgia
tourists—the manager suddenly materialized at her side to
whisk her off into the restaurant's inner sanctum. "Oh, yes,
indeed, Ms. Bolt!" he said warmly. "They've been waiting
for you."

They?

Mariah clutched her silk shawl around her as he led her
through the bar and past an outdoor garden room, then down
the center of two long rows of tables lining a room decorated
in warm terra-cotta and wood. At the end, sitting in a corner
booth with a commanding view of all the action, she saw
Paul's golden head rising above dried-floral arrangements. A
couple was sitting opposite him in the booth, she realized, a
man and a woman. Her first thought was that Paul had
brought along moral support as he prepared to deliver the bad
news that he was giving her the heave-ho. Maybe he thought
she'd restrain herself a little better—no crying or pleading or
slashing her wrists—if he dumped her in front of witnesses.

But when he spotted her and got hurriedly to his feet, his
glance back at the table was fraught with more nervousness
than Mariah would have expected in such a self-assured man.
As soon as she recognized his table companions, his unease
made perfect sense.

The manager announced her cheerfully. "Here she is at
last!"

"Mariah, hi," Paul said, kissing her cheek, his hand cupping her arm and drawing her toward him. "You look beautiful." Mariah vaguely felt his touch on her skin, but she was
so shocked she hardly registered his presence or his words.
He turned to the manager. "Thanks, Chuck, I can take it from
here." As the other man nodded and took his leave, Paul
turned back to her. "Mariah—"

"I don't believe it," she said, facing him at last. "How
could you do this?"

"You mustn't blame him, Mariah," Renata said from her
corner of the booth, her smile both smug and chilling. If Mariah had felt nervous coming in, it was nothing compared to
the abject, unreasoning anxiety she was feeling now—like
Gretel, as the old woman from the gingerbread cottage sized

her up for the roasting pan. "Paul mentioned when he called this afternoon that the two of you were having dinner here. I decided to horn in, I'm afraid. You remember my son, Nolan?"

He was already on his feet, hand thrust out toward her. Mariah nodded slowly as she shook it. Blandly handsome, he was obviously trying to blind her with his megawatt smile. Like Paul's strategy of delivering bad news in crowded places, Nolan's high-potency charm, she suspected, was meant to put her off her guard, short-circuit her defensive reactions. Her brain was still trying to wrap itself around the news that Paul had called Renata that afternoon.

"It's great to see you again," Nolan went on blithely. "I wanted to catch up with you at the Romanov opening, but with all the people there..." His grimace and shrug communicated the weighty burden of *noblesse oblige* that he'd had to carry as host in his grandfather's museum. "I'm quite a fan of your father's work. You must be so very proud of him."

"Oh, endlessly," she replied, wishing he would just sit down and be quiet so she could think. What on earth was Paul doing calling Renata Hunter Carr behind her back? Of all the ways he might have chosen to betray her, surely he had to know this was the only one she'd be hard-pressed to forgive.

Renata, meantime, prattled on, oblivious. "I've known Chuck there forever," she said, waving a ring-decked hand at the manager. He was doing the rounds of the room, glad-handing his way from table to table, checking the wine and satisfaction levels of patrons who all seemed to know each other and him. Old home week in Beverly Hills. "I prevailed upon him to lay on an extra place setting," Renata said, adding an indulgent smile at her son, "and then Nolan happened to show up, too."

"I was supposed to be meeting some people here," he explained. "They'd just phoned to say they were running late when I spotted Mother and Paul."

"Yes, your mother and Paul," Mariah said, relieved they were back to the real issue. "What a surprise."

"If it makes you uncomfortable having me here, Mariah, I

won't stay long,'' Renata said. ''I'll just say my piece, and then we'll leave you two alone to your quiet dinner, won't we, Nolan? You can think about what I have to say at your leisure. If you want, we'll talk again when you get down to Newport. Do you remember where my father's old summerhouse is? Your father brought you there once when you were a little girl.''

Mariah had a sudden image of a many-gabled house high on a cliff overlooking water. She had no memory of her father taking her there, but even as Renata mentioned it, she pictured herself standing on a black-and-white-checked floor in a wood-lined entry hall. She remembered looking up to a Tiffany-domed ceiling that, to a little girl, had seemed miles high. And, she recalled suddenly, there were gargoyles atop the stone pilasters on either side of the big front door. Her father had laughed when she recoiled from their gruesome faces. Who else could they have visited in such a grand home?

''On the Corona del Mar side, overlooking the harbor?'' Renata prompted. ''You can ask anyone down there, they'll point it out to you. Paul, did you give her the keys?''

''Keys?'' Mariah felt the pressure of his hand on her arm, trying to steer her toward his side of the banquette, but she shrugged it off. ''What keys?''

''Why don't you sit down, and I'll explain,'' he suggested.

She was getting a very bad feeling about this. ''What keys, dammit?''

''Paul mentioned you were looking for a beach house,'' Renata said, clearly determined to take charge of the situation. ''I have several, including a couple that are vacant at the moment. I told him you and Lindsay would be welcome to use any one you wanted for as long as you liked.''

''I don't believe this.'' Mariah turned her back on the woman and addressed herself to this man with whom she'd made love only hours earlier, fool that she was. Was this her mother's legacy? Insidious genetic programming driving her into a relationship with an untrustworthy man, like some horny lemming jumping off the cliff of her own stupidity? ''I noticed you moved yourself out of the room,'' she muttered.

"I was afraid you'd react this way," Paul murmured. "I wasn't sure you'd want me there afterward."

"You got that right. For God's sake, Paul! You went to *her* about the stupid beach house? I wasn't that desperate."

"No. The subject just happened to come up when Renata and I were talking a couple of weeks ago—"

"'Renata'? 'Paul'? A couple of *weeks* ago?" Mariah echoed. "I had no idea the two of you were so chummy. How odd that all this time you never thought to mention it."

"I was only trying to help," he said. "Renata got in touch with me recently, looking for advice on how to approach you about your father's papers. When I found out why, I had to help. After all, it was my fault the news leaked out about you finding them. Maybe I shouldn't have interfered, but now that it's done, could you let her say her piece? Let's just get through it, and then you can tell me what a jerk I am."

"Let's *us* get through it?" Mariah echoed. "Why should I have to get through anything? Why would you imagine you could go behind my back like this and I would blithely accept it? You knew how I felt about her."

"Mariah, please," Renata said in the voice mothers use with unreasonable children winding up for a temper tantrum in a public place, "I prevailed upon Paul's good offices to help me contact you before I knew you'd be at the Romanov reception. I told you last night that it was important we talk."

Mariah turned at last to face her head-on. "And I seem to recall saying we had nothing to discuss."

Renata glanced around the room, as if daring anyone to have the temerity to stare. Her son was still standing, wearing that awkward, fixed smile. Renata turned back and locked her bluesteel gaze on Mariah. "You, my dear, are drawing a ridiculous amount of attention to yourself. Would you consent to sit for just five minutes?"

"Here, Mariah, why don't you slip in next to me?" Nolan offered, apparently thinking his charms would succeed where Paul's had failed.

"I'm not slipping in anywhere."

"*Please,*" Renata said, almost as a weary afterthought. "Let me tell you why I think it's in your best interest—and in your daughter's by the way—"

"You leave my daughter out of this."

"Well, I would, but unfortunately, she's implicated, whether you like it or not. I presume she's aware she's Ben's granddaughter, so this will affect her, too. For Lindsay's sake, if not your own, take five minutes to hear what I have to say. Then, if that's your wish, I will go away and never bother you again, let the chips fall where they may. Do you think you could manage at least that?"

She was a dreadful woman, Mariah decided. But as she glanced around, she noticed that many eyes were, indeed, cast their way. Paul stood beside her, arms dangling at his sides, looking more distressed than she'd even seen him. This was exactly the kind of public scene he hated. Good. Let him squirm, Mariah thought. At that point, she could have happily throttled him.

But she grabbed an empty chair, set it down in front of the table and dropped into it. No way was she getting herself wedged into a booth between any of them. "Five minutes," she said, clutching her shawl around her, knuckles white as she gripped her small purse. She glanced at her watch. "Starting now."

Paul settled back into the curved, black leather banquette. "Mariah, this is serious, what she has to tell you."

"Then she should begin, because the clock is ticking."

She leaned back in her chair and waited, but instead of an explanation, the first words out of Renata's mouth were ones Mariah had often heard before, though rarely accompanied by such a wistful sigh. "You look remarkably like your father," the older woman said.

"So I gather. My mother often said the same thing."

Renata froze momentarily, then nodded. "Touché, my dear. I imagine she must have found it as disconcerting as I do."

Mariah glanced at Nolan, feeling embarrassed for him in spite of her own discomfort. How could he feel, watching his mother pine over the memory of a man who wasn't his father? But if he was bothered by it, it didn't show.

"More so, I would think," Mariah said, turning back to Renata. "She was his *wife,* after all, and devoted to him. Loved and supported him for eight long years. Bore his two children, and mourned him with her dying breath, despite the lovers he'd taken over the years they were together." She looked the other woman dead in the eye. "You do know, of course, that you were only one of many?"

"Yes. But thank you for reminding me."

"And you lasted...what? A few weeks before you abandoned him?"

"Two months. And touché again," Renata said. There was a glass on amber liquid in ice on the table in front of her. She lifted it and took a stiff belt. At the precise moment she drained it, a waiter appeared, as if by magic.

"Can I get you a refill, Mrs. Carr?"

"Please," she said, straight-arming the glass.

"And you, madam?" he asked, turning to Mariah. "A cocktail?"

"No, nothing. I won't be staying."

"Oh, well, very good. Mr. Chaney?"

Paul shook his head grimly and waved the fellow away.

Mariah glanced at her watch. "Three minutes left."

"Oh, fine!" Renata snapped. "If that's the way you insist on being, here it is. You can't allow *Man in the Middle* to be published. It's not Ben's work. He stole it from another writer."

"You're referring to the unpublished manuscript I found among his papers, I presume? The one that's supposed to be plagiarized from someone else?"

Renata seemed surprised. "You know?"

"I've heard there's such a theory kicking around, but I've seen no proof. I have seen the manuscript, however, and I'm virtually certain it was produced on my father's old typewriter. There was something niggling in the back of my mind, and this afternoon, I finally remembered what it was. His typewriter had a mechanical eccentricity that lifted the letter E a little above the type line. When I was little, he used to tell me it was his lucky typewriter, and that those were his Magical Flying E's. He took the machine when he moved out. The manuscript is full of flying E's."

Renata waved a well-manicured hand. "He retyped it. But the novel was written by Anatoly Orlov."

"The Russian?"

"That's right. Ben met him in Paris. Orlov was very old. He'd been struggling against the Communist leadership for years, and he knew it was probably the last time he'd ever be allowed to leave the Soviet Union, so he smuggled out a *samizdat* novel and gave it to Ben in the hope he could find a publisher for it in the West."

Mariah frowned. "I don't think so. What I read of that manuscript is in perfect, colloquial American English. I don't know whether Orlov spoke English or not, but even if he did, I doubt any foreigner could have written with that kind of native confidence. Not only that, but I've read his work, in the original Russian and in translation—as much of it as was ever published, anyway. This manuscript is nothing like his stuff. Orlov wrote about heroic Russian soldiers and salt-of-the-earth peasants. It's why he's such a national hero there— that, and the stirring speeches he made to rally the people during the Nazi siege in World War II. From what I read of it, *Man in the Middle* is a futuristic allegory along the lines of *1984* or *Brave New World.* There's nothing particularly Russian about it at all. The country setting is fictional, and even the names of the characters are a hodgepodge of different languages and cultures." Mariah shook her head firmly. "I've given this plagiarism theory a lot of thought since I first heard it, but it just doesn't hold water."

"It's not theory, it's fact," Renata insisted. "I was there when Orlov gave Ben the manuscript."

"Apparently, they met at an international writers' conference," Paul added. Mariah glanced at him, irritated. Obviously, he and Renata had discussed this before and at length. Paul leaned toward her. "Ben could have cleaned up the translation. I'm sure he never intended for the work to be taken for his own. It's all just a big misunderstanding."

Mariah shook her head slowly. "No, I can't buy that. You saw a few pages of the manuscript, but maybe you didn't see the cover page. *Man in the Middle, A Novel by Benjamin Bolt.* That's what it said. He sent the draft to my mother for safekeeping. She packed it away like it was a talisman. I think that's why she always thought he was coming home."

The waiter breezed back with Renata's scotch. "Here you

go, Mrs. Carr! Now, are you folks ready to order, or would you like a few minutes with the menu?''

"We need some time,'' Paul said. "I'll let you know.''

"Very good, Mr. Chaney,'' he said, backing off again.

Renata, meantime, was staring into her glass. "He was,'' she said quietly.

"Excuse me?'' Mariah said.

The older woman took a drink, then looked up. "Ben wanted to go back to Andrea...to your mother, and you and the baby. He missed you. I tried, you know. I wanted to be more than just another lover to him. I wanted to be his patron. His muse. Help him develop as an artist. He was a great, great talent, Mariah, but he needed stimulation. To travel and meet people. He was too isolated. Those were momentous times. Great events were happening all around, while Ben surfed and went to beach parties and tried to come up with new ideas for his novels. His confidence started to slip. He thought his life was frivolous, and that it reflected in his writing. The day he told me he wanted to get away, he'd seen a news report about a Buddhist monk who committed suicide by self-immolation to protest the war in Vietnam. Ben felt small and frivolous in the face of that kind of commitment, like he was just frittering his life away in my little cottage.''

"Your cottage? In Newport?'' Mariah asked. Renata nodded. "You mean, *you* owned that place we lived in?''

"My father did, but he had dozens of properties. I convinced him to give me that one for my own use. When Ben needed a place, I let him have it. I still own it, actually. I keep meaning to sell it off, but I've never been able to bring myself to do it.'' Renata reached down beside her and opened her purse, pulling out some keys, which she set on the table. "If you'd rather have that house, instead—''

Mariah pulled back and shook her head. "Oh, no. Not that one. Not any house of yours, in fact.'' Then she paused, frowning. "My mother stayed on there until she died. She never told me it belonged to you. She just said she stayed because the rent was low and it held my father's memory.''

Renata began to fidget with her rings, lining up a massive diamond solitaire that had slipped around her thin finger, aligning the stone to the center of a wide wedding band of sapphires and diamonds. These were gifts that had obviously not come from the impoverished writer who had preceded her husband. "Ben would have wanted me to let her keep the place, and I was always happy to give him anything he wanted. That's why, when he decided he needed to get away, I took him to Europe." She took another drink from her glass. "But then he changed his mind. He decided that what he needed was his family, after all."

Mariah studied the woman's liver-spotted hands and the tired lines around her mouth. Up close, she looked every bit her fifty-nine years. "That's why you dumped him, isn't it?" she said. "Not because he took up with someone else, as everyone always says. Because he wanted to go back to his wife."

Renata studied her glass morosely, obviously uncomfortable with the direction this conversation was taking. She nodded slightly.

"But he was broke, wasn't he?" Mariah pressed. "He had no way of getting back to this country on his own. That's why he was working so hard those final weeks of his life— to try to produce another novel that would pay his way home."

"I suppose so, yes," Renata said. She looked up at Mariah. "But I couldn't help him, you see. I'm sure you think it was vindictiveness on my part, but it wasn't. I had no choice."

"Of course you had a choice! Would it have been so hard for you to lend him the money?"

"Yes! Because of my father. He absolutely forbid me to see him anymore. He'd never been happy about me being with Ben. Mind you," she added, "he never liked anyone I was involved with. I just did what I wanted, and after he finished grumbling, he usually indulged me. But when he heard that Ben was holding a smuggled *samizdat* novel, that was another story altogether."

"You have to understand, Mariah," Nolan piped up, "my grandfather had extensive financial dealings with the Soviet Union—billions of dollars in investments and trade monopolies. He couldn't be linked, not even indirectly, to anything that might upset the Kremlin."

Renata shifted her attention to Paul, seeking his sympathy

if she couldn't get it from Mariah. "I had never in my life seen Daddy so angry as when he heard about the smuggled Orlov manuscript. He gave me an ultimatum—give up Ben, or give up my trust fund."

"So you threw Ben to the wolves," Mariah said bitterly.

"He wasn't interested in my patronage, anyway," Renata said bitterly. "It seemed an easy enough choice."

"You have to remember, Mariah, my mother was very young at the time," Nolan said.

"You told everyone Ben was running around with other women behind your back," Mariah said, ignoring him.

Renata arched one perfectly tended eyebrow. "Well, one has to save face, doesn't one? The allegation could hardly hurt him, given his reputation—as you've already pointed out."

"Not as much as the humiliation *you'd* suffer when word got around that he'd dumped you for the waitress he'd left behind," Mariah said.

Renata lifted her glass in a resigned toast. "And touché yet again. You, my dear, are a very hard woman, you know that?" She took another long drink. "The point is," she added, setting down the glass, "Ben seems to have decided to take advantage of Orlov's manuscript to get himself out of the financial pickle he was in. After all, Orlov had been evacuated back to Moscow—ostensibly for medical reasons, although rumor had it he was under house arrest. No one knew about the smuggled book, and Orlov was hardly in a position to stand up and defend his copyright, was he?"

"But we don't know for a fact that's what happened," Paul was quick to point out. "There could have been any number of reasons why Ben put his name on the cover sheet. Maybe just to protect the true identity of the author until he could get back to the States and get the manuscript to a publisher. I think we should try to put a positive spin on this," he said to Mariah. "If the publisher is alerted in time, damage control will be a relatively simple matter. In fact, it'll make for a great story. There's no reason why anyone need suffer embarrassment." He laid a comforting hand over Mariah's, frowning when she snatched hers away.

"This doesn't change the fact that your father was still one of the great American novelists of the twentieth century, Mariah," Nolan argued. "What does it matter if this book is published or not? Benjamin Bolt doesn't need it to ensure his place in literary history."

"Ah, yes, that's true," Renata said, "but public opinion is a fickle thing. If the notion gets around that he was a plagiarist, Mariah, I think you'll soon find that he's about as popular on a college syllabus as O.J. Simpson at Pebble Beach. And the residual royalties on his book sales, my dear, will dry up even faster than his reputation. I understand you keep the bulk of those proceeds in trust for your daughter?"

"Is that something else your private investigator uncovered?"

"I do hire the best," Renata said. "In any case, you see what I mean about this affecting your daughter."

"My daughter will survive," Mariah said firmly. "She's a tough kid. But whether *Man in the Middle* is a Bolt novel or an Orlov novel, there's another aspect of this you haven't touched on."

"What's that?"

"The allegation that my father was murdered."

"Oh, God." Renata groaned softly, resting her head in her hands. "Louis Urquhart's gotten to you, hasn't he?"

"So you know him?" Mariah asked.

"Who's Louis Urquhart?" Paul inquired. "Why does that name ring a bell?"

"He's a professor at UCLA," Renata said impatiently. "He won a Pulitzer Prize for his biography of Jack Kerouac, and now the idiot thinks he's infallible. He came to me about this, too. Damn that man!" she exclaimed, glancing over at her son, "I can't believe he's persisting with this nonsense!"

"Mother, don't get yourself upset about him. He isn't worth it."

"Mark my words," Renata said, turning back to Mariah and Paul, "Urquhart's just looking to line his pockets on the profits he'll make if he stirs up a scandal like this. I had him thrown out on his ear when he came to me," she added, waving an arm airily. Mariah sensed she was a little drunk.

"Urquhart's working on a biography of my father," Mariah told Paul. "He wrote to Chap Korman saying he'd uncovered evidence not only of this so-called stolen manuscript, but also that Ben was murdered. I just found out about it yesterday. Frank's looking into it for me.''

Paul's face shifted into something not at all attractive. ''So that's the research he was doing for you. And what the message from him at the hotel was about. You went to him for help. Why? Why couldn't you have come to me?''

''Chap had couriered a copy of Urquhart's letter to my house and I needed Frank to pick it up.''

''And because you trust him in a way you've never trusted me,'' Paul said.

Mariah considered denying it, but as she thought about it, she realized he was absolutely right. ''Yes, I do, as a matter of fact,'' she said, adding, ''With good reason, as it turns out.''

Paul looked severely vexed. Not even the curious stares of other diners were enough to force him to maintain a good front at this point.

Mariah turned back to the other woman. ''You don't credit Urquhart's theory that Ben was murdered?''

''No, of course not,'' Renata said impatiently. ''When Ben died, I made the funeral arrangements myself, my father be damned. I discussed them with your mother, as a matter of fact.''

''You actually spoke to her?''

''Yes. I phoned her from Paris. She was his next of kin, after all.''

Watching her drain her glass again, then nod as the waiter appeared with a refill, Mariah recalled the day she'd come home to find her mother on the sofa, crying after learning of Ben's death. It must have been Renata, she realized, who'd called while she was at school.

''Hepatitis is a contagious disease,'' Renata went on, lecturing as if to the simple-minded. ''Neither the American nor the French public-health authorities were going to allow the body to be transported. Cremation was the only option. I explained to your mother about Père Lachaise Cemetery—how many other famous writers were buried there, and how I would ensure that a suitable monument was erected to his memory. She agreed with me that it would be a better to have his ashes interred there rather than dragging them back to the States. The point is," she added, "there was an autopsy when Ben's body was found. The French authorities were very clear that he died of hepatitis."

"So Louis Urquhart is chasing a conspiracy that never happened," Paul said. "I think you're right, Renata. The guy's a hatchet man." He turned to Mariah. "He'll try to milk this for all it's worth, you'll see."

"Maybe," she replied, "but that doesn't mean I won't listen to what he has to say." She gathered up her purse.

"Where are you going?" Nolan asked.

"Her five minutes are long since up. I've heard all I need to."

"I know this is upsetting, Mariah," Nolan said. "but surely you can see that there's nothing to be served by dredging all this up again now. Those papers you found will only bring grief to you, to your daughter, and damage your father's reputation. Meantime, you're going to drag my family through the muck, too. You have to let this drop."

Renata nodded. "If I made mistakes, it was only because I was young and in love. Everything I did, I did for Ben. I don't want or deserve to be made an object of public speculation. It isn't right. I have always acted with the best of intentions."

"And so the road to hell is paved, they say," Mariah noted.

"That's not fair," Paul said. "You need to—"

"I need to go," she said, pushing back her chair. "And as for what's not fair, Paul—manipulating people for your own interest, that's what's not fair. It's arrogant and presumptuous, and I won't have either of you manipulating my life or my daughter's."

"I'm trying to help," he protested. "We're both just trying to save you from public embarrassment."

"Public embarrassment?" She laughed scornfully. "You know, Paul, that's *your* great bugaboo, not mine. And it's really what's got you worried here, isn't it? The idea that the great Paul Chaney might be publicly associated with a scandal and end up looking foolish. Tsk, tsk! Poor choice of company you're keeping, Mr. Chaney. Doesn't reflect well on you at all. I suppose that's the problem with living your life on a pedestal—you're in constant fear of falling off, aren't you? Well, not me. So you can keep your help, thank you very much. And you, Mrs. Carr, you can keep your beach house. I'll get the keys back to you somehow. Nolan, I'm sorry you've gotten caught up in this. I understand why you feel you have to take your mother's side, but I'm afraid you're backing the wrong horse here. Don't bother to get up, any of you. I'll find my own way out.''

Thursday,
July 4

Chapter
Twenty-Three

Time zones mean nothing to a teenager. Two days after her own arrival in L.A., Mariah's internal clock was still running three hours ahead of Pacific time, and she was waking up long before the first garnet rays of dawn spilled over the San Gabriel Mountains. But Lindsay's biorhythms were another story. Mariah watched the slow rise and fall of the blankets on the other side of the massive bed, where her daughter lay turned away from her, curled on her side in a tiny ball and snuggled down into the pillows. With only a bit of her clipped russet head peeping above the fuzzy tan blanket, she looked like a fledgling bird in a lint-lined nest. A night owl hatchling, whose greatest pleasure was to wander around half the night and sleep away half the day.

This morning, Lindsay had every reason to want to sleep in. Her plane had arrived at LAX nearly forty minutes late, and tension had reared its ugly head the moment she walked down the jet way. Mariah thought she'd steeled herself for the change in Lindsay's appearance, but her shock must have been obvious. Or maybe it was just Lindsay's own regret over her impulsive action.

Mariah hugged her and kissed her, then passed a hand over

the short curls. "It's only hair," she'd blurted, laughing nervously. "It'll grow back."

A very stupid thing to say. Lindsay had stiffened under her
embrace and pulled away. Why couldn't she have pointed out
how beautiful her daughter was? Mariah berated herself.
Lindsay could be bald and dressed in hopsacking, and she'd
still look wonderful by anyone's standards. Why couldn't she
applaud Lindsay's independence of spirit? Because, her heart
replied, it was so hard to let go. Every self-reliant step felt
like the beginnings of flight. But though terrified of losing
her child, she seemed to be doing everything in her power to
drive her away. She could see herself doing it. She just didn't
know how to stop.

Lindsay had retaliated last night by launching into snide
references to Paul as they waited at the baggage carousel,
remarks obviously designed to deflect attention from herself.
She was bright enough to know that the best defense was
always a kick-ass offense.

Mariah had been hard-pressed to defend him after the am-
bush at Spago, but the mention of his name had inevitably
led to the subject of the beach house, and despite her best
intentions to leave that can of worms unopened until the
morning, she'd found herself admitting that she'd refused the
place. The disappointment on Lindsay's face had been shat-
tering to see.

It was one-thirty in the morning by the time they arrived
back at the hotel—4:30 a.m. back in Virginia—not the hour
to launch into a long explanation of why it was impossible
to accept favors from Renata Hunter Carr, a nonperson whose
name Mariah had never even uttered in her daughter's presence. She'd tried to reassure Lindsay that they would come
up with an alternate California holiday plan in place of the
three weeks in Newport—maybe drive up the coast to Santa
Barbara and San Simeon. But, noncommunicative and clearly
exhausted, Lindsay had been interested only in bed. Clinging
to the far edge of the king-size mattress, as far away from
her mother as she could possibly get without actually moving
blankets and pillows onto the floor, she'd fallen asleep in
minutes.

Mariah had slept restlessly, sick at heart, and she'd been

awake for over an hour now, reluctant to disturb sleeping adolescent dragons by stumbling around a room darkened by the drawn, heavy drapes. Instead, she watched over this beautiful, tempestuous child who, in sleep at least, radiated warmth and vulnerability. Resisting with difficulty the impulse to reach out and stroke those baby-soft, spun-copper curls.

This was the infant girl she'd cradled in her arms. The tiny soul whose very existence had inspired a fierce, protective love deeper than anything she could have imagined before Lindsay had come into the world. The toddler whose fat fingers had gripped hers with absolute trust during her first wobbly steps. The mischievous second-grader whose tumbling red hair, gap-toothed grin and sparkling dark eyes had had every little boy on the playground scrambling to be her next victim, a tiny snow queen repelling all challengers from the slippery white hillock left by a rare Virginia blizzard.

There wasn't a moment of her daughter's life that didn't bring a smile to her lips or a sweet ache to her heart, Mariah reflected. She'd already lost the man with whom she'd counted on spending the rest of her life. The prospect of losing this child, too, was more painful than she could bear.

She rolled back with a quiet sigh and glanced at the digital bedside clock. Six thirty-two. Lindsay was sure to sleep for hours yet, but Mariah's own anxiety would drive her crazy if she didn't do something to wear it off.

She moved lightly to her feet, scooping the hotel notepad and pen from the bedside table on her way to the bathroom, withdrawing a sleeveless dress as she passed the open closet. The bathroom door closed behind her with a soft shush and a click, and she turned on the light. Slipping out of her nightgown and hooking it onto the back of the door, she pulled down her Speedo from the shower rod and shimmied into it, then brushed her teeth, washed her face and dropped the navy linen shift over her head and arms. Perched on the edge of the tub, she wrote a note:

Lins:
Gone down to swim laps, then have breakfast and read the paper. If you're up before I get back, come join me.

*I've left the extra room key card on the bureau. Or, if
you'd rather order from room service, go ahead and do
that. Either way, I'll hang around downstairs for a couple of hours so you can sleep in. When you get up, we'll
decide what we want to do today.*
    I love you very much.

                                                              Mom

Switching off the bathroom light, Mariah padded back out
into the room, toes sinking into the soft carpet. After a moment of calculation, she wedged the note into the corner of
the dressing table mirror, wryly recalling the first time she'd
cut off her own hair. She'd been Lindsay's age, come to think
of it, swimming on her high-school varsity team and sick of
the daily struggle with long hair. If Lindsay was anything like
her, it would be weeks before she felt at ease with her own
reflection. After the way things had gone last night, Mariah
thought ruefully, she'd just as soon be out of the room to
miss Lindsay's initial angst when she woke up and checked
herself out.

With the key card in the pocket of her linen shift, Mariah
grabbed her purse and sandals from the closet, took one last
look at Lindsay's sleeping form and headed for the door,
wincing at the clatter of brass on brass as she lifted the safety
latch. At the last second, she remembered to hook the Do Not
Disturb sign over the outside handle.

She was leaning against the wall at the end of the hall,
wrestling into her strappy black leather sandals, when a soft
ding announced the elevator's arrival. A middle-aged man
exiting the car nearly collided with her as he stepped off.
''Sorry,'' he said, reaching out to steady her briefly, then
holding the door while she walked onto the elevator. But instead of releasing it, he frowned. ''Are you Mariah Bolt, by
any chance?''

Mariah studied the unremarkable-looking man before deciding whether to admit she was. His graying hair was very
short, and his mustache was neatly trimmed. Closer to five-
ten than six feet, she estimated. Fit-looking for his age, which
might have had a year or two on hers. His white cotton shirt
was neatly pressed, although the navy blazer over his gray

slacks looked as though it spent most of its time folded over the back of a chair or car seat, to be shrugged into only when absolutely necessary. His tie was department-store silk in a safe, subdued burgundy print, and would probably be considered insufficiently trendy for either a guest or employee in a landmark L.A. establishment like the Beverly Wilshire. So who was he? A reporter? Doubtful. Too tidy for a newspaperman, too bland for TV. One of her own? she wondered briefly before discarding the possibility. Too domestic for the CIA, not buttoned-down enough for the FBI. By rapid process of elimination, she concluded he could only be a police officer, with the pass-anywhere, innocuous look cultivated by plainclothes cops worldwide. Her first thought was that Yuri Belenko's irrepressible nature had finally landed him in hot water, and that her name had somehow come up in the process of investigating his claim to diplomatic immunity.

"I am Mariah Bolt," she confirmed. "And you are...?"

Sure enough, he flipped out a badge. "Detective James Scheiber. I was just coming to see you. Sorry to bother you so early, but I was worried you might check out and I'd miss you. I wonder if you could spare a few minutes to answer some questions?" He nodded back in the direction of her door as he struggled with the oscillating elevator door that was trying to close on his arm.

"What's this about?" she asked.

"I'd just as soon not discuss it in the hallway."

"Well, that may be, but my room's not an option, either," she said. "If you want to talk to me, it'll have to be downstairs. I was going for a swim, but I suppose I could do with breakfast, instead." His skeptical glance at her outfit said he was finding the swim story implausible, but she wasn't about to unzip her dress to reveal the tank suit underneath it. Let him wonder. In any case, he nodded and followed her into the elevator. As the door closed, Mariah frowned and added, "Can I see that badge again?" He retrieved it from his inside jacket pocket and held it out for her. "Newport Beach?" she read, peering at it more closely. "Aren't you a little out of your jurisdiction?"

The detective shoved it back in his pocket. "Funny, that's exactly what Tucker said. I never had the impression you

Company people paid much attention to little things like jurisdictional limits.''

Mariah was sufficiently surprised to ignore the interagency dig. "*Frank* Tucker?''

"So, I gather you do know him?''

"Yes, of course, very well,'' she replied. "When were you talking to him?''

"He broke into your hotel room yesterday evening. At least,'' Scheiber added as she started to protest, "the assistant manager and I thought he had. He didn't try to deny it, mind you, but maybe he was just being pigheaded. He's not the most communicative person I've ever met.''

In spite of herself, Mariah smiled. "That's a fact,'' she said, "but make no mistake about it, he's a good man.'' The idea of Frank being near at hand was the best news she'd heard in a long time. Whatever else could be said about him, his timing was impeccable. The way things had been going for the last couple of days, professionally and personally, she couldn't think of anyone she'd rather see.

"Did you give him a key to your room?'' Scheiber asked.

"I didn't even know he was in Los Angeles. You actually saw him here?''

Scheiber nodded. "I've been trying to get in touch with you since last night. I dropped by a little after eight. You weren't around, but he was, and that's where we ran into one another.''

"I don't suppose you happen to know where he's gotten to?''

The elevator doors opened onto the hotel's rotunda, and as Mariah was stepping off, the detective delivered the news to her back. "He's in an LAPD lockup not far from here. Under arrest.''

She swung around, stunned. "*What?* For being in my room? Don't be ridiculous! He was obviously looking for me, and he's welcome anytime. I'd never dream of pressing—''

"Not for break and enter,'' Scheiber said. "He's being held on suspicion of murder.''

It was one of those time-slowing moments that, by now, Mariah had come to associate with imminent crisis—like the morning she'd been pulled out of an embassy meeting to be told her husband and daughter had been in a devastating car wreck, or the night the hospital had called to say David had been found dead in his bed. Silence enveloped her like a thick shroud, and the only sound she perceived was her mind crying out in protest and disbelief. *Oh, Frank! What have they done to you?*

She glanced back at the hotel lobby, but it was virtually deserted at that early hour, neither the lone clerk behind the big front desk nor the concierge on the phone at his station taking any note of the urgent conversation by the elevator banks. One cleaner was pushing a droning floor polisher around the elaborate circular mosaic at the center of the rotunda, while another polished the already gleaming brass light fixtures.

Mariah took a deep breath and turned on Scheiber. "That's impossible," she said. "Frank Tucker wouldn't murder anyone. There must be some mistake."

"Well, maybe," he conceded reluctantly. "It may be a case of mistaken identity at that."

"I should think so."

"There was a murder near here last night," Scheiber explained, "and Tucker fit the description of the killer, but I just came from LAX. I caught a D.C.-based flight attendant just as she was boarding for the return run and I showed her a mug shot of Tucker. She put him on a flight that touched down here at almost the precise moment the murder was being committed. Mind you," Scheiber added, frowning, "she thought his name was Lewis and that he was a talent scout. He's some joker, your friend."

"There's no way he could have killed anyone, though," Mariah said, slumping with relief even as her mind was racing, trying to think why Frank would have been traveling under a cover name. "So, you *are* going to get him released?"

"That was my next stop. Would you care to join me? I've got a few more questions for you, but the quicker I get over there, the quicker your friend gets a 'Get Out of Jail Free' card."

Mariah hesitated. "It's close by, you said?"

"Ten minutes from here." Scheiber leaned back and

crossed his arms, dipping his head back toward the elevator. "I gather you've got company, but I'm sure you'll be back long before Mr. Chaney wakes up."

Mariah paused, then grimaced. Obviously, the discretion of hotel professionals had its limits, and even off his turf, a smart cop knew how to get around them. "Well, whoop-de-do for your investigative skills, Detective. You look so proud of yourself, I almost hate to tell you your information's stale. That's my fifteen-year-old daughter I left asleep upstairs. She got in late last night."

"So Mr. Chaney did check out, after all?"

"Not that it's any of your business, but yes," she said. Permanently checked out of her life, too, as far as Mariah was concerned, but that wasn't any of this man's business, either.

He shrugged. "Well, anyway, if you'd like to come along with me, we can kill two birds with one stone. If it's a problem, though, we can just leave Mr. Tucker to stew where he is for the time being." He shrugged again, like it made no difference to him one way or the other.

"Oh, God, no," Mariah groaned. Poor Frank. She debated whether to call up and let Lindsay know where she'd be, but it was so early. She and Frank would be back long before Lindsay woke up. At the thought of the two of them, Mariah smiled, remembering how Frank had stuck up for Lindsay yesterday over the hair issue. Having him to act as referee was only one of the reasons she was pleased he was here. Where mother-daughter relations were concerned, she and Lindsay needed all the help they could get, at this point. "Why exactly was Frank arrested in the first place?" she asked, following Scheiber toward the hotel parking lot entrance.

"The LAPD had an eyewitness who thought she'd seen him at a crime scene," Scheiber said. "But it turns out the building where the murder took place was pretty much locked down and running on minimum lighting when the murder happened. It's an old place, and the halls are windowless and pretty dim, even in daylight. By the time the homicide team got there, all the lights had been turned on, so they assumed the witness had had a clearer look at the assailant than she did. Tucker, unfortunately, showed up just when the force was on the lookout for someone big, probably bald or with thinning hair, and dressed in dark clothes."

"Lord," Mariah said, shaking her head grimly. "What a cock-up! And remind me again what all this has to do with you? How did you get involved in it?"

The detective held open the front door. "I'll explain on the way over."

It wasn't entirely kosher to have lured her that way, Scheiber admitted to himself. The subject of Tucker's arrest had come up so early in their conversation, and her concern for the guy's welfare had been so great that it had overshadowed the fact—which he was certain he'd mentioned—that he'd only met Tucker in the first place incidental to looking for her. She was obviously intelligent, though, and the conversation would inevitably return to the reason he'd been looking for her last night. In the meantime, she was preoccupied with the need to serve as a character witness for her friend Tucker and help bail him out of trouble. Scheiber was content to leave it that way until they got to the LAPD's West L.A. Division.

He had no grounds to haul her in just because two people linked to her happened to have died under odd circumstances in the space of twenty-four hours. Fortunately, she had freely agreed to come with him and, even if she'd forgotten about it temporarily, to answer Scheiber's questions. He had a lot of them, but the LAPD homicide detective in charge of investigating Louis Urquhart's suspicious death would be as interested as he was in what Mariah Bolt had to say about the link between the two dead men, her father and her father's possibly missing papers. Sitting her down between Ripley and himself, Scheiber rationalized, was simply the most efficient way of gathering facts.

His cell phone rang as he was pulling his car out onto Wilshire Boulevard, and he expressed a silent word of gratitude to Dave Eckert for giving him an opportunity to postpone explanations a little longer.

"Iris called," Eckert said. "She wanted to let you know

the Korman autopsy's scheduled for around eleven this morning.''

"Good. Tell her I'll be there, would you? You have any luck convincing your contact at the sheriff's lab to rush those tox-screen results for us?''

"She drove a hard bargain. Never underestimate the determination of a mother of the bride. I had to promise to throw in another set of prints and a couple of extra eight-and-a-half-by-elevens of the happy couple, but she finally agreed to put us on top of the pile as soon as the tissue and fluid samples come in from the pathologist. Even so, we're looking at Tuesday at the earliest, you know.''

"Yeah, I know, but it's looking more and more like there's reason to follow this one closely. You remember what I told you yesterday about naked bodies?'' Scheiber glanced over at the woman next to him, but she was making a good show of watching the passing scenery, ignoring his half of the conversation.

"That suicides rarely die naked,'' Eckert said, "because they think it's too embarrassing to have their bodies discovered that way?''

"Exactly. Strange but true. Just another reason the Marilyn Monroe murder conspiracy theory has lasted as long as it has.''

"Hey, that's no theory. It's been conclusively proven. If the CIA and the mob hadn't been so efficient at pushing the big lie that she'd offed herself, her killers would have been tried years ago. Poor old Joe DiMaggio. It breaks your heart to see the guy and know what the Kennedys got away with, you know? I mean, there was never anybody for him after Marilyn, was there?''

"It's a tragedy, all right,'' Scheiber said, shaking his head in bemusement.

"Just imagine if they'd had a better handle on your basic psychology of suicide, huh?'' Eckert said. "There might not have been any debate at all, and poor Norma Jean's murder would've been completely forgotten by now.''

"There you go. Anyway, if we rule out the possibility of suicide in that case of ours we were discussing earlier, it only leaves two other choices, right?''

"That case we were discussing?" Eckert repeated. "How many cases do we—oh! I get it! You've got someone there with you and you can't talk?"

"You're an astute fellow, you are," Scheiber said.

"You sound like you're in traffic. Where are you, anyway?"

"On my way to visit the LAPD."

"You finally link up with the Bolt woman?"

"As we speak."

"She's in the car with you? Why?"

"Long story. I tried to call you last night, but you must have been showing off your Bang & Olufsen again." Scheiber heard Eckert's harrumph. "Anyway, turns out we may be looking at a series of incidents."

"You mean, there's been another hot-tub case?"

"No, but one that's just as inconclusive, on the surface, and with a strong link back to ours. Look, I can't go into it now, but why don't you meet me at the coroner's office for the autopsy and I'll bring you up to speed. And don't worry, buddy," Scheiber added, "we'll get you out in time for you and Iris to see those fireworks and maybe make a few of your own."

"You're all heart, man. Okay, I'll see you in Santa Ana at eleven."

Scheiber disconnected the call and glanced over at the passenger seat. The woman swung around to face him.

"Naked bodies and Marilyn Monroe?" she asked, arching one eyebrow. "Sorry, I didn't mean to eavesdrop, and I don't think I even want to know what *that* was all about. But all I can say is, people say *my* line of work is bizarre. Ha!"

"Ah, well, it's revisiting those cold cases keeps us on top of our game, don't you know."

"Right," she said dubiously. "So, how about telling me what exactly you want, and why you've been trying so hard to get in touch with me?" She frowned at him. "And, by the way, while we're on the subject, I don't suppose it's you that's responsible for the tail I've picked up?"

"You've been tailed? By whom?"

She shrugged. "Some nondescript but official-looking car. Not this one, admittedly. Although..." She paused, frowning.

"Newport Beach P.D., you said, right? Oh, Lord, restore my faith in public institutions here, Detective. Tell me you guys aren't under the thumb of the Hunter family like everything else in that damn city, would you? Because if that's what this is about, and Renata's got you harassing me, too, I swear—"

Now he was confused. "Renata?" Scheiber asked.

"As in Renata Hunter Carr?"

"Why would you think that? I mean, they do have a big place down there, and I gather both Nolan Carr and his mother are pretty active in the community. Personally, I've only been on this job for a few months, but I think I can safely say they don't get any kind of special service from the police department. Why would you think—"

She waved it off. "Never mind."

As she fell silent for a moment, Scheiber vaguely remembered something Eckert had pulled up off the Net during his research into Korman's client, Benjamin Bolt. Wasn't there something in there about Bolt having left his wife for Renata Hunter? Ouch. That would certainly account for the daughter's tetchy reaction.

She, in any case, seemed to have moved on. "Weren't you going to tell me why you've been looking for me?"

"Yes, I was," he said, pulling into the LAPD parking lot, congratulating himself on a masterful stall. "But let's go inside. I've got a colleague here who'd probably like to sit in on our discussion." There were plenty of open spaces because of the holiday. He pulled in right next to the front door and went to get out of the car, but the woman held back.

"Hold it right there," she said suspiciously. "You never said anything about the LAPD wanting to talk to me. What's going on?"

"We're here to get Tucker," Scheiber promised, "and to talk about a couple of cases where your name has come up. This shouldn't take long, I promise. I, for one, have someplace I need to be later this morning, so I'm going to have to hit the road soon. Let's just go have a chat with Detective Ripley and see what we can do about springing your friend at the same time."

Tucker had slept very badly. Detectives Ripley and McEvoy had grilled him for over three hours once they'd gotten to the LAPD divisional interview room—intermittently, because one or the other or both of them kept getting called out of the room, forcing him to backtrack and repeat himself when they returned. It was a deliberate tactic, Tucker knew, to force him to redeliver his story over and over while they searched for inconsistencies and tried to poke holes in it. Since his plan was to tell them as little as possible, it had taken all his concentration as the evening wore on and his level of fatigue rose to maintain his focus and not elaborate on why he was in the city.

The detectives had finally parked him in a four-bed cell with indestructible concrete bunks while they checked out his alibi. Or so they told him. Since it was after midnight at that point, LAX and the airlines were virtually shut down, so Tucker had resigned himself to spending the night on a thin, smelly mattress with dubious roommates for company. He'd shared the cell with a six-foot, black transvestite hooker in a blond wig, muscle shirt, skintight leather skirt and fishnet stockings, and a skinny, acne-scarred guy who'd apparently been caught selling Saturday night specials out of the trunk of his car. Around 2:00 a.m., they acquired a fourth cell mate—an old drunk too iffy-looking to be trusted not to pee in the bunk over Tucker's head. Tucker had ceded the bottom berth and climbed up top, trying to sleep through the drunk's repeated groaning of "Why me, Lord?" Around 4:00 a.m., out of patience, Tucker had bellowed, "Because you're an idiot! Now shut up before I come down and really give you something to moan about!" What was left of the night passed in relative quiet, except for the assorted snorting and snoring noises echoing up and down the concrete cell block.

A guard finally showed up around seven to tell him he was being released. As he dropped off the bunk, the drunk grabbed his arm, urging him to reform his wicked ways. "I'm turning over a new leaf," he said boozily. His rheumy eyes went wide as he added in awestruck whisper, "The voice of God spoke to me in the night." Touching a nicotine-stained finger to his lips, he glanced disdainfully at the other two snoozing reprobates, obviously deeming them unworthy to receive the Good News.

"Yeah, sure, pal. It'll be our little secret," Tucker dryly assured him, head shaking as he walked out of the cell.

By then, he was ready for just about anything—except the shock of being led to an interview room, where he found Mariah, looking surprisingly small and very upset, sitting opposite Detectives Scheiber and Ripley at a long interview table. From the look of the situation, Tucker guessed they'd told her that Chap Korman and Louis Urquhart were dead. When she spotted him, though, Mariah dredged up a smile and leaped to her feet.

"There you are, finally! Are you all right?" When she embraced him, he wanted to hold on to her in the worst way, but he felt grimy and disgusting after the night he'd had. He patted her back a couple of times, then pulled away from her.

"What are you doing here?" he asked gruffly, shooting a scowl over her head to the two detectives.

She relayed how Scheiber had tracked her down at the hotel that morning. "They told me about Louis Urquhart and the mix-up over the witness. And, oh God, Frank, Chap Korman's dead. Did they tell you?"

"I heard, kiddo. I'm sorry. I know he was a good friend."

She nodded. "To me and to my mother," she said, her voice trembling. "He was always there for us. Long before my father's work took off the way it did, Chap would be calling, making sure we were all right and that we had enough to get by...schoolbooks, clothes...whatever. If it hadn't been for him—" Her tears finally spilled over. "My mother told me once there were a couple times we wouldn't have had Christmas without his help. He was such a good person."

Tucker nodded and took her hand, cupping it between his own. "I know," he said quietly. Then he looked up at the two detectives. "We're both free to go?"

"Hold on. We've still got some questions," Ripley said.

"Yeah, well, that may be," Tucker said, "but not now. This has been tough news for Ms. Bolt. You're going to give her some time. And as for me, Ripley, I've given you as much time as I intend to. I'm out of here."

"Tucker, wait!" Scheiber protested. "I got up at four-thirty this morning so I could hit LAX and get a statement from that flight attendant before she took off back to D.C."

"Yeah, well, at four-thirty, I was still awake in a cell with three scumbags," Tucker replied testily. He exhaled heavily. "But thanks. It shouldn't have been necessary for either one of us, but I appreciate you going the extra mile on this."

Scheiber nodded. "It's okay. That's my job. But now, I really need you to tell me what you know about these two cases."

Tucker stiffened. "I didn't—"

"I'm not saying you had anything to do with either Korman's or Urquhart's deaths," Scheiber said. "But they're obviously linked. The common denominator has to be something to do with Benjamin Bolt."

"You said my father's papers were missing," Mariah said. "Are you absolutely certain about that?"

"No," Scheiber said. "I'm not certain about anything. I looked for them after I heard your phone message, Ms. Bolt, but I didn't know exactly what I was looking for. I'm probably going back to Korman's house again later. I wouldn't mind it if you'd come along. It's in your own interest, after all. Those papers do belong to you, don't they?"

She nodded slowly. "I might be willing to do that. But not today, Detective. I just can't. I've got my daughter to think about. She just arrived, and she's going to be upset, too, when she hears about Chap."

"Tomorrow, then?" Scheiber pressed.

"Maybe. Can I call you?"

Scheiber withdrew a business card from one pocket and a pen from another, wrote on the card, then slid it across the table to her. "My office number is there, and I've added my cell-phone number. Call me anytime, night or day. Please."

She took the card and studied it, then slipped it into the pocket of her dress. Tucker took her elbow. "Come on, let's go."

"Tucker, wait, dammit!" Scheiber said, rising to his feet as they headed for the door. "I know you suspect something about how they died. Tell me, for God's sake."

Tucker had his hand on the door, but he paused, then turned reluctantly back to the man. He owed him something, he supposed. "I'm not certain," he ventured.

"I don't need certain, I just need an idea. Tell me what you think," Scheiber pleaded. "Point me in a direction."

"Transdermal toxins," Tucker said.

"Trans-what?"

"Transdermal toxins," Tucker repeated. "Poisons delivered through the skin. When they do the autopsies and the tox screens, have them look for signs of chemicals delivered either through intramuscular injection or via skin absorption."

"I gather we're not talking your average pharmaceutical opiates and such?" Scheiber asked. "We found sleeping pills and antidepressants at Korman's place, and he'd been drinking."

Tucker waved it off. "No, forget that stuff. The poor bastard just muddied the killer's tracks by having that stuff around. They're going to have to look closer. It could be any one of a number of other possibilities. Curare, cobra venom—"

"Cobra venom?" Ripley exclaimed. "Would you give me a frigging break? How the hell would a cobra—"

"You don't need the snake," Tucker said. "All you need is the venom, or a synthetic chemical derivative that acts on the body in a similar fashion." He shrugged. "Or maybe the guy did overdose himself. Like I said, I'm not sure. But if the M.E. can't come up with a conventional explanation for what happened to these two guys, this is worth a look, believe me."

Mariah had been standing quietly at his side, but as her gray eyes widened, Tucker realized she understood where he was coming from. Her back was to the two detectives. "The Dzerzhinksy Borgia?" she whispered, incredulous. It was a nickname western intelligence had bestowed on Valery Zakharov, former KGB colonel, now foreign minister of Russia and well on his way to that country's top office. Like the Borgias of fifteenth-century Italy, Zakharov's route to power was reputed to have been via the noxious chemicals he'd kept stocked in his KGB offices in Dzerzhinsky Square.

Tucker glanced over at the two detectives, but they obviously hadn't heard her. He looked back down at her pale, stunned expression and nodded.

"Wait a minute," Ripley said. "I want to be clear on this.

You're saying someone's going around injecting poison into people. There was no sign of struggle in these cases. How do you pull out a syringe and get a guy to sit quietly while you inject him with God knows what?''

"The killer—or killers—don't need syringes. Remember the case of the guy in London who was stabbed with a poison-tipped umbrella? Anything sharp will do. Say, in the case of Urquhart, his visitor shakes his hand, but he's wearing a ring equipped with a barb on the inner surface.''

Ripley grimaced. "Yeah, right, and two bucks will get you a hand buzzer at the joke store.''

"Roses,'' Scheiber said. When Ripley gave him a strange look, he added, "Mr. Korman's hands were cut up. His neighbor said he'd been pruning his roses. Could that have done it?''

"If someone had dipped the thorns, sure,'' Tucker said. He nodded to Mariah. "Let's go.''

But she held back, looking torn. "Wait a minute,'' she said. "Detective Ripley, do you know the disabled war veterans who sell plants in front of the Federal Building on Wilshire?''

"Yes,'' he said. "What about them?''

"I was walking across the plaza yesterday afternoon when a cyclist nearly collided with me. One of the vets knocked me aside and took the blow. He lost consciousness shortly afterward. They had to call an ambulance. They thought he'd overdosed on something. At the time, it seemed plausible, but now I'm wondering...'' She glanced worriedly at Tucker. "He had a cut on his hand after the cyclist hit him. Maybe it's nothing, but—''

Tucker felt is if he were standing on a sandbar in the middle of a river, an upstream dam collapsing under the weight of her words. It was the Newport detective who voiced the possibility he couldn't even bring himself to contemplate.

"Somebody tried to kill you, too,'' Scheiber said darkly.

"Did you get a look at the cyclist?'' Ripley asked.

Mariah shook her head. "No, not really. He wore a helmet and sunglasses. The vet who took the hit was a big, bearded fellow. His friends called him Martin. I'm not sure what his last name was. Would you look into it?''

Ripley nodded soberly.

Chapter
Twenty-Four

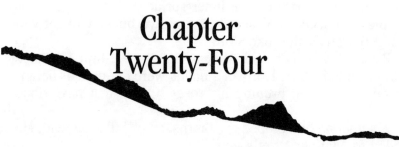

Mariah's day had started badly, and it skidded rapidly down-
hill from there. Before it was over, her very worst fears would
be realized. For now, though, things seemed bad enough, with
the news that Chap Korman had died not long after she'd last
spoken to him, and that the mildewed papers she'd pulled out
of her flooded storage locker had probably sparked a killing
spree, claiming not only Chap, but Louis Urquhart, too.

Her shock over those developments was only slightly
greater than her astonishment at what she was learning about
this man who'd been her mentor, colleague and closest friend
for nearly two decades. "You destroyed them?" she repeated,
incredulous when Frank briefed her on his quick turnaround
trip to Moscow to visit the Navigator and about the files he'd
brought back then shredded. "The evidence of Zakharov's
murderous dealings during his climb to the top? Why would
you do that?"

Frank stared into his coffee cup, as if the answer might be
there. They'd taken a cab back to the hotel, stopping in the
lobby lounge for a quick breakfast and to bring each other up
to date on what they knew. Mariah had snagged a table in a
recessed alcove where their quiet conversation wouldn't be
overheard but from where she could keep an eye out for Lind-

say, who would surely be getting up any time now. Mariah had debated running up to see if she was awake, but before she faced her already troubled daughter to deliver even more bad news, she had to find out what Frank knew. Upset as she would undoubtedly be to learn about Chap, Lindsay was going to take all Mariah's time and attention after that.

Absentmindedly picking apart the flakes of a croissant, she waited for Frank to explain himself. He'd always been taciturn and stubborn, but she'd never known him to behave irrationally. Before now, anyway.

"Zakharov has diplomatic immunity," he said finally. "He can't be arrested here, and he'll never be charged in his own country. Not unless the democratic opposition over there gets its act together to oust him and his ilk, once and for all. Short of assassinating him myself, which is what Deriabin may have had in mind, for all I know, there's no way to touch him."

"Surely Deriabin didn't expect you personally to rid the world of the Dzerzhinsky Borgia? I mean, Zakharov got where he is today by destroying everyone who stood in his path, and the thought of him controlling one of the two largest nuclear arsenals on the planet is pretty scary. But if anything were to happen to him while he's in this country, it would be seen by Moscow as a virtual declaration of war."

"I know, but I don't think it was an accident that the Navigator's handover of those files was timed to coincide with his official visit here." Frank shook his head ruefully. "Who knows what went on in that old bastard's Machiavellian brain?"

He leaned back in his seat, and his hands passed wearily over his face. They were both operating on minimal sleep, but *her* bed, at least, had been comfortable, Mariah thought. The midmorning sunlight streaming through the tall, arched windows emphasized dark circles under Frank's eyes and blue-black stubble on a chin that hadn't met a razor since he'd left home. In any other city, he might have stuck out like a weed in a place as hushed and elegant as the Beverly Wilshire lounge, but L.A. had scruffy down to a fine art form. Frank looked positively buttoned-down compared to some MTV types Mariah and Lindsay had seen checking into the

Presidential Suite when they'd arrived from the airport late last night.

Tired as he was this morning, Mariah thought, Frank seemed a little more like her friend of old, but anyone keeping him under surveillance these past months would have seen how hard the death of his son had hit him. A manipulator like the Navigator might have even imagined him capable, given the right motivation, of being pushed over the edge into some rash act. Even as she thought it, Mariah's chest tightened as she guessed the vulnerability the Navigator may have perceived in Frank. The key to waking the sleeping giant. The fact that Frank had dropped everything to come to her side now was proof of it. If he thought she was in trouble, he would do whatever necessary to help her, consequences be damned.

It was something she'd sensed for a long time without ever allowing herself to ponder what it meant—much less put a name to it. Denial, after all, had been the defining rule of their relationship for almost as long as they'd known each other. When they'd first met, Frank had been married to a dying woman he deeply loved. By the time Joanne passed away, Mariah had been caught up in her life with David and Lindsay. At the time David died, Patty and Frank were an item, and Paul Chaney had been hovering in the wings. She and Frank had been moving in syncopated time for nearly two decades, always by unspoken mutual agreement, damping down the spark they both knew could flare between them, regardless of their other commitments. Personal chemistry is, after all, a volatile thing.

Had the Navigator been watching all that time, she wondered, watching for an opportunity to use that spark to ignite his own schemes?

She reached toward him. "You really wouldn't do that, would you?"

"What? Assassinate the Russian foreign minister?" He grimaced. "Why would I want to turn him into a national martyr?" He hesitated a moment, then slid his hand out from under hers. Mariah reached for the silver carafe, refilling his cup, then her own, relieved to know that whatever other impact his personal crises had had, Frank's reasoning powers were functioning just fine. He folded his napkin on the table, and out of the blue asked, "Has Paul gone home?"

"I have no idea," she said, stirring milk into her coffee. "It's over," she added quietly. Frank was too discreet to probe for reasons, but she gave him a summary of what had happened at Spago, anyway, and what Renata had said about her father and the manuscript.

"Maybe Chaney *was* trying to help," Frank said, granting Paul more credit than she would have expected. It had been obvious from the outset that the two men had had little use for one another, a mutual antagonism she'd put down to an alpha-male thing, frustrated at feeling pulled between them.

"The question is, was he looking to help me or himself by sneaking around behind my back like that?" she wondered aloud. "And then, knowing Renata would be lying in wait for me when I came out here, and not warning me? How could he do that?" She shook her head, disgusted.

"I'm sorry," Frank said, looking as if he really meant it.

She waved it off. "No matter. That stunt was just the last straw. I'd already made up my mind the relationship wasn't going anywhere, anyway. I don't love him, it's as simple as that. I don't think I ever could. I thought it was because I was still grieving over David, or because Lindsay was unhappy about me seeing him, but it's more than that. I could never be myself when Paul was around. I felt like there was some image I was supposed to be living up to, but kept falling short. To be perfectly honest, I'm relieved it's over."

Frank nodded. "Well, that's good then. But I'm still sorry this business about your father had to blow up in your face."

She looked up at him, frowning. "I don't know, Frank, call me crazy, but considering all of Ben's other sins of commission and omission, what does it matter that he attended some Soviet-sponsored writers' conference thirty years ago? Who cares?"

"It's more than that," Frank said. "There was Anatoly Orlov, the Russian writer he betrayed."

She frowned. "Renata said he stole Orlov's novel and was going to try to pass it off as his own. Professor Urquhart also suspected the manuscript I found was Orlov's, but it doesn't sound like he was accusing Ben of anything underhanded. Just that a mistake had been made.''

"Urquhart was being generous, Mariah. I think Renata's closer to the truth on this. The Navigator's files said Orlov was betrayed by an American—to Zakharov, who was the KGB resident in France at the time. It had to be your father. He was Orlov's constant companion at that conference, the only American who was. Orlov's collapse was undoubtedly the result of Zakharov's pharmacology, and it was Zakharov who dragged him back to Moscow. Then, when he died, Zakharov returned to Paris to eliminate the only witness to what had happened.''

"My father," Mariah said, chilled. "Are you sure?"

Frank nodded. "It's what's in the one file I saved and brought to show you. Ben's death probably did look like hepatitis to the French authorities, mind you. There are at least a half a dozen toxins that cause liver damage. Zakharov knows them all.''

"And they would've been harder to detect thirty years ago," Mariah said, sounding more calmly analytical than she felt. Why was this lump forming in her throat? Why should she mourn the murder of a man who'd wreaked so much damage in his brief, selfish life? "I doubt the French even probed very hard," she added. "What would they care about a down-on-his-luck American found dead in some fleabag garret?"

Frank's fingers began to beat a nervous tattoo on the starched linen tablecloth. "All this time, I thought this business was better kept buried. I should have known it would come out sooner or later.''

She frowned. "What do you mean, 'all this time,' Frank? How long have you known about it?''

"The fact that your father had flirted with the Soviet propaganda machine popped up once before, during your initial security clearance," he told her. "I only found out about the Orlov part when I got the Navigator's files.''

"But how is it I was hired? Agency rules should have barred me on the grounds of my father's associations.''

"Should have," he agreed, "but the Writers for Peace conference was ancient history, by then, an unimportant skirmish in the long history of the cold war. Even the undercover operative who'd noted your father's name on the list of attendees was long since dead. At that point, it was just one line in an old file.''

"Still, it must have sent up a red flag.''

"It would have, except I was on the recruiting committee that year, remember? I deleted the information before the final hiring cut.''

"You did *what?*'' she cried. One or two breakfast diners raised their heads at her outburst, but as she glanced around self-consciously, they returned to their own conversations. She leaned forward toward Frank, whispering, "You mean you've *always* been this crazy, going around destroying classified files?''

"Your father had been out of your life for years. He'd obviously had no influence on your politics or your loyalty,'' Frank said stubbornly. "Why should his irresponsible behavior keep you from the career you wanted? Sometimes bureaucratic rules need to be bent in favor of common sense, you know.''

"I don't think everyone in the agency would agree with you.''

"I know that,'' he said, looking glum. "There are brainless fools even now who'll start second-guessing every opinion you utter, every assessment you've ever written. Seems I've screwed up your career, after all.''

"My *career*, Frank? What does that matter? What about justice?''

"Justice?'' He snorted. "Now there's an elusive commodity. Anyway, you're going to have to watch your back from here on in.''

"Seems to me you've been doing a pretty good job of watching it for me,'' she said quietly.

His big shoulders hefted in a shrug. "I may not be around to do it much longer. Geist is looking for me. He knows I shredded the Navigator's files. For all I know, he may think I killed the guy, too.''

"Why did you shred them?''

"I told you, I don't want to be cleaning up Deriabin's messes for him. The Dzerzhinsky Borgia was his creature. He

made use of Zakharov's skills for years. It wasn't just external
KGB targets, but Deriabin's internal opponents, too, who
mysteriously kept getting sick and dying, one after the other
over the years. The Navigator thought Zakharov was his
trained pit bull. In the end, I suspect, the pit bull turned on
the master.''

"You think Zakharov murdered Deriabin?''

Tucker shrugged. "It makes sense, the more I think about
it. Zakharov is powerful enough in his own right now, with
black-arts operatives of his own. He didn't need the old man
anymore. Who says the doctors who diagnosed Deriabin's
liver cancer weren't Zakharov's minions? When I saw Deriabin, he knew he was a dead man, and from the way he
spoke of his doctors, I think he had his doubts about them.
Leaking that information to us was his way of getting re-
venge. Of course, if he thought we'd deliver it to Zakharov's
opponents, he got it all wrong. What he handed over was
leverage over the man who might be the next Russian president. An operator like Jack Geist would love to be in a position to blackmail somebody like that. Would he give up that
kind of control so some unknown could rise to the top of the
pile over there?''

"Not a chance,'' Mariah agreed.

"And what do you suppose the odds are of any real democratic reform if both the old KGB players *and* the CIA back
a thug like Zakharov?''

"Zip,'' Mariah said. "So you shredded the leverage?''

Tucker nodded. "All but the one file that might really make
a difference, *if* it fell into the right hands. The proof that
Zakharov murdered Anatoly Orlov. Ben's betrayal set the
wheels in motion, Mariah, but it was Zakharov's show all the
way. That's what's got him running scared now.''

And why Chap Korman and Louis Urquhart had had to die,
Mariah thought angrily. Damage control. Anatoly Orlov had
been the best-loved son Russia had produced in the twentieth
century, a literary hero who'd inspired his people to resist and
defeat Hitler's Nazi invasion. The idea of his killer running
for president there was about as ludicrous as Lee Harvey Os-
wald seeking office in America.

The resurfacing of Orlov's manuscript posed a problem,

but by eliminating witnesses and the paper trail, Zakharov probably thought he was home-free. Korman's and Urquhart's deaths might have been put down to a couple of old guys succumbing to natural causes if the office cleaner hadn't seen the killer running away. Zakharov's burly bodyguard, Mariah thought suddenly, the one Yuri Belenko had termed a steroid-damaged Olympic wrestler?

"Renata was right, after all," she said. "Ben Bolt's stock is about to crash. The truth has to come out, Frank. At least some kind of justice will be served—not just for Anatoly Orlov, but for Chap and Urquhart, too. Even for Ben. He made some horrible choices in his life. This had to be about the worst of them, but I'm his daughter, and he didn't deserve to be murdered. If Zakharov's diplomatic immunity means he can't be prosecuted here, then let him be held to account in the one place where it really matters to him. That file you saved has to be kept away from Geist and the agency, and sent instead to every national and international media outlet we can contact."

Tucker nodded. "We don't have much time, though. Geist is going to catch up with me sooner rather than later." His expression darkened. "And you'll get caught up in a media tidal wave, you know."

"I know," she said glumly, "but it's the right thing to do." She pushed back her chair. "Come on. We'd better go and wake Lindsay. She needs to know what's going on. And if you're going to meet the press," she added, running the back of her fingers over his sandpaper cheek, "you'd better come on up and have a shower and a shave, bub. You look like you just stepped out of solitary confinement at Alcatraz."

"No," Frank said ruefully. "That's probably my next stop."

While he collected his things from the parking lot, Mariah headed to her room to wake Lindsay, passing a linen cart in the hallway outside the door next to hers. Her own suite was gleaming and bright, the curtains flung wide—bed made, bathroom cleaned, carpet vacuumed. Inside the big closet, Lindsay's suitcase had been moved to a luggage rack, and the clothes she'd just dropped the night before had been hung neatly on hangers. On the closet floor, her clunky Doc Martens oxfords stood neatly at attention next to Mariah's black suede pumps, looking like wide-mouthed twin hippos getting ready to devour a couple of kittens. This was not Lindsay's doing, Mariah knew. Like most fifteen-year-olds, her daughter's preferred wardrobe-storage option was the floor—any old floor would do.

But if Lindsay's things were accounted for, she herself was nowhere to be seen.

Mariah went back out into the hall and found the chambermaid stuffing wet towels from next door into her canvas bin. "Excuse me? I noticed you've cleaned my room."

"Yes, madam. Is there a problem?"

"No, the room is fine, but I left my daughter sleeping and the Do Not Disturb sign on the doorknob. She got in very late last night, and—"

"There was no tag on the door."

"You're sure?"

"I would not have gone in if the sign was saying no." The woman was gray-haired and wiry under her starched, peach-colored uniform, with a brusque manner that suggested she did not appreciate having her professionalism questioned.

"No, I'm sure you wouldn't," Mariah reassured her, "but did you happen to see my daughter? A teenager, fairly tall, long red hair—I mean, short red hair. She just got it cut, and I'm not used to it yet."

"I saw no one, madam."

"Oh. Well, I guess she just woke up sooner than I thought she would."

The elevator dinged at the end of the hall. "Will you be needing anything else?" the maid asked her.

"Maybe a couple of extra towels?" Mariah asked, watching as Frank stepped off the elevator carrying a briefcase and a small duffel bag. The chambermaid followed the line of her gaze, then turned back to her cart and handed Mariah a couple of big fluffy bath sheets. Her expression was blank, except for the tiny muscle above one eyebrow that seemed itching to lift in an arch of disapproval. She moved down the hall as Mariah waited.

"What's up?" Frank asked.

"Lindsay's not here," Mariah said. "She's probably hanging out by the pool. Why don't you go in and use the shower while I have a talk with her, bring her up to speed on what's happened?"

"Are you going to be all right?" he asked, switching his briefcase under one arm so he could take the towels from her.

Mariah sighed. "I'll be fine. We need to have a long talk, anyway—although I'm not looking forward to telling her about Chap. She was really fond of him."

"That poor kid's been through a lot at her age."

"She's been through a lot for someone of any age. I hate having to give her more bad news." Mariah smoothed her linen dress, already creased. It was only midmorning, but it felt like days ago that she'd left Lindsay sleeping to go downstairs for a swim and a quiet breakfast. This was supposed to be the first day of their vacation, she thought grimly. They should have been slathering sunscreen on themselves right about now, getting ready for Lindsay's first run into the Pacific Ocean. "We'll meet you back up here," she told Frank resignedly.

But twenty-five minutes later, after doing the rounds of all the public spaces in the grand old hotel and talking to lifeguards, gym staff and waiters in all three restaurants, Mariah was back at the room. She found Frank in the steamy bathroom, shirtless, but freshly showered and shaved—including his head, she noted, smiling to herself in spite of her rising anxiety. He seemed tired still, but much refreshed. In fact, she thought, he was looking pretty damn good—broad-chested, slimmed down, ready for action.

When he caught sight of her reflection in the bathroom mirror, he whipped a clean navy polo shirt off the towel rack. "Where's Lindsay?" he asked, looking past her as he wrestled it over his head.

"I can't find her. I looked everywhere. Nobody seems to have seen her."

"Maybe she walked out to have a look at the shops on Rodeo Drive?"

"She has no business doing that. I left her a note, told her to have breakfast here or meet me downstairs. Even if she couldn't find me, she knows better than to go wandering around a strange city by herself.'' Mariah checked her watch. ''Ten-thirty. Where could she be?'' She moved around the room, searching the dressing table, the bed, the side tables, the sofa area in the suite's outer room.

''What are you looking for?'' Frank asked.

''I left the note stuck in the frame of the mirror over there. It's not there now. I'm just looking for some sign she actually saw it. For all I know, she thinks I've abandoned her. After some of the stupid things I've done lately, she probably wouldn't put it past me.''

Frank just shook his head and started poking around the dressing table. It was an antique-looking affair, French, Louis-something-or-other. Heavy, with a solid back and a keyhole opening at the front into which a tapestry-upholstered stool fit neatly. ''Is this it?'' he called. Mariah turned to find him with his shoulder pressed against the mirror on the wall, one big arm squeezed behind the table. ''I think it slipped down here,'' he grunted. ''Got it!'' His arm came up, and Mariah recognized her handwriting on the slip of hotel note-paper caught between two of his fingers.

''Shoot! She probably never even saw it,'' she said.

But Frank's face darkened as he examined the note. ''Oh, she saw it all right,'' he said. He handed it to her, and when Mariah turned it over, she found her daughter's scrawled reply on the other side.

Mom:
Couldn't find you downstairs, but I did find out how to get to Newport. I *know* you changed your mind about staying at the beach, but I came all this way, and I'd like to see it, if you don't mind, even if just for a few hours. Anyway, you weren't going to leave without visiting Chap, were you!! I'll meet you at his house. And don't panic, all right? I know *exactly* how to get there. I managed the Paris metro just fine, didn't I?

L

''That's it,'' Mariah fumed. ''I am going to kill her. And then, I'm going to ground her for the rest of her natural life. She's going to have to finish high school and college by correspondence, and then knit socks for soldiers for the rest of her days, because I am *never* letting her out of my sight again. How could she *do* this? Never mind, I know exactly. To prove how independent and—'' Mariah froze. ''Oh, hell, Frank,'' she cried, ''she's going to Chap's!''

He was already gathering up his keys and wallet, stuffing them into his pants pockets. ''Come on,'' he said. ''She can't have that much of a head start. Maybe we can track her down before she gets too far.''

''Dammit, dammit, dammit!'' Mariah wadded up the note and lobbed it at the wastepaper basket. It missed and tumbled along the baseboard. Typical, she thought, grabbing her purse and the room key card. She couldn't do anything right. ''The concierge,'' she said as they rushed toward the elevator. ''That must be who gave her directions.''

When they roared up to his desk and elbowed their way apologetically past a couple of Japanese tourists looking for directions to Frederick's of Hollywood, the concierge admitted that he had, indeed, given out directions to Newport Beach that morning. ''Why, yes, I did talk to a young lady about how to get down there, but I didn't think she was planning to go by herself.''

''Well, she has,'' Mariah said angrily. ''She's only fifteen years old!''

''Really?'' He looked to be pushing sixty himself, with a neatly trimmed goatee and three points of a red silk handkerchief standing at strict attention in the pocket of his double-breasted suit. ''My goodness, she's very well spoken for her age, isn't she? I thought she was eighteen or nineteen. But then, it's often hard to tell with young women these days, don't you—''

''How would she get there?'' Frank interrupted.

He started pulling out Amtrak brochures. ''Let's see...I told her which bus to take over to Union Station to pick up the nine-thirty San Diegan to Orange County. You get off at Santa Ana, and then it's a bus or cab ride from there to Newport.''

''Nine-thirty?'' Mariah repeated, incredulous. ''She was up in time to catch a nine-thirty train?''

''She would have had plenty of time. It must have been

only a little after eight when I spoke to her. In fact, she's probably almost there by now,'' the concierge added, glancing at the crystal-cased clock on his desk.

"Wouldn't you just know this would be the one time she decides to get up before noon," Mariah muttered. She and Frank exchanged worried looks, then simultaneously voiced the same thought. "Scheiber!" She rummaged in her pocket until she found the Newport detective's card. But when she borrowed the phone to call him, she got voice mail. "I'm on my way down there," she said in her message, after giving a brief rundown on her daughter's ill-advised plan to visit Chap Korman. "Frank Tucker and I have more information on your case, Detective. I'll call you when I get to Newport, but in the meantime, I'd be grateful if you'd have your people keep an eye out for my daughter."

As Mariah hung up, she noticed that another woman, blond, wearing a dark business suit, had appeared at the concierge's desk. "I'm Barbara Latham, assistant manager of the hotel," she said, looking askance at Frank as she added to Mariah, "Is this gentleman giving you any trouble?"

"Who? Frank?" Mariah said.

"Ms. Latham and I met last night," he explained. "In your room."

"Oh," Mariah said, nodding. "I heard about that. No, it's my daughter," she added to the other woman. "She took it in her head to visit a friend in Newport Beach this morning. Your concierge, unfortunately, lived up to the hotel's reputation for personal service and advised her how to get there. She's only fifteen and she went on her own. She's never been in Los Angeles before."

"Oh dear," Latham said, shifting her critical regard to the concierge.

"She seemed older," he said. "A very self-assured fifteen, believe me."

"Look, I'm not blaming anyone," Mariah said. "She's my responsibility, no one else's. I just need to find her. Aside from anything else, the friend she was going to see in Newport has died suddenly, but she doesn't know that."

"Oh dear," the assistant manager said again, more strenuously.

"I'm heading out after her right now," Mariah added, "but I'm worried about what happens if she calls here while I'm out."

"I'll have all your room calls routed to my office," Latham assured her, "and I'll call you myself if I hear anything. Do you have a cell phone?"

"I didn't bring it with me," Mariah said. "I was trying to get away from all that." She looked over at Frank, but he also shook his head.

"Didn't bring it," he said.

"Well, we have a few for the use of our guests," Latham said. "I'll give you one, and if your daughter calls—"

"Two," Frank said. "We need two phones, in case we have to split up."

"Two," Mariah echoed. "And two cars, Frank. I'll go after Lindsay while you take care of copying those papers we were discussing. As a matter of fact," she added, turning to the assistant manager once more, "you must have office-support facilities for your guests, don't you? Mr. Tucker here needs to run off some documents."

"Am I to assume Mr. Tucker is now a guest of ours?"

"He's with me," Mariah said firmly.

"I see. Well, then, *two* phones," the assistant manager said, frowning at Tucker, "and someone to assist Mr. Tucker with his paperwork. Anything else?"

"That's all for now," Mariah said. "But please, if my daughter calls, make sure you give her the cell-phone number and let her know I'm on my way. She should just sit tight until I get there."

Chapter
Twenty-Five

The autopsy on Albert Jacob Korman had been inconclusive, Scheiber told his captain by phone after he and Eckert arrived back at the victim's house from the Santa Ana morgue. "No obvious signs of trauma, no gross abnormalities of the internal organs, hardly any water in the lungs," he recounted. "Some tiny broken blood vessels suggesting oxygen deprivation, but the medical examiner was stumped as to the reason for it. Since Korman didn't appear to have drowned and there was no evidence of heart attack or stroke, it wasn't clear why his lungs and heart shouldn't have been working normally."

"So how's the M.E. going to call it?" the captain asked.

"He's not, until the tox screens come back. Thing is," Scheiber added ominously, standing guard over a dead bird on Korman's sidewalk, "Eckert and I are back at the victim's house, checking out a tip I got this morning, and we may have found the culprit. We're going to need a Haz Mat team over here."

"What kind of hazardous materials are we talking here?" the captain asked.

"Damned if I know," Scheiber said, "but it looks pretty lethal. We need a disposal team ASAP."

He and Eckert were at the side of Korman's garage next

to a row of trash cans, and Scheiber was carefully avoiding touching anything with the latex-gloved hand that had lifted the lid off Korman's green waste-recycling bin. He'd set the lid aside on the low wall between Korman's house and the architect neighbor's while he checked to see if the roses the old guy had reportedly been pruning were still there. Thorns, the M.E. had conceded, might account for the cuts and scratches both he and Iris Klassen had noted on Korman's hands.

The bin did hold several pruned rose branches, but when Eckert had moved in to photograph them, Scheiber had shouted a warning to get back. A sparrow that had landed on the damp lid of the green waste bin, pecking at condensed water droplets, suddenly begun to stagger, then keeled over onto the sidewalk. Scheiber and Eckert had watched the bird draw one or two feeble breaths as it lay on the ground, and then its eyes had rolled back in its head and it went still.

"I think it's some kind of biological agent. Potent," Scheiber added.

Johnson, the uniform assigned to stand guard outside the sealed house that morning, suddenly returned from the coffee break Scheiber had sent him on, and as he rounded the corner from the back lane, Eckert urgently waved him away from the dead bird and the bin, telling him in a low murmur what had happened. He'd left the lane gate open, and an old couple strolling by paused to peer curiously down the side yard, drawn by the police cars parked in the lane and the yellow crime-scene tape strung around the perimeter. Spotting Scheiber frowning at them, Johnson returned to his post, herding the old couple back into the lane and closing the gate behind him.

"Okay," the captain said, "I'll call in backup units. Cordon off the area and I'll get onto the county right away to send in a Haz Mat detail. Jesus! Just what we need on a Fourth of July holiday."

"Don't remind me," Scheiber said grimly, disconnecting the call. He dialed once more to check his messages. There was one from Mariah Bolt.

"Now what?" Eckert asked after he'd hung up.

"We wait, I guess," Scheiber said, "and keep a close

watch on the front courtyard, as well. We don't dare leave it unguarded. All we need is for some curious kid or holiday drunk to stumble over the wall into those bushes out there, and we'll really have a disaster on our hands. Speaking of kids," he added, "I just picked up a message from Mariah Bolt on my voice mail. Seems her teenage daughter's run off. She thinks the girl's headed this way. She's on her way down to pick her up."

"You going to call it in to the watch commander?" Eckert asked.

Scheiber grimaced. "Like he hasn't got enough on his plate today. I don't think so. If the girl shows up, we'll make sure she stays put. But I don't even know what she looks like, so I'd be hard-pressed to issue a lookout. She'll probably head for the beach or the Fun Zone, anyway. It's all I need, to be worrying about some famous dead guy's spoiled, runaway granddaughter."

"Jeez! Testy today, aren't we?"

Scheiber ran a weary hand through his hair. "I got up at four-thirty. And I promised my stepson I'd try to bring him down for the fireworks tonight. The way this day's going, I may have to renege, and I hate that. That kid's already got one old man who never comes through for him. He doesn't need another one."

"You might be okay. And if we run late, maybe Liz can drive down with him and meet you here. I can hold the fort while you go over to the beach for a while."

"Thanks, bud. But what about Iris?"

"She's a good fort-holder, too. Anyway, for all we know, crazy holiday like this, she'll probably end up getting called out to work, too."

"Ain't public service a bitch, though?" Scheiber said. A scratching sound at the kitchen window drew his attention, and he turned to find Korman's fat cat whining at him through the glass. "I feel like I'm running a frigging petting zoo instead of a homicide division. All right, all right," he grumbled, adding to Eckert, "You stand guard while I go feed him. I should probably call animal control to come get him, but I hate to think he'll end up being put down."

"Maybe Korman's sons will want him," Eckert said. "Iris

talked to one of them last night. They were trying to get a flight in today, last I heard.''

Scheiber tapped on the glass, ''You hear that? You get a one-day reprieve,'' he told the cat. ''They don't spring you in the next twenty-four hours, buster, it's Kitty Sing Sing for you.''

Mariah made agonizingly slow progress on the holiday-packed roads into Newport Beach. She was on the San Diego Freeway, just entering Garden Grove, fifteen or twenty miles shy of Newport, when the cell phone rang. ''Your daughter just called,'' Barbara Latham, the hotel's assistant manager said. ''She had been to your friend's house and found it sealed. She said there was a policeman there who told her he'd died.''

''Oh, God,'' Mariah said quietly. ''Poor Lindsay. Did you tell her I was on my way down to get her?''

''Yes, I did,'' Latham said. ''I tried to give her your cell number, too, but she didn't have anything to write with.''

''Did she say where she'd be?''

''At a neighbor's. I suggested she just wait there.''

''Which neighbor?''

''I'm not sure, but she said she'd be outside watching for you.''

''Okay, that's great, thank you. And Frank Tucker? Is he still there, do you know?''

''The last time I checked, he had my secretary addressing and stuffing envelopes for him,'' Latham said. ''You do, um, know that there will be a charge for her time and the materials he uses?''

''Yes, go ahead and put them on my bill,'' Mariah said. ''We appreciate your assistance, Ms. Latham.''

''Hmm,'' the other woman said.

''Would you tell him Lindsay called, and that I'll call him as soon as I have her?''

''I'll do that.''

Mariah finally found the Newport exit, but when she crossed over onto the peninsula, the traffic only got worse. Balboa Boulevard was largely unchanged from the way she'd remembered it: two narrow lanes in either direction, both squeezed by solid lines of meter-parked cars along the outer lanes and the median strip. The sidewalks and crosswalks were packed with holiday tourists carrying coolers, blankets and beach chairs, and as she peeked down side streets toward the beach, she saw a solid mass of striped umbrellas and tanned bodies. Lindsay could not have picked a worse day to get lost in Newport Beach.

It was the first time she herself had been back in two decades. While the Balboa strip was still chockablock with souvenir stands, surf shops and restaurants whose grip on life looked fleeting at best, most of the cottages seemed considerably spruced up, a sure sign that the town had shifted from being a predominantly rental and summer cottage community to one of year-round, home-owning residents.

Mariah smiled a little as the Mustang inched through heavy traffic past her elementary school, whose playground consisted of the beach and where the end of recess had always been signaled by the scuffing sound of four hundred small feet tracking sand onto the much-abused red linoleum floors. Magnolia Street, where she'd grown up, was three blocks beyond that, but between cars jostling for nonexistent parking spaces and pedestrians jaywalking with lethal-looking beach umbrellas, Mariah had time to catch barely a glimpse of their old cottage. Or rather, the cottage Renata had allowed them to continue to occupy after she'd run off with Ben, then abandoned him to the wolves, she thought bitterly. Left him to die in Paris so Arlen Hunter wouldn't take away her trust fund.

At Medina Street, she turned away from the beach and headed for the harbor side of the peninsula, where the town's more expensive summer homes sat cheek by jowl on postage-stamp lots. Rather than the sight of the hoi polloi tanning beer bellies on their front step, the residents on that side preferred to overlook their sailboats anchored in the harbor.

But Mariah hadn't gone more than a dozen yards down the side street before she ran into flashing lights and a barricade marked Orange County Hazardous Waste Disposal. A uniformed police officer held up a hand to stop her and wave her down a side street, back out of the neighborhood, but Mariah shook her head and pulled up alongside him.

"The street's closed," he said. "You can't park here."

"I'm looking for Detective Scheiber. Is he here?"

"Scheiber? Yeah, he is. What's your name?"

When Mariah told him, he had her wait while he stepped away and put in a radio call. He was back a moment later. "Okay, he says you can go in. He'll meet you at the corner of Edgewater and Medina, on the water walk. You have to leave your car out here. Park it over there in the alley and stay well clear of the Haz Mat people."

She nodded, tempted to ask what it was all about but figuring she'd find out from Scheiber, anyway. Also, fearing she knew already. She pulled the Mustang over behind a black and white. Climbing out of the car, she spotted a couple of people dressed like astronauts in full, self-ventilated protective gear that covered them from head to toe, only their faces visible through clear Plexiglas masks. They were wheeling two gray steel drums down a ramp off the back of an orange and white van and into the backyard of a house that looked distinctly like the pictures Chap and Emma Korman had sent Mariah when they'd first bought their shingled Newport retirement cottage—not that Chap had ever really been able to bring himself to retire. At the thought of him, Mariah felt tears spring to her eyes.

Scheiber was waiting at the corner for her. The air smelled of charcoal, sunscreen, sea water and diesel. While the streets had been cleared for the disposal operation, the decks of several boats in the harbor were crowded with spectators enjoying the show as they toasted the holiday.

"Roses," he said glumly. He pointed to Chap's front courtyard, a few houses up from were they stood. "It looks like they were recently pruned back from the fence. Looks like your friend Tucker was right about transdermal toxins," Scheiber added, telling her how he'd watched a bird die after coming into contact with the pruned branches.

"Like a canary in a mine," Mariah said soberly. "If you'd touched those branches, you might have been the next victim."

Scheiber nodded. "They're taking out the entire front flower bed—plants and topsoil, right down to the substratum clay. Who knows how much was affected? Depending on what they find, they'll do more soil testing, see whether the whole property has to be condemned.''

Mariah shook her head. "I don't think so. I think they'll find that this toxin has a very brief half-life. If you hadn't found it today, you probably never would have. The traces disintegrate that fast.''

"Why is it you and that Tucker character don't seem surprised by any of this?'' Scheiber asked, frowning. ''I put this question to him, and now I'm putting it to you—is this some kind of Company operation gone haywire here? And don't bullshit me, lady, because this is not remotely amusing.''

"Look, Detective,'' she said just as angrily, ''I've known Chap Korman since I was eight years old. He was the closest thing to a godfather I had, and I happened to have loved that sweet old guy. Believe me, no one is more upset about what happened to him than I am.''

He nodded. "Fair enough,'' he said, ''but you still seem to know a lot about this business. Why is that?''

"There was a similar case in Britain about fifteen years ago,'' Mariah told him. ''A Russian political defector was found dead in his rose garden outside London. Turned out his roses had been dusted with trace residues of a synthesized version of cobra venom.''

"*Cobra* venom?'' Scheiber repeated, incredulous.

"Yes. Same paralytic effects, only twice as lethal and three times as fast-working as the real thing.''

"Jeez, Louise.'' The detective blanched. ''By the way, I had a call from Detective Ripley—the guy you met at the LAPD this morning?'' Mariah nodded, and Scheiber continued. ''He followed up on that veteran you told him about who tried to protect you from the crazed cyclist. Turns out the guy died in the ambulance on the way to the E.R. Funny thing was, they ran a field test for opiates, thinking he was high on something, but it came up negative. Same thing in the E.R. The autopsy's pending, but at this point, they haven't got a clue what killed him. You think it might have been something like this?'' he asked, cocking his thumb at the Haz Mat team. ''And maybe whatever killed him was meant for you?''

Mariah felt the blood drain from her face. "Maybe," she said.

He didn't look surprised, but he didn't look happy, either. "Okay, that's it," he said. "I think it's time you and I and your buddy Tucker had a good long talk. Where is he, anyway?"

"He had some business to take care of while I came to pick up my daughter." Mariah glanced around. "Where is *she*, by the way?"

"I haven't seen her."

"What do you mean, you haven't seen her?" Mariah said, her heart beginning to pound. "I had a call as I was driving down here, saying she'd phoned my hotel over an hour ago. She'd found Chap's house sealed up, and had spoken to a police officer. She was going to wait outside for me."

"She didn't talk to me," Scheiber said, adding as he glanced at his watch, "but I only arrived about forty-five minutes ago. Come on. We'll find the officer who was guarding the place. Maybe he knows something he forgot to tell me."

They approached a small group of uniformed and plainclothes police officials standing a couple of doors down from Chap's, one of whom was introduced as Scheiber's partner, and another, in uniform, as Johnson. The officer frowned. "There were a lot of people stopping to ask what happened," he said. "It's not like South Central L.A. here. People don't see houses strung up with crime-scene tape every day."

Mariah pulled her wallet out of her purse and opened it to show him Lindsay's school picture. "This is my daughter— except her hair's short now. Red. She's slim, quite a bit taller than me, around five-eight."

"Oh, yeah," Johnson said, nodding at the picture. "I did talk to her, as a matter of fact. She seemed pretty shocked to hear Mr. Korman had died, as I recall. I thought she was just a neighbor or something."

Mariah snapped her fingers. "A neighbor! That's it. She said she was calling from a neighbor's house. She was supposed to wait outside there until I arrived."

Scheiber's partner, Eckert, shook his head. "We went door-to-door to evacuate the houses in the immediate vicinity when the Haz Mat team arrived,'' he said. "Standard operating procedure. Nobody was home on either side of Mr. Korman's house. I didn't see her at the houses we cleared across the back lane, either.''

"Yeah, but come to think of it," Johnson said, "I did see her again a little later. Maybe it was before you guys got here. She was petting a dog—one of those Hush Puppy dogs, you know?''

"A basset hound?" Scheiber asked. He and Eckert exchanged knowing looks.

"Yeah, a basset, that's it. Some guy was walking it and stopped to talk to her.''

"Balding? Dressed in black?" Sheiber asked. Johnson nodded.

"The architect," Eckert said.

"What architect?" Mariah asked.

"Mr. Korman's next-door neighbor, Douglas Porter," Scheiber said. "But like Dave here said, he wasn't in when we went door-to-door. He seems to have been pretty friendly with Mr. Korman, though. As a matter of fact, Porter knew you and your daughter were coming. He mentioned how much he'd been looking forward to meeting you.''

"Apparently a big fan of your father's," Eckert explained.

"That must have been whose house she was calling from," Mariah insisted. "Maybe you just missed them while they were out with the dog.''

Scheiber nodded. "Could be, although I'd be surprised if they returned without being seen. But let's go check again," he said, starting up the walk of the house next door to Chap's. "Just stay clear of that property line," he added, nodding in the direction of the other yard, which was beginning to look like a war zone.

Not that this one was much better, Mariah thought. They crossed a starkly landscaped courtyard and rang the doorbell of a dour, angular house obviously designed to be intellectually interesting rather than welcoming. Between the extraterrestrial appearance of the house and its landscape, and the space-suited Haz Mat technicians working next door, Mariah felt as if she'd been dropped into a bad science fiction movie. The doorbell gonged, deep and throaty, but there was no answer. Scheiber rapped sharply on the bloodred steel door, but met only silence.

"No dog, either," he noted. "It went crazy when we came to the door yesterday."

"Do you mind?" Mariah asked, indicating the big window to the right of the door. When the detective nodded, she walked over and cupped her hands around her eyes, peering inside. It looked like a living room–cum–office, but it was nearly as stark and uncomfortable-looking as the front courtyard. There was precious little furniture, and only one or two pieces of artwork, but the walls were half covered in what looked like blueprints and aerial photographs of a massive construction site.

"It's some resort he's working on over in Europe," Scheiber said, peering in alongside her. "Somewhere on the Mediterranean, I think."

Mariah peered around for a moment longer, then pulled away. "I don't like the fact that this guy seems to have just wandered off with my daughter," she said. Despite her best efforts to stay calm and to reassure herself that Lindsay was fine and merely walking a basset hound on a beach somewhere, a steady stream of pimps, rapists and serial killers was already intruding on her thoughts, like a horror movie running on fast forward.

"If it's any comfort to you, we think the guy's gay," Scheiber said.

Mariah pulled back, frowning. "Do you happen to have a daughter, Detective?"

"Yeah, as a matter of fact, I do."

"Then you know that's small bloody comfort."

"Yeah, I do," he said, chagrined. "You want to give me that picture of your daughter? I'm sure she's going to turn up any minute, but just in case, I'll get my partner here to take it in and scan it into the system and make up some copies."

Mariah waited, but Lindsay still hadn't shown up an hour later when Eckert returned. He met them at a nearby drive-in restaurant where she and Scheiber had gone ostensibly to grab a bite to eat—although food was the last thing on her mind—while she brought him up to speed on what she and

Frank thought the motive might be for the murders of both Chap Korman and Louis Urquhart.

As Eckert slipped into the red vinyl booth next to Scheiber, he slid a digitally retouched picture of Lindsay across the table, one that substituted a cap of short copper curls for the long hair in her school photo. "I hope this is a close approximation of what she looks like now."

"My God, yes, this is great," she told him gratefully.

"It's what I do," he said, blushing a little. "Every Newport cop on foot, bike or cruiser duty is getting a copy. The watch commander sent it over to the sheriff's department, too."

"They won't do much with it over there, I have to warn you," Scheiber added, "except add it to an already long inventory of runaway teens."

"She's not a runaway, Detective," Mariah insisted. "Would a runaway have phoned the hotel to let me know where she was?"

"But you did say you'd had an argument, and that she's been upset lately?"

"Yes, but it wasn't anything we couldn't work out. We would have been well on our way by now to doing just that," she added, pushing away the sandwich she hadn't wanted, anyway. "I wouldn't have had to leave her alone at the hotel if you and your LAPD buddies hadn't done such a damn stupid thing as arrest Frank Tucker for murder."

"Where *is* he, anyway?"

"I don't know," Mariah said. That was troubling her, too. She'd been trying to reach him for the past hour, but the phone he was carrying was either malfunctioning or turned off, because she kept getting a recorded announcement saying that the cellular customer she was calling was unavailable. Finally, Mariah had called back to the Beverly Wilshire, but Ms. Latham had informed her she'd personally checked both phones before handing them over that morning. She also said Frank had left the hotel at least a couple of hours earlier, after having asked her to find him a courier service that would be open on the Fourth of July holiday. Service at the Beverly Wilshire and the American entrepreneurial spirit being what they were, she had been able to do that. So, Mariah thought, if Frank was just dropping off copies of the Navigator's remaining file for delivery to media outlets, why wasn't he answering his phone? The answer, she realized, might simply be that, technophobic as he was, he'd forgotten to turn the damn thing on.

"Look, I can't stand just waiting around anymore," she said, grabbing one of Eckert's photos of her daughter. "I'm going to walk over to the beach and see if I can spot her and this bloody neighbor and his dog."

"Dogs aren't allowed on the beach," Eckert pointed out.

"Fine. I'll take the car and look anywhere a dog might be. The point is, I have to move. But I'll have my cell phone on and you've got the number, so please, if she shows up, call me, all right?"

Scheiber sighed. "We'd better get back over and see how they're doing at Korman's, anyway. But Ms. Bolt? To coin a tired old phrase, don't leave town, okay? I'm not even close to running out of questions for you."

Mariah stood in her bare feet in the sand, fingers looped through her sandal straps, watching with a large crowd of onlookers as half a dozen daredevil bodysurfers challenged the crashing waves of The Wedge. Situated at the very end of Newport Beach, where a long jetty protected the inlet to Newport Harbor, The Wedge had some of the most famous and most dangerous waves in southern California, created by the strong crosscurrent of the incoming tide and the backwash off the jetty. She'd ridden those waves herself when she was young, but posted signs warned that only the very strongest swimmers should attempt them. For those who could handle it, the rush made the risk worthwhile, but at this point, Mariah thought, she'd had about as much death-defying experience as she cared to experience in one lifetime.

She'd spotted the large group of people on reaching the end of the peninsula, and had quickly pulled over, risking a ticket by parking illegally in a red zone while she rushed over to see if Lindsay had by chance made it this far down the beach and was enjoying the spectacle with the rest of the crowd.

It would happen as easily as that, Mariah kept telling herself. She would suddenly spot Lindsay's copper curls, and find out she'd wandered off and lost track of the time, as kids were wont to do. That she was safe, and this nightmare was over. She wouldn't even get angry, she promised herself. She'd just hug Lindsay, and tell her she loved her, and they'd go somewhere and have a good, long, honest talk.

Please, God, let me just have her back.

But Lindsay wasn't in the crowd at The Wedge. Sick at heart, Mariah turned back toward her car. And then, froze. Across the inlet, in Corona del Mar, high on a cliff overlooking the harbor and all of Newport, sat the massive summer home of the late Arlen Hunter. And as she looked across the water, remembering the sight of it, an old children's skipping song came into Mariah's head, one that she had always associated with the woman who'd taken her daddy:

On the mountain stands a lady,
Who she is I do not know.
All she wants is gold and silver,
All she wants is a fine young man.

It seemed more appropriate than ever, she thought grimly, remembering Renata's balancing act between her fortune and the young man before whom she'd dangled her money like a lure. Back at the car, she hurried to dust the sand off her feet as a little green parking warden's van approached along the line of cars, looking for expired meters and illegals like herself. She was cramming her feet into her sandals when her cell phone rang.

"Frank!" she cried when she realized who it was. "Where are you? I've been trying to reach you forever."

"I'm on my way down there. I turned off the phone for a while. I was doing a little surveillance and I needed to be in silent running mode. Did you find Lindsay?"

"No, and I'm getting really worried. She was at Chap's house, and then she was seen with his neighbor, but she's vanished."

He cursed softly, and then added, "She's not the only one."

"What do you mean?"

"Zakharov and most of his delegation up and left last night."

"I thought he was staying for the Pacific Rim conference. It kicks off tonight with a gala reception on the *Queen Mary*."

"Apparently Zakharov decided he needed to be back in Moscow, tending his political fires and maneuvering for the prime minister's job."

"You said 'most of his delegation.' Who's still in town?"

"Your Mr. Belenko, for one. I gather he's going to carry on at the Pacific Rim conference. One or two other support personnel. Not only that," Frank added, "but the *Pushkin*, the ship Zakharov was staying on while he was here? I just left the port and it looks like it's making ready to leave."

"Because of the murders," Mariah said, fist clenching. "Zakharov's got my father's papers and Urquhart's research, and now he's out of here, leaving his mess behind. Doesn't need his base of operations anymore."

"That would be my guess," Frank agreed.

"You got the file copied, I hear."

"It'll be delivered first thing in the morning to every American and international media outlet and foreign correspondent I could find—including *Pravda, Izvestia* and half a dozen of the new, autonomous Russian press outfits."

"Good. Some of them are bound to run it. Zakharov's going to get a nasty surprise when he opens his paper in the next day or so," Mariah said. "I'd be happier if he could stand trial here for what he and his people did to Chap and Louis Urquhart, but at least—"

"That's a bit of a problem," Frank interrupted.

"How so?"

"I spoke to a friend of mine in FBI counterintelligence. We were in the navy together. He's been involved in keeping Zakharov and his people under surveillance this week. He says there's no way any of them could have killed Korman, and probably not Urquhart, either."

"*What?* How is that possible? Both killings have all the hallmarks of the Dzerzhinsky Borgia. And, get this—Scheiber stumbled across a toxin in Chap's roses. The M.O. sounds identical to that case in London several years back where the

Russian defector was poisoned in his rose garden. That was Zakharov's handiwork, through and through.''

"That may be," Frank said, "but my guy in the Bureau has all the Russians present and accounted for. All except your friend, Belenko, that is. He gave them the slip once or twice, but only for brief periods.''

A puttering sounded behind her, and Mariah glanced in her rearview mirror to see the parking warden moving up on her bumper. "Hang on, Frank, I've got to move or I'm going to pull a two-hundred-dollar standing violation.'' She dropped the phone on the seat beside her and quickly started the engine, pulling out of her illegal space with a squeal of tires just as the meter maid was climbing out with her ticket book. In the rearview mirror, Mariah caught the woman's scowl. She headed back down Balboa Boulevard, picking the phone off the seat once more. "You still there?" she asked.

"Still here," he said. "Tell me where you are.'' She gave him Chap Korman's address and told him to watch for the Haz Mat unit. And to drop Scheiber's name to get in. "I'll be there inside the hour,'' Frank said.

It hit her suddenly, with the brute force of a tsunami.

After she'd finished talking to Frank, Mariah was driving around in the late-afternoon sun, searching for Lindsay with a sick, growing fear that there was some terrible clue she'd missed, and that her daughter was lost to her because of it. At the same time, she was mulling over Frank's surprising news that neither Zakharov nor any of his delegation might have been responsible for the murders of Korman and Urquhart.

And then she remembered something one of her history professors had once said about tyrants down through the ages. The truly great tyrant, he'd suggested, is the one who inspires zealous disciples to do his bloody work for him. Alone, a Ghengis Khan, a Stalin, a Hitler is nothing. But give them dedicated fanatics to lead, and they become a terror. To that principle, Mariah added a particularly American corollary— *follow the money.* And suddenly, in one of those blinding moments of insight that come to mere mortals once or twice in a lifetime at best, she understood both what had happened thirty years ago and in the last forty-eight hours.

Instead of making another circuit of the beach area, she drove off the peninsula and headed down the Pacific Coast Highway to Corona del Mar, thinking about her father. The man should have been required to wear a warning label. Loving him had been hazardous, trusting him downright dangerous. After everything he'd done to those who'd loved him, there was a certain poetic justice to his having ended up broke and utterly alone when he died. But that said, had he been a thief, and therefore guilty of betraying his friend and fellow writer? Would he have stolen Anatoly Orlov's work? She didn't think so. The only thing he'd ever dedicated himself to and believed in wholeheartedly was the power of the written word. He'd never suffered any doubt where his own talent was concerned, and he'd been a prolific writer. Why steal another man's work? For the money, to pay his way home? Then why send it to his wife and tell her to hold it for him, instead of to his agent or publisher? It made no sense.

Crossing the Newport inlet, Mariah took her first right turn, driving by instinct. Once she turned onto Deep Cove Drive, it was easy enough to pick out the place she was looking for. Even if the stone wall that isolated the sprawling compound hadn't given away its location, Arlen Hunter's initials woven into the wrought-iron gates would have done the trick. Pulling into the wide drive, she leaned on the intercom button, surprised to hear Renata herself answer after a few moments.

If Renata was shocked to find Mariah at her gate, it wasn't obvious by her voice. A buzzer sounded and the massive gates swung inward, the wrought iron *A* and *H* parting in welcome. As she drove up the circular red brick drive, Mariah saw the front door of the house open and Renata come down the broad front stairs to meet her.

"So you came, after all," the older woman said, watching her get out of the car.

"You knew I would," Mariah said. "I want my daughter."

"Your daughter? I don't know what you're talking about."

"I think you do."

Renata frowned. "I have no idea why you would think that, but why don't you come in and we'll discuss it? I'm pleased you came. A little surprised, but pleased," she added, watching Mariah climb the steps. "I'd actually hoped to invite you out so we could get to know each other, but last night didn't go quite the way I'd planned. Have you eaten? I'm not much of a cook, but I'm sure we can pull something together."

"I'm fine," Mariah said.

Despite her superficial ease, Renata seemed to feel the need to fill the silence with chatter in the form of a tour commentary. "My father had this house built in the forties, right after the war," she said. "William Boyd was the architect, but Daddy added several specifications of his own design. I think it drove Boyd crazy, but Daddy was what you'd probably call a control freak. We spent summers here, when we weren't traveling. After my father died in '88, I started staying down year-round. You can still see the Hunter Oil rigs from the front gallery. They were some of the first offshore rigs ever built in California."

She was dressed in a sleeveless, tan linen dress and a filigree gold necklace and earrings. As she held out a matchstick arm to wave her inside, Mariah noticed the wattled flesh on its underside.

"We're on our own," Renata told her. "I gave the staff the day off. I wish my son were here, but unfortunately, he's out with his friends."

"Is Nolan your only child?"

"Yes."

"I gather he's become very involved in running your father's companies?" Mariah asked.

"Yes, he seems to have quite a knack for it," Renata said. "One of those talents that skips a generation, I suppose. Personally, I always found business a little boring. My husband handled things briefly after Daddy died, but then he died, too, and it all fell to me. Ten years I had to carry the Hunter trusts and corporations all on my own. I'm delighted that Nolan seems eager to take on that load now. Can I offer you a drink, Mariah? I was just filling the ice bucket actually."

"No, but go ahead," Mariah said.

The older woman led her across that broad, black-and-white-tiled vestibule of Mariah's childhood memory, waving her fingers in the direction of the sinuously curved staircase, continuing her tour commentary. "The wood is South American mahogany. The balustrade was hand-carved in France, then shipped, and reassembled in—"

"Renata?" Mariah said, interrupting her.

"Yes?"

"I really don't care."

The older woman glanced at her sharply, then nodded. "No, of course you don't. This way." She led Mariah through a door at the back of the stairs, along a serving hall that connected to the dining room, then into a massive kitchen. "Have a seat while I find the ice bucket," she said, opening cupboards, one after the other. "I know it's here somewhere. Are you sure I can't get you a drink?"

"Quite sure, but you go ahead." Whatever it took to grease the wheel of candor, Mariah thought.

"I think I will," Renata said. She busied herself with finding a glass and, apparently abandoning her hunt for the ice bucket, on trying to figure out how to get a few cubes out of the refrigerator-door dispenser. Mariah had the sense the woman rarely stepped into her own kitchen. "You know," Renata said as a couple of ice cubes finally tumbled into her glass, "your father never did, either."

"Never did what?"

"Care." Renata waved a hand. "About all of this. In my entire life, I think he's the only man I ever met who didn't give a damn about my father's money. The only one who couldn't be bought. It was a little disconcerting, at first. In the end, though, it's what I loved most about him."

"I think you overestimate him," Mariah said. "After all, you bought him for the price of a ticket to Europe."

Renata shook her head. "Don't imagine it gave me any control over him. He did exactly as he pleased. He went along because it suited his needs at the time, but when I tried to tighten that golden leash, he just slipped out of it and walked away. He wouldn't be owned."

"You must have felt used."

"No. Well, perhaps at first," she amended, disappearing for a moment and then reappearing with a bottle of scotch in her hand, the one commodity in her house whose location she seemed sure of. "In the end, I suppose I loved him more for his independence. It was quite refreshing. With everyone I ever met, before or since, the question was always there— were they interested in me, or in my father and his money and power?'' Renata was filling her glass, but she paused, looking up. ''Surely you've run into the same thing? It can't be easy, being the daughter of someone as famous as Ben.''

Mariah shrugged. ''I've been lucky. I met my husband in college. He was a physicist, brilliant in his own right. My father's celebrity didn't mean much to him. He'd been raised in a big family, and they were loving, close and sufficient unto themselves. When David and I got married, they just folded me and our daughter into their clan. My work is fairly esoteric, too, so it's not often I meet people I haven't known and worked with for years.''

''Well, then, you *have* been lucky. You must miss your husband.''

Mariah nodded. ''Very much.''

''I never had anything like that. Except for that short while with Ben, I was never allowed to forget I was Arlen Hunter's child and heir. They were all just so fascinated with Daddy,'' Renata said bitterly. She capped the bottle and lifted her glass. ''Cheers. What about Paul Chaney?'' she asked after a sip.

''What about him?''

''Well, I'm sure he doesn't need your money. He's very accomplished in his own right. But he has that overly impressed quality about him, too, doesn't he? I picked up on it right away. You must be quite attuned to it, yourself. It's an intensity that comes into their faces, isn't it, as they probe your life? If pressed, I'm sure Paul would say it's the newsman in him, drawn to the human-interest side of men like our fathers. But in the end, in his own way, he's one of the starstruck, too, isn't he? I'll wager he enjoys telling people he's seeing Ben Bolt's daughter.''

Mariah shrugged. ''Doesn't really matter. We're history.''

''Oh, dear. Not because of me, I hope?''

''That was just the proverbial straw. I don't think Paul was in it for the long haul, anyway.''

''That kind rarely is.'' Renata took another drink. ''You're sure you won't join me?''

''No, thank you.''

"I see," Renata said, arching one of her well-shaped eye-brows. "So, you came here to visit, but you're not sure about socializing with the heartless home-wrecker, is that it?"

Mariah exhaled heavily. "I'm too tired to fight with you, Renata."

"Why *did* you come, then?"

"I told you, I want my daughter back. Chap Korman and Louis Urquhart are dead—"

"Urquhart's dead?" Renata said anxiously. "How?"

"Poisoned, I suspect. Sound familiar?"

The other woman began wiping the island countertop with one hand as she maneuvered her glass to her lips with the other.

"Renata?" Mariah pressed. "You know who did it, don't you?"

"No. Why should I know anything?"

"Because you know about my father's death. And Anatoly Orlov," Mariah added. "Orlov was murdered by the KGB—by Zakharov. There's no doubt about that anymore. The proof is coming out, and when it does, Zakharov will be unelect-able. I thought it was my father who ratted on Orlov, and that he did do it to steal Orlov's manuscript and pass it off as his own. But I just don't believe it. Ben had too much pride in his own writing abilities to put his name on someone else's work. Besides which, if he'd had a critical Orlov manuscript, Zakharov would have demanded he hand it over immediately, then killed him then and there. He wouldn't have left him hanging around for three months. So, if Ben didn't betray Orlov to Zakharov, the American who did was someone else. You, maybe?"

"Me? No!" Renata said indignantly.

"Could have been. You were losing Ben. You must have known people in the Soviet embassy through your father's dealings with them. When Orlov gave Ben his manuscript, you might have reported it in a fit of pique, knowing the Soviets would yank Orlov back to Moscow. Only Ben was killed, too."

"No! Ben died of natural causes. He told me he did!"

"*He* told you? Who?"

"I mean *they* told me," Renata stammered. "French police."

"No, Renata, you said 'he.'" Mariah nodded, her suspicions confirmed. "Your father. He's the one who told you Ben died of hepatitis, and said his body had to be cremated. And it was your father who betrayed Orlov, after you told him about the smuggled manuscript."

"He wouldn't have done that."

"Don't be ridiculous, of course he would! You said as much last night to Paul and me. Your father had billions tied up in joint ventures with the Soviets. He couldn't afford to antagonize the Kremlin. He also wanted Ben out of your life—especially after the business with the smuggled manuscript. So your father betrayed both Orlov and my father to Zakharov."

"Not Ben!" Renata cried. "He swore he didn't say anything about Ben's involvement!"

"Come on, Renata!"

"Anyway, Ben died long after Orlov was taken back to Moscow."

"Orlov was sent to a sanitarium after his 'collapse' in Paris," Mariah said, "a psychiatric clinic, the kind of place they generally sent people suffering from what they called 'reformism of a paranoid nature.' Nobody survived those places, Renata, especially when they were checked in by Zakharov. Nothing was secret there. Nothing. You can be sure Orlov cracked and told them where the manuscript was. Then he was executed. And while the Kremlin planned a great public funeral for the 'hero of the people,' Zakharov went to retrieve his manuscript."

"No—"

"Yes! My father died in Paris on the same day Orlov was buried in Moscow. You can't believe that's a coincidence."

"My father told me it was hepatitis!" Renata sobbed. "He swore it! He was concerned about Ben. He said he went to check up on him, even took him some antibiotics from home—"

Mariah slumped onto a stool across from the older woman, stunned. "He did it himself? Oh my God," she breathed. "Your father injected Ben with the toxin himself." Renata was crying, and Mariah herself was shaking like a leaf. She forced herself to take a deep breath. "What about Louis Urquhart?" she pressed.

"What about him?"

"Did he suspect what your father had done? Was that why he came to you first, Renata? To try to blackmail you? Is that why he had to die? To protect your father's name?"

"My father's name?" the older woman repeated with a bitter laugh. "My father was a ruthless scoundrel. That's hardly a national secret. Have you seen some of the biographies that have come out since he died? He made a fortune—several fortunes—dealing with dictators, propping up the Soviet regime. Don't think Ben and Orlov were the only blood on his hands. There's nothing Urquhart could have done to blacken my father's name more than others already have—more than the old bastard blackened it himself. I would hardly murder a nonentity like Louis Urquhart to protect the name of Arlen Hunter."

"But *somebody* murdered Urquhart. I think you have a good idea who that somebody is. Who else knew that he was getting ready to reveal the truth? Who would suffer dire consequences if Zakharov fell from grace? Who did you tell about Urquhart coming to see you?"

"My son," Renata cried. "But I had to."

"Why?"

"Because they wanted me to contact you and get you to withdraw that novel. I couldn't imagine how it had even popped up after all these years. Who knew there was an English translation? I tried to tell Nolan it would be all right, that no one would ever find out it wasn't Ben's work. After all, even his agent thought it was his. But Nolan said Zakharov was insisting it was like pulling a loose thread in a garment. There was always the risk everything would unravel, and the whole truth would come out."

"And when it did," Mariah said bitterly, "guess who would be standing naked for the world to see, in all his wicked glory? Former KGB Colonel Zakharov, responsible for the deaths, among countless others, of not only Ben Bolt, but also of Russia's beloved national hero, Anatoly Orlov. Not a winning presidential platform, I wouldn't think." Mariah exhaled heavily. "And if Zakharov falls, so does your son, doesn't he? Nolan and his buddy, Porter. The architect moved in next door to Chap not long after the press found out about those papers I'd found. He was assigned to keep an eye on things. That was before any of you knew Urquhart had already stumbled onto the truth. The police thought Porter was working on a resort project in the Mediterranean, but I saw the site photographs in his house, and I just suddenly realized I've seen them before. Our satellites have been tracking the Nova Krimsky project since ground was first broken in the Crimea two years ago. The Russian mob is planning the largest gambling and money-laundering operation in the world there. Zakharov will provide governmental cover for the project in exchange for a percentage of the take, and he picked your son, Nolan—Arlen Hunter's clever grandson—to head up the consortium of developers." Mariah shook her head bitterly. "The more things change, the more they remain the same. Nolan brought in Porter. If Zakharov is ousted, they both stand to lose a fortune."

"We all do."

"I beg your pardon?"

"The entire Hunter empire. I told you, I was terrible at business. I hated it."

"Are you saying you ran the Arlen Hunter fortune into the ground over the decade you ran things?"

"Depleted it somewhat," Renata said petulantly. "A lot, actually." She reached for the phone.

"Who are you calling?"

"My son," Renata said. "I'm scared."

"Renata, listen to me," Mariah said, staying her hand. "Porter has my daughter. I think he—and Nolan, too, I would imagine—thought they could convince me to walk away and forget I ever heard about Orlov or Zakharov or the manuscript. And maybe I might have, too, except it's too late. The proof of what Zakharov did has already gone out to the media. The proverbial is going to hit the fan in the next twenty-four hours. There's nothing you or I can do to stop it. But you can do the right thing and help me get my daughter back."

"I can't."

"Dammit, Renata, you can!" Mariah cried. "You stole my

father! Do you have to take my daughter away from me, too?''

"I loved Ben!''

"And your father murdered him! Are you going to let your son hurt his granddaughter? Is that the kind of family you are, every last one of you?''

"You don't understand! Zakharov will kill Nolan!''

"Zakharov's left the country, Renata! In any case, his days are severely numbered. I can't imagine his mob cronies are going to look very kindly on this sort of publicity. If you go to the police and the FBI right away, you can get yourself and Nolan into some kind of protective custody before this hits the fan. But you have to work fast. You have to convince Nolan it's over so he and Porter will give themselves up now and release Lindsay before Zakharov finds out his goose is cooked.''

"Do you really think Zakharov is finished?'' Renata asked fearfully.

"I do, yes.''

"Then my son would be safe from him. Oh, wouldn't that be wonderful? He's held us all—my father, me, Nolan—in his grip for so long.'' Renata exhaled a long, shuddering sigh. "All right. I'll do it. But Mariah? Would you come with me?''

Mariah nodded. "I'll drive you.''

Renata finished her drink, then rose slowly from her stool. "Just let me go and powder my nose,'' she said. She left the kitchen, heading back for the front hall. Mariah was picking up her glass and putting it in the sink when a loud bump sounded from the front hall.

"Renata?'' she called. "Are you all right?'' She shouldn't have let her drink so much, but it had seemed like the only way to break down those haughty defenses. Seen in this light, in fact, Renata seemed old and pathetic. Whatever else could be said about her, she did sincerely appear to have loved Ben. For that alone she deserved some empathy. Mariah hurried out of the kitchen, thinking she might have taken a tumble on the stairs. Oh, God, she thought desperately, what if she had? What about Lindsay then?

But when she got to the hall, she halted in her tracks. Renata's eyes were wide above the hand clamped over her mouth—a massive hand belonging to Mr. Lermontov, Zakharov's steroid-enhanced bodyguard.

Mariah heard a sound coming from behind her, but before she could turn to find the source, a vicious blow knocked her to the floor. She struggled back to her knees, but a second blow flattened her, and her face struck the cold, hard tile. As her head began to spin, she had a vague sensation of being lifted up and tossed over a shoulder, then carried down, down, down on an endless flight of stairs. Then she lost consciousness entirely.

When she again came to, briefly—hours later it must have been, because night had fallen— she smelled seawater. She was on a boat, she realized, lying on a rocking bunk in a dimly lit stateroom. From overhead, she heard angry shouts, and then a woman's cry. Or was it a seagull? Mariah wondered as a symphony of color and noise exploded outside, lighting up the portholes around her. She had a brief memory of standing on the beach at night with her mother and father, all of them laughing and waving brilliant Fourth of July sparklers.

Then the darkness slipped over her once more.

Friday,
July 5

Chapter
Twenty-Six

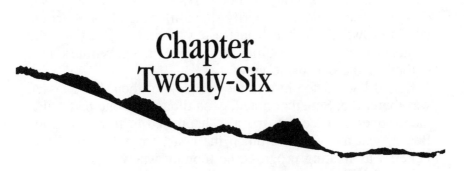

The phone next to Scheiber's bed rang at 2:00 a.m. Considering that this was supposed to be the new, improved version of his life, he thought, grabbing to silence the thing, it sure felt a lot like the old one. Liz and Lucas had driven down to watch the fireworks on the beach with him. He'd managed to stick with them from the opening salvo to the last rocket's flare, but then he'd had to give them a quick kiss and rush off, leaving them to find their own way home while he rejoined the search for Mariah Bolt and her daughter—both of whom had vanished into thin air from practically right under his nose. He and Eckert had finally packed it in about midnight, planning to take up the hunt again at first light.

It was the night watch commander on the line. "Hey, Detective," he said. "Thought you'd want to know. Old Buddy Higman found himself a girlfriend." Buddy Higman was the resident drunk of Newport Beach—forty years old but looked like sixty, missing half his teeth, and possessed of the ruddy, bloodshot look of a man whose roof generally consisted of a refrigerator crate. "Only one problem," the watch commander added. "She's dead."

"Yeah, well that's about his speed, I guess. Where?"

"Washed up on the beach, bottom of Seventeenth, about halfway between the piers."

"Is it the Bolt woman or her daughter?"

"Worse. You'd better get on down."

Jeez, what now? "I'm on my way," Scheiber said.

"Do you recognize her?" Dave Eckert asked Scheiber as they stood over the body of an elderly woman. The night was dark, moonless and hazy, eerily silent after the mass of people who'd crowded the beach just a few hours earlier. Only the white, rolling, low-rumbling surf broke the gray-black monotony of the oceanside view.

Eckert had beaten him to the scene—but then, Iris Klassen was there, too, Scheiber noted, even though no one had called the coroner's office yet. Iris also happened to live in Laguna Beach, just a few miles down the coast from Newport. Old Eckert was making progress, he thought wryly.

Eckert had gotten some floodlights set up over the scene while waiting for Scheiber to arrive. The body of the woman on the sand was thin and well maintained, her facial skin artificially tight, although the looseness of the pasty gray flesh on her neck and hands, where little surgical help can be had, put her in her early sixties, Scheiber estimated. She was wearing some expensive jewelry—a filigreed gold neck chain, solid gold earrings and three heavy rings, two of them studded with chunky diamonds and sapphires. And that was *all* she was wearing.

"Can't say I know her," he said, smoothing down his mustache as the woman's blind blue eyes, gone milky, stared up at him from the sand, looking a little startled to be there.

"Renata Carr," Eckert said, adding when he still drew a blank, "Renata *Hunter* Carr? Of Hunter Oil? The Hunter Trust? The Arlen Hunter Museum? Newport society's leading lady?"

And Ben Bolt's onetime lover, Scheiber thought, recalling Mariah Bolt's resentful references. How many more people linked to her would die before he got to the bottom of this?

"What's wrong with you guys?" Scheiber grumbled to the assembled cops in general and no one in particular. "I thought I was coming down to work a cushy nine-to-five.

Can't you keep things under control better than this?'' He crouched down on his haunches and peered at the body. "Buddy Higman found her just like this?''

Klassen and Eckert joined him. "So he says," Eckert said.

"Looks like she took a bullet in the shoulder," Scheiber said. "Doesn't seem like a killer shot, unless somebody got lucky and hit an artery. Obviously not a suicide bid, either."

"No kidding. Did you notice her foot?" Klassen asked. "Don't think that's the way I'd choose to do it."

"Her foot?" Scheiber's gaze moved down the naked torso to the legs. The right one was stretched out, nothing unusual about the foot. The left was bent at the knee. He crouched to get a closer look at the foot, which seemed, in the harsh shadows cast by the floodlights, to be half-buried in the sand. Then he recoiled as he realized it wasn't buried at all. "Jesus! The toes are gone!"

"Shark," a sonorous voice pronounced over his head. "You mark my words, that's what it was." Scheiber looked up to see Buddy Higman shaking his shaggy head. "Met a great white myself once. Took a piece-a my surfboard and a half-a my thigh." He rubbed his leg absently as one of the patrol cops, catching Scheiber's grimace, led the man back up the beach a little ways, away from the body—taking care, Scheiber noted, to stay upwind of the limping drunk.

"Out of the mouths of babes and old sots," Klassen said. "I think ol' Buddy could be right."

"Welcome to Amityville," Eckert said, grimacing.

"Probably just a small thresher or a mako," Klassen said matter-of-factly, "drawn by the blood from the shoulder wound. Losing her toes like that would probably have been enough to bleed her out, though. Enough for her to lose consciousness, anyway."

"Yeah, but what was she doing naked in the water in the first place?" Scheiber pondered. "And wearing all her jewelry?"

"Now there," Eckert said, "is your puzzle for the day."

The answer came faster than Scheiber could have hoped, and from an unexpected source. Although, given Tucker's talent for being in all the wrong places, he shouldn't have

been surprised when his cell phone rang while he waited for
Klassen to do a more thorough exam of the body. Tucker
asked him—no, told him—to meet him over at the dead
woman's house in Corona del Mar.

"Where've you been all night?" Scheiber asked him.

"Where do you think?" Tucker said. "Searching for Mariah and her daughter. Where the hell did you get to?" Tucker
had shown up at the Korman house around dinnertime the
night before, not at all happy to find that the mother, as well
as the daughter, was now AWOL. Scheiber had searched till
sunset, then slipped away to meet his family. Still, they'd
found no trace of Mariah Bolt, her daughter or her rented red
Mustang.

"I caught another case," Scheiber said, feeling evasive and
guiltier than he should. There'd been a lookout notice for the
girl and the woman issued to every cop on the beat that
night—and the department had been out in force, given the
usual holiday burst of beach activity and incident reports. He
had no cause to beat himself up for getting a couple of hours'
sleep, did he? "What are you doing at the Hunter Carr
place?" he asked, changing the subject.

"I got a phone tip," Tucker said mysteriously.

Scheiber was tired of playing Twenty Questions with the
guy. Hell, he was tired, period. But he needed to interview
Nolan Carr, anyway, to find out what he knew about his
mother's activities last night. Might as well catch him early,
before he left for wherever it was that millionaires went in
the morning. "Okay, I'll meet you outside the house in ten,
fifteen minutes," Scheiber told Tucker, waving Eckert over
to the car.

"I'm not outside the house," Tucker said. "I'm inside."

"With the woman's son?"

"No, he's not here. Nobody's here. The house is empty."

Scheiber scowled. "Then what the hell are you doing inside, Tucker? That's private property. Unless you've got permission to be in there—and what makes me think you
don't?—you got no business—"

"Don't you guys have some kind of principle of hot pursuit
in your line of work? Something that lets you enter private
property if you think there's a crime going on inside?"

"Yeah, but *you* don't," Scheiber pointed out.

"Well, then, say thank you, Detective, because I just gave you cause to enter this place without a warrant. Don't dawdle," Tucker added just before he hung up.

Scheiber felt his teeth grinding. "I think I hate that guy," he told Eckert.

Tucker paced the terrazzo entry hall like a caged bear, waiting for the Newport detective to show up. He'd closed the front gates so as not to draw the attention of the private security forces patrolling the neighborhood, but he'd already located the inside terminal of the gate security system. As soon as he saw Scheiber's car pull up on the closed-circuit TV, Tucker buzzed him through, then opened the front door and waited for the detective and his partner. The sun was just up.

"Tucker, goddammit," Scheiber said, coming toward him, "give me one good reason I shouldn't arrest you right here and now. Because this time, this *is* my jurisdiction."

"This is where Mariah disappeared from. I found her rental car in the garage, hidden under a tarp," Tucker added, nodding at the six-bay unit at the end of the drive.

Eckert loped over and stretched himself up to look through the window. "It's there all right," he told Scheiber.

"They were probably planning to have it disassembled and dumped just as soon as they got back," Tucker said.

"They? Who 'they'?" Scheiber demanded impatiently.

"Nolan Carr, Douglas Porter. Maybe a couple of other associates on the Russian casinos project. I'm not sure how many are involved, but I know Carr's front and center."

"Mariah told me she thought Korman's and Urquhart's murders had something to do with the Russian foreign minister," Scheiber said. "Something about covering up some information that might keep him from being elected president."

"It's more than that. Zakharov has associates in this country—Carr and Porter chief among them—working on a scheme to build a massive gambling resort in the Crimea to launder money for the Russian mob and anyone else with a need to recycle cash. Zakharov's supposed to be a statesman now, so he keeps his hands clean and lets other people handle his dirty work. In the case of Korman's and Urquhart's murders, it was Nolan Carr. And Porter, Korman's neighbor, who also kidnapped Mariah's daughter.''

''And Mariah?'' Scheiber asked.

''I think she came last night to warn Nolan's mother that the jig was up and try to bargain for Lindsay's release. Only they took her, too. I think I know where.''

''Why am I not surprised?'' Scheiber said dryly.

''There's a Russian ship, the *Aleksandr Pushkin,* that moved from Los Angeles into the Port of Long Beach last,'' Tucker said. ''Zakharov's left but the ship is housing what's left of the Russian delegation for a conference that's getting under way there this morning. I think Carr and Porter took Mariah and her daughter up there last night under cover of darkness and handed them over to the *Pushkin*'s crew. They'll be held there until the conference ends. Then, once the *Pushkin* is on the high seas, they'll be dumped overboard like yesterday's garbage. Unless we get them off first.''

He watched the color drain from Scheiber's face as the detective and Eckert exchanged worried looks. ''I don't know how to tell you this,'' Scheiber said. ''We may be too late.''

''What do you mean?''

''Renata Carr's body washed up on the beach last night. If she was taken with Mariah—''

Tucker felt his world beginning to implode, but he shook his head angrily. ''No. She and Lindsay are still alive. I'm going after them. I want you to call the Coast Guard. Have them search both the *Pushkin* and Porter's boat. It's a sixty-foot cruiser, apparently, called—''

''*Wright Think'r,*'' Eckert said. ''He showed us a picture of it.''

''How are you planning to go after them?'' Scheiber asked.

''Follow me,'' Tucker said. Scheiber and Eckert followed as he led them into a library off the center hall, a large, circular room overlooking Newport Harbor. Its walls were fully lined with dark wooden bookcases filled with tomes and bric-a-brac from around the world. Deep leather chairs sat in front of a massive stone fireplace paneled on either side with highly polished mahogany. In the center of the room, a table inlaid with intricate marquetry held a large Russian silver samovar.

Tucker walked around the table and stood by one of the shelves on the room's inner wall, near the fireplace. "Read any good books lately?" he asked. *"War and Peace,* for example?" Running a finger along the leather-bound spines, he located the title and pulled the top of the book toward him. It resisted for a moment, and then they heard the soft snap of a catch releasing, and the wooden panel on one side of the fireplace popped open. Scheiber walked over next to him, opened the hidden door wide and peered in. As his head passed through the opening, a light switched on, activated by a motion sensor. The smell of the sea wafted in through the open passageway.

He pulled his head back and turned to Tucker, one eyebrow cocked. "Very slick," he said. "How'd you know about that?"

"Old Arlen Hunter lore. He was pretty notorious in his day. Care to go down and take a look?" Tucker said. "You'll need this for your blotter report. I presume they make you do that kind of paperwork on these hot-pursuit cases?"

"Gee, thanks for thinking of that," Scheiber said. He followed Tucker through the narrow doorway, and they started down a circular wrought-iron staircase, Eckert close behind. The smell of the ocean was strong now, and Tucker felt a distinct movement of air. At the bottom, an open door led out onto a wooden dock inside a cave that had been carved out of the solid granite cliff on which the house stood.

"A hidden boathouse?" Eckert exclaimed. "I had no idea this was here."

The cave was low-ceilinged, barely high enough for a tall man like Tucker to stand upright. Maybe forty feet long, he estimated, and half as wide. The wooden dock ran down one side, capable of tethering a couple of speedboats, although a black Zodiac inflatable was the only tenant at the moment, lashed to a stanchion on the dock, bobbing gently on lapping waves. A sixteen-footer, the rig had a couple of forty horsepower motors clamped to the stern of its fiberglass hull.

"Arlen Hunter had this boathouse built even before the house was constructed," Tucker said. "He used it to move

certain kinds of cargo, like smuggled Russian icons and assorted other contraband that he regularly slipped past U.S.
Customs. With the house set the way it is, the opening is
hidden from prying public eyes. It wasn't a complete secret,
mind you, but Hunter had people convinced he just used the
boathouse to store his yacht tender so he could get to and
from the local yacht club without having to drive.''

The rocks outside would have to be maneuvered around,
Tucker calculated, studying the opening now that the light
was better. He'd been down once already, loading what he
needed into the Zodiac while he waited for Scheiber to arrive,
but it had still been dark outside then. Getting beyond the
rocks would be a tricky operation for any but the most agile
of small craft. He had been no fool, this Arlen Hunter. No
weekend sailor would risk approaching the bluff and being
smashed on the rocks.

Tucker walked down to the end of the dock. Beyond it
stood a set of stone gray steel double doors, opened inward.
They operated, he'd already determined, on electronic hinges
activated by remote control, like a garage door. He glanced
·back into the Zodiac. He'd found one control there, stowed
in a forward storage locker. There was another one inside a
storage cabinet bracketed to the wall of the cave.

''Scuff marks,'' Eckert called. Tucker and Scheiber turned
back. The investigator was in the passageway leading from
the stairs once more, peering at the walls. Scheiber walked
over to him. ''Here,'' Eckert said, pointing to a dusty imprint
about three feet up the passageway wall, just the other side
of the door. ''It looked as if someone carrying heavy lead
might have braced a leg against the wall, propping whatever
he was carrying on his knee to free up a hand to open the
door.''

Eckert pulled a flashlight out of his pocket and passed it
along both sides of the passageway. At the door, he paused
at the middle hinge, halfway up the frame. ''There's hair
caught here. Looks blond,'' he added, pulling out a pair of
tweezers and an evidence bag and dropping it in.

''Renata Hunter Carr was a blonde,'' Scheiber said.

''So's Mariah,'' Tucker said grimly, standing next to the
wall closet. He opened it. Oil, gas cans, oars, life vests and

various other bits of boating paraphernalia hung inside. On a hook was a set of keys. While Scheiber and Eckert were still examining the blond hair sample, Tucker palmed the keys. Then, moving back down the dock, he stepped into the stern of the inflatable.

"Okay, I'm sold," Scheiber said. "We'll contact the Coast Guard, but—" He frowned as he turned and spotted Tucker. "Get out of there."

"I'm just looking," Tucker said, his hand idly priming the gas line as he glanced at the console. A zodiac this size held about a thirty-gallon fuel tank, suitable for long excursions. The gauge on the console read full.

"You shouldn't be leaving your footprints," Scheiber said. "Dave here's going to want to go over it."

"Yeah, you're right. Sorry," Tucker said, moving toward the port gunwale.

"I think there might be a couple of drops of blood here," Eckert said, crouched on the floor of the passageway.

"Blood? Where?" Scheiber asked, turning back.

Tucker released the line at the stern of the boat.

"Here on the frame," Eckert said. "It's—"

They both jumped as the powerful outboards roared to life. Tucker had the bow line off the stanchion and the boat moving in reverse, away from the dock, before they could reach him.

"What are you doing?" Scheiber yelled.

"Call the Coast Guard!" Tucker ordered. "I'll meet you out there. Remember, the Russian ship's the *Aleksandr Pushkin.*"

"Fine! But we'll go together!" Scheiber called, racing down the dock alongside him. "Don't be a damn cowboy, Tucker!"

"Just meet me out there!" he bellowed over the roar of the outboards. He turned the wheel hard to port, and the Zodiac reversed direction. As he slammed her into forward, he heard Scheiber holler for Eckert to find a way to close the outer door. But he had the throttle all the way forward, and the speedy little craft was out of the cave and planing neatly around the rocks at the entrance long before Scheiber and Eckert could find the controls.

The sun was rising over the eastern foothills as he sped up the coast toward where he estimated the *Pushkin* and Porter's boat would rendezvous. Somewhere off Long Beach, about midway between Newport and the Port of Los Angeles was his guess. There was enough maritime traffic there that a couple more craft in the water would attract little attention, even in broad daylight. The Zodiac was fast, light and stable. Lightly loaded as she was, her twin outboards barely strained to keep her skimming over the waves.

But as he approached the Port of Long Beach, he slowed, knowing the waters off the port would be crawling with Coast Guard, Secret Service, FBI and L.A. County Sheriff's patrols, standing guard over the twenty-odd foreign ministers gathered for the meeting of Pacific Rim States being held at the Long Beach Convention Center. The great cruise ship *Queen Mary,* now a permanently berthed tourist attraction in the port, had been the site of last night's opening reception. Over at the convention center, he spotted dark-suited officials milling around on outdoor terraces, smoking their last cigarettes before the first meeting of the international conference got under way.

Good. With the rump Russian delegation at the convention center, most of the stripped-down security contingent left after Zakharov had departed would be with them. If he was going to board the *Pushkin,* Tucker realized, it was now or never. All he had to do was locate the Russian ship among all the others berthed in the port, and not draw attention to himself in the process.

It should have been an easy enough task, especially in daylight. He knew the *Pushkin* well. The vessel had been in service for nearly a quarter of a century, involved in both legitimate oceanographic research and dozens of covert Pacific spying operations from Vladivostok in the north to Tierra del Fuego in the south, and all points between. U.S. Navy and Coast Guard officers were taught to recognize it by sight. Tucker kept his speed down as he moved along the quays, alternately scanning the profiles of ships and keeping an eye out for patrol boats.

After forty fruitless minutes, he was about to risk moving in closer when it dawned on him. Paranoid as he was, Zakharov never allowed the *Pushkin* to be berthed, much to the chagrin of the Russian crew, no doubt, who would have been counting on some shore leave. In Los Angeles, Zakharov had ordered the ship to drop anchor offshore for the duration of his stay aboard. There was no reason to believe he wouldn't have left similar orders for Long Beach. Sure enough, when Tucker moved farther away from the quays, he soon spotted the outline of the vessel about a half mile offshore.

He idled his engines while he searched the onboard tools and lockers, preparing a boarding kit for himself—a wrench, some wire cutters, a length of chain and some duct tape, wrapping all of it in one of the heavy-gauge plastic zipper bags someone had sensibly stored there. A zippered nylon pouch containing the Zodiac's foot pump provided a handy carrying case. After loading everything inside the pouch, Tucker unfastened his belt, threaded it through the bag's nylon handle loop, then rebuckled.

Then, he brought the Zodiac around in a wide arc, approaching the *Pushkin* from the seaward side, reasoning that whatever the official security protocol, the natural human inclination was to look for danger from the shore. He could make out the heads of a couple of crewmen relaxing on deck, enjoying the urban view.

Cutting the engines entirely, he drifted in the last few yards, paddling lightly with a small, collapsible fiberglass oar from under the rear bench. At the side of the ship, he glanced up, but the ship seemed to be operating on minimum crew, and there was no sign his approach had been spotted. Pulling himself and the light craft hand over hand, Tucker passed along the lowest line of portholes, mostly unlit, peering into one after the other. Even research vessels had rooms deep in the bowels of the ship that served double duty as a brig. He found the *Pushkin*'s almost at the stern of the ship. Dimly lit as the small room was, he could just make out two slight forms. Mariah was lying on her side and she seemed to be asleep, although there was a small dark spot on the pillow near her head. Unless he was mistaken, that was dried blood. Lindsay was sitting beside her, watching over her, looking very worried.

Tucker tied up the Zodiac to the *Pushkin*'s anchor chain,

then slipped out of his jacket, shoes and socks, and tossed them aside. After checking the tool bag at his waist, he slipped silently into the water.

His first order of business was the speedboat he'd spotted tethered to the other side of the ship. Hugging the *Pushkin*'s hull, Tucker approached the unoccupied craft. He withdrew the pliers, wrench and chain from his belt bag, then slipped over the side of the Zodiac and went to work, submerging several times to get at his target. A frogman once more— although he could have done with his old scuba gear, he thought when he finally finished, breathless, and made his way back to the Zodiac, guiding it to the rear of the ship once more.

The *Pushkin* hadn't even been built the last time Tucker had shinnied up an anchor chain, and it hadn't been easy even then. But where he'd had youth working for him in those days, this time he had motivation that went well beyond a desire not to look weak in front of his men.

He launched himself off the Zodiac's deck and up the anchor chain. A few minutes later, he was on the deck of the ship, dripping wet, padding softly toward the aft stairs.

Mariah awoke to a dull thump outside the cabin door. She'd lost track of time, drifting in and out of sleep since being brought on board the larger ship. She kept trying to stay awake, for her daughter's sake as much as anything. Lindsay's immense relief at seeing her brought aboard Porter's boat had quickly shifted to anxiety as her mother's step had faltered. Mariah's focus had kept going blurry, and her head had been pounding since the moment she'd been struck from behind in Renata's library. The more she tried to concentrate on staying awake, the sleepier she became, until she would drop off once more.

The outside bolt on the steel door of their cabin prison slid open with a dull, rasping scrape. Lindsay jumped up, and Mariah pulled herself to a sitting position, determined not to look vulnerable when their guards returned. When the door opened, a pair of broad shoulders backed in, carrying something—a dinner tray, Mariah guessed. Oh, joy. Feeding time at the zoo.

But then she saw a pair of sprawled legs dragging along the floor. The burly man backing in was pulling a prostrate man. Another prisoner? Mariah got to her feet, ignoring the searing pain in her head. "What did you do to him?" she demanded.

He dropped the load and straightened.

"Uncle Frank!" Lindsay cried.

He turned and gave her a smile, but put a finger to his lips. When his gaze shifted to Mariah, she felt her face break into the world's widest grin. He was wet and barefoot, shirt plastered to his skin, but he was the most wonderful sight she'd ever seen.

"Shh! Keep your voices down," he whispered, cutting off her cry of relief. "Lins, get the door." He pulled the prostrate man farther inside. It was one of the guards, the one called Sergei, Mariah had gathered during a moment of lucidity. Lindsay leaped over the man's still form and yanked the door shut, then turned back as Tucker lifted him and dumped him unceremoniously on the bed.

"Is he dead?" she whispered, wide-eyed.

"No, but he's going to have a bad headache."

"I know the feeling," Mariah said.

"We think Mom's got a concussion," Lindsay said. "I've been trying to keep her awake."

Tucker straightened. He walked over to them and accepted their hugs, and then his hand gently probed Mariah's head. "Ouch. That's a real goose egg. The skin's broken."

"What are you *doing* here?" she whispered. "Not that we're not thrilled to see you."

He shoved his hands deep into his pants pockets. "Thought you ladies might need a lift out of here," he said, rocking back on his bare heels.

"You're a piece of work, you are, Frank Tucker."

"Yeah, well, you can sing my praises if we get out of here in one piece," he said, pulling up sharp as the man on the bed groaned and stirred. "Help me tie this guy up."

"With what?"

There was a blue nylon bag hanging off his belt. He unzipped it and withdrew a roll of duct tape, handing it to Lindsay, who picked at the ends to get it started, then ripped off a long strip. Tucker, meanwhile, handed Mariah a pocket-knife. She cut another strip of tape, slapping it across Sergei's mouth while Tucker held the waking man down. Lindsay, meantime, whipped off a third strip as calmly and efficiently as if she did this every day, slinging it around his left wrist and the bedpost Tucker was holding it up against. Then they did the same on the other side.

"They jumped Renata and me at her house," Mariah said quietly. "Chap's neighbor kidnapped Lindsay."

"I know," Tucker said, taking a long strip of tape from Lindsay to bind the guard's ankles.

"Porter told me he had Chap and Emma's cat Rochester on his boat," Lindsay said, "and that he was just on his way over to feed him. He said the cat was afraid of him and the dog, and he asked if I'd help while we waited for Mom to show up. Then he tied me up and gagged me. I'm so sorry, Mom," she added. "Sorry I ran off, and then fell for such a lame con."

Mariah put her arms around her, ignoring the ache in her own head that throbbed with every movement. "It's all right. You couldn't have known. Chap thought the man was his friend, too, and Porter poisoned him. He's a terrible person."

"You were taken along with Renata?" Tucker asked her.

Mariah nodded. "She'd agreed to go to the police about Porter and her son, Nolan, and their connection to Chap's and Urquhart's murders. Lermontov, Zakharov's bodyguard, is still in the country. He grabbed Renata. Somebody else knocked me out. I'm thinking maybe it was Yuri Belenko."

"I'll tell you about Belenko after," Tucker said.

"Lindsay says Renata jumped off Porter's boat. I was down in the cabin, out cold, for most of the trip over here."

"The lady was screaming at her son and the others," Lindsay added. "About me and Mom and a man named Urquhart?" Mariah and Frank nodded. "Next thing I knew, there were fireworks exploding overhead and when I turned around she was gone. Just jumped overboard in the confusion. Porter pulled out a gun and fired. They spent quite a while looking for her, but I think she got away."

"Time to hit the road," Tucker said.

Mariah touched his arm. "Frank? Do you know if she made it?"

He shook his head. "No, she didn't."

"Oh, God..."

"Come on," he told them. "Let's get out of here. Forget your shoes," he added as Lindsay started to slip her feet into her sneakers. Mariah had lost her sandals somewhere between being hit on the head the previous night and waking up on the Russian ship that morning, probably in the course of being manhandled.

Tucker opened the door and peered out into the passageway, then took Lindsay's hand and headed out, Mariah following close behind. They made it as far as a staircase at the end of the hall, but just as they started up, they heard voices approaching the stairwell from the top. They backed down quickly, and finding nowhere else to hide, ducked behind the open stairs.

Their luck held. At the bottom of the stairs, the crewmen headed straight down the passageway without a backward glance, moving in the direction from which Frank, Lindsay and Mariah had just come. Frank nodded, and they left the alcove again, padding swiftly up the steps. If the two crewmen noticed the guard missing outside her door, Mariah knew it would only be a matter of seconds before they found him trussed up inside and sounded a general alarm.

Sure enough, a split second later a muffled shout echoed up the stairwell. Then came the sound of running feet.

"Up one more level," Frank said as they turned on a landing and fled up the next flight of stairs. "If we get separated, head aft—to the back, all right?" Lindsay's copper curls bobbed energetically. "There's an inflatable boat tied to the anchor on the starboard side," Frank added. "The key's in the ignition. Don't wait for me. If you can't get to it, jump overboard and swim like hell for shore. Just get away from this ship, you hear me?"

"All of us together," Mariah said as they reached the upper deck.

Shouting voices and pounding feet sounded in the stairwell behind them.

"Aft!" Tucker said, letting go of the girl's hand and pushing her forward. "Grab your mother, Lindsay, and run!"

They ran as fast as their legs would carry them. When they got to the back railing, Mariah looked over and made out the form of an inflatable boat about thirty feet below, bobbing against the side of the big ship.

"Okay, you guys, we jump," she said. "Ready?"

Lindsay grabbed her arm. "Mom! He's not with us!"

The deck was alive with pursuers now, and they heard Frank shout from the far side—the *port* side. Mariah turned toward his voice. From a tower high above the deck, she caught the movement of a rifle swinging in his direction as he yelled at them again. "Jump!"

Dammit, Frank, you said starboard! Mariah's brain cried as she saw him freeze against the opposite rail. What kind of an ex-navy man doesn't know his port from his starboard? He remained still for a second, his eyes locked on hers as he mouthed two words. *Love you.*

Then Frank pressed himself against the railing, and leaning backward, he tipped into the water like the frogman he'd once been. At the last second, a shot rang out. A patch of red exploded on his shirt, but the point of no return had been reached, and his momentum carried him over the side.

"No!" Mariah and Lindsay screamed in unison. Other voices shouted. Shaken out of her stupor, Mariah saw half a dozen crewmen running toward her and Lindsay. Overhead, the barrel of the rifle turned in their direction. "Lindsay, jump!" she cried.

They were up on the railing and over as the first shots rang out. Mariah's stomach heaved at the roller-coaster drop of three stories, and when she hit the water, she landed awkwardly, arms and chest slapping painfully against the cold surface. She sank down and down, the salt stinging the cut on her head. But when she resurfaced, she knew she was fine, her senses cleared by the shock of immersion.

The Zodiac was only a few feet away, and Lindsay was already at the side of it, looking around frantically for her. Mariah swam as hard as she ever had, ignoring shouts from above as she grabbed the stern cleats and scrambled over the rear-deck platform. Stumbling over the back of the pilot seat, she grabbed for the mooring line. A crack of gunfire sounded overhead, and the ping of metal on metal told her they were firing down. If the shooters hit the boat's inflatable tube, they were sunk—literally.

The mooring line finally dropped free, and Lindsay pushed them off from the side of the hull while Mariah turned the key in the ignition. The outboards roared to life, and she found the gearshift, slamming it into forward, then throttling up the engines.

Hugging the *Pushkin*'s hull line, she ran up the starboard side to the bow, then spun the wheel hard to port, rounded the bow and headed back down the other side. Frank had told them to get away from the ship, but that was before he had decided to take a backward swan dive off the opposite side. In Mariah's view, that made all previously agreed-upon deals null and void. He was in the water somewhere on the other side, and she intended to find him.

Suddenly, she heard the distinct *fwapping* sound of a helicopter overhead, and then the roar of other outboard motors. Straight ahead of her, she saw with a shock that Lermontov, the burly wrestler, was at the wheel of a speedboat, getting ready to push off in hot pursuit. Mariah had to cut her engines and yank the rudder hard around to avoid running into him.

Lermontov was still trying to move his craft away from the ship, but while the engine roared, the propeller refused to kick in. From where Mariah stood, it look as if his propeller had gotten itself tangled up in something.

Lermontov handed over the wheel to another man while he leaned over the stern of the speedboat to check out the problem. He shouted something in Russian, then started making a wild go-backward gesture. The man at the wheel finally caught on, as police patrol boats began closing in from all sides. He slammed the gears into reverse. The propeller finally kicked in, churning the water while a chain that had somehow become wrapped around it thrashed the surface. Mariah immediately thought of Frank and that little nylon bag of tricks at his waist.

Lermontov was still hanging over the back of the boat, shouting directions. When the whipping links rose into the air he tried to jump back, too late. A mighty metallic whack to the head dropped him overboard like a stone. The chain continued to gyrate like a crazed snake for a couple of revolutions, and then Mariah watched as an extraordinary thing happened. The propeller unscrewed itself from its shaft and sank unceremoniously into the ocean.

The crewman stared, dumbfounded, at the impotent, roaring engine as Coast Guard officers boarded his craft.

As other police and Coast Guard vessels closed in, returning fire to the *Pushkin,* the deck of the Zodiac rocked violently. A helicopter dropped low out of the sky, and Mariah grabbed Lindsay to keep her from toppling overboard. They held on to the console for balance. Another hand suddenly landed beside Mariah's, and she peered through the whipping wind to find Detective Scheiber, standing awkwardly next to her on the Zodiac's deck, having apparently dropped from the sky. He was holding a gun, keeping a wary watch, and looking about as at home on the boat as the proverbial fish on a bicycle.

"Ms. Bolt, and Lindsay Bolt-Tardiff, I presume?" he shouted over the roar of the helicopter. Lindsay nodded. A few last sporadic shots of gunfire sounded from the deck of the *Pushkin* as Mariah searched the water frantically for some sign of Frank.

"Are you one of the good guys, I hope?" Lindsay yelled back at Scheiber.

"I like to think so," he said, nodding. Police boats were in the process of dragging a very limp Lermontov out of the water, although he was obviously alive. Above the mayhem, Mariah heard him shouting two words, over and over. "Diplomat! Immunity!"

"Where's Tucker?" Scheiber bellowed.

"He was shot!" Mariah cried. "He went into the water!"

The waves were choppy with the beating of the helicopter blades and the churning of cruiser engines as one patrol boat after another converged on the scene.

"Mom! There!" Lindsay cried, pointing off to one side.

Mariah spotted Frank, the top of his head shining like a small beacon on the water. She was over the side of the Zodiac in a flash, and reached him in a few strong strokes. He was limp, but his big frame was buoyant in the water. She flipped him onto his back so his face was clear of the water. Pulling his head back, she put her mouth over his and exhaled hard. Then, hooking one arm across his chest, she side-stroked furiously back toward the Zodiac, crying with each stroke, "Don't you dare die on me, Frank Tucker! Don't you dare!"

Scheiber and Lindsay had spread-eagled themselves over the pontoons, and they hooked their hands under Tucker's arms to keep him afloat while Mariah climbed up and began mouth-to-mouth in earnest. "Come on, Frank!" she urged between breaths. "Breathe, dammit!"

It seemed to take forever, but finally he drew a strangled breath, then gave a couple of wet coughs. "I thought I told you to take off," he gasped.

"I had to stick around to see that trick with the propeller," Mariah said, mustering a smile. "Now, be quiet, would you?" As his eyes closed, she looked up at Scheiber, mouthing worriedly, "He's bleeding." His shirt was plastered to his chest, streaked in blood.

Scheiber pointed up. "Air ambulance is on the way."

The Coast Guard had boarded the *Pushkin,* Mariah noted, and things seemed to be fully under control overhead. As the police helicopter withdrew to a safer distance, a second, with a big red cross on its side, landed on the ship's helipad.

Mariah watched every shallow breath Frank drew, until finally, an eternity later, a basket was lowered. A dozen hands appeared to help maneuver the basket under him and strap him down. As it rose again to the deck of the ship, Mariah and Lindsay scrambled up the *Pushkin*'s ladder to meet it at the top, Scheiber close behind.

"You two better go along and get yourselves checked out," he said, adding to Mariah, "Your head's bleeding."

She reached up and touched the back of her head. When she brought her hand down, it was covered in blood. "It's not serious," she said. But she let them lead her toward the hospital chopper, so she and Lindsay could be with Frank.

Tuesday,
July 9

Epilogue

The gray slate deck warms her feet as Mariah shrugs off the thick hotel terry robe and drops it on one of the butter-yellow lounge chairs by the Beverly Wilshire pool. The chairs are lined up in two long rows to catch the sun. The pool is Romanesque in design, and the vine-covered archways around its courtyard look transplanted from the Via Appia. Waxy palm fronds rustle softly overhead. It's going to be another gorgeous day, but at this early hour, Mariah and the attendant are the only people around. He's laying a thick, folded towel on each of the chairs, and they exchange friendly greetings as he hands her one. By now, they know each other by name.

Lindsay is still fast asleep upstairs, her copper curls a striking contrast to the white down pillows and the shimmering blue-black fur of the cat curled up at her side. She has inherited Emma Korman's fat tomcat. The Korman sons, it turns out, are allergy-prone, so Mr. Rochester is going to live in Virginia. Lindsay has already begun to spoil him shamelessly, and Rochester is in love. Hotel management is turning an indulgent blind eye to his presence. The cat is unobtrusive, after all, unlike others in this ever-changing entourage.

Mr. Rochester is not the only orphaned animal to have found a new home this week. Detective Scheiber has decided to adopt a tricolor basset hound named Kermit. He told Mariah he only meant to take the dog home overnight, but his six-year-old stepson refused to give it up. He and the boy have decided they will enroll Kermit in obedience classes, which may not do the headstrong, lovable dog much good, but could help cement a new bond that seems to be forging between father and son.

The dog was spotted—or rather, his mournful baying was heard—late Friday night by a fisherman, who came across a sixty-foot sloop called the *Wright Think'r,* floating adrift and apparently unmanned about a mile off the coast. On boarding her, he found not only the dog, but also the body of the owner, Douglas Porter. The UCLA cleaning lady, shown a photo of the tall, bullet-headed Porter, conceded that he could well have been the man she saw outside Urquhart's office the night the professor died. Forensic testing has confirmed the architect died by his own gun, found next to the body. A brief suicide note also showed up, although Scheiber is troubled by the fact that the apparently left-handed Porter was shot in the right temple.

It's not the only unsolved mystery of this affair. Porter's erstwhile partner on the Nova Krimsky casino project, Nolan Carr, has vanished since the incident on the *Aleksandr Pushkin.* A small yacht tender belonging to him was found the next morning, hung up on the rocks below his estate. There is speculation that he was trying to slip back into the cave boathouse under cover of night, possibly to get some emergency cash discovered hidden behind a false panel in an equipment shed—nearly three-quarters of a million dollars in mad money stashed away for such a time as this. However, Scheiber himself had closed the doors of the boathouse when trying to stop Tucker's escape in the Zodiac, inadvertently hitting the security lock, which prevented the door being opened from the outside. Newport police have kept the house under surveillance ever since, but Nolan has not shown up.

Hunter Carr assets have been frozen, meantime, pending investigation by the FBI, the IRS, the Securities and Exchange Commission and the Treasury Department. Their creditors are screaming. Arlen Hunter, it seems, should have spent less time indulging his only child and more teaching her to manage his murky empire. His heirs have dissipated his fortune in about a third the time it took the old brigand to build it. Young Nolan managed to dazzle their bankers temporarily with predictions of fabulous profits from Nova Krimsky, but with him now unaccounted for and yesterday's announcement in Moscow that Nolan's development consortium has been dumped from the project, the vultures are beginning to circle over what remains of Arlen Hunter's empire.

Mariah approaches the sun-dappled water. Wide, tiled steps lead into the shallow end of the turquoise pool, but she prefers the deep-water plunge. She hesitates at the edge for a moment, stretching out her muscles, gingerly massaging her temples. Her head aches a little. The doctors have told her the concussion will take a few weeks to heal completely. In the meantime, it is a painful souvenir of Nolan Carr's fury at finding out she'd convinced his mother to turn him in.

It could have been worse, Mariah thinks. Nolan might have killed her outright when he snuck up behind her that night. Maybe he held back a little because the gilded wooden icon he'd grabbed from the hall table was irreplaceable and had once belonged to Catherine the Great. Or maybe he just didn't want to deal with the mess. That was Lermontov's job, after all. Nolan had borrowed the big Russian enforcer and brought him home as an unsubtle reminder to Renata of the importance of keeping her mouth shut—only by the time they got there, it was too late. His mother had already betrayed him.

Nolan's attack on Mariah and Porter's spontaneous decision to kidnap Lindsay were the knee-jerk reactions of weak men who were in over their heads. Having dealt profitably with Arlen Hunter for decades, Zakharov had learned too late that the grandson was not cut of the same cold cloth. It was his second biggest mistake, Mariah decides. The first was murdering Anatoly Orlov. Of all Zakharov's victims, Orlov was the one who would come back to haunt him. A nation does not forgive the murder of its heroes.

Yuri Belenko has been by to apologize to Mariah for what she and her daughter have been through. Zakharov, he says, went back to Moscow expecting to be named premier, next step to the presidency itself, only to find his backers beginning to desert him in droves. The mob also considers him too great a liability to be a figurehead for Nova Krimsky any longer. Belenko confides that he suspects Nolan Carr has been permanently silenced. He thinks Zakharov will need to watch his back, too, because organized criminals do not care for the kind of public attention he is getting.

In publicizing the Orlov/Bolt file, Frank Tucker has done exactly what the Navigator hoped. As for Belenko, he was Deriabin's spy inside the Zakharov camp, it seems. Arranging for Mariah to be introduced to the foreign minister was, he admits mischievously, an unsubtle but perversely pleasing bid to rattle the man. And by the way, Belenko adds, he is grateful for Mariah's offer of alternative employment, although he won't take her up on it at the moment. Things are in a state of flux where he is, and opportunities abound. But who knows what the future will bring? He only hopes the two of them will run into each other again.

And the other files Deriabin gave Frank? Belenko has told Mariah they were mere filler—accurate enough in their portrayal of Zakharov's crimes over the years, but useless in terms of getting rid of him. Then why not just give Frank the one file that mattered? Mariah asked. Because, Belenko explained, the Navigator calculated that Tucker would resist such blunt manipulation. He had to believe he was picking his own battle. From what he knows of Mr. Tucker, Belenko is not surprised to learn he destroyed the rest of the files rather than let them fall into the wrong hands.

Belenko has also given Mariah a gift—her father's papers, including the manuscript for his novel, *Man in the Middle,* stolen from Chap Korman by Porter, his killer, to hand over to his new Russian friends. And it *is* Ben's novel, Belenko says firmly, handing her at the same time another yellowed, Russian-language manuscript—*Man at the Edge,* by Anatoly Orlov. This is the novel smuggled out of the Soviet Union and entrusted to Ben Bolt in an act of defiance that got both men murdered. The KGB, hidebound bureaucracy that it was, had filed Orlov's novel away rather than destroy it. Now, says Belenko, it's time for this great joint project of two brilliant writers, conceived during that long-ago meeting in Paris, to be published as they always hoped it would—as a tandem set, parallel visions of a Utopian future. Creative, hopeful hands clasping across a great ideological divide.

Mariah, unspeakably moved to know the truth at last, has promised to deliver them both to her father's publisher.

She knows there are tears running down her face when she dives into the pool, but as her body tenses at the first shock of the plunge, they are quickly washed away. Ben did not betray Orlov. And he had wanted to come home.

She surrenders to the buoyant, silken cool, and her feet kick off the smooth tile. She does two laps of breaststroke to warm up before settling into the rhythm of a strong freestyle, feeling more contented with every stroke than she can remember having felt for a very long time.

She'll do her laps, then go up and have breakfast with Lindsay. The hotel has moved them to a larger, two-bedroom suite—partly because it is on a floor with more security, which they need right now, given the media onslaught they are going through.

One reporter is conspicuously absent among those clamoring for interviews, however. Paul Chaney did telephone after news broke of the incident on the *Pushkin*. The brief message he left on her hotel voice mail said he hoped Mariah and Lindsay—and Frank, he added reluctantly—were all doing well, and that he and Mariah would have a chance to talk soon to clear up any misunderstandings between them. In light of the breaking scandal, clips from his interview with Zakharov—probably the Russian's last—are getting wide airplay. But Chaney has announced he feels honor bound, in the name of objectivity and given his personal link to some of the players, to refrain from commenting on either the fall of the Arlen Hunter empire or the much-anticipated final literary triumph of Benjamin Bolt. Only Mariah knows how humiliated Paul must be at having misjudged things so badly, but she will never mention it.

The other reason Mariah and Lindsay have changed hotel suites is in anticipation of Frank's release from hospital in the next few days—maybe even tomorrow, the doctors have said, amazed as they are by the man's indomitable constitution. In the meantime, Mariah and Lindsay will head down to Long Beach Memorial Hospital later and spend the afternoon with him, as they've done every day since he rescued them from the *Pushkin.*

The bullet Frank took passed almost right through him, finally coming to rest a scant two millimeters from his spine, breaking a rib and nicking his diaphragm en route. But he looks set to make a complete recovery. Even Ms. Latham, who was ready to have him arrested only a few days earlier, asks after him every day and wants Mariah to apprise her of anything he might need when he arrives at the hotel.

Frank thought he was resting up in preparation for his inevitable incarceration, but that seems unlikely. Jack Geist was in town on Sunday. While he is not pleased with Frank's unilateral decision to destroy the Navigator's files, he seems willing—almost eager—to promote the view that they consisted of unreliable material, possibly even outright disinformation. In any case, legal action against Frank is out of the question. The CIA, Geist said firmly, does not air its dirty linen in public. Congress does not want to hear about rogues inside an agency that receives billions of dollars annually from the public purse.

After Geist had left Frank's hospital room, Mariah cornered him privately in the hall, pressing him to reveal what he had planned for Frank. After all, she pointed out, the man could hardly be relegated to a danker pit than he'd already been occupying before this happened. Geist thought about this. It was true Frank's talents were being underutilized, he said. Perhaps that was part of the problem, and needed to be rectified. But first, Frank needed to decide that the agency was still where he wanted to be. If so, there would be a position waiting for him appropriate to his experience and seniority. In the meantime, Geist said briskly, Saddam Hussein was once more massing tanks in the Middle East, and the president required briefing. He had to get back to Washington.

Mariah has also noted that since Geist's departure and the end of her assignment to recruit Belenko, she has lost her ever-present tail.

She starts down her final lap of the pool. Frank has to decide about the future. So does she. Whatever decisions they make, she suspects, they will be making them together. She smiles at the notion. There is a certain comforting inevitability about it, a sense of events running a course they were always meant to follow.

Lindsay is already trying to convince her mother they should drive back home across country. All of them—Mariah, Lindsay, Mr. Rochester and Frank. She could help with the driving, Lindsay has hinted broadly. Maybe they could stop in Las Vegas. It's not a place Mariah has any great desire to visit, but Lindsay thinks it would be great to see the Strip and catch some shows and Elvis impersonators. Maybe check out those drive-through wedding chapels, she added mischievously, her dark eyes dancing from one to the other as Frank and Mariah find themselves uncharacteristically red-faced, suddenly tongue-tied and shy with one another. How did that daughter of hers ever get to be so clever? Mariah wonders.

She reaches the end of the pool and hauls herself out, energized. Ready to start the day.